CW01498165

THE TYRANT ALPHA'S REJECTED MATE

THE FIVE PACKS: BOOK ONE

CATE C. WELLS

Cover art and design by Clarise Tan of CT Cover Creations
Edited by Nevada Martinez
Proofread by Kayla Davenport

Special thanks to Lily Luchesi of Partners in Crime Book Services, Kara M., Julia B., Elizabeth L., Elisabeth J., Layne K., Jennifer S., Stephanie H., Leslee N., Sara B., and Kate A.

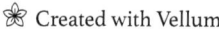 Created with Vellum

1

UNA

"Una! Come get this!"

I hunch over and text quicker.

I've got a guy from the city willing to drive down and pay three hundred dollars for five pounds of dried morel mushrooms. I'm getting ripped off. He's going to turn around and sell them to some fancy restaurant for six hundred, minimum, but three hundred is a nice payday when technically, I'm not allowed to handle human money.

Or talk to human men.

Or own a phone.

Or leave pack land without permission.

I'm probably not allowed to harvest morels, either, but there's no rule, and his highness Killian Kelly never deigns to notice what mere females do all day while he and the males train and spar and condition.

I'm not mad about it. Now that Killian has the males fighting on the circuit, there's food to eat besides what our wolves can catch and money for gas and electric. When Killian's father was alpha, we did the laundry by hand in rain barrels and lived on venison and rabbit.

Unmated and unprotected females like me still rank low, but back in the day, I'd be working on my back, not bussing tables. That's progress. We're almost out of the Middle Ages in the Quarry Pack.

"Una!" Old Noreen snaps her fingers and points her hooked chin at a tray with five plastic pitchers filled to the brim with foam.

Now that's a challenge I'm likely to fail. My arms are strong, but my bad leg plays hell with my stability.

Old Noreen must read my look of dismay. "You'll be fine. It'll save you having to make another trip in twenty minutes, and then you can bury your nose in that phone to your heart's content. Come on, girl." She snaps a few more times.

My phone vibrates. The human—Shroomforager3000—confirms the deal is on. Three hundred dollars. My heart soars. I send him the time and place.

It's not my turn to make the run into town this week. Annie's up. I'll have to swap with her. It wouldn't be right to ask her to break the "no human male" rule. If we ever get busted selling to the vendors at the farmer's market in Chapel Bell, it'll be bad enough. I can't imagine what Killian would do if one of us were caught with a man.

A sliver of fear skates down my spine. It would be bad. Killian believes in making examples. If a packmate breaks the rules, if he doesn't work hard enough, if he shows weakness—he's dirt. Killian is fearless, unrelenting, and merciless. His life's goal is to bully everyone else into being the same.

If he caught us in town, trading with humans—it wouldn't matter that we're females. There'd be hell to pay.

I breathe through the anxiety. We won't get caught. We haven't yet.

I power off my phone and tuck it in our hidey hole

behind the crockpot. Then I head for the pitchers of beer, my bum leg dragging behind me, shoe rubber squeaking against the tile. I hoist the tray and find my balance.

"You got it?" my youngest roomie Mari asks over her shoulder. She's at the sink up to her elbows in suds.

"Yup." My bad leg can't take my full weight, but I can use it like a crutch to hobble along. It's not graceful, but I manage.

I take a steadying breath and shoulder through the swinging door into the great room. Beer is already sloshing over the brim of the pitchers. I'm going to get dirty looks for that.

Killian's lieutenants don't think much of me. They respect strength. Dominance. The wolf. I've got none of that.

Well, I do have a wolf. I can feel her. But for some reason, I've never gone into heat, so I've never shifted.

Abertha, the pack's crone, says that some wolves come later than others. Maybe back when I was a girl, during the attack that mangled my leg, my wolf got skittish, and in good time, she'll find the courage to shift. Or maybe I'm just a late bloomer.

I want to meet my wolf. I've watched a three-legged dog in town, and it keeps up with the others. Abertha says my bad leg will manifest in the wolf, but she thinks only one limb will be jacked up. It's a fear of mine—that I'll finally shift, and two legs will be useless.

It's the kind of worry I don't spend much time on. No heat, no change, no wolf. And there's no sign of my heat, so it's kitchen duty and the old maid's cabin for me.

I don't mind since the alternative is mating one of these meathead assholes.

I slowly make my way between the tables. None of the males bother to move their stretched legs out of my path.

Wouldn't want to acknowledge my weakness. That'd be rude.

They avert their eyes as I pass, otherwise ignoring me. Which is fine. I feel bad for their mates, stuck on their laps or crushed to their sides, forced to listen to them recount old fights in excruciating detail—for the umpteenth time.

I'm skirting the edges of the great room, focused on the task at hand, when Killian's voice booms from his makeshift throne on the dais.

"Lochlan." He snaps and points to the open floor at his feet. Lochlan's crew goes nuts. Shouts shake the rafters.

"And—" Killian pauses for dramatic emphasis. "Tye."

The shouts turn to howls. Folks stomp their feet. Everyone has been waiting for this match. Lochlan Byrne has been picking fights, challenging wolves closer and closer in rank to Killian. Lochlan's working himself up to a beta challenge and everyone knows it.

Tye is our beta now. If Lochlan wins, he can demand the rank, and Killian would be going against tradition to deny him. If Tye wins, Lochlan has to step back down. For now. My stomach aches. I spend a lot of time worrying about what would happen if Lochlan and his backers took over. It wouldn't be good for me and my roomies, that's for damn sure.

Killian's a dick, but Lochlan is a "back in the day" type. You know, "back in the day" bitches presented at command. None of this mating-for-life bullshit. "Back in the day" the alpha put down defective wolves. For their own good. This, of course, is always said within my hearing while eyeing my bum leg.

I'm not afraid of Lochlan, but I'm terrified of all the packmates who think like him and keep it on the down low.

I'm scared they'll outnumber Killian's crew, and I won't see it coming in time to run.

I can live with our current level of backwards, but I'm not going face down, ass up because some higher-ranking male wants to scratch an itch. Screw that. I've got cash in a jar buried behind my cabin. I've got options.

As Tye and Lochlan make their way to the center of the room and square off, Killian bends forward in his metal folding chair, bracing his forearms on his thick thighs. It might as well be a throne. The huge fireplace at his back frames him in stone and fire, and no one dares approach unless he gives them the nod.

Tye and Lochlan bump fists and crouch. It's gonna be a wrestling match. I edge along the wall. They're cutting off my direct route, but I can pick my way to the table that needs the beers.

With a grunt, the males collide.

Killian's cruel lips soften into what might be considered a smile, but it's a lot closer to the look a snake has after it swallows a rat.

I don't know why I'm watching Killian. Usually, I avoid eye contact with higher ranks at all times. Saves a lot of getting asked to fetch something.

Killian's not looking at me, though. He's intent on the fight. There's no clear favorite at the moment. It's a two-man rugby scrum.

My arms are getting heavy, and somehow, it's hotter in here than the kitchen. Sweat trickles down my temples, and I can't wipe my face.

I inch further toward the front table, but as soon as I step near the open floor, the fighters sprawl in front of me. Tye scrabbles for dominance. There's a crackle in the air—like he might shift.

I'm stuck. If I venture closer and they change, I'm wolf meat. If I'm in their way, they'll plow me over.

Sweet Fate, someone needs to crack a window. Now there's sweat dripping down my back. Standing puts more pressure on my leg than moving, and my thigh muscles are starting to ache. This is miserable.

Why did I wear a flannel? It's sticking to me. So gross.

I need to drop this tray and get some air. What if I just skirt them—

Lochlan slams Tye into the ground, barely missing my foot. Okay. Guess I'll wait right here.

After several long moments of grunts and growls, Tye gains the upper hand. Half the room roars. Then there's a reversal; Lochlan wrangles Tye into a headlock, and the other half goes wild.

Killian watches, fingers steepled, gaze flickering from male to male. Our king. He's wearing a plain white tank top, faded jeans, and tan work boots. It's pretty much a uniform in this pack.

Killian should look basic, but he doesn't.

His shirt clings to every defined muscle, and like his gargantuan wolf, he's in a whole other weight class than the other males. His jeans hug his thighs, and they're more solid, too. His sculpted shoulders are broader, his posture more arrogant, his dusky blue eyes flintier.

Every angle on his face is harsh. His nose is crooked, his Adam's apple pronounced, his lips a slash. Even when he smiles, they barely curve.

I'm really thirsty. I swallow, but my mouth is bone dry.

Why am I looking at Killian Kelly's lips?

I drop my gaze, and my face blazes. It's the heat in here. It's muddling my brain.

Killian Kelly is strong, but he's not attractive. He looks mean —which is what he's always been. He's only two years older than me. I've known him since the day I was born, and I've never been into him like the other females. I'm not a rank groupie.

I shake myself off as best I can with a full tray. Tye and Lochlan are still blocking my way. I could go back, circle around behind the tables, but that'd take forever. It's getting muggier and more humid by the second, and my shirt is sticking to me. I'll wait a few more seconds. Tye looks to be making his comeback.

He's not going to lose. Killian wouldn't have ordered him to fight if it wasn't a sure thing. Killian and Tye are closer than brothers, and in this pack, everything goes the way Killian wants.

That's because unlike the other packs, Quarry Pack is ruled by strength, not blood. Any male can challenge for rank at any time. Theoretically, Killian could have to fight every day to keep the lead, but he doesn't because he cannot be beat. It's a fact.

Besides having the biggest wolf in the five packs, Killian's a flip-shifter. He can change from skin to fur and back again whenever he wants, without effort, in the blink of an eye. It's an unbeatable advantage.

Abertha says flip-shifting isn't magic, but it sure as hell looks like it when he morphs back and forth mid-air. No one wants to challenge an alpha touched by the moon.

A flash of heat crashes through me. It has to be at least ninety degrees in here, and behind Killian's makeshift throne, the fire's roaring. Why does no one open the windows?

Probably because the mated and protected females are perfectly comfortable. They're allowed to wear short sleeves, and per usual, the males who aren't wearing tank tops are bare-chested.

My wrist is so tired. I switch so I'm holding the tray in two hands. My palms are getting slick. It'd serve them right if I dropped the tray, and they'd have to go get their own damn beer. The folks at the far table are already casting me dirty looks—like why don't I wade through the shifter fight?

Ugh. I press my legs tight together. Sweat is dribbling down my inner thighs and tickling the back of my knees. And my stomach's doing something weird. Do I have a fever? I can't get sick. I've got a mushroom deal in the works.

Fortunately, the match seems to be wrapping up. Ivo Bell is squatting and squinting between Tye and Lochlan's entangled bodies. I'm not sure why he doesn't call the match. Tye is howling at the ceiling in victory, and Lochlan's face is beet red, fur sprouting from his collar. There's definitely a winner and a loser, and if Ivo doesn't call it, there's gonna be a wolf fight in the great room.

I can't stand here any longer. I need air. All this male musk is making me queasy. I'm gonna yak. I grip the tray and pick my way around them, praying Lochlan doesn't break free at the very last second and topple me ass over tea kettle.

Luckily, I make it past them to where Killian's lieutenants sit next to the dais. From the way everyone treats the table like sacred ground, you'd think it'd be special, but it's like the others—worn laminate top, backless benches, wheels. The tables came with the building when the pack bought the property in the 80s and stopped living in dens.

"Took you long enough," Finn Murphy gripes as he grabs a pitcher, knocking my hand as he helps himself. I set the tray down and unload it. I don't bother to respond. I don't talk to dicks.

"Get us some more." Finn shoves an empty bread basket at me. He doesn't meet my eye, just gnaws on a drumstick while he watches Tye help Lochlan off the floor.

"Bad call," he grumbles under his breath. He's just sore because he's in cahoots with Lochlan. From where I was standing, Tye won without a doubt.

I snag the basket and turn to go. I'm going to "forget" about the bread and duck out the back. The sun is setting. There'll probably be a breeze from the foothills. I can cool down.

I want to be outside so bad. The desire hits me so hard, it's a longing. I need open sky. I want to breathe in the night air. I want to bask in the moonlight.

Mostly, I want out of these clothes. My bra straps are digging into my shoulders, and my khakis are damp and too damn tight. They must've shrunk in the wash. Or I've ended up wearing Annie's again by accident.

I take a step toward the kitchen, but before I head back, I glance up at the dais. I have to. I'm called. It's instinct even though no one said my name.

But there's only Killian, staring at me.

Heat bursts from my core, surging down my limbs, leaving my toes and fingertips tingling. I hold onto the empty tray for dear life.

Why is he checking me out?

No, he's got to be looking at the table behind me. He's probably deciding who fights next. The sparring is incessant, at least until it gets late and drinking and groping take center stage.

There's no need for me to linger here. I'm acting like he gave an alpha command, but he's just scowling like usual. If I don't move, he's going to flick his hand imperiously to get out of the way like he does. Killian never deigns to speak if he can grunt and point. I don't think he's ever said an actual word to me.

I should hustle back to the kitchen as quickly as I can, but for some reason, I can't make my feet move. I'm hyperfocused on the linoleum floor now, cheeks burning, stuck. Because his eyes are on me.

My heart thumps, echoing in my ears.

And there's a new delicious aroma weaving through the usual beer and roast meat and other earthy pack smells. It teases my nose, warm and sweet and sticky in the best possible way. It's not coming from the kitchen. It's—I don't know where it's coming from.

The ache in my leg fades. There's a pleasant buzz in my head now, softening everything. The constant grating ruckus of mealtime in the lodge fades—the fluorescent lights overhead, the shrill laughter of the females, and the braying of the males. It's all muted. Like an old talkie movie in black and white.

I peek up out of the corner of my eye. Is Killian sitting taller? He's still glaring, and his hard, almost craggy face has become thunderous. He's pissed. That's my cue to leave, but still—still—I can't go.

He's too freaking *interesting*. His chest rises and falls, stretching the crisp white cotton of his shirt, and it's mesmerizing. What would it feel like against my cheek? Under my nails?

My claws?

I lick my dry lips. I can taste the yumminess in the air. It coats my tongue, and I'm salivating. It's so. Damn. Tasty.

Am I drunk? I feel tipsy, but I only partake at the cabin with my girls. Lone females aren't allowed to drink.

I inhale deeply, trying to shake off this weirdness, but now the lush, decadent scent is in my lungs. Excitement shoots through my veins, a flood of heat rising up and cresting, crashing through me.

Heat.

Of course. Oh, Fate, it's beyond obvious. That's why my brain is so slow.

I'm going into heat.

My wolf's ears shoot up. She yips and chases her tail. She's not really moving—it's how she feels. I'm anthropomorphizing her emotions. Or whatever it's called when a spirit lives inside you. It *feels* like she's dancing, though. She's ecstatic. She can finally come out and play.

I want to meet her so bad. Hope swells in my chest. She's gotten quiet these past few years, deflated, but she's letting herself be heard now. She's demanding. Whining.

Outside, outside, outside.

And then she changes her mind. No, *him.*

Him, him, him.

I raise my eyes to Killian's, and even though I know better, I can't force my gaze to lower. You don't meet an alpha's eyes. That's a challenge. Even from a lone female. It's ingrained in our DNA. I shouldn't be able to help but defer. He won't be able to stop himself from knocking me down if I don't.

Shit. I focus as hard as I can until my neck bends, but I'm still gazing up from under my lashes. I can't stop. He's *fascinating.*

I bet he tastes like melted toffee. Or taffy.

I bet he feels like when a summer storm rolls in and the clouds race and there's the sizzle in the air from the lightning.

Mine, mine, mine.

My wolf paws at my ribs. She wants out. I don't know how to let her, and this is crazy. I'm scared and shaking, but wild horses couldn't tear me away from devouring my alpha with my eyes. I *need* him.

I'm sopping wet. Between the legs. My hand reaches down, searching. Oh, Fate. What am I doing? In the middle of the frickin' lodge? I snatch it back to my chest at the last second.

What's wrong with me? That's Killian Kelly. He's a tyrant, and a dick, and all he cares about are the fights. He's the reason Moon Lake thinks we're backwards, and they're always making noise about how it'd be better if their pack absorbed ours.

I've known Killian my whole life, and every year, he's worse.

Mate.

No. He's not *my* mate. No way. I'd have had an inkling.

Wouldn't I?

Wouldn't he?

He slowly rises to his feet, chest thrown back, a fighting stance. A growl rolls from the back of his throat. He scrubs his pecs with the flat of his hand like he has indigestion. His brow furrows. He's as confused as I am. This doesn't make any sense.

My wolf replies with a rumble.

She makes a noise!

It's kind of a sassy purr. I press my palm above my breasts. Holy crap, my solar plexus is vibrating. Whoa. She's really in there. She's not a figment of my imagination. I didn't somehow eat her in utero like a vanishing twin.

My eyes prickle. I'm going to shift. *Finally*. I need to get out of here. I need wide open spaces, room to run, and—

Out of nowhere, without waiting for his nod of approval, Haisley Byrne saunters to the dais, steps up to Killian, wraps her arms around his neck, and shoves her boobs into his side. Then she rises up on her tiptoes and kisses him full on the mouth. He goes rigid.

He doesn't avert his eyes. He's looking at me while she sucks his face.

No.

Ours.

An inhuman wail—both a yowl and a roar—fills my ears from inside my skull.

My spine rips out of my skin.

Pain cascades through me, bursting from the inside out, an explosion of splintering bone and shredding muscle. I'm dying. I'm being torn apart.

I scream, collapsing to the ground. My joints break with a sick pop, and I lay powerless against the contortions, staring unblinking at the dais. Haisley's jaw has dropped. Killian's—holding himself back?

His fists are clenched, his teeth gritted, as if he's straining to control himself.

My vision is like a camera focusing. Everything is small and far away, and then it's close and bright and too vivid. I can see the cracks in the linoleum. Dust motes suspended in the air. The golden rings around Killian's pupils blow wide and then contract into pure black.

In the kitchen, a dish shatters. Everyone's heart is beating in an uneven rhythm. It's a roar filling the room, a wave beating against a shore.

I can smell everything. Meat. Blood. That bitch. Her coconut shampoo and her vanilla lotion mixed with sweat. She's touching my mate, rubbing her scent on him.

A faint, panicked voice, far away, pleads to stop, think, wait a minute, but she—I—don't listen. I am the wolf, and she's encroaching on our mate.

I leap, baring my fangs, snarling, every movement an

agony as my body tries to reknit mid-motion, joints and sinews mending as I simultaneously rip them anew. I mean to lunge, attack, but there's something wrong with my back leg, so I have to drag the useless limb as I go for that bitch, snapping my teeth.

I can't stop. Everything's in the wrong place, the wrong proportion, and there's no color, but scents swirl and speak.

I'm weak—I know I am—but she can't touch him. He's *mine*.

I raise my muzzle and howl.

There are hoots and catcalls behind me. She says human words from her fake red mouth.

I bark at her. *Shift, bitch. Fight me. Let him go and come. I'll tear your pelt from your hide. I'll destroy you for touching my mate.*

Through sheer determination, I drag my aching carcass close enough to take a swipe at her. She laughs and toes me in the ribs with her high-heeled boot. Compared to all the other pains, it's nothing. I manage to nip her calf and get a taste of denim.

Not what I want. I lick my muzzle. I want blood.

She snarls. Someone snaps, "No!" But in a moment, she's gone, and in her place, a snow white she-wolf is looming over me.

She's big. Three times my size, at least.

She doesn't hesitate. She goes for my throat. Her fangs sink into my collarbone, a new, searing pain exploding through my already reeling brain, and I struggle, I fight like hell, but she's so much stronger, and I'm a mess.

She rips a hunk of flesh from the bone, and I scream. She doesn't let go, flinging me side to side, slamming me against the floor.

I snap my teeth, but my mouth closes on air. My claws glance off her thick coat and tough hide.

I'm losing blood, fading by the second. The stink of copper is everywhere. My pack is going to let me die. They're going to watch me bleed out while they sop their dinner plates clean with bread I baked.

I'm cold. And tired. I let myself go lax. I can't win, and there's no sense in giving them a show.

"Enough," Killian roars.

Haisley tears her fangs out of my flesh and straddles my limp body, drooling on my side, the strings of her saliva pink with my blood.

"Shift," he commands.

My bones instantly obey, cracking again, even the broken ones, snapping back into place. For a few seconds, the pain dims everything.

Am I going to pass out? Oh, please, let me just fade away. Too soon, my shifter healing kicks in, and I'm snatched back from darkness. I can't escape.

I try to curl into a ball, but I can only raise a knee a few inches. I still have an unobstructed view of the dais, so I can watch, collapsed and naked on the floor, as Haisley accepts a T-shirt from her mother Cheryl, our alpha female.

Haisley smirks, licking blood from her lips. Her mother fusses over her while she glares at me, lip snarled.

I'm on the ground in a pool of blood. Scraps of my red-soaked shirt and pants litter the floor. I'm shaking hard, my teeth clattering. I struggle to sit, but I can't get my muscles to contract. Nothing's attached right, and I'm so weak. I huddle, my knees as close to my chest as I can raise them, trembling arms wound around my calves.

No one offers me a shirt. They've backed far away from me as if I'm contagious.

Moon mad.

I dare to peek up at Killian. His angular face is stone, chin lifted slightly as he glares down his sharp nose.

Somehow, despite the stench of blood, I can still catch his scent—a mix of sweet, soothing things. Sugar cubes. Bubbling hot butterscotch. A drop of caramel on the tip of your tongue.

My wolf mewls for him.

Help.

His lip curls in disgust, but his eyes flicker blue to gold.

"Stand up," he snarls.

I can't. I don't have the strength, and everyone will see everything.

"Stand up, or I'll drag you up."

My gaze careens around the great room. Males leer and smirk. Some of the females, too. The elders are tutting behind their hands, scandalized and disapproving. Old Noreen and my girls are crowded in the kitchen door, horror on their faces. They don't dare come out.

No one is going to help me.

Killian growls a warning. It's a question. *You dare defy me?*

Summoning every scrap of energy I have left, I roll to my stomach and push up on my good knee. I can't just stand; my bad leg won't let me.

I stagger to my feet, exposing my butt, my belly, the wicked scars on my thighs and calves. The shame scalds as hot as fire.

There's a lump lodged in my throat. I wish it would choke me out. I wish I would lose consciousness right now and wake up yesterday or tomorrow or in the middle of the ocean.

What did I do to deserve this?

I do what I'm supposed to do. I keep my head down, follow all of the stupid rules—mostly. I get my work done, and I don't make trouble. How am I here? How is this happening?

Why did I do something so ever-loving *stupid*? There's no planet or alternate reality where my runt of a wolf could beat Haisley Byrne's she-beast.

I can't live through this moment. The humiliation blisters every inch of my skin, but my heart keeps beating, and so I have to. Ghosts from the past pluck at the edges of my awareness. *You've survived worse*, they murmur. *Just hold on.*

"What the *fuck*?" Killian finally bites out, his voice dripping scorn.

I open my mouth, but no words come out. My wolf wails, pacing her confines. Why isn't he helping?

She doesn't understand, so she cries, piteously, and Killian's face shifts from disdain to anger. I try to swallow the sound down, but it's coming from my chest. I can't even muffle it.

"Why attack Haisley?" he demands.

He knows why. Mates know each other instantly. Females go into their first heat, and it triggers some kind of magical chemical reaction. The male recognizes his fated mate, and then she recognizes him, and they fall in love and have young and live happily ever after. Or something like that.

Most of the mated females *say* they're happy. They don't smile much more than us lone females. You kind of have to take them at their word.

The point is—if I recognize Killian as my mate, he recognizes me now, too. He gets why I attacked Haisley.

It was a dumb, dumb, *stupid* move, but wolves can't tolerate their mates being scent-marked by rivals. It's basic psychology. Biology. Whatever. Apparently, it's hella stronger than the survival instinct.

My wolf still bristles at Haisley hovering nearby. If my wolf were stronger, she'd go for round two. Dumb, dumb, *stupid* wolf.

Killian lets out a growl that makes the tables wobble on their wheels. He's losing patience.

"Speak for yourself," he says.

"You know why I did." It's almost a whisper.

He stalks down from his dais to stand above me, stance wide and arrogant, as if he needs extra space for his dick to swing. He folds his arms, and his biceps bulge. I lick my lips.

"Humor me," he says.

I swallow. My throat is still tight, and my mouth is bone dry. I'm scared, and my wolf is flinging herself at the walls, desperate to get loose and jump on him—I'm not sure whether to claim him or rip him a new one. She's out of control, and I can't calm her down. It's all I can do to stop her from trying to take our skin again.

Killian cocks his head expectantly.

"You're my mate," I say.

It had gotten almost quiet in the great room, but at my words, a wave of gasps, and a few sputtering laughs, ripple through the crowd.

I hug an arm to my breasts and try to cover my pussy with my other hand. This isn't the gathering at the end of a midnight pack run or a dip in the river on a hot day. I'm the only one naked, and it's full bright.

Everyone can stare at my mangled leg at their leisure. They take every opportunity to gawk usually. I'm a car crash to them. A shifter with scars. Doesn't really happen, so they can't help but look. Even the packmates I'm cool with.

My good leg wobbles, and my stomach heaves. I can't

throw up. I have to live through this moment to get to the next one, and I can't do that standing in a puddle of puke.

I force my back straight. I'm not really here. I'm in the future, and this is a memory. It can't hurt me.

I ball my fists, nails digging into the meat of my palms.

"What was that?" Killian arches a brow, his dusky blue eyes daring me.

"You're my mate."

I know it like I know how to breathe. My wolf is even more certain. She's frantic, howling for acknowledgement. Rescue. Touch. A carcass she can maul and take her messy feelings out on.

I can't help her. There's nothing I can do. I try to soothe her, but she's lost in her agitation.

Killian's lips press into an unforgiving line. He glances at his lieutenants. They're all standing now, too, staring at him, shoulders squared. Awaiting orders.

The whole pack is waiting with bated breath to hear what he's going to say.

Dread crawls up my spine with spidery fingers.

"It is known that I have no mate," he says.

The words slam into me, rocking me back on my heels like a cannonball to the chest, not with surprise, but with a physical force. For a second, I lose balance, but my good leg doesn't fail. It firms right away. I'm still upright.

My wolf wails.

"If I had a mate, would she be weak?" He rakes his gaze down my front, lingering on the red puckered scars on my outer thigh.

"Would she be incapable of defending herself? I am alpha." He gestures toward all the people gathered around, craning their necks to see better. "Would Fate give us you to lead by my side? To protect us?" His tone isn't cruel or mocking. It's coldly reasoning. Like he's speaking to a child. Or a mad woman.

He waits as if he's expecting an answer.

I can't speak. It hurts. My she-wolf's pain echoes off my own, and none of this makes sense.

I don't want to be his mate. I'm *not*. If I have a choice, I refuse, but every atom in me knows there's no choice. There's a flow of energy between us, my breast to his chest. How does he not feel it?

Of course, I'm the last female to rule a pack. I didn't pick this. But that's not the way this works, and he *knows* it.

His angular jaw clenches. He's perturbed that I'm not taking it back. Should I? I don't want this. Not in any way.

"I've killed for this pack," he says. "I've brought light in the dark and heat in winter. Water that runs clean. I've been challenged eight times, and I have emerged victorious with the flesh of my rivals filling my belly. What have you done? How have you earned the rank you claim?"

His voice is even, and there's pity in his eyes. He shakes his head.

"You're confused. Go back to the kitchen."

And that's all the time he has for me. He snaps for his lieutenants and turns back to his dais. I'm dismissed. Thrown back in the water with my head ripped off like a too-small fish, guts leaking, lungs still screaming for air.

Inside me, everything that makes me, that holds me up and keeps me going day to day, crashes to the ground and splinters. The pain is a gaping hole. An unfathomable *wrong*.

The connection between us is there, throbbing and alive, and he doesn't seem to feel it at all.

I wait for my heart to sputter to a stop. It can't endure. It isn't possible that it's still beating.

But it does. Thump. Thump. Steady and sure. As if nothing happened.

As if the universe hadn't told me, in the most basic of terms, that I'm less than nothing.

The silence in the great room is suffocating, and then chaos breaks out. There are catcalls and hoots and laughter. Killian snaps his teeth, and the pack lowers the volume until the derision and amusement is a dull roar filling the room.

"Get her out of here," Killian says to his lieutenants. They try to out-stare each other until, finally, Tye huffs, strides over, and grabs my elbow. He marches me out, hauling me back to my feet when I trip, steering me across the open floor and down a corridor to the rear exit.

He kicks the screen door open and thrusts me into the dark.

"Go home," he says, his voice surprisingly free of scorn. "Don't come back around for a while. Let things cool down."

He doesn't wait for an answer. He goes back inside, letting the door slam behind him.

I'm alone in the dark, naked and trembling, and the worst is that now the danger is past, heat is creeping through my veins again. Warm want and longing rise as the adrenaline ebbs. Slick drips down the insides of my thighs.

I squint into the night. My senses are sharper than they've ever been—there's a new richness to the faded green and brown rust of the dumpsters, to the musk of the raccoons that circled the container and ambled off into the trees.

Oh, hell. I've been thrown out with the trash.

Well, I'm not going to stay here. I head into the woods. There is no way I'm going back around front to the path so I can stumble naked past the old males smoking cigars on the porch.

Killian's words ring in my ears. *What have I done for this pack?*

Endured it for twenty-seven years. Cooked their food. Cleaned their lodge. Washed their clothes. And in between I taught myself—and then the other lone females—how to make preserves, and keep bees, and dry herbs, and raise hens for eggs, and forage for mushrooms.

I figured out how to drive and how to sell our goods at the human market, and then I figured out the internet. I made money. Money for phones and books and whatever we want. Money so that we don't have to ask the males for anything, and we owe them nothing.

We paid for Old Noreen's massage chair. A rental on the far side of town so Kennedy can shift in private. Annie's books and music and movie subscriptions. Video games for my old foster brother Fallon that he resells to all his friends who haven't made the cut to fight on the circuit yet.

I force myself to count so I don't drown in the hole Killian shoved me into. I'm dangling, holding on for dear life, nails dug into a slippery edge, but I'm not *nothing*.

I might not be male or mated—I might not have a father or uncle to "protect" me—but I have something to show for my life.

The coop and bee yard at Abertha's cottage. The patches of strawberries, blackberries, raspberries, and rhubarb. Our plot of medicinal herbs—calendula, peppermint, lemon balm, and chamomile. The greenhouse that the girls and I built ourselves.

We all have phones. Even Old Noreen so she can call her sister in Moon Lake whenever she wants.

Kennedy's video game consoles. Mari's sexy party dresses and high heels that she can only wear around the cabin and the melatonin so she can sleep.

The chasm yawns, and my life feels so small—*I* feel so small—but I'm *not*. I mumble that over and over as I stagger through the underbrush, aimless, heat itching at my skin, breasts full and aching, my wolf still mewling for help.

I'm not. I'm not. I'm not.

Where am I going?

I could leave.

I have cash in a jar, hidden in the knot of an oak tree behind our cabin.

I have a phone. Four hundred minutes, pre-paid.

I could live in the human world. I don't want to, but if I kept to myself, it could be tolerable. But, dear Fate, the noise and the smells—My stomach turns, and somehow, that ignites a spasm between my legs, and it's so wrong, so disjointed.

I'm devastated, not turned on, but my innards have gone haywire. My wolf cowers and weeps.

Yes. I have my wolf now. That means I have another choice. I could go feral. Live on my own in the foothills like Darragh Ryan.

Leave my girls to fend for themselves.

Be alone. Always.

I've considered my options a thousand times. Some days, staying seems impossible, but I don't have the strength to cut off my leg to escape the trap. This is a shitty pack, but I was born to it. Shedding it would be like shedding my own skin. Wolves are pack animals. My girls are more than family. They're pieces of my *self*.

I don't want to leave them. Or Old Noreen or the elders who are kind or the males like Fallon who aren't the worst.

I can't go back to the cabin, either.

I stop, lean against a tree, and take in my surroundings. The woods are dark, and the night creatures—the bullfrogs by the river and crickets and owls—hush as I stagger through. I'm a predator, and that is such a joke.

I'm weak. Defective. Rejected.

I reach for anger, my plans, my blessings—the handholds I usually cling to when I can't take it anymore, but there's nothing there. Only grief and shame and stupid longing.

Mate.

I have no mate.

How far can I run with three good legs?

I let the wolf take my skin, and I whisper, "Go. Go." The shift is an agony, but I welcome the pain.

I can't escape what I am, but maybe I can run until it's nothing more than a speck in the distance.

Maybe there's a choice I've never seen before now.

A way out.

My wolf stumbles forward, too broken to do much more than drag our bad leg behind. And I was wrong. There's nothing but the same paths I've known my whole life, the same river and foothills in the distance, the same boundaries that never, ever change.

2

KILLIAN

I drive my fist into the punching bag. Gael's holding it. He sways on his toes. I deliver a side-kick dead center. He staggers back a step. Almost got him.

Una Hayes kept her feet at the end. She's not as weak as she seems. Then again, she can't be. She went after the alpha female's daughter in front of the whole pack. And then after she got her ass handed to her, she in essence declared herself the alpha female.

Saying I'm her mate. Holy hell. She's moon mad.

I puff out a breath and fall into a rhythm. Jab, hook, cross punch, kick. Amuse myself with Gael clinging to the bag to stay upright. Repeat.

I don't have a mate. It is known. Besides, wolves find their mates when the females go into heat around sixteen or seventeen. Sometimes a little earlier, a little later. But not ten years later.

Una's close to my age. We rode the bus to the Moon Lake school together back in the day. If we were mates, I would've torn those vinyl seats from their moorings to get to her at the first hint of heat. It never happened.

She's either deluded, or she's a liar.

Given, it's a weird lie to tell. Strange time and place to tell it, too. It was never gonna end well for her. She's never shifted before. Folks figure her wolf is as fucked up as her leg.

She's always on the outskirts of pack life. Keeps to the lone females. Avoids gatherings except sometimes she shows up at the end of a run for a dip in the lake. She's got decent tits.

I clumsily adjust my dick with a taped fist, and then I nail the bag. Gael grunts. Sweet. Got him in the gut.

Turns out Una's wolf is a scrapper who likes to punch above her weight. I sniff and swipe my nose to clear the sweat.

Her animal is a scrawny mutt, gray with no markings and pointed, tucked ears. She lost that fight before Haisley even shifted.

Una's probably going feral. Lone females lose their minds sooner or later. Something about having no men in their lives—no mate, no father, no uncles or brothers—unbalances them. They start talking to ghosts. Refuse to shave their legs and shit. As far as I know, she's never gotten dick from any of the pack males—

"Son of a bitch!" Gael shouts as he sails backward through the air, landing on his ass. The bag swings so high it nearly comes off the S-hook. Damn. I put a lot more power behind that one than I intended.

"Should've moved with the bag instead of bracing," I point out.

He flips me off from the mat.

"Well, come on," I say. "Hop up."

If he takes this long to get up during a match, I'm putting him back on the maintenance crew.

After playing it up and plucking my nerves, Gael finally springs to his feet, showing off, and resumes his position. I fall back into a pattern. Jab, hook, cross punch. Watch Gael flinch. Kick.

What was I thinking about?

Oh, yeah. Una Hayes has gone nuts. I better pay a visit to Abertha. See if there's an herb or a spell or something.

Una may be unhinged, and not much more than a mouth to feed, but she's pack. I'm not gonna exile her to the foothills to die like my dad would've done. I don't know what we're gonna do with a crazy female, though. This pack doesn't lock up females anymore. For any reason.

The bag flies again, and this time, Gael soars a good six feet and crashes into a metal beam. My chest rumbles.

"What the hell, man?" Gael touches the back of his head. His fingers come away dripping blood.

This time I go help him up. "My bad. Must be the wolf."

I know some people talk to their wolves, give 'em personalities and shit, but mine is simple. He's an animal. He wants meat and blood. He sees it; he wants it; he goes for it. He's never let me down, so I give him free rein. Never had a complaint. We don't need to commune. Feel each other's feelings. We just—*are.* As it should be.

But he can get rambunctious.

I twist Gael's head, check out the cut. I can't see skull. He's fine. I punch his shoulder. "Let's go bench."

I'm trying to get him up to middleweight by the North Border fight. He could be competitive. Or he could get mauled and thanked for it by a Canuck if he doesn't stop flopping like a soccer player every time he gets whacked by a punching bag.

"Can I spot first?" He staggers a little on the way to the equipment.

"Nope." And he's doing double reps for asking.

While we're doing sets, Tye and Alfie come back from patrol. Ivo and Finn must have relieved them early. Definitely Ivo who made that call. Finn's a lazy shit. Thinks 'cause he kisses Lochlan's ass, he's special.

He's special 'cause he's currently top ranked in the circuit for cruiserweight. When his laziness inevitably costs him the title, he's back to mopping the ring and stacking towels with the rest of B-roster.

I slap Gael's ass. "Good work. Hit the showers." Gael's relief is visible. Dude needs to work on his game face. "Fallon. You're up."

I rack my weights and wave the pup over to the ring. He comes. Reluctantly. Scared as a rabbit as my grandad used to say. Kid needs to work on his game face, too. He's eighteen now. By his age, my father had been entering me in the New Moon fights for years.

I start today's lesson with an uppercut to the jaw. It'll be harder for the others to tell he's a pussy if his face is swollen.

Fallon's got potential, natural talent for days, but no strategy. He goes for the duck every time. I wait for his head to go down and nail him with a hook around each time he does it, and he still can't figure out what he's doing wrong.

It'd be entertaining if it wasn't gonna get him mauled in the ring.

At least Una Hayes has the excuse of inexperience. She sprinted right into Haisley's open mouth. Fuckin' delivery service. I had to fight my wolf hard not to intervene. He must've thought a pup was being attacked.

The whole thing still doesn't sit entirely right with me, but if you're big enough to go after a packmate, you're big enough to take your beating. I wasn't gonna let Haisley kill her or anything. For a second there, I almost tagged in, it was so hard to watch. I would've never lived it down, intervening in a female fight.

I have to talk to Abertha. If Una's not all there in the head, exceptions need to be made for her. We don't hurt females, young, or the defective anymore. I ended that shit.

Not everyone likes the new world order, but everyone is free to challenge me if they want to go back to the old ways. I only had to put a few males in the ground before the rest decided they could acclimate to change. Fear is a powerful motivator.

Speaking of—Fallon's getting too complacent. He's clinching so much, he should've bought me dinner beforehand. I throw a flurry into his gut, alternating with some pity pat shots to his thick head, and when he gets nice and disoriented, I drive an uppercut into his ribs and smile at the nice, clean crack.

He groans piteously as he taps my shoulder. "Enough, Alpha."

I follow up with a sharp jab for good measure. I say when it's enough. It'll be enough when he learns he's not safe in the ring and hugging is for the bitch he's banging.

"Stop clinching." I jab him again, right in the broken rib, and he yelps. "Stop ducking."

I meant for it to be a quick lesson, but I guess my wolf's got the taste of blood. I have my fist drawn back again when Tye grabs my forearm. When I snarl, Tye immediately drops his hold and shows his neck.

I growl from the chest. My wolf flashes his fangs. Tye lowers his gaze to the ground.

My heart pounds for no reason. Fallon Campbell isn't a challenge. He's hardly more of a workout than the bag most days. And Tye is my beta, my right hand. I don't need his submission. I need him to check my ass when I lose it.

But out of nowhere, aggression is rolling off me like it's fight night. The hairs on the back of my neck are standing on end. It's not a full moon, not even close. I take a few breaths, bounce on my toes, and throw a few punches into the air. I'm unsettled. Is there a threat I'm sensing?

"You didn't smell anything when you were out, did you?" I ask Tye. He's lounging against the ropes, the fraught moment passed.

"Nope."

"No tracks?"

"None."

"No signs?" I push, a dog with a bone.

"A woodchuck took a dump near the old dens. Is that what you want to know?"

"You can tap gloves with me anytime, pretty boy." I bare my fangs and lick the tip of the incisor.

Tye raises his hands. "You saw me last night. I almost let Lochlan Byrne pin me."

"Yeah, what was that?" Tye should've finished off that upstart in one round. I'd forgotten about it in all the drama afterwards.

Tye shrugs. "Too much turkey and gravy? Fuck if I know. It was a strange night."

"That it was." I duck between the ropes and slap his back. "Sauna?"

He nods, and we make our way to the locker room. I kept most things the same when I became alpha, but I did have the old gym restored and the facilities updated. We've got a sauna and hot tub now, and I had a ring built in the middle of the basketball court. When you can leap ten feet from flat-footed, dunking isn't really a thrill.

Before I was born, this camp used to be a nature retreat for school children, church groups, and the like. In the 80s, there were budget cuts, and the county was forced to sell the lodge, a dozen cabins, and fifty acres, including the river, ponds, a tract of virgin forest, and a cross section of Quarry Pack's claimed territory.

Earning the money to buy our land from the government was my father's greatest accomplishment. And it made our males what we are now—prizefighters mostly, bounty hunters and hired muscle on the side. It could be worse. We could wear suits and sniff human ass all day like Moon Lake Pack.

It's an impossible balance—the old ways and the new, the human world and our own. There is no balance, really. It's not unlike Una Hayes' gait—steady only because we keep it movin'.

There are only a few in the pack who realize how tenuous our hold on all of this is. Humans are weak, venal, and undisciplined—and they outnumber us by billions. That's an unstoppable force. They've been content to profit off us where they can—bet on our fights, sell souvenirs to the lookie-loos—but how long before they eye our territories?

Our DNA?

Humans are never content to coexist. I see Moon Lake, and I think Man has already conquered us. Wolves in suits. Humans must know they don't need to do much but let their ways infect our minds. We'll corrupt ourselves.

I strip, drop my sweats on a bench, and pad out the back of the locker room to the free-standing sauna. The door creaks on its hinges, and I inhale the cedar, sinking down on a hot, dry bench, not bothering with a towel.

Rowan Bell kneels by the fire, ladling water over stones. She casts me a sly look from under her thick lashes and arches her back so her perky tits nearly fall out of her tube top. I close my eyes and tilt my head back to lean against the wood paneled walls.

Rowan's mated to Liam Hughes. She doesn't care for the hand she was dealt, so they're one of those "strictly for heat" couples. Even if I was interested, I wouldn't go there. I've seen "strictly for heat" turn into "my one and only" too often, and I never want to make an enemy of Liam. He's too good with the engines.

Tye lets the door slam as he comes in and makes the maximum possible noise settling next to me. Hope he's got a towel wrapped around his waist. He's got no concept of personal space.

Not content to just harsh my mellow, he digs an elbow into my ribs. "Check out our little sauna maid over there. She's got something she wants to show you."

I rest my clasped hands on my belly and exhale. "Not interested. You're welcome to it."

He snorts. "Liam's fixing my alternator."

"I see we're in accord." I open my eyes and snap my fingers, catching Rowan's eye. She curves her lips into an invitation. She's got her tits out, shirt bunched around her waist. I jerk my head toward the door. Her smile falls, and she huffs while she yanks up her top, but she goes.

"Rowan better watch herself," Tye says. "Haisley's gonna do to her what she did to Una Hayes."

A snarl escapes my lips. I cough, clearing my throat. I don't know where that came from.

"I put no claim on Haisley."

"Don't matter. The females have their own way of enforcing rank."

Yeah, and it doesn't usually involve blood in the dining room. That's a great way to rile the males. If this shit becomes a trend, I'm gonna have to put the hammer down again like when I first took over the pack.

Tye keeps going. "Maybe it's time to put the females on the circuit since they're so eager to throw down."

We both laugh. Things ain't changed that much. If I let a female train and fight for real, Eamon Byrne would have no trouble convincing every male to take turns on me until I bled out, honor be damned.

"I wouldn't give Eamon the satisfaction."

"He's the one pushing Lochlan to challenge for beta." Tye tells me something I already know.

"Eamon wishes it was the good old days." There's more than a few like him. What the hell do they miss about living in caves, shitting in the woods, and freezing all winter?

Tye shakes his head, changing the subject. "I've never seen anything like that last night. Una didn't stand a chance."

"You take her to her cabin?" I don't know why I'm asking. Or why I'm suddenly anxious for the answer.

And it's not just me. My wolf's ears are perked, too. Maybe this is all him. He's got some weird attraction to crazy chicks.

Of course, that's not possible. The wolf and I are two forms, but one being. We don't have different concerns. That's a faulty construct. Like pain. It's in your head. It's not real. We are our wolves. Period. Every pup who was raised right knows that.

Your wolf's hungry? You're hungry. You're pissed? Your wolf's pissed. Simple.

"I dropped her behind the lodge," Tye says.

"By the dumpsters?" My shoulder blades clench. I have to focus on the muscles to relax. The heat isn't doing it.

"Haisley and her crew were gathered up front. I figure I'd give Una a head start."

"Goddamn."

My father never had to deal with this kind of shit. Females would have never dared to shift unbidden. Or approach the alpha and lay claim to him in front of the pack.

Or rub up on him uninvited, for that matter.

"Haisley's getting above herself." It's my fault. I guess I've let her suck my dick a few too many times.

Tye settles his arms along the back of the bench. "You should talk to Dermot."

"She's not gonna listen to him."

Dermot is Haisley's mate. They're "strictly for heat," too. He's forty years older than her and kind of done with the drama. She does what she pleases, and he's happy to let her.

"Maybe it's time to tell her to move it along, then." Tye cracks his neck and stretches his legs, spreading wide. My wolf rumbles. He narrows his spread.

"Maybe it is."

"Pack comes first, right?"

"Always," I agree. That's why I'm careful not to get too close to any of the females. A blow job is one thing, but you don't want to give anyone any ideas. Packs are built on rank, and there's two ways to gain status—who you fight and who you fuck. Clearly, I've given Haisley too much of my favor.

I need to diversify the roster.

I've never touched Una Hayes.

I mean, why would I? It wouldn't be right. She's got that messed up leg, and obviously, there's something wrong with her wolf. And now, maybe her head.

She always seemed smart. She was one of those kids who was early to the bus stop and sat right up front behind the driver. Teacher's pet. Always eating lunch in the classroom so she could play on the computer.

In my grandfather's day, she wouldn't have gone to school. My generation was the first to send the females, and only because Moon Lake Pack wouldn't let the males go if the females didn't.

At least my father saw the value in education. There were plenty of packmates who thought schooling was a waste of time for males as well, but if we didn't know enough math to grow the money we make on the circuit, we'd still be huddling in piles to survive the winter.

Soft gray fur, wriggling and warm. Tucked ears. Small paws kneading my belly.

My breath catches in my lungs, and my wolf growls low. Almost a purr. What the fuck?

Tye drops his arm and raises his eyebrow. I scrub my chest and toss a shoulder. "I don't know, man. He's been making weird noises."

"You hungry?"

"I mean, I could eat, but it's definitely my wolf, not my stomach."

"Hot for your new mate?" Tye snorts.

Aggression crackles along my nerves. I punch his shoulder. "She's not my mate."

"Obviously."

I nod and force myself to chill out. This is bullshit. Now I'm hot, sweaty, and uptight. And I got a semi from thinking about a sleep huddle, and Tye's eyeing it.

"If she were my mate, I'd know." The bond is unmistakable. That's what everyone says.

"Of course."

"I wouldn't have been able to reject her." A male cannot resist his mated female. It is known.

Tye nods slowly. He's not saying something. He's got that douchey know-it-all look he gets when he's watching his mouth.

"What? Spit it out."

He runs his fingers through his hair. He's got so much gunk in it that it stays perfectly messy. He gets my cousin Ashlynn to do it for him. Vain bastard.

His musk is annoying. I don't want him near—

I shake my head to clear it. The heat's getting to me. I don't notice male musk. I spend eighty percent of my time in a gym.

"Say what you're gonna say," I tell him.

"I don't know, man." He moves, bracing his forearms on his thighs and staring at the cedar slats. "The old timers say a lot of shit. You know your mate at her first heat. There's only one. You can't fight the bond. It's the greatest happiness a wolf can know."

"Yeah." That's the way it works.

"But, I mean—" He slides me a glance. "Haisley's sucking your dick. She's banging Finn. Jaime."

"So?" We've got rules for the lone females to keep the peace and keep them safe, but if a female has a father or brother or mate to make sure shit doesn't get out of hand, she can do what she wants.

"Dermot doesn't seem to mind." Tye raises an eyebrow. "And she's happy enough."

'Cause she likes to lord "my favor" over the other females. "And your point is?"

"Jimmy is mated to Dierdre, but he's living with Conor," Tye goes on.

"Ain't our business." Eamon and the other elders keep bringing it up, and I keep tellin' 'em that love is love. Got that off a dude's shirt at a cage match down in the valley.

"Dierdre's been sneaking off on runs with Liam."

"No shit?" I don't know anything that's going on in my own pack. I guess if folks keep a lid on the drama, I don't have to.

"All I'm saying is if you open your eyes, there's a lot of evidence that the old timers don't know what the hell they're talking about when it comes to mating."

"That fits the pattern."

The old timers are—collectively—morons. They want to be back in the dens. They think it's disrespectful that a female won't present on command. I installed solar panels on the lodge to cut the electricity bill, and they're worried the place will catch on fire. You know, like ants under a magnifying glass—'cause that's how solar energy works.

"All I'm saying is—" Tye draws in a deep breath to make the pause all dramatic. "What if she's your mate?"

"She's not my mate." If she was, my wolf would've claimed her. Period. End of story. He ain't shy.

"How sure are you?"

"Completely."

"I looped past the lone females' cabin on my way back from patrol."

"Yeah?" My adrenaline spikes. I'm only interested because every packmate is my concern.

"She wasn't there."

"I'm sure she's got work." The females are always doing something.

"She's not in the commons."

That's not surprising. She's probably running the woods now that her wolf's wide awake. And she's got to be embarrassed. She's not gonna want to bump into Haisley or her mother any time soon.

"Una's scent is stale. She didn't go home last night."

I snarl. My incisors descend, pricking my lip. "Son of a bitch." I suck the cut. I didn't see it coming.

That's not possible.

My wolf and I are one. We act as one.

I've already got hair sprouted all up my back and my vision's going dichromatic. I fight the shift. I'm not going to track Una Hayes and get people's jaws flapping again. That's not happening. She can go hide in the woods and nurse her wounds if she wants.

It doesn't bother me.

It shouldn't.

"Hey-oh!" I holler. Fallon sticks his head in the door. Not the male I'd have chosen, but he'll do. "Go find Una Hayes."

"And then what?"

"Come back. Report."

"You want me to bring her here?"

"I want you to come back. And *report*." I don't hide the irritation in my voice.

"Yeah. Right. On it." Finally, he shifts and races off. He's fast. I'll give him that.

I settle back against the wall. I'm amped. The steam's doing nothing for my tension. I'm not gonna go chasing off after Fallon Campbell and rend him limb-from-limb. That's crazy. He's just a kid, and he's just doing what I asked.

I'm going to sit here and relax.

Nothing's changed. I am who I've always been.

I don't have a mate. My wolf and I are one—the only flip-shifter in three generations.

Everything is as it should be. As I've made it.

The pack is good. All is well or soon will be.

A low rumble sounds in my throat. I swallow it down.

3

UNA

I wake up in a bramble. I'm not me. I'm her. *Us.*

There are stickers in my fur. *Our* fur. There's a thorn in the pad of my paw. It hurts.

Everything hurts.

The light is too bright. The sun is directly overhead. I'm hot. Burning up. Cramps seize my belly, twisting tighter and tighter. I'm swollen between my back legs. I'm tender there, aching and slick.

I want and I need and I *hurt.*

Killian. If I can speak, I can call. He'll come. He'll help.

There are no words in my mouth; my tongue is dry and coarse. I'm so thirsty. I'm dying from it. I need water. And Killian. He'll bring me water.

I whine and arch my back, raising my haunches. I have to. This is what I'm supposed to do even though everything is wrong. A branch scratches my side. The hurts twine—pricks, aches, a piercing longing that cuts and never eases, no matter how I shift my body.

The air is sweet, but not the sweet I need. Blackberries. I'm in a blackberry patch.

I whimper, wriggling forward, but the prickles scratch my underbelly. I can't move anymore.

Where's my pack? Where are the others?

It's not right to be alone. We're defenseless here. Except for the thorns. They'll give us some protection until our mate comes.

And he will.

I *need* him. I howl, but the sound is thready. He won't be able to hear. I grope blindly along the bond. He's there. Not very far away. I can feel him. He's strong. Willful. Mine.

Come.

He jerks at the word, but he doesn't move. His wolf howls, and it echoes through the woods, faint by the time it reaches my perked ears.

Come *now*.

The heat is ratcheting higher. I can't wait much longer. I need him. I lay my muzzle on the ground and present. I'm ready. Past ready.

He can soothe this ache. He can unwind this coiling agony, this drumming, throbbing need.

But he doesn't come. His howl fades to nothing, and my guts heave, my throat convulses. I'm sick. It's sour and sharp in my nose, and I heave again and again until my stomach's empty. I turn my muzzle so I'm not laying in it. It's all I can do.

I'm facing a clump of blackberries now, and their ripeness cloys. Offends. I want my mate. I want Killian's sweet toffee, molasses, thick and sticky caramel scent. I cover my snout with my paws and press closer to the dirt.

The pain won't stop. It crashes into me in incessant waves—the pricking thorns, the agonizing heat, my spasming leg, and worst of all, the torn and jagged wound where my bond begins. How could he hurt us and not feel it? Something is terribly wrong. Unnatural. Out of order.

Where is he?

He's not here. He won't come.

My wolf doesn't understand. Grief overwhelms her. He must be dead. He must be trapped or hurt or else he would come. She is certain. She knows this in every fiber of her being.

Her heart breaks, and her heart is mine, so it doesn't matter that I know Killian Kelly is garbage, and that he's rejected us. I shatter, too, as I sweat and whine, haunches raised, ready, longing for a male in a way I never, ever have before.

The woods are silent except for a faint breeze rustling high in the canopy.

I don't know how long I'm here. A long time. When a sharp scent breaks me out of my delirium, the sun is low in the west. There's a voice, curt and strong, familiar. I call out, but nothing escapes my lungs but a wheeze.

"You can go back," a female says. It's Abertha, the crone. My friend.

"Killian says I need to report," a male argues. Familiar, but wrong. I huddle small.

"So report."

"What am I gonna report?" The male's voice grates like radio static.

It's Fallon, the youngest brother from my last foster family. We're close, but dear Fate, has he always smelled like milk gone bad?

"Tell the alpha that his mate is in heat in the woods."

"I ain't tellin' him that."

"Then make something up." Abertha's exasperated. She's close. A yard or two away. There's a slight easing, not in my body, but in my mind. She'll help me. She'll know what to do.

"Like what?"

"I wouldn't dare think for one of the alpha's minions." Abertha doesn't even try to not sound sarcastic.

"Yeah, that wouldn't—" Fallon's voice trails off. "But if you *were* gonna give him a report?"

"I'd say his mate is in heat in the woods."

Fallon growls. I tense, and all my joints scream at once. Because of the wounds from the fight? Shifting? Heat?

From all of it and the loneliness salting every wound.

"Don't growl at me, pup. I'll curse you."

There's a long silence.

"I'll tell him she's with you," Fallon finally says.

"You do that," Abertha replies.

"Is she—" He clears his throat. "Is she okay?"

"What does it smell like to you?" Abertha asks, curt, clearly done with him.

"Like something's wrong."

"Go ahead and tell him that."

"He won't care." Fallon's voice is bitter.

Abertha doesn't answer. There's a rustling and the stink of sour milk fades. I suck down a deep breath.

And then I see scuffed boots and the hem of a patchwork skirt.

"Oh, you poor thing." Abertha squats, peering through the thorny branches. "How long have you been in there?"

She clucks. I can't even raise my head to acknowledge her. I've collapsed to my side, panting, tongue hanging from the corner of my mouth.

"Let's get you out of there." She reaches in, yelping when a thorn scratches her forearm. "I'm sorry Una's little wolf. This isn't going to be as gentle as I'd like."

She grabs my hind legs and drags me out from the underbrush. I whine. The pain is so all-encompassing, my bad leg hurts no worse than the other.

"There we go." Abertha plops on her butt—as always, amazingly agile for a female her age— and she cuddles me between her legs, smoothing a hand over my flanks. I whimper.

"You need to shift back, Una, love. I can't help you like this."

I don't want to. I don't want to think as well as feel. Feeling is already too much.

"Come on, now, brave girl. Come on," she coaxes. I lie there, spent and shivering. She sighs. "It'll go easier on you if you decide to do it yourself."

I can't. I don't have the energy.

Abertha scoots back, giving me space. "Well, don't say I didn't warn you. Now, *shift!*"

There's power in her voice. I have no choice. My body buckles, limbs unfolding, and I bow with the intensity and scream. I'm ripped from my own hide. I'm dragged from my form, and there's no way to stop or slow, no respite from the stabbing biting pain that goes on and on and on.

Energy crackles through the bond, a surge of strength that isn't my own finally allows my muscles to knit together.

In her agony, my wolf exhales. *Mate. Alive.*

And then I'm sprawled, naked, in the dirt. Abertha's sitting across from me, knees bent, a thick silver braid hanging over her shoulder. She peels off her T-shirt and hands it to me. I catch a strong whiff of patchouli.

I struggle to sit and take the shirt. It's so hard to wrangle it over my head, but I'm freezing. My teeth are rattling even though my core is on fire.

I ease myself to rest on my hip so there's no pressure on

my pussy. It throbs. I press my thighs tight together. I can't meet Abertha's eyes. I'm a mess, dirty and caked with dried blood.

"So you've discovered you're the alpha's mate." Her lips quirk and the wrinkles in the corner of her eyes deepen.

"No. He rejected me."

"He did?" She raises a thin eyebrow.

"Abertha." I drag in a ragged breath. "It *hurts*."

I'm sweating so hard, already the cotton is sticking to my back. My core spasms, and it's worse than any cramp. It's a contraction. A thrusting knife.

I want Killian. I *need* him. And he won't come.

I *hate* him. I want to claw my skin from my bones. I want to dash my head against a tree, but I'm too weak to do anything but huddle and shiver.

"I can take you to him. I'll need to go get a wheelbarrow or something. To carry you."

I moan. "He rejected me. I'm weak. Unworthy, he says. I've done nothing to earn the rank."

It hurts to say, but the sting lessens as the words pass into the space between us. They can't cut as sharp out here in the open as they can inside.

Abertha's brows fly up. "What kind of bullshit is that?"

A sad, tired chuckle escapes my lips. "Typical. It's typical Quarry Pack bullshit."

"Well, he's gonna rue the day." Abertha snickers. "I can't lie, I would have paid to see this play out. Might have to move some things around on my calendar." Her voice fades, her gray eyes going vague as she stares over my shoulder.

Another spasm racks my body, and I moan, hunching into a ball.

"Hurts like a son-of-a-bitch, doesn't it?" She scoots

closer, her voice gentle. She smells like the things I love—the garden, the beehives, herbs, bubbling jam.

I whimper. "Can you make it stop?"

"I can get Killian. Make him come."

My wolf howls, drowning out my words. She *wants* that so badly. She *needs* him.

We need him.

He can make it stop hurting. He's ours. Our fated mate is our *right*. It's wrong that he's not here, his scent not even on the wind. My wolf loses faith, keening in grief again. *Dead. Our mate. Dead.*

What do I do?

I can't bear this much longer. I'm going to drag myself to him. Beg. The heat is incessant, burning hotter and hotter, like a wildfire racing through a dry forest, spitting and crackling as it encroaches. The smoke fills my lungs and stings my eyes, but I'm not engulfed in flames. Not yet. But soon. Very soon.

I'm going to abase myself in front of that arrogant asshole, crawl to him, and plead for his cock. I won't care who's watching. I can feel the point where I lose control rushing toward me.

I retch, but there's nothing but acid in my gut.

This isn't rock bottom. There's lower I can go. And I won't. I'm not nothing.

I provide for my girls. I protect them. I've made us strong and self-sufficient. I am not begging a male to mount me. Never.

"Knock me out."

Abertha shakes her head. "The heat will still be there when you wake up."

"Please." My voice is weak. "Help me."

"I can't. This is fate."

"*Please.*" I put everything that's left of my *self* into the word.

She lets out a long, gusty sigh and stares up at the passing clouds. "I shouldn't—"

She thinks for a long time, gray eyes reflecting the waning sunshine, and then she lifts a shoulder, suddenly at ease, as if she's come to some accord with herself.

"Well, in for a penny, in for a pound," she says. It makes no sense.

She stretches her arms high above her head like she's warming up in gym class.

"This is going to feel a little like three wishes." She cracks her neck, twisting to one side and then the other. "And maybe a little like that sea witch from the Little Mermaid."

"What are you talking about?" Abertha isn't always the clearest. She's mystical, and she smokes a lot of weed.

She gets on her knees in front of me, hovering her palms above my body, sensing my aura like she does when I'm sick.

"I can, for lack of a better term, *yank* the bond out."

"Do it." I'd do anything to make this all stop.

My wolf is pushing at my skin. She demands that we run to him, find him. If he's dead, avenge him. If he's living, present, thrust our pussy in the air, ass up, face down, and beg him to mount us. The picture is starkly vivid in my mind. It makes me want to puke again.

Our weakness is the only thing that's stopping her from running to him. We don't have enough strength left to shift.

It's horrible—the pain, the humiliation, the heat, the rejection, all twisted and jumbled. I'm so close to losing control.

"Do it now."

She chews her cheek, considering. "It can't be undone."

"Good."

"If I yank it out, you won't be able to use the bond to bring him around."

"I don't want him." My wolf howls her dissent. "I *don't*."

"You can only have young with your fated mate. No mate, no young."

I didn't think I ever would. I'd come to terms with it. But —another pain slices through me, sharp and deep. A loss, a terrible longing. Despair.

Abertha seems to note my hesitation. "There might be— side effects."

"I don't care." Another spasm racks me and my womb cramps, knotting my guts, stealing my breath. Nothing is worse than this. Nothing.

"I can't really predict what might happen."

"Please." Tears stream down my cheeks.

"The Fates have a tendency of getting their way in the end."

"Abertha, you said you could *help*."

"No young," she says again.

I wail. I'm past being able to argue. I can only beg. "*Please*."

She blows on her palms and rubs them together. "This might hurt."

I'd laugh if I could.

She places her right hand against my upper chest, splaying her fingers. She closes her eyes, balancing her weight and inhaling through her nose.

"I've never actually done this before—" Her other hand hovers above my heart, fingers twitching. "I'm not sure that—" She closes her eyes and sways. "Got it!" She clenches her fist and yanks her arm back, flinging it behind her.

Somewhere in the woods behind us, there's a crack, like a thick log is split by an axe.

And it's gone.

The pain is *gone.*

All of it. The heat. The pain from shifting. The scrapes from the thorns. Haisley's bites and scratches. The only thing left is the dull and familiar throb of my bad leg.

"Oh, wow." I blink.

Abertha grins wide enough to reveal the gold tooth in the back of her mouth. "To be honest, I didn't think that would work."

"You did it." There are tears in my eyes. "Thank you."

"I am an uncommonly powerful female."

"You are." I struggle to my feet and offer her a hand. She takes it.

She's agile for her age, but she's not too proud to accept a little assistance.

"A legend, some might say." She brushes off her skirt. She's wearing a white cami. Thank goodness. I don't want to give her T-shirt back. I'm raw in my body and my mind. I don't want to be naked.

Memories flash in my mind of the great room, surrounded by the pack, covered in blood. Killian's unwavering voice.

I have no mate. It is known.

I shiver. He doesn't now. I can feel the silence inside me where the fledgling bond had been.

"Thank you." I grab Abertha's dry hand.

She shrugs. "You'll pay me back."

"I will. I promise."

Abertha already takes a percentage of everything we make at the market. Lately, I've been debating whether to

cut her in when I figure out how to do online sales. I'm definitely cutting her in after this.

"Let's get you some tea," she says. "And pants."

We pick our way through the thick underbrush back to
one of the trails. I don't remember crawling into the thicket.
It was a smart move. In my heat, I was defenseless. At least
the brambles offered some protection.

We aren't far from Abertha's cottage. I must have been
heading there when I lost it. It's reassuring to see our
wooden beehives busy with activity, and the herbs bushy
and tall in the raised gardens.

I'm mostly numb. I feel like a rung bell. And I'm
parched.

Abertha leads me inside, and I sink down at her familiar
oak table, tugging her shirt as low as it'll go so my bare
rump doesn't touch the chair.

Her cat Apollonia winds a figure eight around my
ankles. It's strange, a cat who tolerates wolves, but Abertha
is strange. She's a crone, but she's nothing like any of the
other lone elders I've met. She's wise as hell, but she curses,
gives zero shits about pack politics, and she never sighs
when she sits.

And she disappears, sometimes for days or weeks at a
time.

Annie and Kennedy think she goes on spirit quests. I think
she has a lover in another pack. We don't ask, and she lets us
do whatever we want on her cottage grounds. The rest of the
pack steers clear of this whole area. Wolves are superstitious,
and everyone knows that old, unmated females are bad luck.

Abertha rummages around the kitchen, filling the kettle
and hanging it above the fire before she prods the embers
with a poker.

"So I guess I missed an interesting dinner last night, eh?" she says over her shoulder.

"I finally shifted. My wolf attacked Haisley Byrne. I lost."

Abertha chuckled. "I heard."

"From who?"

"That gaggle of girls you live with. All three of them showed up in the middle of the night, looking for you."

"They did?"

Abertha nods and opens the trunk at the foot of her bed. Her cottage is open concept, so to speak. It's one big room with a low ceiling. Very reminiscent of a hobbit hole.

She takes out one of her long hippie skirts and throws it at me.

"Thanks."

I have to admit, my heart warms a little. Kennedy I can see walking through the woods past curfew, but Mari and Annie are still afraid of ferals and bugbears. They were pups not that long ago.

"That short, squealy one wanted me to go down to the commons and talk to Killian."

"Mari's—" Well, she's hopelessly naïve, but that seems cruel to say. "Mari's a good egg."

"*Egg*." Abertha snorts. "You're on the internet too much. You're starting to talk like a human."

I shrug. I don't mind humans. They're easier to deal with than shifters.

"You can't live with them, you know," Abertha says. My gaze flies up. She sees too much.

"I know."

"You'd end up hurting one. Your wolf will never understand that they're not prey."

"My wolf listens to me."

"Was she listening to you just now in the thicket? Or last night?"

I sigh and rub my temples. She's right.

I breathe deep and let the scent of lavender and sandalwood calm me.

"I don't want to be here anymore." My heart tugs. No shifter wants to be alone. It's not how we're made. Still, it's the truth. This place is tainted.

I can't go back to the commons. I can't look Haisley and her mother in the eye. Act like shame isn't corroding me from the inside out. It doesn't matter that Haisley's mean and stuck up—she's pack. I didn't have the right to go after her. Not when she didn't know she was touching another female's mate.

And I guess, she wasn't. Now.

Abertha sets a steaming cup of tea and a big bottle of sports drink in front of me. "Hydrate while your tea cools."

Then, she shuffles back to the kitchen and comes back with a plate of muffins, placing them between us and easing herself into a chair. "You don't have a choice. This is home."

"I could ask for a trade."

Abertha doesn't bother to reply. She knows that's a nonstarter. No pack would trade an unmated female for me, not with my bum leg and doubt about my status, and we both know it.

"How do I do this?" I glance out a thick-paned window. The garden is peaceful, overflowing with green and bright bursts of red and orange and blue. It's beautiful. Hours and hours of hard work and sweat, but it yields good fruit.

Why doesn't my life work that way?

Abertha gives me a wry smile. "The same way you do anything. One foot in front of the other. One day at a time."

My shoulders slump. I'm so tired. "He's my mate."

"He *was*."

"I just don't get it. How can he reject me? Mates are fated. Am I wrong? Is this moon madness?"

A primal fear chills my blood. It might take decades, but eventually, moon madness is a death sentence. Either it eats your brain to Swiss cheese until you forget how to breathe, or you're exiled, or the pack puts you down because you've become a rabid animal.

Abertha nudges the muffins toward me. I shake my head. I can't eat.

"It's not moon madness. And mates are—complicated."

I've noticed. The story is you sense your mate, you can't resist each other, you fall in love, and you have babies. But there are a lot of—aberrations.

"So Killian and I aren't mates?"

"No. You definitely are."

"I don't get it."

Abertha lets out a long, gusty sigh.

"Is this one of those things like the man and the wolf where everything I've been taught as a pup is wrong?" The more I hang out with Abertha, the more long sighs I hear, and the more life gets confusing.

"Yup."

"So what? There's no such thing as mates?"

"Obviously, there are. Don't doubt your own experience, Una. I thought I'd drilled at least that into your head."

She drills a lot. Sometimes it's hard to separate the wheat from the chaff.

"There are mates," she goes on. "It's kind of like—" She looks around the room, and her gaze settles on the tea and sports drink in front of me. I haven't touched either, yet.

"So you've just run a marathon—that's heat, right?—and there is a beverage perfectly formulated to meet your biological needs." She points at the sports drink. "Ta da. *Your mate.* Nothing else will hydrate you. And, usually, a parched, um, runner will really, really dig the drink that quenches their thirst. What's not to love, right?"

"Sports drink tastes like ass."

She snaps and points at me. "*Exactly.* So when the sports drink doesn't appeal beyond the physical, some people will hold their nose and guzzle it and suffer for life. Some people drink until they're hydrated and then switch it up. Decide they prefer tea."

"Like Dierdre and Jimmy."

"Yup."

"And Liam and Rowan."

"Uh-huh."

"And Haisley and Dermot."

"I see you take my point."

"So why does everyone say mates are fated?"

"Well, I mean, in a sense, they *are*. In a biology as destiny sense. It's almost impossible to have a pup with anyone else."

Almost impossible, but there are stories about it happening. In other packs. A long time ago. I always thought the stories existed as an excuse for insecure assholes to accuse their mates of sleeping around.

"But the Fates are also—complicated."

"Are they like sports drinks?"

"No lip from you, little missy," but Abertha smiles as she says it. Some of the worry that's been haunting her face since she found me in the thicket disappears. "But yes. They are like sports drinks. And tea."

Abertha relaxing helps me let go a little. Breathe a little deeper. I take a sip from my cup. It's sweetened with honey. Just how I like it.

"First off, it's not Fate, it's Fates. Plural. And they aren't necessarily working together. You've got the sports drink Fate who is all about the results. Hydration by whatever means necessary. Pups, pups, pups. That's all she cares about. But then there's the tea Fates."

"Tea Fates?"

Abertha is warming to her analogy. Her gray eyes start to dance like they do when she's enjoying herself. "Uh-huh. Tea Fates are about the *journey*. Pups are great, but they're interested in the bigger things—love and destiny and balance and justice. Destroying all sentient life and returning the world to its natural state. That kind of thing."

"Sounds like a mess."

"Oh, yes. It is. Look around. Obviously, the powers that be have to be working at cross purposes, right?"

"So why do we all believe that mates are fated?"

"'Cause they are."

"And when they're not? Like Jimmy and Dierdre?"

"They still are. The story's just more—complicated. But people don't want to think about that too much. Strains their little pea-sized noggins."

"My little pea-sized noggin is strained."

"I bet. Drink something." She smiles wickedly. "Your choice." She taps the plate of muffins. "And eat."

"So Killian and I are fated mates?"

"Yes."

"But he doesn't think we are?"

"Appears so."

"And we're not anymore. You severed the bond."

"I did sever the bond."

"So I'm good with the Fates. None of them have any interest in me now, right?"

"Wouldn't say that."

"Abertha."

Abertha shrugs. She's got a mouthful of baked goods.

Mates or not—fated or not—it doesn't really matter. I can't bear the thought of going back to camp.

"Can I stay here?"

Abertha takes a moment swallowing. "I don't do room-mates." She pats my hand to take the sting away. "I don't like people eating my food."

"And yet you're pushing these muffins pretty hard."

"They're three days old. If we don't eat them, they'll go to waste."

"Wouldn't want that."

"No, we wouldn't." Abertha grabs another one and carefully peels the paper cup. "Don't worry. Killian will be sorry before all is said and done."

"I don't want him to be sorry. I just want to never see him again. Or if he was eaten by bears. That'd be okay."

"No bears around here. Just wolves and rats."

Abertha stands and crosses the kitchen to the fridge. A wave of exhaustion crests over me.

"It was humiliating," I confess to her back. "He asked what I'd done to earn the rank I claimed."

He's an asshole, but in the end, he's right. I've won no challenges. Matter of fact, I'm zero for one.

Abertha snorts. "For all that Killian Kelly's a thousand times smarter than his father was, he still knows nothing. He's gonna learn, though. Or maybe I should say 'remember'."

I can't follow her mysticism right now. I eye the plate, but instead of taking the offering, I lay my head in my hands. I don't have enough energy to grab the butter, and I can't eat a three-day old muffin dry.

"He's going to live happily ever after," I mumble into my

elbow, yawning. "Getting pawed at by females and barking orders from a metal folding chair."

"I doubt it." Abertha plops a crock of home-churned butter in front of me and drops into a chair with way too much oomph for a sixty—seventy?—year old woman. "I yanked the mate bond out of you." She waggles her arched eyebrows. "Didn't touch his now, did I?"

ABERTHA LETS me sleep in her bed—just this once, she's careful to say—and in the morning, I'm stiff and sore, but the scalding humiliation is—well, it's freaking awful, but at least it's a little less visceral. I'm not glowing red anymore.

I lie still for a minute, staring at the bundles of herbs hanging from the cottage's exposed beams to dry, inhaling the lavender and sage as I listen to Abertha snore.

I want to sink through this sagging mattress, under the floorboards, down and down until I pop out the other side of the earth.

How do I face the pack?

I went from top of the lowest quartile to dead last in rank the instant Haisley's fangs sank into my shoulder.

How do I serve in the lodge, or hell, pass Killian in the commons, without cringing to death?

The thorn patch is a blur, but I remember forcing my beaten, bloody carcass to present. For my mate who never came. I wish you could scrub memories from your brain with sandpaper.

I count to three. That's how many more seconds of self-pity I get.

I'm alive.

I'm healing.

The humiliating heat is gone.

I've picked myself up after worse things before. Like the attack that mangled my leg.

I force myself to remember what I can. I was only seven. Da had already passed, and Ma was bedridden and failing fast. There was no cure for wasting sickness back then.

Ma had sent me out to play in the commons so I'd stop making a racket in the cabin. Rowan Bell and I were weaving dandelion crowns. Rowan was supposed to be watching her baby cousin Mari, but she didn't want to, so she stuck her in a straw laundry basket.

Mari was the sweetest little critter with the perfect button nose, wobbly chin, and blue saucer eyes. I wanted to hold her, just nibble her fat cheeks, but Rowan wouldn't let me. She didn't want to play with Mari, but she didn't want to share her, either. I contented myself with staring.

I was painfully lonely, even then. I hadn't learned to live with it yet. I wore it on my sleeve. It made me weak. Easy to dominate.

Rowan had wandered off when Mari's father, Thomas Fane, staggered down the lane, drunk and raving. He was shouting about his mate fucking Declan Kelly. She may well have been. Killian's father considered it his right as alpha to rut any female in the pack if she wasn't in heat.

Thomas Fane probably would have stumbled on past if Mari hadn't cried out, but she heard his voice and startled.

He stomped over, peered down at her and sneered. I will never forget his expression. He said, "No child of mine."

Then he kicked the basket, flipping it, and as he aimed again, this time to stomp, I ran. My wolf was a pup. I couldn't shift. I was only as quick as a human, but somehow, I landed between his boot and Mari's small body. I huddled over her and braced, but the second kick never came. Instead, there was a snarling and cracking and unholy howl. And then claws and teeth.

I don't remember anything else. Ma told me that I kept Mari tucked to my belly, wildly kicking while Thomas Fane mauled me. Eventually, Declan Kelly came and killed him. They thought the leg would heal, but I suppose I was too young, or maybe there was something in Fane's saliva that infected the wound.

The bite and claw marks faded into scars, but the muscles never knit together properly again. My hip bone mended wrong, too, but I walked again in time.

When Ma passed, I moved in with the Malones and then the Butlers and then the Campbells. They were all kind, but back during Declan's reign, you ate if you won fights, and eventually, every male would have a string of bad luck, and I became one too many mouths to feed. That's why I learned to do for myself. Hunt mushrooms, gather berries. Trade for meat.

I get knocked down a lot. I always get back up.

So what if this feels unbearably heavy?

No one promised me an easy go of it. No one's ever promised me anything.

I swing my good leg over the side of the bed. My shoes are long gone. In the thicket? No, they're in pieces back at the lodge.

At least I have clothes for my walk of shame.

I force myself to stand and take the first step to the door.

I used to dream about running away. I'd go to Moon Lake with their sparkling mansions on the lakefront. Or I'd run all the way to North Border and live with the elk and bear. But a shifter can't run. You need the pack. Lone wolves go feral, kill innocents, and destroy themselves.

Long ago, I came to terms with the fact that running was

a child's fantasy. I make sure to close Abertha's door firmly behind me.

There's nowhere to go but home.

Besides, my girls are there. They're worried. And we've got business. I might have gone off my rocker, but the mushroom deal is still on. I hope someone remembered to get my phone from behind the crockpot.

I take my time walking back. The sun is still rising, and there's dew on the grass. It's quiet. Peaceful. It feels like a fever has passed, and I'm shaken, but gaining strength by the minute. The place where the bond was is raw, but not painful.

The closer I get to camp, the stronger the sweet scent of toffee. It's nice, but it's not what I crave. My stomach growls. I need meat.

My wolf prances, sniffing the breeze. She seems oddly unaffected by recent events. She's super excited to go back to camp. I want to let her out, but I wince thinking about shifting again so soon. Maybe this evening. That puts a spring in my step.

I skirt the commons and follow the ridge, approaching my cabin from behind. Only elders are up this early, and I really don't want to see them after yesterday's naked mortification. Or was it the day before? Time's a little fuzzy.

I round the cabin, and I'm almost to my front steps when a throat clears. I jump and whirl. Thankfully, I've already grabbed the banister, so I keep my balance.

It's Killian, leaning against the outbuilding across the path. He's wearing a gray sweatshirt, hood up, and his customary faded jeans that cling to his thighs. My heart beats faster, but in the way it always does around him. He's built and scary and objectively hot. It's a normal female reaction.

I scan my body. No sign of heat.

I exhale and stare at his boots. It's as close to a bent neck as he's getting today.

"Where were you?" His voice is brusque but even.

He doesn't come closer. He's propped one heel on the wall, and with another male, it'd look casual, but with his air of raw power, it's menacing as hell. I hug my arms to my chest.

"Abertha's."

Where I go is none of his damn business—and now it never will be—but I'm not stupid. He's alpha, and I have too much riding on my freedom of movement to antagonize him. The sooner I go back to being invisible to him, the better.

"For two days?" He lowers his leg and takes a measured step toward me. It's a dominance thing. I'm supposed to get nervous and back away.

I mean, I *am* nervous, but he's also transparent as hell.

I shrug a shoulder. It's an old wives' tale that shifters can taste lies, but—I'm as superstitious as the next wolf. I'm not risking it.

I keep my mouth shut and let him assume what he wants while I stare at his feet. They're huge, but propor-tional. Not like a clown's or anything.

That would be ridiculous.

So now I'm picturing him in oversized shoes and a red nose. All of the stress of the past forty-eight hours is balling up into one self-destructive, manic urge to bust out laughing.

I chomp down on the inside of my cheek.

There is nothing funny about this.

If I laugh, I'll look insane. When Killian's father was

alpha, they exiled wolves with moon madness. A few still live in the foothills. You can hear them at night.

"Why are you smiling?" He stalks closer, but not too close. Maybe three clown feet away.

I shake my head and literally bite my tongue until my eyes water.

"Are you crying now?"

"No."

"Have you gone mad?" My gaze flies to his. He's serious.

He doesn't really joke. To be honest, back in school, I always thought he was kind of dense. I had a few classes with him, and whenever the teacher asked him a question, Tye or Ivo would call out the answer.

"I'm fine." I make my face look sincere.

I'm a hot mess, my hair is in tangles, I'm clearly wearing someone else's clothes, and I'm doing the walk of shame smelling like herbs and blackberry juice, but in my experience, folks accept the answer they want to hear.

Killian scrubs his chest. There's a very faint growl coming from his wolf. "So this bullshit about being my mate?"

"I—" The stab of pain surprises me. I breathe through it. Why should I care that he thinks it's bullshit? It is now.

He waits for an answer, frowning. Irritated.

"I made a mistake," I say, mentally crossing my fingers.

"Yeah." His frown deepens. He's only two years older than I am, but he already has thin lines bracing his mouth, as well as the ones at the corners of his eyes. He looks like he's pushing forty, not thirty. "What were you doing at Abertha's?"

A chew on my lip. What do I say? His gaze darts to my mouth. His wolf rumbles. He swallows.

Might as well stick to the truth. "Nursing my wounds."

He rakes his gaze down my front as if he's trying to see through my wrinkled T-shirt and sagging hippie skirt, but in a very critical, and not at all in a lascivious way. His lip curls. He does not approve of my outfit.

Screw him. I swear he's been wearing that same pair of jeans since before graduation.

He folds his arms and glares down his nose. "You were foolish to attack Haisley."

"Oh, I get that now."

"She's got forty pounds on you, at least."

Tonight, before I go to bed, I am going to replay that line in my head and snicker and be very disappointed in myself.

"There's no way you could've won," he adds.

"I know."

He grunts.

My agreement seems to be pissing him off. He starts pacing. "You've got to compensate for weakness."

What is happening? This feels like a lecture, but we're alone, and the dynamic is weird. He's dominant, the most dominant wolf I've ever met, including his father. My blood-lines are solidly middle pack going back generations. Nature demands that I recognize him as a threat, but I'm not scared or intimidated. Neither is my wolf. She's—basking. There's no other word for it. She's just happy to be here.

I should be getting a crick in my neck from bending it. I'd hate it, but I shouldn't be able to resist, not with an alpha this close and obviously upset. But I feel no compulsion to show my submission.

Is this because the bond is gone? Did Abertha rip out my survival instincts when it comes to him, as well?

Could I just walk into the house? Let him lecture a shut door?

It's a heady thought—as warming as a shot of tequila.

I'm not in his thrall. I could just—go inside. Make a sandwich. Take a shower.

Fate knows, I don't want to be standing here. I'm worn out, and I stink. I'm not wearing panties, and I'm overripe downtown. There's no way he doesn't notice, but I guess he doesn't care.

He's almost ranting now.

"It's basic self-preservation. Never leave your underbelly exposed. In this case, your—" He waves at my bad leg. "If you've got a gi—, uh, shit, a disabled limb, don't go on offense. No such thing as the best defense is a good offense if your carotid is in some bitch's teeth. Understood?"

He glowers at me. His eyes are strange. Hard. Unforgiving. But they're also light denim blue and crinkled. And there's a thin band of gold around his pupils. I'd never noticed the ring before the other night. It's the color of his wolf's eyes.

A shiver zips up my spine. I tense. Is that heat? Oh, no. Please, no. I don't ever want to feel that again.

Killian drones on, and slowly, I relax. There are no more shivers or zips or zings. I'm warm, but I'm standing directly in the sun. I'm fine. Abertha fixed me.

"So you need to think before you do stupid shit. If folks figure you're moon mad—well, you don't want that. Just— buck up. Rub some dirt in it. Walk it off. Understood?"

He's finally paused, and he wants a response.

I have no idea what he means. Rub dirt in what?

And moon mad? He *knows* I'm his mate. He must. Else why the speech about how much I suck? If he thought I was just nuts, he would've skipped to the part where Tye bounces me out the back exit.

A flicker of anger flares in my chest. For a second, it's on the tip of my tongue to tell him to shove it, but I learned young to watch my mouth. Males don't haul off and pop you anymore on a whim, but they used to, and there's no rule about it. They could. If Killian and his crew aren't around, the elders will still backhand you if they don't like your tone.

So I grit my teeth.

"Do you understand?" he repeats, taking a step closer until his shadow falls on my face. My bonkers wolf gets excited. Like *joyful* excited.

I'm supposed to say yes. If I'm really cowed, I'm supposed to throw in a yes, *Alpha*.

I don't want to.

He already won. I got smacked down, and I'm not claiming him as my mate anymore. But he needs a pound of flesh, too? Total submission?

My skin tingles, and hidden in the folds of my skirt, I ball my fists.

I hate him.

I hate that he gets whatever he wants, and does whatever he wants, and everyone shows him their neck and kisses his ass, and he *still* needs to stand here in front of my home and call me crazy and stupid.

I was alone in a thicket—my eyes burn. Nope. Not gonna go back there. Not with him so close that I can smell him. It's such a sweet scent, but nothing special. Nothing I can't get in a candle or scented dryer sheet.

I am fine now. Heat was a bad fever dream.

"Una." He grabs my chin and forces me to meet his eyes. "What's wrong with you?"

I try to jerk from his grasp, but his fingers dig in. I let out the smallest whimper. Almost a hiccup. Out of nowhere, a growl explodes from his chest. Really loud. So loud there's movement in the cabin and a curtain flutters. Probably Mari and Annie. I bet they've been eavesdropping this whole time.

Killian drops his hand to his side.

"What's wrong with *you*?" I ask, rubbing my face. It doesn't hurt at all, but it's the principle. Dick.

He seems—thrown. Like the growl took him by surprise, too.

"Can I go now?" I ask.

"No. Stay." He raises his hand, slow and tentative, his forehead furrowed. He stares at me. My nerves sizzle. Then, with the lightest touch, he traces my jawline. Two rough fingers graze my cheek, his thumb caressing my neck. Shivers and tingles race through me, straightening my spine, seizing my lungs, curling my toes.

My wolf purrs, low and languid, and rolls onto her back, exposing her belly.

The little fool.

He stares at my lips. I nibble the bottom one. It's instinct.

He stiffens. A vein pulses at his temple. His wolf's rumble kicks up until it sounds like an engine.

Killian gently tilts my head from side to side.

"I didn't hurt you," he murmurs.

That's such a lie. For so many reasons.

"Alpha!" A voice booms from the head of the path. Eamon, Lochlan, and Finn. The three douche-kateers. I step back, but Killian's already dropped his hand and turned toward them.

He holds up a finger. "Gimme one."

Then he rounds back to me, face hardened. Cold.

He grabs my chin again. "Don't leave the commons."

"What? Why—"

"You don't ask questions. You say, "Yes, Alpha.""

He raises an eyebrow and waits.

He can wait all freakin' day. *Dick.*

I stare at the dirt path.

The males whisper amongst themselves.

Finally, Lochlan calls, "Alpha, you want us to go on ahead?"

Killian lets go of my face with a very slight shove.

"You attacked a packmate without provocation." He steps back, squaring his shoulders. "You're probably halfway to moon mad. You stay in the commons until I tell you that you can leave."

I'm grounded. Like a pup.

White-hot fury fills me as he strides off without a backwards glance. The males greet him like they didn't just see him yesterday, slapping his back, falling in behind him. I eat the rage. You have to if you want to live in Quarry Pack. If you let yourself really feel the injustices, your day is ruined, and I've got things to do. A mushroom deal to confirm.

Behind me, the door creaks open.

"Una? Are you okay?" Mari whispers, even though they've already disappeared down the path.

"I'm fine," I lie as I seize the banister and mount the first stair, hauling my bum leg up after.

"Do you need help?"

"I've got it." Stairs take me a second, but I can do them no problem. It's steep declines that suck.

When I get inside, all my roommates are huddled on the sofa. They've been snooping.

"What did the alpha want?" Kennedy asks.

"Are you exiled?" Annie worries the hem of her shirt.

"Why would I be exiled?"

"For attacking Haisley."

"There is literally a fight every night during dinner."

Killian usually picks the competitors, but brawls break out often enough that my point holds.

"But you claimed him as your—" Annie glances around the rooms as if someone might overhear. "*Mate.*"

"Yeah."

All three females are staring at me, Mari's blue eyes swimming with concern, Annie trembling, Kennedy's arms crossed, cranky as always. Kennedy is twenty-three, but she never grew out of the phase where she thinks everything and everyone is bullshit—always—in every way. If I had to pick, she's my favorite.

My young roomies want an explanation.

I sigh.

I flop down in the armchair. "I made a mistake, okay?"

"So he's not your mate?" Mari asks.

I shrug. I don't want to lie to them. Not if I don't have to.

"You can't reject your mate," Annie says.

"I guess you can."

Annie's face contorts in horror. A lot of her anxiety manifests around the mate thing. She's terrified that she'll never find him, or she'll mate with a male thirty years younger or something.

I used to be tormented by the same late-night thoughts. Maybe my mate died as a pup. Maybe he's a male from the Last Pack, and I'll never meet him because he's living in a den somewhere as a wolf twenty-four seven. Maybe Fate miscounted and had one female left over when she paired everyone up.

Maybe there's something wrong with me that makes me fundamentally unlovable.

There's so much to be afraid of that's totally beyond your control. But I was lucky. I discovered the farmer's market. There's no time to worry about males when you need to harvest enough honey to fill the orders for the Pumpkin Festival.

That's not going to be much comfort to Annie. She's got to find her own farmer's market, so to speak.

For now, her fear of dying alone is stinking up the place.

"Your mate isn't going to reject you." I muster the most reassuring smile I can.

We all know there's no way of knowing, but—shifters are superstitious. Say it and it will be so. And I'm older. Strange as it is, they look up to me.

"Oh, Una. I'm so sorry." Mari's lip wobbles.

"I'm not. Who wants to be mated to Killian Kelly?"

Kennedy shudders. "I'm not sure if he smells like the gym, or if the gym smells like him."

"He yells a lot," Annie adds.

"And all the females always talk about his dick." Mari wrinkles her nose, disapproving.

My wolf snarls. She can pipe down. It's the truth. Killian's a manwhore. It's nothing to us.

"I heard his wolf had his first kill when he was only nine years old," Mari says.

"That's impossible." Males don't shift until puberty, just like females. I didn't appreciate until now how much physical stamina it takes to move from one form to the other. There's no way a pup could do it.

"Killian Kelly can flip-shift," Mari argues. "And that's impossible."

It should be. Your brain can't even process what it's seeing when he does it. He'll be fighting, and one instant he's a man, the next a wolf, and then a man again. All the while, he's striking, kicking, leaping. Common wisdom holds that the wolf is always stronger, but a man can swing and throw and strangle. Handle a knife. Shoot a gun.

When Killian flip-shifts, he's supernatural.

That used to frighten me when I was little. Then it only made me nervous. Wary. But something's changed. I'm not intimidated anymore. At least not now that he isn't right in front of me.

I guess Abertha plucked out my fear with the bond.

It feels good. Liberating.

"That's enough about Killian Kelly," I declare. "We need to talk mushrooms."

Mari groans. Kennedy reaches for her video game controller.

I raise my shoulder and look at Annie. She shrugs in return.

I'm not fearless enough that I'm going to ignore an alpha command, and I'm grounded, so Annie's going to have to make the delivery after all. This rejected mate debacle is not costing me three hundred bucks in addition to all my dignity. Not this week.

4

KILLIAN

I feel cooped up all morning. The gym is stuffy. Reeks of socks and jocks.

I take B-roster down to the ravine to train on a downed oak lying across a dried-up creek bed. Put them through their paces. It's always fun to watch males who think they're badass eat dirt 'cause they can't find their center.

Conor and Gael are coming along, but Fallon might be better suited to the maintenance crew. It's a shame. The kid has heart. No fuckin' balance, though.

Una gets along well, considering how jacked up her gait is. I was never clear on how her leg got mangled. Thomas Fane was involved somehow right before my father put him down.

She could probably improve function with consistent training. I'd start with heel and toe raises, lifts and crunches. Put her on a treadmill. Maybe some yoga. Jimmy's been doing that to maintain flexibility as he bulks up. He's had some decent results.

Other than the leg, her musculature is decent. She's got

a female's round hips and soft belly—you don't wanna mess with that—but there's definition in her arms. Her posture's good. And she's got those sweet tits.

I don't remember them being so ripe. Earlier, she was wearing a white T-shirt that clung to the slopes of her breasts. It was so thin you could see her fat, dark areolas. Big as half dollars.

My mouth waters. Up on the log, Fallon teeters. Conor gives me a side eye. Did I growl again?

My wolf's antsy. I already let him run along the river for a few miles, but he's still making himself known. He knows he can help himself, but he's not interested in food or a fight to work off some energy.

This is Una's fault. She's disturbed the force. She seems so innocent. Stays in the kitchen, keeps her head down. So why's she so thick with the crone? Haisley and her crew wouldn't be caught dead up at the cottage. They ward against the evil eye when they so much as hear Abertha's name.

And now that I think about it, she gets around. Doesn't stay in her own circle like the other females. She's tight with the other lone females, but I also see her around Old Noreen's and the Campbell's cabin. Some of the quieter elders will call her over for a word at the lodge—I've seen her and Nuala with their heads together. Una gave her some honey or jam or something. And last month, wasn't it, I saw her talking to Liam at the garage. What business does she have with him?

And why do I care? She's not breaking any rules.

It's this mate bullshit. It's gotten in my head. I accepted a long time ago that I'm destined for something else. The flip-shifting. How I have my own ideas—I don't want to do shit the way it's always been done. I figured the cost of greatness was no mate. No young.

It isn't what I would have chosen, but that's the thing about Fate—she's got her own mind.

It's a bitter pill, but I deal with it.

And Una wants to stand in the middle of the pack, claim me, and nearly die for the insubordination. Haisley's teeth were real fucking close to her carotid. If Haisley had seen Una as a real threat, she'd be dead.

What a cluster.

I've got a riled wolf inside me, an unsettled pack, and there's no fight to look forward to. The next match is a month from now in North Border.

I sigh. Fallon pinwheels his arms and falls into the river for the sixth or seventh time.

Too far from the commons.

My senses jolt. The hairs on my arms stand on end.

I sniff the breeze. "Do you smell that?"

"What?" Conor and Gael twitch their noses. "Dinner?"

I inhale again. There's a faint hint of smoke and beef in the air. Maybe that's what caught my attention.

"Get back up there, Fallon. Front snap kick. Go." I clap a few times. He groans. I nod to Conor to partner him.

Get back to camp.

I pop my ears. The voice—if that's what it is—is silent.

The sun's still high, the sky is blue and cloudless, and the woods are peaceful. Birds chirp. Beavers are building a dam a half-mile downstream.

Shivers creep up my spine.

A black dot swoops across the horizon, riding a current. My fangs shoot out.

"Damn." I suck the cut. It's just a hawk, not even a very big one.

It's like I'm jittery. I don't get jitters. I get stoked. Aggressive.

Fallon lands a high kick, forcing Conor back a step. Fallon stumbles, falls on his ass, squashes his balls, shrieks, and then tumbles off the log as he curls up like an armadillo.

It's funny as shit. Conor and Gael crack up, but I hardly break a smile.

I'm missing something.

We should go back to camp.

"Conor, check him for a concussion. If he's good, ten more. See you back at the gym." I don't wait. Once I make a decision, I go. I shift and lope north. They'll catch up.

I race east, and instantly, some of the tension eases. The wind riffles my fur, and the soil and leaves, wood and water, all the sights and sounds of my territory sift through my senses, unraveling the knot that's been coiling in my gut.

Maybe I'm spending too much time training the males and not enough time roaming the pack lands. Bad things happen when you stifle the wolf. You start hearing voices, for example.

When we trot into camp, I expect him to give up our skin. The wolf doesn't like buildings. He keeps his form, though. I don't fight him; I never do. He sniffs, noting the fresh venison in the shed we use to butcher meat and wet pussy from a cabin along the common. Rowan and Lochlan.

Lochlan's supposed to be patrolling the southwest quadrant with Tye. Are we abandoning our posts to bang females now? That's the kind of self-indulgence that leads to fuck ups.

I figure the wolf will handle it, take out some of his nervous energy on Lochlan's ugly hide, but he canters straight through the commons, up the path along the ridge, winding past the laundry and the elder cabins. He's got a destination in mind. The garage.

Liam's out front under a truck, country blaring on the radio. Only his legs are visible. The place reeks of oil and metal. What scent is the wolf tracking? I can't make anything out under the chemicals.

The wolf snuffles around a tire and plops on his haunches, scratching his hindquarters like he's got nowhere else he'd rather be. We have shit to do. Training. Meetings with elders. Finances. Phone calls. All the other crap I avoid by training B-roster.

But I guess I'm gonna scratch my ass by an old tire.

Then I hear giggles. Females.

Una and Annie walk around the corner of the garage, and the instant they see my wolf, they freeze. Guilty as hell. Annie's eyes go round as dinner plates. She has the most skittish wolf I've ever met. Una steps in front of her.

My wolf doesn't move, but he barks an order.

Shift.

Annie shifts immediately. Under the truck, a curse devolves into a pained yelp. My bad. I guess Liam shifted, too.

Una is still standing on two feet.

My wolf barks again, louder. She lifts her chin.

My wolf growls a few more times for good measure.

Shift. Shift now.

Liam wriggles out from the undercarriage on his belly. Annie cowers, trembling, gaze averted, neck bared. As is right.

Una is frozen in place, wearing a pale-yellow blouse, rolled up past her elbows, and a long jean skirt. There's something balled in her left fist. Her brown hair shines, wisps framing her face. She's tied it back in her usual braid.

My wolf pads closer to her very slowly. Almost cautiously. She tenses. My wolf stops, sits, and—*whines*.

My wolf *never* whines. He's a huge silver beast with pure white markings, bigger than a dire wolf. We fear nothing and no one. We're unbeaten in battle. Sought by all females. Alpha.

What witchcraft is this?

My wolf stares at Una. Una stares at us.

He strides forward. One pace. Another. Like he's trying to be casual. Annie scuttles backward, whimpering.

Una cocks her head slightly to the left. My wolf pauses, patient, watchful. He wants her wolf to come out. Badly. He's frustrated, but he's being very careful not to let on.

For the first time that I can remember, he is not me at all. *I* want to force her down to her knees, snatch that braid and tilt her neck until I can see the vein throb in her exposed neck. Make her submit.

She's mad, and she's gonna get herself hurt. You don't bait a monster like mine. He has mauled males for less provocation than this. It's not in his nature to ignore a challenge.

But he's not giving up the skin. And for some reason, he's not responding to her defiance with aggression.

I don't get it. And I don't understand why he's so keen to see her wolf. It was painfully small and scrawny with a gnarled hind leg. The thing looked underfed.

And how can she resist shifting at our command? Only another alpha can defy our compulsion.

This can't be a mate thing. I don't feel a bond. I'd know if we were connected in that way.

My wolf rumbles low in his chest, a sound used to soothe the newly born. Una stands, all false bravado. Her knees knock, swaying her skirt. I can smell her fear. Neither my wolf nor I like it. It burns our nose.

My wolf pads toward her, closer, closer, until there's no more than an inch separating us. He lowers to his haunches, almost to eye level. Una's pupils are huge, eating up her irises. What color are they?

I try to recall, but all I can picture is her gazing down or scurrying away, like all the lone females. And then a memory—an old one—pops up from nowhere. Brown. They're a dark, hickory brown.

Without warning, my wolf darts forward and buries his nose in her hand, snuffling and slurping.

She yelps. Her fear spikes, and then it retreats, disappearing with her abrupt laugh. My wolf is smug with satisfaction.

She snatches her palm away and wipes it on her thigh. "That's so gross. Your nose is wet."

He nudges her again, nuzzling her hip, trying to reach the hand she's now tucking behind her back. I understand why. She smells delicious. It's subtle. I couldn't pick it up a foot or two away, but this close, it's fucking amazing. Delicate and earthy. Like vines and shade and pussy.

And her taste? So good. Unbelievably good.

My wolf butts his snout into her again.

She sighs and peers into our eyes, brow furrowed. I don't know what she sees, but her demeanor changes. She relaxes.

"You aren't him, are you?" she says. She stares a moment longer. "No. You definitely aren't."

My wolf whines. She actually smiles, and then she tentatively offers me her palm. I dive in, licking, covering her in my scent. She tastes—homey. A hint of salt and warm, light things. Bread straight from the oven. Melting butter.

Now he's whining and nuzzling like a pup until she gives in and scratches behind his ears. I haven't asked for this since my mother was alive. I'd forgotten how it feels.

My body goes boneless. I flop on the ground at her feet. She laughs softly. It's a pretty sound. Tentative and delicate.

Behind us, Annie perks her ears, curious.

My wolf growls, but it's playful. He nips at the hem of Una's skirt.

"You're as bossy as he is," Una says, awkwardly lowering herself to the ground so she doesn't have to bend. "And you're big, too."

My wolf scoots himself forward with his rear legs until he's draped across her thigh. I tense, preparing to fight him for our skin.

Is he lying on the jacked up one? Does it hurt her?

No. He's flopped on her good leg.

"What are you doin', big guy?" she murmurs. He kneads her belly lazily with his front paw.

A short giggle escapes her lips. "Hey. That tickles." She grabs the paw and puts it back.

My wolf wriggles higher on her lap and sticks his snout under her arm.

A peal of laughter rings out. "You did that on purpose!"

She shoves him back, her fingers slipping into his thick fur. "Oh. Wow. You're so soft."

I'm not. If I were in human form, my cock would be hard as a rock. As it is—I try not to think about it.

She plunges her fingers deeper into my pelt and scritches. My wolf's tongue lolls, and he stops messing around, resting his muzzle on her upper thigh so he can sniff her pussy. He's so damn happy.

I've never really felt his feelings before. We're usually on the same page. Irritated. Aggressive. Excited. Horny. Somehow, he's developed a mind of his own. Preferences.

I like big hair, big tits, a little effort. High heels and shit. I'm not into, like, homesteader chicks. But my wolf digs this female.

Mate.

It's not possible. The wolf and the man are one. If the wolf has a mate, so does the man.

Mate.

I'll be damned if my wolf doesn't sound patronizing as hell. Like he's talking to an idiot.

Annie cautiously creeps closer. My wolf ignores her. She's not a threat.

Una glances at Annie. My wolf butts her. He wants all her attention.

She smiles, indulgent. She's not scared—at all —anymore.

"Look at these paddles." Una lifts my foreleg and measures herself against my paw. It eclipses her hand. Her palm is exquisitely soft against our rough pads.

Annie burrows into Una's side and gawks. Between Liam and her, the whole pack is gonna hear about this by dinnertime.

Una's gone back to smoothing my sides and scratching behind my ears. She's humming under her breath, her expression dreamy. She's pretty like this, unwary, unhurried. She seems younger. And when she leans to reach my far ear, her tits brush my flank.

Why did I never let her show me a good time?

For one, I guess she never came on to me like most of the other females. I'm not so lazy that I won't make a move if I'm interested, but I never sniffed after her.

I'd say it was because I never noticed her, but we're a

small pack. Everyone's on my radar, especially wolves like her who stick out.

She's the lone female who sat at the front of the bus. The female who never shifted. The one with the tidy braid down her back. And obviously, the one with the busted leg.

If I'm gonna be honest, over the years, I've thought about her a lot. And little Mari and Old Noreen and the other lone females. And Conor and Jimmy and Kennedy. All the ones who would have been exiled, tormented, or exploited under my father.

Fixing that shit took years. Almost a decade, and I'm not half as far as I thought I'd be when my father passed and I beat Eamon Byrne to become alpha. Spared his life to set a new precedent—pack over ego. Pack over everything.

What my father never understood—and the elders refuse to grasp—is that subjugating and abusing your own packmates leads to a weak pack.

We've got Moon Lake to the east, growing fat off human money, snapping up land as quick as they can buy it. How long before they get the idea that Quarry Pack territory should rightfully be theirs? Might makes right.

If your pack has a bunch of broken females and cowering young, you look weak. I want plump, happy females swollen with young, and well-fed pups with thick coats yipping and wrestling in the commons.

In my father's time, I'd only ever see it from the window of our old yellow bus as it rolled up to the Moon Lake school, but I knew it was good. It was *strength*.

So, yeah, I've *considered* Una a lot, but never in a sexual way. She's damaged. It'd have been wrong.

My wolf doesn't see her as off limits. He's getting playful, and he's not watching his strength like he should. He's wriggling up on her lap, propping his paws against her chest to lick her face. She'd be knocked flat on her back if she wasn't bracing herself on her arms.

He slurps right across her lips, and she shrieks, reaches up, and whacks him upside the head. I freeze.

He doesn't even snarl. He plops back and rests his head on his paws, makin' eyes at her, a contrite whine in the back of his throat. And then when she reaches out to pet him, he lunges up and slobbers on her face again.

He loves her shrieks.

He thinks this is the best shit ever.

And she's smiling.

Maybe I'd be, too. If I were in my human skin. It would be a sight to see. A giant wolf teasing this small female as if he's a pup.

This whole interaction is blowing my mind.

Generally, when I'm the wolf, my mind is blank, my consciousness deep in the animal. I'm along for the ride, brain disconnected, enjoying the experience.

Not now.

I'm hyperaware, and I'm baffled. I don't get his motives.

He wants something from her, but he's not pushing. He's just messing with her.

He wants to get his rocks off, but he's deferring the urge. He *never* defers the urge. We never have to.

Annie's getting bored. She trots away to sniff Liam. He's already shifted back to skin and working on the truck.

Eventually, my wolf has had enough of making Una squeal, and he rests his head in her lap. After a few seconds, she starts stroking the top of his head.

"You're not scary at all, are you?" she says.

She's a hundred percent wrong. My wolf and I have more kills than any alpha in North America. We've taken on a pack of ferals alone and left their drained carcasses in a heap. The sun-bleached pile of their bones still sits on the border of the southwest quadrant as a warning. The male pups dare each other to go there and steal a bone. It's become a rite of passage.

I am a once-in-a-hundred-years flip-shifter, alpha at eighteen, bigger and stronger than any competitor I've faced on the circuit. My wolf and I show no mercy to those who threaten the pack. We rule with an iron fist.

And my wolf is drooling through this female's jean skirt, luxuriating in the scent of her ripe pussy.

"I like you." She runs a finger down my muzzle and fuckin' boops my nose. My wolf flops and wriggles until his upper half is plastered to her lower abdomen—her womb, where she'll grow our young.

Is that the wolf's thought?

Mine?

She's still propping herself up with her arms, and they're wobbling, but she lets him lounge on her. He doesn't have any concept of his weight. I'm gonna need to force him out of the skin if he doesn't back off soon.

There's nothing but birdsong and the distant ratcheting of a wrench, so when she speaks, I startle.

"You have to make Killian leave me alone," she says low, almost under her breath.

What?

My wolf growls. He doesn't like that either. We don't take commands.

"We're not mates anymore," she goes on. "Abertha fixed it. Tell him to ignore me. Okay?"

Abertha fixed it? What the hell is she talking about?

She's not moon mad. The wolf can smell that rot a mile away. She's not making sense either. No one can "fix" a fated mating.

"Tell him he doesn't have a mate now. He can do whatever he wants. He should leave me alone. I won't cause any more scenes in the middle of dinner."

She laughs, and it's self-deprecating. Sad.

The wolf does not like how she's talking. Impulsively, he bites her shirt and yanks.

She smacks him—hard—and says, "No."

Immediately, she freezes, sucking in a breath. *Now* she shows her neck.

I'm summoning my skin, ready to wrestle control back, when my wolf very deliberately licks all the way up her exposed neck and then bites the shirt again, tugging back and forth, gently so as not to rip it, sly as hell. Teasing away her rush of instinctual fear.

It's hard to think. Her taste explodes in our mouth. Our heartbeat kicks up, groin tightening, balls swelling.

He wants her. He nudges her. Growls a command. *Roll over. Present.*

She's breathless. Nervous. Unsure. She scrambles away from us.

I don't want that.

He lets her go, dropping his muzzle to his paws and pricking an ear. Holy shit, he's trying to be cute.

She's doing the complicated maneuver that she did after the fight to get herself back to her feet. Roll from her hip to all fours. Push up on her bad knee. Rise to her good leg. Take the pressure off the bad one and balance.

My wolf keeps his distance. *We* keep our distance.

What is he going to do? Somehow, we're split for the first time in our lives. I don't know what he's going to do next, and I don't trust him near her when she's vulnerable. She's unsteady on her feet. I stay back. I don't draw attention to her weakness.

Why is my wolf giving her space after being all up on her? I have no idea.

"It was nice to meet you, Killian's better half." She speaks softly, her lips curved. "Tell him I'm not a threat, okay? I'm not going to attack anyone else. It was all a mistake. Everything can go back to normal. Please?"

Her brown eyes are big and round, and damn if they don't remind me of something. A place and moment a long time ago, just beyond memory.

THIS ISN'T NORMAL.

Everything's out of whack.

My wolf's gone rogue. My brain is on the fritz. Abertha the crone is somehow involved.

And Una Hayes tastes fucking *amazing*.

5

UNA

Annie is a lot craftier than I give her credit for. I took her to the garage to show her how to get the Ford's engine to turn over. Liam won't let us take a pack vehicle to the market because the males would smell us in the cab, so we have to take an old junker. The Ford's the best of a bad bunch.

When we rounded the building and Killian's wolf bounded up, the keys were in my hand. There's no explicit rule against us driving, but females aren't allowed to leave pack land, and we aren't taught to drive like the males. Except for my girls—who I taught—none of the females except Abertha knows how.

She's the one who taught me on the trails by the old quarry. I don't know where she got her rusty hippie van, nor do I know how she kept it running as long as she did, but I miss that old girl. Liam tore it up for parts a few years ago.

Anyway, the keys would lead to questions I don't want to answer. I figured I'd bend my neck and make a quick escape, but then Killian's wolf got friendly. He wanted to play. I swear, he was just like Fallon when I used to live with the Campbells, all paws and slobber.

Killian's wolf is a beautiful animal. Like snow cast with moon shadows. And soft. *So* soft. It's clear as soon as you look into his golden eyes that he's nothing like Killian.

My wolf and I are similar. Not identical. I'm more cynical and world weary and cautious—for obvious reasons. She still has a pup's enthusiasm. Maybe because she hasn't been able to run free yet. At the end of the day, though, we're the same. She's the inside, I'm the outside, but we share a soul.

Killian and his wolf are *completely* different. His wolf is canny. His playfulness was a ploy. He wanted close to my wolf, and since he couldn't force me to shift, he figured he needed to make friends. Killian doesn't know how to do anything but bark orders. His wolf, though—he's slick. Observant.

Until the other night at dinner, I don't think Killian's ever really *looked* at me, but his wolf is completely tuned into everything. I was panicking at first. The keys were in my fist, and my palms were sweating like crazy. The wolf was nudging my other hand. I pet him to distract him. Luckily, that's what he was going for—pets.

I smile, remembering. That gargantuan killer beast wanted rubs.

Annie was terrified. At one point, I scented piss in the air, but she pulled it together and wriggled up to me. I dropped the keys in the grass, and she crawled right on top of them. I don't know how she picked them up, but when I finally peeked down, they were gone, and she was hanging out with Liam by the truck.

She might actually be able to pull off the mushroom run.

Maybe things are turning around. I lay low for a while,

and my new buddy Killian's wolf convinces him to ignore me like he used to. This could all be a bad dream, and I can get back to business as usual.

I'm actually feeling pretty good as Annie and I turn onto the path that leads up to our cabin, but then I catch a scent on the breeze. Male sweat and Bengay. My wolf's hackles rise, and a nervous whine erupts from Annie's chest.

Striding towards us down the path are Eamon and Lochlan Byrne. Annie shuffles closer to my side.

It's weird to see them here. No one uses our path but us. There's nothing except our place and the groundskeeper's shed at the top. Maybe they're cutting through after patrol.

I don't like Lochlan, but I hate Eamon. Once, when I was younger and staying with the Campbells, they had him over for dinner. He was a big deal then. Declan Kelly's beta. He leered at me all night, and then he said to Dan Campbell, "It's a pity about her legs, but I guess they'll spread just fine."

Eileen hustled me off to the kitchen to help her with the dishes.

The past decade hasn't been kind to him. His knuckles are gnarled, and the hair on his head has receded, although his mutton chops are as bushy as ever.

Lochlan is his nephew. Eamon raised him. They're two of a kind. They walk the same, hunched but swaggering, arms swinging. Like wiry, foul-tempered chimpanzees.

As they plow forward, I get no sense that they're going to make way. Annie dodges into the tall grass, but I'm not that nimble. I'm still in the middle of the path when they come to a stop, inches from me.

My wolf growls, baring her teeth, and my heart thunders. I shrink back. She's going to get us killed. We're alone.

I make to step aside, but Eamon grabs my upper arm,

digging his fingers into the muscles. His sneer is echoed on Lochlan's face. Both their noses flare. They must smell Killian.

"Not so fast." Eamon rakes his eyes down my front, pausing at the white and silver hairs I didn't manage to brush off. I jerk my arm, but he squeezes tighter, the tips of his claws snicking, ripping my sleeve.

Instinctively, I reach for the place the bond was, but there's nothing there.

My wolf wants to fight. She's riding some kind of high from taming Killian's beast. I tamp down hard. That's not reality. We're outranked and outnumbered, and I can taste the malice wafting off these two.

In my periphery, I see Annie skulking away. Both males are focused on me. She's going to bolt.

Go, girl. I need to distract them.

"What do you want?" I force the words out of my tight throat.

A rumble sounds in Eamon's chest. "What was I just telling you, Lochlan? When I was beta, bitches didn't speak unless you asked 'em a question. Shit's gotten way too lax around here."

Lochlan nods in full agreement. From the corner of my eye, I see Annie inching farther up the path.

"If you have a problem, take it up with the alpha." I brace for a cuff to the side of the head. I've seen Eamon deliver those blows to his mate for as long as I can remember. I can hardly breathe; my chest is so tight.

"And if a bitch didn't learn when to keep her mouth shut, well—" Eamon grins at Lochlan. "Hard to talk with no teeth."

Lochlan nods again. "Some bottom feeders have gotten real comfortable around here. Attacking their betters."

He's talking about Haisley.

"No matter what Killian Kelly does, you can't change the reality of rank in a wolf pack," Eamon says.

He extends his claws just enough to prick my skin. Annie has disappeared over the crest of the hill, and I'm sweating bullets, but I can breathe a little better now that she's safe.

Eamon leans down to whisper in my ear. His sideburns scratch my cheek. "Strength rules. It always has. It always will. And you and your band of rejects aren't very strong, now, are you?"

He straightens, retracting his claws and dropping my arm, and gazes up at the blue sky. Then he steps off the path and waves me forward. "Enjoy this while you can, female. Change is coming. Something tells me you and the other sluts up the hill aren't gonna like it very much."

He slams his shoulder into mine as he passes, knocking me back, and by the time I steady myself, they're gone. My blood is thundering in my veins, and my crazy little wolf is leaping, snapping her teeth, straining to attack. It's all I can do to hold her in.

And then Annie, Mari, and Kennedy's massive beast of a black wolf come racing down the path.

My heart stutters with relief, and then gladness. When he comes to a halt beside me, I plunge my fingers into Kennedy's thick, silky pelt. He stares toward camp with his unearthly silver eyes, lips peeled back from inch long incisors. It's clear he wants to go after them, but that he won't leave us to do it.

"You came to my rescue," I murmur. This is such a risk for Kennedy. The wolf growls low in the back of his throat, and then he licks my hand.

"What did they want?" Mari asks. "Were they messing with you 'cause you attacked Haisley?"

"Kind of?" Haisley is a Byrne—Lochlan's cousin and Eamon's niece. They've never seemed to give a crap about her before though. "Eamon was, like, doing a whole villain monologue."

Mari shudders. "His sideburns are creepy as shit."

"Agreed."

"A-are you going to tell Killian?" Annie asks.

I wrap an arm around her waist as we turn to walk home. She's shaking like a leaf. "Why would I?"

"So he can tell them to leave you alone."

I shake my head. I'm not opening any can of worms with Killian Kelly. That was bad and scary, but it's just words. We've all heard it before, and we will again. *In Declan Kelly's day, blah blah blah. You females better watch out because blah, blah, blah.*

I don't want to say that, though. It might be true, but I don't want to ever tell my girls we just have to 'suck it up, buttercup.' So I say, "Killian's not my mate."

"But he is your alpha," Mari pipes in.

I'm not sure why the point makes me grumpy, but I get quiet, and when we get back to the cabin, I turn down a beer and excuse myself to take a shower before kitchen duty.

I've got wolf drool and hairs all over me, and my clothes reek of Killian's wolf. That's probably why the Byrnes decided to hassle me. I walk the blouse and skirt to the hamper while I run the water, and because I'm weird, I hold them to my nose and sniff.

All the lingering disquiet from the encounter with the Byrnes dissipates, and my wolf's tail wags, excitement thrumming in my middle.

Killian's scent is awesome. Like the one night each summer growing up when the elders let us pups go to the fireman's carnival in town—humid haze, velvet darkness, candy apples, the tantalizing trace of plentiful prey, and happy howls.

The scent drags me back in time, uncoiling the anxious knot in my belly and winding me up at the same time. It's dark magic. Tempting. Familiar.

Intriguing.

I dangle the clothes over the hamper lid, but I don't let go.

I should soak them in the sink so the place doesn't reek of male. Laundry day isn't until Friday. The other girls don't want to catch a whiff of alpha every time they use the bathroom. Talk about harshing your mellow.

I *should* do that, but instead, I walk them back to my bedroom, fold them neatly. and hang them over the chair by my bed where I put the clothes that I figure I can get another wear out of before washing.

It's dumb and embarrassing, something a girl would do right before her first heat, the kind of nesting mimicry that girls always got teased for in high school. It's a ridiculous thing to do, but my wolf approves wholeheartedly. It gives her ideas.

I head back to the shower, and while I scrub briskly from head to toe, rinsing off the fear scent with scalding hot water, she bounces around—the Byrnes forgotten—spitballing. We should go for a run with Killian's wolf. Sleep huddled up next to him. Wear the skirt to dinner so the other females know he's ours.

I put the kibosh on that. *Not ours. Don't want.*

She growls, but her heart's not in it, the silly, giddy, ball of sunshine.

Not ours. Leave him alone. No fighting.

I flex, force her to recognize that I'm serious. She whines, and then she tucks herself in a corner, grumbling.

She's not actually going to act on her ideas. She's chastened. Haisley's wolf tore her up. She's painfully aware of her limits now, and besides, I don't think she can take me by surprise again. I know the sensation of an oncoming shift now. I'll be able to stop her if she tries to take our skin.

I'm sorry that she's disappointed, but she'll get over it. We both will.

I hustle back to my room, wrapped in my towel, after listening to make sure Kennedy's playing her video games out front. Mari, Annie, and I don't mind a little nudity—or in Mari's case, a lot—but Kennedy is bashful.

I sit at the vintage school desk I use as a vanity and take my time brushing and braiding my hair. Old Noreen never really needs us until it's time to serve. She says we get under foot.

My oval mirror hangs on a nail from the wall. I scavenged it from the white elephant table at the farmer's market. My seat is a step ladder that I found in the outbuilding across the path. Mari's terrified of the place, but it's just an old groundskeeper's shed. There's not much in there except cans of dried-up paint and glass jars filled with cobwebs and nails.

Sometimes I wonder what the other female's rooms look like, the ones who mated at first heat, or the ones with fathers or uncles to live with. The "protected" females. Do they have nice, matching furniture? Framed pictures and padded satin hangers for the clothes they buy from town?

I watch HGTV. Do they have an accent wall? A window seat filled with pillows?

I'm not jealous. Not much. In a way, it's my worst nightmare. I don't want to be accountable to a male for where I go and what I do. But I do wonder. What's it like knowing there's a powerful male looking out for you?

A memory flashes. Killian's wolf laying sprawled on my lap, his sharp eyes taking in everything—me, the garage, Liam and Annie, the birds overhead, the distant forest hoots and cracks and snaps. I wasn't alone. No one would have dared approach us. Touch my arm. Prick my skin with their claws.

I rub my biceps. The nicks are already healed.

My wolf yips and waggles and rolls. She likes remembering. She wants me to rush down to the lodge. Find him. Lick *his* face. Tickle underneath *his* chin with our fur.

Down girl.

I purposefully picture the other night. Haisley's wolf leaping for my wolf's throat. Killian watching. Not moving a muscle.

She whimpers and slows her roll. It's tough love, but she's going to have to learn. He's a dead-end street.

I take my time picking out my outfit, settling on a periwinkle blue maxi dress with long sleeves and sandals. It's a synthetic fiber, but I like how it flows when I walk. Silky and soft. I don't have a lot of sensation around some of my worst scars, so I like soft fabrics that whisper over the skin I can feel.

I wash a cereal bowl Kennedy left full of milk in the sink, and I fold a quilt Mari dropped on the floor, laying it on the back of our secondhand sofa. I shut the windows. There's a hint of an approaching thunderstorm in the air. Then, finally, when I can't think of anything else to do, I stop putzing around and head for dinner.

The evening is cooler than it has been. There's that undernote of rain, but the sky overhead is cloudless and almost purple as the sun sets.

I can't imagine living anywhere else. The ridge, the ravine, the river, the caves, and the foothills. The seesawing mountain breezes and valley breezes. It's my territory. It runs through me like veins, connecting all my parts to the earth.

But I also wish I was a million miles away.

With each step, my dread grows. The pack is going to stare. Talk shit. Laugh. I lost a challenge, and that's how a pack works. It teaches you your place.

And the Byrnes will be there, smug that they've put me in my place.

I'd happily skip dinner, but Annie, Mari, and Kennedy expect me. They went ahead, always anxious about being late. God forbid a male wants a beer and has to get it himself.

I shouldn't be so critical. I was just like them when I was their age. Being a lone female messes with your mind. You're consigned to the kitchen, the furthest cabin from the commons, the jobs where you don't have unsupervised interactions with unmated males—in other words, the sucky ones. You're pack, but not. You're a satellite.

Easy to pick off.

Humans like to talk about "alone time" as if it's a good thing. That's how far they are from their herd origins. "Alone time" means you've been left behind. It means you're on your own, and no one has your back. And there are predators out there. Still.

An old memory of gnashing fangs and screams surges from my subconscious. I slam it back down and walk a little quicker the rest of the way to the lodge. The evening has shadows now, and strange sounds. A shiver zips up my spine.

When I slip through the screen door, Old Noreen is

piling serving dishes on trays. Annie and Mari are shoveling food into their mouths while standing at a counter, and Kennedy's squatting on an overturned bucket in a back corner, absorbed by her phone.

"Took your time, eh?" Old Noreen swipes her forehead with a dish towel. "Come on then. This isn't that movie with the hot beast in highwater pants. The dishes aren't gonna dance themselves out."

Kennedy snorts from her corner. Mari wrinkles her button nose and says, "I don't get it."

I grab a tray. There's a knot in my stomach.

This is it. The last time the pack saw me, I was naked and covered in my own blood. This is step one in painting over that picture. It needs to be done, so therefore, I can do it. That's my mantra.

My face burns. It feels like forever ago, but it was only three nights. Pack memory goes much, much longer. They'll be reminiscing about the time my wolf went suicidal for years to come.

I can't hide from it. All I need to do is push open the door and walk through. Piece of cake. Done it a hundred times. The sooner I get to it, the sooner I can trade places with Kennedy and go back to researching mushroom cultivation. The pack can be awful, but if I fall back in line and tuck my tail, they'll go back to ignoring me.

"Do you want a kick in the ass to get you moving?" Kennedy pipes up from her corner.

"Kicking it myself," I mutter.

I square my shoulders as much as I can carrying a huge round tray, and then I knock the swinging door open with my hip and hold it for Mari and Annie.

A hundred heads swivel. Voices hush except for a nasty laugh here and there.

Against my will, my gaze flies to Killian. He's in his place on the dais, his bulk overwhelming the metal folding chair, legs cockily sprawled as he lounges on his throne.

He has two modes when he's up there—the pissy lord of all he surveys or the arrogant emperor willing to be entertained. Based on his posture, I'd say tonight we're in for the latter. That's good. Usually that means less blood to mop off the floor at the end of the night.

Ivo is crouched beside him, bending his ear. I venture out into the great room, and Killian glances at me for a split second. Then he casually—and very deliberately—looks away, replying to Ivo, dismissing me from his notice.

My heart drops.

Cool. That's cool.

The pack takes it as a cue. Conversations resume. I'm no big deal again. There's some pointed snickering, but the mood in the room mellows, the focus returning to food. I lower my eyes to the floor and keep moving.

Killian's giant silver wolf is only a vague presence in the background tonight. Killian the man is in full control, and he obviously has no interest in me.

Good.

That's what I wanted.

I swallow past the lump in my throat and make my way to the front of the room. Serving the lieutenants and the other fighters is my job. Mari takes the elders and pups. Annie and Kennedy trade off on the others.

Serving the lieutenants isn't an honor or anything. The unmated males hit on everyone but me and Old Noreen, and it makes Annie and Mari anxious—and skeeves Kennedy out to no end—so I take one for the team.

The unmated fighters sit at two tables by the dais—A-roster and B-roster. A-roster is closest. The lieutenants and a few other favored fighters are always seated there. They make room for Jaime if he's on a winning streak and Alfie if he hasn't pissed off anyone lately. And then there are the high-ranking females. Ivo's sister Rowan. Killian's cousin Ashlynn. Haisley.

Haisley's mother Cheryl is the alpha female. She eats with her mate at the high-ranking elder table and then floats around the great room, ostensibly "supervising." Mostly she makes us fetch things until she gets drunk and forgets about us.

The B-roster table buffers A-roster from the elders so the lieutenants don't have to listen to their stories. B-roster is generally younger. Dominant, but not oozing aggression like A-roster. There are no females at B-roster's table—they don't rank high enough to draw female interest—and yet, overall, they're a lot better behaved.

Tonight, I serve B-roster first. Finn and Alfie shoot me dirty looks, and I smirk on the inside. I take my time going back to refill my tray. Packmates whisper as I pass, but if I don't focus, I can't make out what they're saying. I keep my eyes straight ahead and think about mushrooms.

Besides the product I have ready to sell now, I have maybe six or seven pounds drying in the shack behind Abertha's. They'll be ready for market in a month. If the deal with ShroomForager3000 works out, I might have a steady buyer. That's another four or five hundred dollars. The girls and I could upgrade our phone plan to unlimited data. Or we could reinvest the profits.

The morels were a lucky find, but they're going to run out. I want to cultivate them. You have to capture the spores in a slurry—which sounds foul and probably smells rancid—and then after you seed the right area, it takes a couple years for the mycelium to form, but then you're golden. A cash crop with minimal upkeep. What else am I doing with my life? Beats the hell out of bees. The competition with honey is getting too fierce.

Suddenly, there's a tan work boot in my path.

I dash left, quickly skirting the leg. While I was passing, Alfie stretched into the aisle with no warning. Inconsiderate dick. It was a close call.

What was I thinking about?

Mushrooms.

With the whole farm-to-table, slow food, locavore movements, there's a growing market. I wish I could brand them as Quarry Pack morels. Shifters still have a mystique, even if it's faded since the packs came out in the 50s. We get the occasional fanatic trying to sneak onto our territory, and Chapel Bell, the nearest town, has made a cottage industry out of wolf tchotchkes and New Age "moon power" crap— crystals and dream catchers and essential oils and tarot cards.

Why shouldn't we cash in, too?

The elders go on and on about the dignity of the beast and pack pride and the mandate of destiny, but at the end of the day, the pack pays its bills by charging humans and rich shifters to watch our males maul each other and bet on the outcome. Dignity my ass.

The uptight elders don't want females making our own money because then we'd have options, and they'd have less control. It's about status. At the end of the day, *everything* in pack life is about status.

There are plenty of elders who see things differently, though. Nuala trades me berries from her garden for chocolate and liqueur from town—and I know she turns around and trades them to her friends for twice as much.

I'm feeling kind of cranky, so when I get back to the

kitchen, I take a bathroom and phone break before I go back out with A-roster's dinner. The great room is ringing with talk and laughter, and it feels normal. Everyone is shoveling food into their mouths except A-roster. As I pick my way to the front of the room, I'm very careful not to smirk.

When I approach the table, Haisley stands and glares at me with her arms folded. I figured she'd say something.

My wolf instinctively shrinks, but she doesn't show her neck. That's weird. I'd prepared myself for that. We did get owned. By all rights, my wolf should be sniffing Haisley's butt, but she's managed to hold onto a few scraps of pride. Good girl.

As for Haisley, I ignore her. I expect her to give me shit. That's part and parcel of losing a challenge. You get to eat dirt until there's a new loser.

As I start passing out dishes, she lifts her chin and gives me her back. That's cool. Better than I expected, actually. I figured she'd run her mouth—take a few pot shots at my leg or how small my wolf is—but I guess I'm supposed to feel bad because I'm not even worth hassling.

Sweet.

I set the vegetables in front of Finn, and then I limp down to the other end of the table to unload the meat as far from him as possible. Haisley saunters past me, pats my shoulder, and struts over to the dais.

She pauses, smirking at me, making damn sure she has my attention, and then she licks her glossy lips. My wolf alerts, rigid from tail to ears, teeth bared. She's indignant, but for some reason, she's not trying to take our skin. I reach out to test the edges of my control, and they're solid.

The place where the mate bond used to be is raw—like the pink flesh after the scab falls off a skinned knee—but it doesn't throb or hurt or react at all.

Haisley props a high-heeled black leather boot on the single shallow step leading to Killian. She makes the pose work. Her apple bottom gets a lift, and so do her perky boobs. She tosses her loose blonde curls. It's like a 90s music video to the soundtrack of shifters snarfing down brisket and talking with their mouths full.

I set the last dish on the table, intent on heading back to the kitchen, but my wolf can't tear her eyes away. And I guess I can't either. There's a sinking sensation in my stomach. My wolf whimpers. There's nothing we can do but watch.

Haisley says something to Killian. He's still in a tête-à-tête with Ivo, but he doesn't wave her away. She approaches him. He glances up and offers her his usual tight smile, not much more than a softening of the lips.

No. Our mate.

I ignore my wolf. She's growing more and more agitated, but she's not making a move to shift. I'm good. Nauseous, but good.

Whatever's going on up on the dais has nothing to do with me.

Haisley and Killian hook up. Everyone with a nose knows, as they say. Killian's also been with Rowan and Tierney and Finley and Iona. He's alpha. Alphas take what they want and females are happy to give it.

Nothing is different now than it was last week or last month or last year. I'm not going to puke. Or cry. I'm gonna march my ass back to the kitchen and play on my phone until it's time to clear the tables. Like every other night.

But instead, I stand in the aisle with the tray dangling at my side while Haisley straddles Killian's lap. She arches her back, rising up on her pointed toes. Putting on a show. He frowns, probably because she's distracting him from his conversation. Ivo wraps it up, clapping him on the shoulder and striding away.

Killian's eyes find mine. They're pure, dusky blue.

His wolf isn't there. It's all him. His face is inscrutable. No emotion.

Haisley winds her arms around his neck. He lets her, watching me. There's a challenge in his eyes. Why?

I swallow down the puke creeping up my throat.

Is this a test of my wolf? To see if she's feral enough to attack again? Or if I'm strong enough to hold her back?

Or is it a message? He's not mine. We're not mates. Know my place.

Alfie elbows me in the side. I glance down. He jerks his chin toward the elder's table. Cheryl's there, waving at me, her thin, painted eyebrows arched to her hairline.

I give myself a shake and head over, scurrying to avoid Finn's chair as he takes the exact moment I pass to push back from the table. He doesn't even notice me. He's still recounting some story over his shoulder as he makes for the bathroom.

I'm somewhat out of breath by the time I make it to Cheryl. She points at a bowl of potato salad. "Heat that up," she says, not bothering to look at me. "It's gone cold."

"It's a cold salad." I watched Old Noreen take it out of the fridge and dump it out of the plastic tub myself.

"I didn't ask for your culinary expertise. Go stick it in the microwave for a few minutes. Dermot wants it hot."

Right. Shit flows downhill. I forgot for a second. I grab the bowl.

"And bring more brisket when you come back," she calls after me.

"And a pitcher of beer," Dermot adds.

"Make it two," another elder tacks on.

At least I have something to do. Haisley's still grinding up on Killian, but that's not my business. My wolf is prowling back and forth as if my body's a cage, whining in distress, but I'm solid. Test passed. Challenge accepted.

He does what he wants. I do what I want. Thanks to Abertha, we're not mates.

I wouldn't want him. He has no sense of humor, and he's boring. His interests, as far as I can tell, are the shifter circuit, boxing, MMA, Brazilian jiu-jitsu, cardio, strength training, and "bulking." He's the prototypical Quarry Pack male. Even if he weren't a massive dick, I wouldn't be into him. He's not my type.

My wolf disagrees, but she's judging on different criteria —mostly smell.

She won't let me check my phone when we get back to the kitchen. After I stick the potato salad in the oven—Old Noreen won't hear of microwaving it—my wolf drives me to stand at the kitchen door and peek out the square window.

Haisley's turned herself around, so now she's sitting on Killian's lap facing the open floor. They're watching Gael and Conor spar. Killian's barking at Gael. "Fists up. Step into him. Quit dancing."

His arm is loosely wound around Haisley's waist. She's draped back against him. His fingers rest an inch above her hip bone on the bare strip of skin below her belly shirt.

I don't care if he's touching her stomach. If it feels like a horse kicked my gut, that's because my brain hasn't gotten the message yet that the bond is gone.

I have to think about something else.

Killian's nails are bitten to the quick and his cuticles are raw and red.

How can I see his nails from back here? It's like I've got wolf vision. I try to focus on something farther away—the taxidermied falcon on the mantle above the fire. I can't make out where his talon meets his toe. Weird. Do I only have binocular vision when it comes to Killian? That's crappy.

I don't want to see what he does super clearly. I don't really care, though. This doesn't hurt. It's just phantom limb syndrome. Biology on the fritz.

Now Haisley's whispering in his ear. Her lips graze his cheek. My wolf lunges, slams into her limits, and crumples. My hands twitch. My stomach aches.

He's not my mate.

And that's good. It's so good.

Remember the thicket?

It was agony. I was torn and beaten and aching, and if I'd had the strength, I would have dragged myself on my belly to Killian's door and begged him to mount me. I was alone and bleeding in a briar patch, and where was he?

He's not my mate. He can touch whoever he wants. He can bend Haisley Byrne over up there on the dais, and I might puke, but I won't care.

Not. My. Mate.

Kennedy taps my shoulder, and I nearly jump out of my skin. "Potato salad's ready."

"Shit. I need two pitchers of beer, too. I'll get it." I make for the keg, but Kennedy grabs my wrist to halt me.

"You just keep growling at those assholes. I'll pour."

"I'm growling?"

"Sure are." She gives me a small sympathetic smile. "Don't let the bastards get you down."

I love Kennedy. Sometimes we hang out, late at night, out on the porch after Mari and Annie have gone to bed. We talk about life. Leaving. And why we stay.

Pack life is easy in a way. Rules, taboos, status, rank. It's all laid out for you from the day you're born. You know where you belong, minute to minute. You don't have to make hard choices.

But what if your heat and your wolf never come?

What if you're female but your wolf isn't? What are you then? Are you pack? Are you only pack if you follow the rules? If you don't draw attention to the part of you that doesn't fit?

Or can everyone see that you don't really belong, and it's only a matter of time before exile? Wouldn't it be smarter to get the hell out of town before that happens?

No one has been exiled since Killian's father's time, but that wasn't so long ago.

And we need a pack. Pack isn't just Cheryl and Killian and Haisley and the assholes at the A-roster table. It's also Abertha and Mari and Annie and Old Noreen and Liam and Fallon. It's the Malones and Butlers and Campbells. It's the pups. It's the elders who remember my Ma and Da and will tell me new stories about them I've never heard before, even now after they've been gone so long.

I rest my forehead on the cool door. It's an equation Kennedy and I do over and over again. The packmates we love minus the packmates we hate. The rules that crush our spirits minus the fact that we belong even less in the human world, and their ways are even more intolerable.

"Here you go, fighter." Kennedy prods me with a filled tray. "Go get 'em."

I give her the finger before I take it from her.

Back in the dining rooms, packmates are howling and cheering. Conor has Gael on the ground. Killian's riveted, oblivious to Haisley and me. She's smiling, smug as hell, watching the fight with her arms over her head, draped around Killian's neck.

My stomach sours. I hate this. I need to think about mushrooms, but I can't. My wolf's given up. She's done with this bullshit. She's huddled in a corner, back to the world. I want to join her.

I trudge toward the elder's table. The leg, again, comes out of nowhere. This time, I can't avoid it. I trip. The tray goes sailing through the air. I can't help but put my full weight on my bad leg, and it gives in. I fall, my shoulder slamming into the floor.

"Watch that last step." Lochlan Byrne smirks as he stares down at me. "It's a doozy."

I push up on my elbows. My tailbone aches. There's beer down my dress. Potato salad on the floor. The bowl broke, and there are shards everywhere.

"Una, what on earth are you doing?" Cheryl peers down at me, hands on her hips.

My leg throbs. I wrenched it as I fell, and I landed on my bad side. I have to get up, but I can't. I need a second. I'm in between B-roster and a pup table, but we're close to the edge of the open floor. Everyone has a great view. There's laughter. Murmured disapproval.

Lochlan Byrne's lounging in his chair, smirking down at me. Finn slaps his back. I don't look up at the dais. I don't want to know.

I'm not even embarrassed or mad. I've switched to automatic pilot. I just want to get up off the floor.

I flick a chunk of potato off my calf and push up until I'm sitting upright. The aisle's narrow, and the table top is too high to use for leverage. There's not enough room to do my usual sitting to standing routine. It's gonna be awkward as hell getting back on my feet. Good thing my feelings are switched to off.

I'll feel the humiliation later.

Maybe I can grab a chair leg?

"Lochlan, what the fuck? She's got a bad leg, asshole." Gael abandons the fight and trots over. He elbows past a gawking Cheryl and bends over, grabbing me under the arms and hoisting me up with zero finesse.

For a second, I feel a flash of gratitude. And then Killian howls so loud that the plates rattle on the tables. He leaps from his chair, transforming into the wolf mid-air, and Haisley goes flying, landing on her butt a few feet away.

I don't have time to do more than tense before Killian's silver wolf bowls into Gael. Everyone scrambles for distance.

Gael flings me out of the way as Killian's wolf smashes him into the B-roster table. Laminate cracks. People scream and scatter. Half of B-roster, including Conor, shifts. The other half freezes, cowers, and shows their necks.

The past and present collide. Snarls, cries, shouts, and blood. I freeze, too.

And then Ashlynn Kelly—who I hadn't even noticed tonight—seizes my forearm and uses her whole weight to drag me across the floor, out of the way.

Gael somehow manages to shift. His wolf is big, but he's nowhere near Killian's weight class. Gael is so out-matched, he might as well be another species. A cat fighting a lion. Blood spurts, fur flies. Screams and howls fill the lodge.

"He's gonna kill him," Ashlynn pants.

We're huddled behind an overturned table, stuck between a wall and the fight. Packmates in human form have clustered along the far wall. The lieutenants have all shifted. They're circling, darting forward, trying to distract Killian's wolf from Gael's flagging body, but they're uncertain, and the wolf pays them no mind.

Killian is mauling the smaller male. Gael's wolf is limp, head bent to show his neck, his flanks rising and falling rapidly as blood pools around him. The fight was over before it began, but Killian's wolf is unsatisfied. He growls ferociously, shaking the rafters, and then he paces, taking lazy swipes at Gael's prone carcass.

"Do something," Ashlynn hisses at me. Like what? Like a rodeo clown or those guys who distract the bull from a matador?

Killian's wolf plants a paw on Gael's bloody haunch and howls. It's a warning. Everyone bends the neck.

He bares his fangs, and I can see clear as day what he's going to do next. He's going to rip out Gael's throat.

Gael helped me.

Out. My wolf paws at her walls.

This is wrong. This is bad.

"I can't watch." Ashlynn buries her face in my shoulder.

Let me out.

I don't know what else to do, so I let my wolf come, bracing myself. She's so small. There's nothing she can do against a giant.

My bones crack, my muscles tear, and there's the strange pulsation as my heightened senses come online. The shift is over more quickly this time, and it hurts less.

At first, my wolf does nothing. She's totally calm. She sniffs the air a few times, and then she trots out from behind the overturned table as if she doesn't have a care in the world.

She's trembling inside. *We're* trembling. But she isn't afraid. Not of him. She's terrified of what he'll do. She's also kind of—irritated with him.

She stands at the edge of the open floor, careful not to get blood splatter on her paws. She's panting. Despite it all, she's happy to be out. She's happy to see *him.*

Mate.

Inside, I steel myself. My breath stills.

Killian's wolf falls silent. He glares at her, every inch bristling with righteous indignation, and then he surveys the pack through narrowed, golden slits, reveling in his dominion over all of us. He raises his muzzle to the ceiling and howls, a ferocious bellow of power and command.

Submit.

Every packmate bends lower. The reek of piss and terror assails my nose.

My wolf kind of checks out what's going on behind her, and then she sits, careful of her bad back leg. She doesn't cower or run. The happy idiot plops down on her rump and begins to lick herself.

I like her. We're gonna die, but she does *not* care. She's not gonna let Killian's wolf see her sweat.

Killian's wolf howls again, louder, the command now an imperative.

Submit.

She blinks up at him and lets out a snippy little yip, the kind of bark a dam gives her pup when he's testing her nerves.

Killian's wolf growls in the back of his throat, and then he bounds off Gael's prostrate form and stalks toward us, fur bristling, the tips tinted red.

My wolf better know what she's doing. She's not as cool as she's acting. Our heart's racing, and butterflies are zooming in our belly. Butterflies is a weird reaction to imminent death. I hold my breath.

Killian's wolf butts our shoulder with his muzzle. Mine snaps her teeth, barely missing him on purpose. Oh, my sweet Fate. He could kill us with a swipe of his paw. He could literally bite our head off, and my wolf is nipping at him. She *is* moon mad.

Behind us, Ivo and Tye dart forward and drag Gael's wolf away. Gael is young, and his shifter healing is at its peak. His injuries aren't fatal, but it looks horrible. A few feet away, Gael shifts, shrugging the other males off so he can walk away under his own steam.

Killian's wolf butts me again. I can't understand what he wants. My wolf licks herself and ignores him, although she's —we're—amped up almost past our endurance.

I don't know what to do.

Killian's wolf butts us a third time, harder. My wolf huffs and grazes his side with her teeth. It's a brief nip. Perfunctory. Irritated and indulgent.

And the air changes. The big wolf's golden eyes fade to dusky blue. There's a crack of bones, and Killian's movements are masked by the weird fast-forwarding effect as he flip-shifts. In a split second, he's looming above my wolf, buck naked, fists balled, every muscle tight and cast in sharp relief.

His teeth are bared. He's furious.

He doesn't waste a second. He scoops my wolf up in his arms like a naughty pup and strides toward the doors.

~

"Shift!" Killian commands.

My wolf instantly abandons our body. I barely stifle a scream as our spine breaks and reforms. It's over in less than a minute this time, and the hardest adjustment is the return of color vision and the dulling of my sense of smell. I have to blink and sneeze a few times before the world comes back into focus.

I'm in a darkened alcove by the lodge's front entrance, buck naked and shivering, and Killian's looming, blocking me into the corner, so much wider and taller than me, furious. *Seething.* I'm almost more scared of the man than the wolf.

I hug an arm around my bare breasts and press my knees together, bending a little to hide whatever I can. I hate this. My wolf hates it. She has no hang ups about nudity, but she hates the feeling of being exposed and defenseless. She wants her fur.

I'm not showing my neck, but I am staring at Killian's bare feet. He's not fazed by his lack of clothes in the least.

"What's wrong with you?" he booms.

My gaze flies up. He's glaring.

"Lochlan tripped me. You attacked Gael." I don't know what the answer's supposed to be.

He snarls. "Not that." His chest rumbles. "Stop. Shaking," he grits from clenched teeth.

"I can't." The adrenaline has ebbed, and I'm a ball of raw nerves. Every inch that I'm not holding onto for modesty is trembling.

He growls again. "Don't move."

And then he stalks off, back into the lodge, taut ass flexing, shoulders thrust back, arrogance personified.

I should run now while I have the chance, but my wolf is frozen in place. There was enough alpha command in Killian's tone that I don't think she'll let me bolt. I'm impervious to Killian's orders, but she's in his thrall. To a degree. She did act like a rodeo clown for him just now.

The moon is full and high, and everything high is illuminated—the tops of the trees, the roofs of the cabins—and everything low is cast in shadow. The commons look ethereal, like the village in a Van Gogh painting. The storm never materialized, but there's a stiff breeze whipping down from the foothills. I huddle in my corner and wait.

No one comes out the lodge's front entrance until Killian, a few minutes later. He throws an orange cardigan at me.

"Put that on."

I'm already buttoning it. It smells like Nuala, an elder who trades me for Bailey's Irish Cream. It's tight, but it covers my ass cheeks. Just barely, but it does.

Killian got himself a pair of athletic shorts, but he didn't bother with a top. He's got his arms crossed, glaring again, his pecs and abs and the V dipping into his shorts all carved with precision. There's a fine dusting of fair hair down the valley of his six pack, disappearing into his waistband. It looks soft. The muscles look rock hard.

My fingers twitch. I quickly cross my arms, tucking my hands tight against my chest.

"We're not mates," he spits, finally breaking the silence. It sounds like an accusation.

It cuts, but no worse than a splinter or a bee sting.

"I know," I say.

His jaw tenses into a sharp line. His expression is now beyond forbidding—it's menacing. "This is the second time you've been the cause of disruption in the pack."

How's that?

I don't actually reply. Pack protocol is so ingrained.

"I could have killed Gael."

He's putting that on me? No way.

He's gearing himself up for something, pacing short steps, left and right, glowering at me in contempt.

Shit. Is he going to exile me?

"I will not tolerate this, this—disorder. You cannot—"

I panic. "Bullshit." It flies from my lips.

He freezes mid-step, eyebrows slowly raising. I interrupted him. Oh, crap. Well, in for a penny, in for a pound.

I hug my arms tighter. "You can't blame me because you can't control your wolf."

"*I* can't control my wolf?"

"Or your males." If I'm getting exiled, I'm laying it all out. "Lochlan tripped me on purpose. Are you okay with that? 'Cause I remember having to sit through a bunch of lectures about how only pussies hit females and pups."

It was early on, when Killian had just secured alpha rank, fending off three challenges in a row, including Eamon. Declan Kelly had passed a few months earlier. The power vacuum had made bad wolves worse, and all the males were posturing and jockeying for status. A lot of females and young were taking beatings from mates asserting dominance.

Killian was nineteen or twenty, and not anywhere near as articulate as he's become, and he mostly grunts and curses now. Someone would slip back to the old ways, and he'd call everyone out to the grassy lawn in the middle of the commons, and spend an hour or two ripping the pack up for being a bunch of "limp dick bitches who can't fight someone their own size."

Then, he'd tell the females to go home and get back to work, and run the males along the pack land perimeter until they were too exhausted to mess with anyone.

At the time, I thought maybe things would change. Killian would be a new type of alpha. He stopped the beatings and got the males focused on the circuit, but that was it. Females still had to stay home and ask a male for anything they wanted. I was disappointed, but I was younger then, too. Naïve. I thought a wolf could rise above his nature.

Eamon's right about one thing. In a pack, at the end of the day, strength rules.

I'm so lost in my head, that it takes a second for me to

realize that Killian has closed the space between us. The scent of blood and fury fill my nose.

Instinctive fear saps my strength. I let the wall hold me up, and I fight the terror. I don't want to be afraid. I'm mad. Pissed, actually. I'm not the one in the wrong this time.

Killian's lips peel back. His fangs have descended, but he shows no other signs of becoming the wolf. Flip-shifter weirdness.

"I control my males," he hisses, threat lacing each word.

I need to shut up. Nod. Make this be over. But now my mouth has its own mind, too. "Was it your idea for them to trip the female with the bad leg, then?"

He snarls. "I'll deal with it."

"Gael dealt with it. You were busy with your dinner and a show." I know when you're in a hole, you're supposed to stop digging, but I can't stop myself from adding, "Playing Haisley Byrne's chair."

He slams a palm into the wall beside my head. There's no give. The lodge is made of solid pine logs. Still, I'm thrown, but not by the display of aggression. From the heat emanating off his body and his breath on my cheek.

He smells even more like toffee. Hot toffee. Drizzling, thick, delicious toffee.

"Be careful, female. I don't think that little wolf of yours can back up that big mouth."

He sneers. My "little wolf" perks up. Her ears prick, and she has prancing feet. Whatever this is, she's here for it.

I don't know what possesses me. I swear I don't have a death wish. Maybe Abertha took my filter when she yanked out the mate bond.

"I don't need my little wolf," I say. "I have your big one."

He growls.

"Your wolf likes me." I lick my dry lips, and plunge ahead, right over the cliff. "He saw someone touch me, and he did something about it. You're mad because you were asleep at the wheel, and he went after the wrong guy. I own going after Haisley the other night. That was on me. But this was you."

"You're gonna tell me how to lead my pack?" He gets right in my face, his gaze skewering me, challenging me, daring me.

I've seen him do this with his males a hundred times. He forces them to look him in the eye, and then he eye-fucks them until they can't help but lower their heads. It's a dominance move.

I should be squirming, itching to bend my neck. But way back, I sense his wolf, calm now, attentive, and pleased as shit that I claimed him.

Killian narrows his eyes, and for all that he's a massive dick, they're the softest faded blue and the rings around his pupils shine like liquid gold. Someone so awful shouldn't have such pretty eyes.

I have no urge to drop my gaze. None. The opposite. I want to keep looking.

My stomach flutters.

What did he ask me? Oh, it was meant as a rhetorical question. About telling him how to lead his pack.

But yeah, I have thoughts.

"Somebody should. You need to rein in the assholes. Unless you want to be the alpha of a pack so pathetic the males have to trip a female with a bad leg to make sure she knows her place. 'Cause I'm such a threat to the natural order. With my killer wolf and all."

I tense—you don't talk to a higher-ranking wolf like this, *never*—but at some point, Killian's expression has lost the aggression. He's still pinning me with his gaze, but it's more measuring. Considering.

He edges forward, pressing his broad chest to my folded arms. There's nowhere to go. My back is to the wall.

But I'm not panicking. I'm—curious? My wolf is very interested. She's right up against the border between us. Peering through the fence slats.

There's a prod at my belly. What is that?

Oh, shit.

I know what that is. It's his cock. He's hard. I'm making him hard.

What's happening?

I don't look down. My face would literally burst into flames. I'm not—unfamiliar—with dicks. I'm not a virgin. There was a human male who used to sell glass pipes at the farmer's market. He was friendly, and he lived in an RV. He invited me to check out his personal collection. Afterwards, I went to the lake to wash off his scent, and it was a wonderful afternoon—alone and alive and self-determined and free.

He's in the Pacific northwest now. He has kids and a job with computers. We're friends on social media.

And there was a visiting male from North Border who stayed with us for training. I thought I'd miss him, but I didn't. Turns out, it was the sneaking off to the woods that was exciting, not him.

So, anyway, I know about cocks. But not cocks this size. Alpha cocks.

I gulp. My cheeks burn.

Thankfully, he shifts back a hair so I can't feel it anymore.

"You're wrong," he finally says, low and intent. "You're a threat."

I shake my head.

"You've got an alpha wolf enthralled. How the fuck did you do it?" His Adam's apple bobs as he speaks. He's so chiseled, even his neck exudes strength, the cords, the vein running the length. My mouth waters. I want to sink my teeth into it.

I'm losing my mind.

I know this is an important conversation, but my attention keeps slip-sliding away. His body is fascinating. The deep ridge where his shoulders meet his pecs. The trail of darker, crinklier hair that starts just below his belly button—

He gently tilts my chin up.

"Eyes up here." His voice is bemused. "What's going on, Una Hayes?"

I swallow. "You're reaming me out."

"Kind of feels like the opposite."

"Well, if I were alpha, I wouldn't let assholes like Lochlan Byrne kick people when they're down. And you're lucky you didn't kill Gael—"

"I wasn't trying to kill him. I was making a point."

"Which was?"

He frowns. "I ask the questions."

"How's that workin' out for you?"

Did I just say that? Am I cruisin' for a bruisin', like my Da used to say?

He reaches for my face. I flinch. He hesitates for the slightest second, and then he brushes my cheek with his fingertips, grazing my temple. Shivers follow in the wake of his touch. Then his eyes harden, and he reaches behind my head, grabbing my braid by the base.

He drags me into his chest, winding my braid around his fist, forcing my back to arch, my hips to press into his.

I can feel him again. His length. His hardness.

My scalp stings. I whimper, searching his pupils for the gold of his wolf. It's nowhere. My own wolf has lowered her head, almost purring she's so pleased with his display.

"Let me go," I whisper. I could sass him when there was air between us, but now that I'm plastered to his heat, my wolf's instincts are rising. Submit. Present.

"No." He tugs my braid, tilting my head further back, forcing me to show my neck. It should be humiliating, but it's not. Some primal part of me wants this. Craves it.

I swallow again and babble, desperately reaching for a handhold on reality. "Trip the girls. Pull their hair. What, are we back in school?"

"I never pulled your braid, Una Hayes. You hid up by the teacher." He bends and nestles his nose in the crook of my neck, inhaling. Tingles zip down my spine. "Why don't you smell like arousal?"

I don't? Good, good. That would be too humiliating. But I feel something. New and powerful and terrifying.

But no, I don't want to have sex with him. He's Killian Kelly. I just got publicly humiliated. Again. And we're out in the open. Anyone could walk past. There's a bug zapper hanging a few feet away. I'm wearing an old lady's sweater, and it smells like mints.

And yeah. He's Killian Kelly. My mate who rejected me. I'm not turned on.

I try to pull my neck away from his nose, but his grip on my hair is too tight.

"I don't like you," I say. It's such a stupid argument.

He nips at my shoulder. "You don't have to. Do you think half the females in this pack *like* me? I'm the alpha."

"I think it's bigger." My voice is breathless. Wobbly.

He stops messing with my neck and rises to his full

height to gaze down at my upturned face. His forehead wrinkles. "What?"

"The number. It's definitely more than half."

Why am I baiting him? Is this how moon madness starts? With bad jokes and me getting my head ripped off by the braid, buck naked except for a borrowed cardigan?

He doesn't laugh, but he doesn't snap my neck like a twig, either. He kind of cocks his head. "Why don't you like me?"

"Well—" I don't know where to start, but I do know that saying pretty much anything honest would be a huge freakin' mistake. "I mean, for one, you're pulling my hair. It hurts."

He stares at me for a long second, and then he smooths my braid so it hangs over my left shoulder. He tugs off the elastic, and with one hand, he undoes the sections, careful not to yank.

He combs his fingers through the loose strands. Slowly. Gently. His fingertips glance down the slope of my breast. It's too light and fleeting to be full-on copping a feel, but I don't think it's accidental, either. Goosebumps break out down my arms and bare legs. No one touches me like this. Ever.

Nobody ever really touches me.

"I could make you hot," he says. "Your wolf's panting for it."

She is—at this point, she's presenting—and it's beyond awkward. I'm not paying her any attention. If I did, my face would spontaneously combust.

"We've agreed to disagree on this one," I mumble.

"There's no division between the man and the wolf. That's a heresy." Killian says it like he learned the words by rote. I bet he did. It's what the elders preach. The man and the wolf are two sides of the same coin.

Abertha teaches us differently. She says everyone's connection to their wolf is unique, a creation of their own making. When people are fucked up, it's because of an imbalance in the relationship. She says that's what's wrong with a lot of folks in this pack. Their heads are up their wolf's ass.

But I don't say that. I hedge a little. "I don't see it that way."

"And you know better than your elders?"

"There's a division between you and your wolf." It's as clear as the color of his irises. And the fact that his wolf actually likes me.

"Is that so? And how do you know?"

Because he's a cocky asshole, and his wolf is a giant, homicidal snuggle bunny.

"Because your wolf is in my thrall." I almost gasp when I say it. It's way more truth than I intended. I brace myself. That was a challenge. He can't possibly take it any other way.

His already angular jaw clenches, throwing those neck muscles into even sharper relief.

Why did I say that? What is possessing me? This whole conversation is bonkers. I should apologize for whatever I did or didn't do, according to him, and go on to live another day.

But the moon is casting the world in blue, and everything feels hyper real. Heat radiates off Killian, and I've never had an alpha this close to me before. I'm not "aroused" as he put it, but I'm—interested.

It's like my inhibitions—some of them, the filter on my mouth, for one—are fading. I forget to defer. That should be impossible. Submission to rank is hardwired into our DNA.

At least that's what the elders believe.

I wait for Killian's response, a knot coiling in my belly, fear and—anticipation.

He slides a finger along my temple, tucking my hair behind my ear. Then he traces the shell. I shiver. His mouth softens into something almost like a grin.

He leans close, and when he whispers, his lips brush my earlobe.

"And what are you going to do with him, little wolf?"

A husky whine escapes from deep in my chest, a demanding, impatient sound dripping with raw lust. I press my palm to my mouth, cheeks flaming, and Killian laughs, backing off.

Somehow, the spell is broken. A mask I didn't even realize had been lifted returns, making Killian's face cold and hard again. And almost—worried.

He jerks his chin toward the lodge's front doors. "Come on."

He doesn't wait for a response. He heads inside, fully expecting me to follow, the elastic from my braid around his corded wrist.

I wait a full three seconds before I scurry after him.

NUALA'S SWEATER is a really lovely pumpkin color, but I feel like a neon orange emergency cone when I trail Killian back into the great room. People are back at their seats, finishing dinner, but as soon as I walk in, there's a massive clatter of forks and the hushed chatter dies.

Killian points to a spot by the elder's table. "Stay there."

He doesn't bother to look back at me when he gives the order. He's striding toward the A-roster table with a purpose.

I clutch the hem of the cardigan, stretching it as low as it can go.

People are staring at my messed-up leg. Thomas Fane's fang marks should be old news to everyone, but packmates still ogle the scars, and I still squirm inside.

Besides Killian, I'm the only one standing. I catch sight of Annie, Kennedy, and Old Noreen at the window in the kitchen door. I bet Mari's in the back, hiding her eyes.

Is he going to exile me now?

But he's not focused on me. He stalks right up to Lochlan Byrne, whacks the back of his head, and grunts, "You. Me. Now."

Then he goes to stand in the middle of the open floor.

Lochlan shrugs and smirks across the table at his buddy Finn as he pushes back his chair, feigning unconcern.

Of all the males, Lochlan is built most like a human fighter—wiry, slightly bow-legged. He has a quick walk and a buzz cut. Between the two of them, Annie and Mari have crushes on all the lieutenants, but neither of them like Lochlan. Kennedy says he smells like entitlement and drug store body spray.

However, Eamon is his uncle, so he comes from beta stock. He's won titles on the circuit. He's in the same weight class as Killian. And the fight with Tye was closer than it should have been. He's a contender.

The entire pack holds its breath.

Is this an alpha challenge?

It feels like it as they face off, steely-eyed, expressions unreadable. They don't tap fists. One moment, they're staring at each other, the next, Lochlan swings.

It's an obvious shot, not really meant to connect, just to

start the action. It's not surprising when Killian sidesteps the blow. I expect a counterpunch. I don't know a whole lot about fighting—I'm not interested in the slightest—but you don't grow up in Quarry Pack without developing a sense for how these things go.

Killian keeps his fists up, protecting his face. He bounces on the balls of his feet.

Lochlan swings again, this time launching into a combination. Killian ducks and sweeps Lochlan with his leg at the exact moment Lochlan throws a right cross. Lochlan wobbles, almost staggers, but he's too good. He recovers instantly.

Killian bobs and weaves, fists in guard position. Lochlan lands a series of jabs to Killian's torso and a right hook to his face.

Both males are sweating now, their chests vibrating with the growls and snarls of their pent-up wolves. Blood trickles from the edge of Killian's eyebrow. Lochlan smirks. You can see the confidence swelling in him. He thinks he has a chance.

He doesn't, does he?

My muscles are so tight they ache. My good leg is taking all my weight, and my thigh is so tired, it's a knot. At least no one is looking at me anymore. Everyone is riveted by the show on the floor. The alpha is getting his ass handed to him, and he doesn't seem the least bit fazed.

Lochlan lets an uppercut fly. Killian ducks, sweeps his leg again, this time driving an elbow into the side of Lochlan's knee at the same time. There's a crack. Lochlan stumbles. Weaves.

He's not smirking anymore.

But Killian—Killian's grinning now. His eyes are bright gold with pale blue rims.

"Get off on tripping lone females with bad legs, eh?" he pants.

Lochlan's a good fighter. He ignores the taunt and goes after Killian with a vengeance, throwing combination after combination, driving him to the edge of the open floor. Killian takes blow after blow to the face, the ribs. He's jerking back and forth like a rag doll, but he never loses his balance, not for a second.

He spits blood on the linoleum. "Rules don't apply to you, eh?"

Lochlan raises his fist, and Killian sweeps his leg again, this time with so much power, Lochlan collapses and rolls. He jumps back to his feet, showing no pain, swiping his nose with his thumb.

He doesn't launch immediately into another attack. Lochlan studies Killian, the wheels turning. Killian's stance hasn't changed. He's still bouncing lightly, fists in guard position, cool and collected despite the blood and sweat streaming down his face.

My wolf is riveted. The twisted little monster is *into* this. She wants popcorn.

Lochlan glances behind him at the A-roster table. Finn and Alfie are grinning at him, barely containing their glee. They still think Lochlan's winning.

Behind me at the elder table, there's a hushed murmuring. They know better.

Lochlan lunges. Killian kicks, driving his foot into the side of Lochlan's knee. There's a crack. Lochlan slams into the floor.

Panting, Lochlan slowly raises himself. He has to do it like me—awkward and step-by-step. When he's upright, Killian lets him land a few more shots.

Now Lochlan understands what's happening. His face is

twisted with frustration, and he starts fighting dirty, aiming for the throat, the groin. Killian flip-shifts for split seconds at a time, easily avoiding the below the belt blows.

The murmurs become a whisper. "That youngster better watch himself. Alpha will kill him."

"He shouldn't have tripped the female. Alpha won't stand for that."

My wolf strains forward in anticipation.

Lochlan throws a haymaker. Killian snaps a kick, slamming his bare foot into Lochlan's other knee. It crunches. Lochlan topples to his side, and this time, he stays down, teeth grit, neck bared.

"Get up," Killian snarls.

Lochlan bares his neck further.

"Get up!" It's a command. Lochlan has no choice.

He slowly rolls to the knee that isn't bent at an unnatural angle, his neck still exposed, face blanched and sweat dripping onto his white shirt. Unlike Killian, there's no blood splatter on his chest. It's his jeans that are soaked red.

Lochlan stands there, broken but unrepentant, waiting. Cheryl, his aunt and the alpha female, sidles up behind Killian. She reaches out to touch his arm. He snarls over his shoulder, the message so powerful and clear that even I trip back a step.

"We do not harm females," Killian says, voice meant to carry through the lodge.

"Yes, Alpha," Lochlan mutters resentfully.

"Or the young."

"Yes, Alpha."

"Or the defective."

I can hear the pack's heads turning to stare at me. Oh, ouch. He's talking about me.

"Yes, Alpha."

"Gael?"

"Yes, Alpha." Everyone searches for the voice. I'd have thought he'd be in the infirmary, but he's in his usual seat at B-roster table, though considerably worse for wear. His face is black and blue and swollen past all recognition. He's upright, but he's cradling his right arm to his chest.

"There's a seat open in A-roster." Killian points to the metal folding chair across from Finn where Lochlan always sits.

The pack mutters. For a moment, nothing happens. Then Gael's seat screeches back, and he drags himself the few feet to resettle at the table of honor. Tye claps him on the back. He winces, but he smiles. He's missing a tooth.

I figure that's the end. It has to be. But then Killian raises his arms to his side like the statue of Jesus on top of that mountain in Brazil.

"Well? You wanted your shot, Lochlan. Take it."

Lochlan's gaze shifts. Finn. Alfie. Eamon. His aunt. You can see his mind racing, getting nowhere. He's backed into a corner. He either falls to his shattered knee, or he swings.

Quarry Pack are fighters. If he doesn't want to sink lower than me in rank, he doesn't have a choice. He has to swing.

He draws in a ragged breath and throws a left hook. Killian flickers, the flip-shift so quick it's almost invisible to the eye. Lochlan's fist meets nothing but air as Killian casually extends his leg and drives his foot into Lochlan's good knee. A bloodcurdling scream echoes from the rafters, and bone tears through flesh, a rain of red spurting through the air.

My stomach heaves. My wolf howls in delight.

Behind me, an elder, maybe Nuala, says, "He should've taken a knee. At least then he'd still have a working one."

"You don't mess with defectives," an old male opines.

"That's just plain wrong. Everyone knows that."

My wolf falls quiet, her glee deflating like a punctured tire.

That's me they're talking about again. *Us.*

Fuck this shit.

Suddenly, a weight descends on my shoulders. I didn't ask for this.

Am I supposed to be impressed? Vindicated?

'Here, Una, stand right here all alone by the elderly, and I'll remind everyone not to pick on weak folks like you.'

Thanks, Alpha.

My leg aches. Given, not as bad as Lochlan's must right now, but I've had enough. I'm going home.

Killian's talking to Tye, gesturing as if he's dissecting the match, while Lochlan's friends get the stretcher down from its hook on the wall.

No one seems to be paying attention to me, so I shuffle toward the door. I have no pants on, my hair is wild, and I'm so damn tired.

I'm focusing on my balance—at this point, my bad leg is close to giving out—so I'm at the entryway before I glance back and notice Killian. He's standing on his dais, arms folded, face severe and unperturbed, Ivo and Tye at his sides. The males are talking to him, but he's staring straight at me.

My belly flutters.

I force my spine to straighten, hike my chin, and give him my back as I leave the lodge.

If I sway my hips—and I never sway my hips on purpose —but if I do, it's my wolf. She's smug as hell.

She's not the least bit humiliated.

Good mate. Avenge. Protect.

The little idiot. She's got it all wrong.

6

UNA

After texting ShroomForager3000 to confirm the time for tomorrow's meet, I shower off the lingering scent of potato salad, braid my damp hair, and put on a plain, white cotton nightgown.

I'm moving painfully slow. My bad leg throbs. There's an ugly bruise on my hip from where I hit the floor, but it'll be gone by morning. I flip off the overhead and plug in the fairy lights strung across the ceiling. The room fills with a soft, mellow glow, and I climb in between the clean, crisp sheets of my twin bed and exhale.

I'm home. Safe. Surrounded by my people. My things.

My fancy custom label maker. The rose petals, lavender, and orange peel I'm drying for potpourri. I've got Mari sewing some cute sachets with wolves on them. I'll probably be able to sell the lot to the souvenir stand for at least two hundred bucks.

My trunk sits against the wall under the window. After Ma died and the Murphys claimed our cabin on the commons, I lived out of that trunk. Now I keep my jars and other supplies in it.

Everything feels different after the past few days, but it isn't, really. I'm still a lone female. Bottom of the pack. And that's *good*. I can do what I want. Make my own way. Nothing needs to change.

Annie is going to do the run into town tomorrow, but honestly, I bet I could get away with going myself. Despite the present weirdness, I can't imagine anyone would come looking for me during the day. Literally no male ever has.

I *really* want this deal to work out. Crafts and such are a great side hustle, but mushrooms could be a real business. Everyone sells honey these days, but morels—they don't grow on trees.

I smirk at my own joke.

My brain's whirring. I fluff my pillow and turn on my good side so I face the window. The curtain is slightly parted, and I can see the moon. It's high tonight. Waxing gibbous.

Why is the moon sometimes high and sometimes large and close? I'd search it on my phone, but I'm stingy with my data at the end of the month. I need it for work.

If I use the mushroom money to get us unlimited plans, I could search whatever I want whenever I want. Moon facts. New herbs to grow.

I could watch videos of the shifter fights.

Killian was brutal tonight. He took every bit of punishment Lochlan dished out as he waited for an opening. His face was totally intent. His eyes were pure blue. No gold. His wolf had nothing to do with it.

When he kicked, the control in his body, the force and fluidity—I shudder. He's a powerful guy. He always has been. I've never had the urge to watch him fight before.

But I want to watch him do it again.

So does my wolf—she whines in agreement. I want to

watch. I want the slow motion replay, to watch frame by frame, see Killian's head snap back as Lochlan drives a fist into his jaw.

Not just 'cause I want to see Lochlan eat the floor again. Or Killian take a few punches in the face.

I also want to watch the bunching of muscles as Killian spun and kicked Lochlan's leg out from under him, how he smoothly returned to standing, bouncing ever so slightly on the balls of his feet, no victory or even exertion in his expression, only cold intent.

A shiver slides down my spine, curling into my belly.

I don't like Killian but that doesn't mean I can't admire parts of him. I wish I was strong enough to kick Lochlan's ass.

And it's not like Killian did that for me. He's the alpha. Lochlan broke his rule about females and young. Killian was making an example of him. It wasn't about me—no matter what my wolf thinks.

She's oddly reserved considering her earlier excitement. I thought she'd be urging me to shift and go hump his leg.

She was excited enough when he was doling out the beatdown. And there was a moment—when he delivered the first kick to Lochlan's leg, and I figured out what he was doing. I got excited, too. Not *sexually*. But there were tingles. I know he didn't do it for me, but that hopelessly naïve part of me that's never grown up could pretend, for a second, that he's our champion. *Ours*. And nobody better fuck with us.

Now I'm the silly one because the idea stirs something between my legs. What would it hurt if I let myself daydream a little? Only until I drift off to sleep.

Killian shifting in a rage when another male dares to touch what's his.

Killian breaking a male who made the mistake of messing with me.

Another chair on the dais for me, a place of my own. He glances down. I nod. And then he destroys my enemies. Fangs and claws. Muscles and fists.

It's a seductive fantasy. Dangerous and impossible. The stirring grows and spreads, though, growing wings, fluttering and swooshing below my navel. The stiff cotton of my nightgown teases my hardening nipples. My hand slips between my legs.

I'm restless. I part my thighs. I'm wet. I slip my fingers between my folds and find the stiff, aching nub.

I picture Killian's wolf bowling into Gael, murder and possession blazing in his golden eyes.

There's a howl from the porch right outside my window. My heart leaps into my throat.

I snatch my hand back and snap my knees together.

It's him. Even without peeking through the curtain, I know.

The window's cracked. Oh, Fate. There's no way he can't smell my arousal. It's thick in the air.

Killian's wolf howls again.

Come outside.

I scramble for resolve. My wolf is gonna bolt. She's awake and on edge, and he's so close, and she's—*I'm*—so off center. So needy.

There's a scuffling at the window. He's wedging his snout into the opening. Thank goodness the wood is old and swollen. The sash is not gonna budge.

He growls in frustration, and then backs off to howl again.

Let me in.

I tense my muscles, prepare to fight my wolf for our skin.

But she doesn't make a move. She plops herself down, and puts her snoot in the air. She's ignoring him.

More howls, so loud they shake the window pane.

Come out. Come out. Come out.

My wolf lets forth a series of yips and snarls.

Go. Go to the other female. Go on. Go.

Then, she daintily crosses her paws, rests her chin on them, and dramatically closes her eyes.

No way. She's *pissed* that he let Haisley rub up on him. I guess the rush of his dominance show has worn off, and she's remembered that she has beef.

His wolf is quiet for a few moments, but then he howls again, louder, blustering and bombastic. I don't need my wolf to understand him. He sounds like any male called on the carpet by his female—it wasn't his fault the other female came onto him. My wolf's being too sensitive. Making a mountain out of a molehill. He's sorry, but he didn't do anything wrong, and my wolf's being a real bitch, but he won't do it again.

Since she's so mad.

Over nothing.

She has no more time for him. She snuffs and lets herself fade in my consciousness.

He howls like he's been done all kinds of wrong.

I'm jumpy—he's a monster, and he's losing it on my porch, and I can't forget what he interrupted—but I'm not *scared*. Because my wolf's not scared. She's put his wolf in time out. And I'm a million miles away from cracking a smile, but—it's funny.

After a few more minutes of Killian's wolf howling at the moon, I creep over and shut the window. He keeps on going, but it's somewhat muffled.

I return to bed, tug the sheet up to my chin, and wait for

him to give up. My "phases of the moon" clock ticks on the wall. After a while, Mari and Annie come knocking on my door.

Mari pokes her curly blonde head in, squinting toward the window. The moon reflects off Killian's silver coat. He paces the porch, and his howls have become more plaintive. Almost grumbly.

"How long is he going to do this?" she whispers.

"I don't know," I whisper back.

"Should we let him in?"

"No!" Kennedy shouts from the other room. "Or at least gimme a minute!"

"She's hiding her consoles," Annie explains, squeezing past Mari to come sit on the edge of my bed. I scoot over.

"We're not letting him in," I reassure her.

If he shifted to his human skin, he could barge right in. He's alpha; we couldn't stop him. And honestly, he could easily break our door down in wolf form. Or come through the window.

But he doesn't. He trots back and forth, growling, casting aggrieved looks at the cabin every now and then.

Mari joins us, sliding under the covers. When Killian first moved us to the cabin, she was only eleven, and she'd come looking for midnight snuggles a lot. She hasn't done that in a long time.

"How much trouble are we in if he finds the consoles?" Mari asks.

"And the phones." Annie keeps a wary eye on Killian's wolf.

"And Kennedy's weights." Mari pulls the sheet to her chin. "And the liquor."

"And the mushrooms." Annie's actually trembling.

How is she going to drive to Chapel Bell by herself and

do the deal with ShroomForager3000? He'll take one look at her and rip her off.

"He's not coming in. He's just, I don't know, hanging out?" Killian's by the stairs now, looking up at the moon. He's grown quiet.

"What's he doing?" Mari asks.

"He wants me to shift, but my wolf doesn't want to."

"Una, you have to get him to leave." Kennedy appears in the doorway, breathless. "If he comes inside, we're busted."

It's true. Except for Kennedy's game systems, we keep the sitting room pretty clean, but he'll be able to smell the bar we keep in the pantry and Kennedy's marijuana gummies.

Lone females aren't supposed to drink. There's no rule about gummies, but I can guess what it'd be.

Our cabin is pretty much bursting with contraband. Nothing but the alcohol and phones are explicitly forbidden, but the place is full of evidence that we have access to human money and that we've been leaving the territory.

"Shit." I swing my good leg over the side of the bed.

"That's our fearless leader." Kennedy grabs a green knit shawl from a hook and drapes it over my shoulder as I pass. "I'm sure he just wants to talk."

A howl shakes the window frame.

I check in on my wolf. She's pretending to sleep. Guess I'm on my own. I wrap the shawl tight around my shoulders.

As I step onto the porch, I hear the girls fighting for seats on my trunk. I guess whatever happens, I'll have an audience.

I shut the door quickly behind me and lean against it. There's a bite to the air, and a crispness to the night sounds —bullfrogs and rustling leaves and a distant hoot.

Killian's wolf turns to glare at me expectantly, the gold blazing.

"She won't come out," I tell him.

He pads over, noses my belly, and then gazes soulfully into my eyes. He's really bummed. I shouldn't care, but I'm not made of stone.

"I'm sorry."

He cocks his head.

"She's tired."

He snuffles, and it sounds exactly like a human snort.

I sigh. "She's mad that you let Haisley rub up on you —him."

He peels back his lips, revealing his fangs. I stiffen. He's pissed. At me? My wolf?

He paces to the edge of the porch and howls again, a litany this time that drags on and on.

And then, suddenly, silence falls and Killian is standing there, moonlight bathing his chiseled back. His sculpted ass. I curl my bare toes. They're cold. That's why.

I clear my throat. "I—uh—did you, um, want something else?" I reach behind me for the door knob.

For a moment, he doesn't turn, and when he does, my breath catches. I can hear the girls gasp through the closed window. So can Killian. His gaze flies over my shoulder. The curtain sways. Kennedy lets out a wolf whistle.

My face flames. I step forward, holding out my shawl. "Here. You can, er, cover up."

He doesn't move to take it. He stares at me, searching for something. I fight the compulsion to bend my neck. If I did, I'd be looking straight at his dick.

How is he so confident? My face is on fire, and he's just standing there in his birthday suit with a massive erection, lord of all he surveys.

It's a long, thick, ruddy erection.

Not that I ogled him. Only for a second. I couldn't miss it. It's—

I swallow.

It's notable. I noted it.

I shake the shawl at him.

"What am I supposed to do with that?" he asks.

"Tie it around your waist?"

He raises an eyebrow. "I'm not doing that."

Mari giggles. It's abruptly cut off. Probably by Annie's hand.

Killian snatches the shawl and wraps it around himself like a towel. Now his cock is making a huge tent, stretching Nuala's cat's paw stitches.

But I'm not looking.

"Your face is red," he says.

My gaze flies to Killian's face. Shit. I was totally looking down.

"I, um, do you, uh, need something?"

His lips soften the slightest bit. A Killian smile. "You got pants?"

"Not men's pants. No."

His eyes darken, and there's a low rumble in his chest. He steps towards me.

Muffled by the glass, Mari blurts, "What's he doing?"

Annie hisses at her to shush.

Killian grabs my elbow and leads me to the far corner of the porch. At the edge, he glances down. There's no railing, and it's maybe three feet off the ground. There's a flower bed below. Purple allium and lavender and phlox.

He seems to consider, and then he leaps down, grabs my hips, and before I can react, he sets me gently on the edge. Then he vaults to sit beside me.

There are two big footprints in the flowers.

"You crushed the phlox," I say.

"What's *phlox*?"

I point below us. The moon casts a spotlight on the blooms, the illumination turning the petals into glowing jewels. The scent of lavender rises from their broken stems.

"Oh. My bad."

I don't know what to do with my hands. He's too close. I can't rest them on the ledge.

It's chilly out, but I don't want to hug my arms. I don't want him to think I'm intimidated. Or that my nipples are hard because of him. They are hard, but it's because of the chill. I'm not wearing a bra, and the cotton of my nightgown is thin.

I don't know why I care what he thinks. He's the one being weird.

I settle on clasping my hands in my lap. It feels awkward.

We fall into an uncomfortable silence. If he's waiting for me to say something, I'm at a loss. I already asked him what he wanted.

Finally, he says, "I'm not your mate."

It hurts, but this time, it's only a twinge. It passes quickly. I swear, my wolf snorts.

"But, ah, my wolf—apparently, he's into your wolf." He almost sounds embarrassed. Like his wolf's a pervert or something.

He's such a dick.

"She's not interested." I hike my chin.

He's quiet again. He stares down the path toward the commons. The lodge is still ablaze, but most of the cabins are dark. The families with young have long since put them to bed.

"He won't—" Killian clears his throat. "He won't let me leave."

Oh.

I dart a glance at his face. His jaw is rigid. His temple's ticking.

"You're pretty far out up here," he says.

Where's he going with this? The back of my neck prickles. This isn't good.

"It's peaceful." And there's no one to watch us come and go.

He sighs. "You know, I put you guys up here to keep you away from—" He cracks his jaw. "From, uh, males who'd take advantage."

I never knew why he did it. We'd been living various places until one day, Cheryl told the four of us that Alpha said to pack our shit and move up the hill.

Seems weird, though. To put all us lone females out here alone for our protection.

Killian seems to read my mind. "My cabin's straight down wind. Anyone approaches, I know."

Oh.

"And I got the patrols overlapping up there." He points to the crest of the ridge behind our cabin.

I had no idea. Oh, shit. Why don't we scent them? They can definitely smell us from that close. Kennedy smokes her pipe on the back deck.

Killian cracks a slight grin. "We know you ladies cut loose sometimes up here."

"I—"

He raises a hand. "Keep it up here, and we don't have a problem."

"We didn't—Why can't we smell the patrols?"

"If they didn't have the sense to stand downwind, they wouldn't make good scouts, would they?"

I guess that's true.

"Listen. I know what you all think, but I do shit for a reason. Do you remember what it was like before?"

I was sixteen when his father died. I remember. I kept my head down. Mixed with the pack as little as possible. If I wasn't at school, I spent my time in the kitchen, the laundry, and up at Abertha's. You couldn't avoid the gossip, though. Packmates disappearing, coming back hurt and not saying where they'd been. Packmates who didn't come back. And you saw the bruises.

And the females who broke down and cried in the middle of dinner.

"Yeah, I remember."

"Males—they took what they wanted. Females got hurt. Young got beaten."

I know it used to be worse.

"I changed that," he says. "You're safe now."

He pauses. Does he expect me to thank him?

I guess he deserves it.

Old Noreen is always bringing up the bad old days. She thinks we're ungrateful, so she reminds us—in Declan Kelly's time, that male would have bent you over the table. Be happy he just slapped your ass.

In Declan Kelly's time, if a babe was born small, they'd leave him out in the woods. If he was still alive in three days' time, his dam could keep him.

And don't get her started on the dens. In the dens, females weren't allowed to wear clothes, except furs in winter. In the dens, enforcers didn't just eat first, they ate their fill. Low rank got scraps—if there were any left.

We all roll our eyes, but we're not unaware that we're lucky. Even though it doesn't feel like it.

Killian hasn't gone on, so I say, "Um. Thanks?"

He huffs, annoyed, clasping his hands behind his head and stretching. He tilts his head up toward the moon. "I don't need your thanks. I'm just saying you're safe here."

"I've got the patrols above on the ridge at fifteen-minute intervals. I keep my window open so I can scent any approaching threat at night. I keep you all in the kitchen or the laundry, away from the males. They know not to get near any of you alone."

They do? I guess that's another reason the run in with Eamon and Lochlan was so unsettling. Males will be gross at dinner or at the swims after runs, but they don't corner us.

I don't understand what he's getting at, though.

"You're safe," he says again, emphatic. He glances over at me, his eyes intense. "So why can't I leave?"

I blink.

He wants me to answer? I don't know.

"Well, maybe your wolf—"

He cuts me off. "It's not just my wolf." He sort of pounds his chest once with his fist. "*I* can't leave."

"Oh."

A surge of something, something tingly, almost sparkly, rushes through me. My belly flutters.

"Well, um, we are perfectly safe here. Like you pointed out." I sniff the breeze. "I don't smell anything."

He inhales, and his eyes drift shut. He groans softly. "I do."

Now he blinks. He glares at me, tense, frustrated. "You smell like bread."

"Thank you?"

I guess it could be worse. I try to casually duck my nose toward my shoulder and inhale. I don't smell anything but fabric softener.

"Maybe you should come back to my cabin," he says.

His voice lowers. His expression is somehow less alpha. It's not exactly friendly, but he's set aside the usual domineering bluntness. He's trying for charm. It doesn't quite work, but it's interesting to see.

I've seen him look at females at the lodge like this, late at night. Then they follow him outside.

"No." I swallow past the tightness in my throat.

"It'll be good. I'll do you, too, if you want."

What does that mean?

There's a rumble to the words. He strokes the tip of his fingers down my cheek, and while my brain spins, every inch of my skin comes alive.

"No, thank you."

"Aren't you curious?" he says.

Am I?

I can't afford to be. I don't *want* to be.

But sitting next to him is like sitting next to an energy source. Sensation arcs in the space between us.

He's so strong, so above everyone else. We've lived together all our lives, but his orbit has never intersected mine. But now he's here.

It's like sitting on a jetty in a stormy sea.

The power makes you feel small and magical at the same time.

My body is responding. My belly swirls. My nipples rub against the cool cotton, creating an achy heat. My pussy lips swell. I press my thighs together as hard as I can, but the next time he inhales, his nose quivers.

His lips rise until they're almost curved. "You are, aren't you?"

"No. I—" I shake my head, but inside, my body hums in agreement. I clasp my hands until my knuckles blanch white. This is a bad idea. Dangerous. Stupid.

My wolf isn't feigning sleep anymore. She's alert and pissed and letting me feel it. *Bad male. Go to the other female's cabin.* She huffs and turns her back.

Killian twists his torso, reaches over, and gently lifts my chin. Then he bends down and brushes his firm, dry lips against mine.

Time freezes.

I exhale a sighed, "Oh."

And suddenly, I can feel it all at once, his touch shining a floodlight on the emptiness inside of me, the years of touchlessness after Ma and Da passed when I was fostered, the cold ache that settles into your bones, and remains, no matter how much your friends care for you when you're grown.

It's the place left when Ma no longer brushes your hair for a hundred strokes. When Pa's no longer there for you to rest your head on his furry belly and scratch behind his ears.

It's raw, always—still—and Killian's touch exposes it and soothes it at the same time.

It's what I needed.

What I missed.

And the thoughts don't make sense, but it doesn't matter because I'm rapt.

He draws his nose along the side of mine and then kisses my forehead. His hands stroke over my shoulders and down my back. He draws me closer. My fingers land on his bare chest. It's hot to the touch.

My heart pounds. We're both breathing heavily, and it stirs the air between us, creating a heat, an urgency.

An intimacy.

I let my fingers explore, slide up his pecs, and they twitch and tense. His lungs hitch.

I did that.

There's a rumble in his chest, and I lay my cheek against it to see if I can feel it.

I can.

He smooths my hair, dropping a kiss to my hairline, the tip of my nose. I sigh and cling tighter, winding my arms around his neck, lifting myself so I can kiss him back.

This is perfect. This is designed. This can make up for it all if I let go, if I just give in to the mysterious swirling rising inside me.

He's exploring, traveling from my lips to my temple to my jaw, as if he's tasting the differences, as if he's swept away, too.

We're thigh to thigh, the shawl bunched and tented as we twist to reach each other. I want more. I want to touch everything. I grab his shoulders to lift myself, but my leg is stiff, and I can't get a good enough grip. I growl, frustrated.

He chuckles. "I got you." He picks me up and resettles me sideways in his lap, returning my hands to his shoulders and then massaging the thigh of my bad leg.

He kisses me, eyes closed, as he cradles me, and I feel floaty and surrounded and gobsmacked. I feel *held*.

He's so strong. I run my fingers down his bulging arms, the veined tops of his hands, his hard knuckles. He has a fighter's hands, a fighter's body. But he's docile beneath me. Patient. Coaxing.

Waiting for me.

For what?

He nips my bottom lip with his sharp teeth, and something inside me bursts open.

Oh, now I know. For *this*.

I *want*. Heat courses through my veins, and I squirm.

I don't like this position. I want to be able to climb, crawl, roll.

I dig my fingers into the bunched muscles of his shoulders and lift up. This is too slow motion. I know what I need. He knows too, that's why he matches me, urges me closer, cradles my neck in his palm.

I lick his mouth, and when he parts his lips, I devour him. I clutch him, plastering my breasts to his hard chest, inhaling with him because he's air, he's home, he's everything.

I *need*, and he has what I want. The deprivation is a chasm inside me, and he can fill it, he has it, and I can make him give it to me, with my mouth, my hands.

He folds his arms around me, tight, and rubs my lower back, soothing me and murmuring, "You taste so good, baby. Let's go back to my place. We'll get this out of our systems."

Yes.

That's the best idea.

We need space. So I can put things in order, and we can touch all over, and we can—*get this out of our systems*.

My brain crashes headfirst into the words. There's almost an audible tire screech.

Hold up.

Wait a minute.

I'm the only one swept away here.

He's in full control.

He's smirking, self-satisfied, tugging the shawl where it's bunched under my thigh.

Oh, hell. I'm making a fool of myself.

I've never stood so quickly. I hop down into the phlox, landing with my weight on my bad leg, and thank goodness, it holds me. My wolf is snarling, raging, utterly pissed on my behalf. I'm gonna barf.

I stumble through the flower garden toward the stairs.

My hands are shaking. I wipe my mouth. I want to spit him out. I want to suck on a bar of soap.

What's wrong with me?

I trip. He reaches to steady me—he's right behind me— but I stagger forward, putting as much distance between us as I can.

He keeps following, but a few more steps behind. When I get to the steps, he lifts me up then backs off again.

"What's going on?" He's genuinely confused.

I don't know. The mate bond is gone. I'm not in heat. My body's gone bonkers—and my feelings are all over the place —but this isn't like back in the briar patch. I never want to feel that way again. And yet, here I am, thirsting after this asshole like a teenage fangirl, gobbling up any crumb he throws my way.

I tell the roomies all the time—just because this pack treats us as less than doesn't make it true. But no matter how much I tell myself that, no matter how far I've gotten from the "poor lone female" mentality, here I am, my lonely orphaned self, clinging to the alpha, desperate to feel less abandoned.

This is more humiliating than the briar patch.

"Nothing. I want you to leave. Just go."

His brow furrows.

"My wolf does, too," I add like that'll help.

I stare at his feet and the rough wood planks beneath them.

"Una. Look at me."

My name on his lips stokes the strange excitement in my chest, and it doesn't make sense. I'm hurt. Bristling. And awake and aware in a way I've never been before, not even on a full moon.

I jerk my head no.

He sighs in exasperation and paces a few feet away. "You gotta tell me what's going on in your head. I'm not a mind reader."

It comes out so easily. He's definitely said this to a female before. My wolf growls and tosses her head. I'm with her.

"No, I don't," I say to the weathered porch boards. "I didn't come to your house. I didn't howl outside your window. I didn't start any of this, and I—" My voice breaks just a little. "*I* don't have any problem leaving."

I turn toward the door so quickly that I catch Mari's wide eyes as the curtain falls back into place.

I stop mid-stride and take a deep breath. I'm not going to run away like I'm scared. I force myself to look him in the eye. "I'm not your mate. You said so yourself, and you're the alpha. And I don't want a 'with benefits' kind of thing. Or any kind of thing with you."

"What's 'with benefits?'" he asks.

"And you're not in my system."

"Hold up. Go back. What benefits?"

"There aren't any. That's what I'm saying. You do your thing, and I'll do mine, and just, just—get off my damn porch."

I fumble with the door knob, and when I get it open, it slams into the wall. My insides are sparking. I carefully shut the door so it doesn't seem like I'm upset, and I drive the deadbolt home.

Mari, Annie, and Kennedy huddle in the hall, gawking.

"H-He can break down that door," Annie says.

"We should put the couch in front of it." Kennedy's already pushing up the sleeves of her sweatshirt.

"We can't take him just the three of us," Mari says, her sweet voice quavering. "I'm gonna call Abertha."

And whoosh, the temper drops out of me like a row in Tetris. I'm not accustomed to anger. Big feelings aren't my register. I'm calm, cool, and collected.

And my roomies are the best. I've done okay with them, I think. We're taught every day to bend and show our necks, but all three are making to move the couch. They've got my back.

"You don't have to. The kitchen door's right there." I hike a thumb over my shoulder. "And I don't think he's going to bust in."

Mari peeks outside. "He's sitting on the edge of the porch again."

"Wolf or man?" Annie asks.

"Man."

"What's he doing?" Kennedy elbows Mari away so she can see for herself.

"Staring at the moon."

They're all looking to me, but I don't know what to say. "I think he's guarding us. He'll probably go home in a little bit."

They seem skeptical.

"What do we do?" Annie asks.

"Go to bed. I'm sure everything will go back to normal in the morning."

From the looks on their faces, none of them believe me. I offer what I hope is a reassuring smile, and head back to my room.

I glance quickly out the window as I pull the curtains closed. Killian is still there, his shoulders curved, a sprig of lavender in his hand. He's popping the flowers off, one by one.

His posture isn't defeated or upset. If I had to say, I'd call it contemplative.

I touch my lips. They feel the same as they always have.

I let my mind skim the place where the mate bond used to be. No difference there. Tender but healing. No pain.

But there's a new rawness in me, beneath the confusion and hurt. My wolf is so confident in Killian's wolf. She's snoozing now, perfectly happy and assured that he's miserable.

Killian's rejected me a handful of times at this point.

But he's sitting in human form on my porch.

I turned him down, but he didn't get angry. He didn't force the issue.

And he didn't stick us out here in this cabin because we don't belong. He did it to protect us.

I do remember what it was like, even though the memory feels much longer ago than it actually was. I remember the Butlers and the Campbells forbidding me to walk anywhere alone.

I remember Eileen Campbell hurrying me past the commissary one afternoon. She hissed at me to look down. There was a circle of males out back by the picnic table. A female was sobbing.

There was always a feeling of dread anytime the pack met—at meals or bonfires or full moon runs. That's where I learned to be small. And quiet.

If anyone was trying to change things, they were doing it in secret, and I was too young to know.

Then Killian came to power, and overnight, the rules were different. He burned the picnic table behind the commissary. The unprotected females were moved to this cabin.

Why did he change things?

I'd like to know, but I can't imagine asking.

Even after tonight.

The kissing.

He's alpha. I'm a lone female. We're never going to talk like equals. On the most primal level, we *aren't*.

I crawl under the covers, certain that it'll take forever to fall asleep, but I drift off right away. I have strange dreams, and I wake often and steal to the window.

Each time, Killian's there, staring at the moon, and then later, lying on his side, sleeping on a bent arm, my shawl bunched around his middle.

When the sun rises, he's gone, a pile of plucked lavender next to where he sat.

I sweep them into the flower bed before the others wake up, and I can't stop my lips from curving.

The alpha of Quarry Pack slept on my porch. And he took my shawl when he left.

7

KILLIAN

I wake up with my left side numb, my face plastered to a wood plank with drool. The sky is lightening over the foothills. Down in the commons, elders are stirring. A baby cries.

I feel hungover as shit, but I haven't drunk a drop.

As mysteriously as it hit me, the compulsion has eased. I can leave if I want. I swing my legs over the side of the porch, crack my back, circle my shoulders.

Una is sleeping. She doesn't say much when she's awake, but she was mumbling and cooing all night long. Except for when she woke up and checked to see if I was still out here. My wolf woke me. He wanted me to make a move. He doesn't realize we both got shut down hard.

Obviously, I said the wrong thing. I don't claim to know how to sweet talk. I don't have to, and I prefer to be straightforward.

My cock is hard as shit, worse than morning wood. I can scent Una from here. She smells drowsy and soft like she's fresh from the oven. Her essence wafts through the cabin walls, through the gaps in the door and window frames.

When's the last time we had the maintenance crew up here to check the insulation? We're not so flush with cash that we can afford to heat the whole damn camp.

And she must get cold when the wind blows down from the hills.

She needs to be in our bed.

Reaching for us when she wakes up, hungry and demanding like she was for that too brief moment last night. If we'd been in a safe place—my cabin or up in the dens where I could sense an enemy approach—I would've had her riding my cock before I could fuck things up with my mouth. But my wolf and I are in perfect accord on one thing. Her safety comes above all else.

And we're not gonna piss her off anymore than we already have. If possible.

I scrub my face. What the hell is going on?

She's not my mate. I would *know*. I'm sure as hell not in love. I never have been. I fight. I lead. I don't sniff after females like Tye.

If I were to fall in love, she'd be an alpha. A badass with big ol' titties.

Una's no badass. I mean, she's all right. Even though she kind of went nuts there for a minute, she's got good sense. For years, she's kept the drama to a minimum and the other lone females off the radar. And I'm grateful for it.

Three things keep me up at night—Moon Lake moving to usurp our territory, Last Pack deciding to join the shifter circuit, and the lone female cabin.

If Moon Lake makes a move, we're gonna lose males, and we're not guaranteed a win. They stockpile human weapons, and they see nothing wrong with using them.

If the Last Pack starts fighting, we're gonna have to find a new livelihood. Rumor says they can all flip-shift. Not any day at any time like me, but as a hat trick. Three times in a match would be all it takes to beat every single one of our males.

And if some drunk night when I'm away, Lochlan or one of his buddies decides to rally the unmated males, head up to the lone female cabin, and take what they want? What Eamon and a lot of the other elders have been telling them for years is their due?

Well, I put 'em all in one place, didn't I? Like fish in a barrel.

That's why if I'm away, Tye or Ivo is here. And at the end of the day, they're safer together with Una to keep an eye on them. She's a good packmate. Keeps her head down. Does her work. She's solid.

But she's not my mate.

Yet, for some reason, all of a sudden, I want to fuck her so bad I can taste it. The mate bond is deeper than that, though. Right?

The bond is a flower, rooted in two souls, blossoming with the first onset of a female's heat. Or some such shit. I don't pay a lot of attention during worship.

I need answers. Which means I gotta go see the crone. Not my favorite thing. She speaks in riddles, and she always wants me to drink tea.

I clear my throat, and Gael trots over from where he's been hanging out in the trees behind the outbuilding across the way. I've smelled him there for the past hour or so.

"Tye send you?" I ask him in a low voice. I don't want to wake the females.

"I volunteered."

I nod at his face. "You look like you got run over by a Mack truck." His nose isn't gonna be the same. Looks better now. It's got character.

"Worth it," he says.

"Yeah?"

"Now I get served first at meals, don't I?" He grins. A few teeth haven't grown back yet. "My drumstick and leg days are over. It's only breasts and thighs from here on out."

I see he's gotten chattier since his elevation in rank. That's gonna be annoying.

I stand, catching the shawl before it falls. "I've got shit to do. Watch the cabin."

"Okay." He goes to make himself comfortable on the porch. My wolf growls.

This is our territory now.

"From over there." I point back to the woods he was skulking in.

"Seriously?"

My wolf rumbles. I don't bother answering. Gael bends his neck and scrambles back to where he came from, holding up his jeans. I don't see how pants can be so skinny in the leg and droopy at the waist. Kid needs a belt.

And I gotta take a piss. My wolf is fine with spraying all over the flowerbed, but I'm not an animal. I relieve myself in the bushes beside the cabin before I head home for a change of clothes.

After coffee, I rub one out in the shower. It feels wrong to think about Una, disrespectful somehow, but I can't help it. She's in my head. Her soft lips. Quiet whimpers. How hard she mashed her tits against my chest and how tight she wrapped her arms around my neck. She wanted it. She needed it from me.

I come hard, jizz splattering on the tile. I gotta splash a few times to rinse it all down the drain.

Fates, a few minutes necking with Una Hayes was the most intense sexual experience of my life. Given, I've never actually fucked a female, but I've gotten my dick sucked plenty, and I've been getting hand jobs from alpha groupies since junior high. And it's fine. It takes the edge off. But it's never been like this.

I've never wanted to be *inside* so bad before. And I *wanted*. Hell, I *needed*. And then I opened my dumb mouth.

But she's not my mate.

Though I'm less certain of that each time I think it.

I've got good reasons for not getting my dick wet. It'd fuck with pack rank. Sucking cock is one thing—not much in the way of bragging rights there—but if I favor a female with my seed? She's not gonna shut up about that. Cheryl would feel the need to put her back in her place. It'd be a whole thing.

And our relations with the other packs aren't so chill that I can be rutting their females without certain expectations arising.

And also, I've never felt the need. Until now.

I want to take Una Hayes to my bedroom, watch her build a nest on my bed, fuss and straighten and toss sheets around. And then I want her to present. Call to me over her shoulder. Press her round tits with the saucer nipples to the mattress and hike that thick ass in the air.

I want my cock slick with her cream. I want to dig my fingers into those hips, leave red half-moons in her pale skin as I drag her back to take me.

I want to feel how hot she is inside. How tight. How those muscles feel when they clench. When they spasm.

Oh, Fate. I gotta get out of here before I end up jerking off again.

I don't bother with anything besides brushing my teeth. I throw on some shorts and a T-shirt and jog halfway to the crone's cottage, working out the kinks in my muscles still lingering from a night on the ground. The morning sun has burned off the dew, but there's a mugginess to the air.

When the woods thicken, I strip and shift, hanging my clothes from a branch. Immediately, my wolf scents Una. It's stale. Days old. Disturbing.

It's too faint for a human's sense of smell, but to my wolf, it's a neon arrow.

He follows his nose, up a mossy bank, through oaks with trunks wound in ivy, down into a gulch filled with a black-berry thicket.

What was she doing out here? It's on the way to the crone's cottage, but it's not the direct route, and the stickers are impenetrable. Bushes are crushed where she tunneled through. There are tufts of bloody gray fur stuck to some thorns.

My fur ruffles, and I bare my fangs. Uneasiness roils my guts.

Something bad happened here. Fear still taints the air. And shame.

I don't want to see, but I have to.

I crouch and wriggle down the path she made.

Did she come here to lick her wounds? It's not a smart hidey-hole for an injured animal—no water, no cover from the elements, and all the damn thorns—but her wolf is not the brightest.

A picture flashes in my head of the little gray creature licking her hindquarters, ignoring me while I balanced on Gael's carcass. Her indifference pissed me off and calmed me down at the same time. Despite my rage, I could still sense her fear. She was being daring. And her fear made me rein it in.

So maybe she's not dumb, exactly. Maybe she's the kind of brave that looks like stupidity from a certain angle. I've got more than a few fighters who are the same. They're my best fighters.

The narrow passage she made opens to almost a burrow. The scents smack my nose. Heat. Slick. Blood.

Fuck.

My wolf licks the matted stems. He howls. He circles the nest, nosing everything, flustered. Upset.

It's been strange lately, his feelings separate from mine, but in this, we're of one mind.

This is wrong.

There's a sense of loss. A memory that floats just out of reach. A word stuck on the tip of our tongue.

She was alone here, in pain and need, and where were we?

We want to fight someone, and there's nothing but stickers and crushed berries collecting flies.

We want to go back to Una. Assure ourselves she's safe now. No permanent harm done. But we need to know the truth.

She's okay. She doesn't want anything to do with me, and Gael is there. The patrols pass above the cabin on the ridge every quarter hour. Tye and Ivo are in camp. She's as safe as she always is.

Not enough.

I agree with the wolf. We will fix it. Move her into the commons. And the other lone females, as well. But we need answers now. *I* need answers.

My wolf could give a shit. He wants Una. Fur or skin. Soft and warm. Quiet and watchful. Unbending. Shy. He wants her scrawny gray wolf with the nervous ears and quivering nose.

I need to talk to the crone.

Go back.

No.

The wolf snarls and howls, but when I don't bend, he changes tack. He starts digging, furiously scrambling at the dirt, covering the stems soaked in Una's scent.

Like we're hiding a crime.

This isn't right.

But he won't leave until he's obliterated the evidence of whatever happened here. And even then, I have to drag him away. He rages at me while I force his paws further from camp, step by step. It's like dragging a semi.

Then, when we reach the crone's, for some reason, he chills out. Una's scent is all over. It's like it's coming from the garden somehow, and it isn't laced with pain. It's faint and mellow. Sweet.

We didn't get here a moment too soon. The crone has an electric blue hatchback backed to her front door, and she's stowing a suitcase in the trunk.

I shift, trotting over to help. She doesn't need it. The witch has a wiry strength, and I doubt she's as old as she acts. She hasn't aged a day in as long as I can remember, and she listens to human music that sounds like it's made by robots.

Still, you show respect to your elders. Especially to a female with powers.

She's wearing linen slacks, a classy silk shirt, and gold in her ears and around her neck. Her hair is coiled in a slick bun, not the braid she usually wears.

"Visiting Moon Lake?" I know she's got a side hustle over there. Wouldn't surprise me if she's got herself a cozy cottage in all of the pack lands.

She smirks. "Might be."

"Did you plan on asking me?" It's a joke. The crone doesn't recognize my authority.

"Asking, no. Telling—" She pats my arm. "Also, no."

"Who's watching the cat?"

I've never actually seen the bugger, but I can smell him. He takes one whiff of me and bolts.

"My girls will keep an eye on them."

"And who's gonna keep an eye on your girls?" I know they come up here all the time. I figured it was fine. The crone herself is better protection than my scouts. But maybe I need to rethink that.

We're almost a mile from the commons, and less than half that from the boundary of Quarry territory.

Strike that maybe. I definitely need to reconsider. At least rework the patrols so they crisscross the crone's land.

"You will, won't you?" The crone winks. "A real close eye on one in particular."

Her amusement doesn't amuse me, but I don't let my displeasure show. You can't dominate the crone. It was the one decent lesson my father taught me. He said witches dance between raindrops. Any male who thinks to control one doesn't understand nature.

"That's why I've come," I say.

"I figured. I thought I had a day or two more. I should've left last night." She sighs. "Well. You're here. I'm busted. Cup of tea?"

"If you're so inclined."

Tea's not my thing, but I'm not gonna be rude.

She leads the way to her front door, and once inside, she throws me a pair of athletic shorts before busying herself building a fire. I make myself comfortable at her kitchen table.

Like the crone, the cottage hasn't changed from when I was young. My mother used to bring me up here. The females would go out to the shed for some female business, and I'd be left inside with a cookie and a glass of goat's milk. My mother warned me not to touch anything, but she needn't have. I felt then like I do now—like an alien on a strange planet. And all the shit could be poisonous. How would I know?

It doesn't smell like pack in here. It smells like earth. Herbs. Dust and age and wood and sunshine. It confuses the nose, clings to your hair and skin.

If a predator was stalking me, he'd be able to get damn close before I clocked him. That's dangerous.

I was always happy to leave after my mother had her cup of tea and chat with the crone. After I shifted the first time, she didn't bring me with her anymore, and that was fine by me.

The crone disrupts my reminiscences by setting a plate with cookies in front of me. Oatmeal. Same as I remember.

She raises a gray eyebrow. "Your favorite, weren't they?"

I nod.

"What did my mother come here for?" We always left with a small brown bag. I had a child's lack of curiosity. To be honest, I'm not really sure why I'm wondering now.

"Not my tale to tell."

"She's long gone." Wasting sickness got her in the last wave.

"That's one way of looking at it."

It's my turn to raise an eyebrow. "There are others?"

"Always." She goes back to the fireplace to hang the kettle.

"You know why I'm here."

"I do."

"Is Una Hayes my mate?"

"Did you ask her?"

Did I? I definitely did. Didn't I?

She said I wasn't. She agreed with me that she wasn't. I search my memory for the exact words. It's never this hard with males. I hate semantics. "I don't know. She said you fixed it. What does that mean?"

"At the risk of repeating myself—did you ask her?"

I grab a cookie and take a bite. It's good.

"Is there a reason you're busting my balls?" I say after swallowing. The crone laughs, and she comes to sit across from me. She breaks a cookie in half and begins nibbling.

"Besides entertainment value?" She leans back in her chair. "I'll answer your questions if you answer mine first."

"Fine. Shoot."

"What do you remember about your first shift?"

"Pain." It's a strange question, but I've been asked it before. I shifted at nine years old. That's unheard of, and wolves are nosy.

"What else?"

"Blood. Screams. I thought I went blind for a while."

"Do you remember what happened before the shift?"

"Not really. It was a normal day."

"Do you remember after?"

"Nothing. It's a big blank. Where are you going with this?"

She smiles and rests her hands on the table top. For an old woman's, they're smooth and straight. "I'm going to tell you a story. It's also not my tale to tell, but—" She lifts a shoulder. "Rules are made to be broken, right?"

I disagree, but I nod anyway.

"It's hard to know where to start." She sighs.

"How about the beginning?"

"'Beginning' is subjective, isn't it?" She looks to me for a response, but philosophy is not my thing.

She sighs. "I guess I could start with a sunny day, a

young male playing on the commons, waiting for his friend. Or the night sixteen months earlier when your father snuck into the Fane cabin to take what he felt was his due from his lieutenant's mate? She was in heat after all. And Fane was at a fight in Moon Lake."

"You're talking about Thomas Fane." That's Mari's father, the last male my father put down for moon madness.

"I am." She eyes me like she expects something. Eventually, I guess when I don't give her what she's looking for, she leans to rest her elbows on the table. "I'll start on the sunny day. Una and Rowan Bell were braiding daisy chains. Rowan was watching her baby cousin Mari. Rowan wanders off home to get a snack."

She tilts her head. I can picture it, but it's not in my memory.

"Thomas Fane was getting wasted at the lodge. He was listening to his alpha, your father, brag about his conquests."

My father was a righteous prick. This isn't news.

"The alpha's son—" She waves a hand at me. "He was throwing a ball as high as he could and still catch it, waiting for a friend."

"I was waiting for Tye." I catch a glimpse. Hiking the hard old pigskin I'd found in the woods into the blue sky, frustrated to be kept waiting.

"Thomas Fane had enough. He cursed your father and left. Stumbled home. And on his way, he came across a little girl and a baby in a basket."

My gut knots. My memory offers nothing, but my wolf is alert. On edge. Like he knows what's coming.

"Fane staggered over and punted the baby's basket." The crone sneers in disgust. "He would have stomped his own child to death if not for Una Hayes. She put her little body between Thomas Fane's wolf and that baby, and she nearly died. She would have."

Abertha pins me with blazing eyes.

"Except?"

"Except for Killian Kelly. The alpha's nine-year-old son. He raced to the rescue, and on his way, he shifted for the first time. His wolf was a beast. He rent Thomas Fane limb from limb. It took Declan Kelly and three enforcers to drag him away from the corpse."

"Bullshit." That's the kind of story that gets told at every bonfire. I've never heard it before. And I sure as shit don't remember it happening.

"If the pack knew you shifted before your heat, you'd have a target on your back. Your father knew this. The others wouldn't wait for him to die to challenge you. And you might have a beast inside you, but in human form, you were seventy pounds soaking wet. Eamon or Dermot or anyone with ambition could've easily beat you so many times, no one would've looked at you and seen a possible alpha. You'd be out as a contender before you could grow a beard. So your father swore his enforcers to secrecy, and it was never spoken of again."

"My father would have told me about it."

"Would he?"

The kettle whistles. The crone rises to take it off the fire.

I don't think about my father much. He was an asshole. He started me sparring at five and let the males a few years older whale on me. He got off on watching me come back and take them down. He thought he taught me how to recover, and in a way, he did. He put me on the ground plenty before he put me in the ring.

He was always clear that I was to succeed him as alpha. His seed was the strongest. I was his trophy. His belt.

You don't explain shit to a belt. So, yeah, maybe he wouldn't have told me.

"How do you know all this? You were there?" The crone avoids the commons like the plague, and everyone is cool with that.

She comes back to the table, setting mismatched tea cups in front of us both. I give her a nod of thanks.

"I see all." She rounds her eyes, and then she snorts. "Your mother brought you and Una up here afterwards. You were almost dead. You both were."

I'm surprised my father let her. He was big on rubbing dirt in it.

"Fane didn't get the chance to leave a mark on you, but your wolf tore you up."

"He's a monster."

The crone uses her spoon to strain the tea bag and then sets it on the saucer. I follow suit and put my thumb through the wet sack. Now there's flakes in my cup.

"There wasn't much I could do but treat the pain. There were a few days—" Her eyes grow distant. "We didn't think you'd make it."

"But I recovered." I always do.

"You did. But you weren't the same."

"First blood changes a male." It is known.

She shakes her head. "No, that's not what I'm talking about. You weren't the same as other wolves anymore. It was as if to let him out, you had to consume him. Become one with him."

"The wolf and man are one." It's such a common saying, it's out of my mouth before I think.

She rolls her eyes. "Don't bring that bullshit into my house. That's just how backwards folk justify behaving like animals to each other."

"Don't tell the elders that. They'll burn you at the stake."

She snorts. "Not a single one of those mouth breathers could catch me when they were in their prime."

"No doubt." I've seen her wolf. She's sleek and silver, and she's got uncommonly sharp fangs.

"What I'm trying to say is that I thought it'd undo. Repair in good time. I thought the Fates would prevail. But I was wrong. You aren't like other males."

"Yeah. I'm a flip-shifter."

"I'm not talking about that. You're—" Her face scrunches like she's searching for the right words. "You're getting in your own way."

"Yeah? Maybe so, but I've done all right so far." I abandon the tea and lean back.

"Have you?" The crone sinks back in her chair, mimicking my posture. "Is everything *right*?"

What kind of philosophical bullshit is that?

"Listen, I came with a question. Are you gonna answer it? Is Una Hayes my mate?"

"You honestly can't tell." Her brow creases. There's pity in her gray eyes. "Yes. She was."

Every muscle tightens, and I push back, the chair screeching on the hard wood. "What do you mean—was?"

"Sounds like she told you. I pulled the mate bond out of her."

I bound to my feet. "You what?"

My wolf is choking my voice. The words come out a garbled growl.

The crone doesn't move. My rage fills the room, clogs my own nose, but she's unaffected. She takes a slow sip of her tea.

"You knew this. She told you she was your mate. You rejected her. She told you I fixed it. You must have found her nest in the woods. I can scent traces of her heat on you. You know *all* of this. But you're deaf to it. Because you are getting in your own way."

My clenched fists shake. Fur has sprouted up my spine, and my bones are stretching, my muscles swelling.

"Your wolf recognizes his mate," she says.

"I *am* my wolf."

The crone tuts. "Don't start lying to yourself now, Alpha. Your wolf and you are like that mutt Eamon lets his mate keep in the backyard. You coexist."

"Why didn't I feel the bond when she shifted?"

"Do you let yourself feel anything?"

I do. Every nerve in my body is screaming. I have to wade through the thoughts whirling in my brain.

"You pulled the mate bond out of her?" I spit the question through elongated fangs.

"What would you have had me do? You scented her nest. She was in pain."

"You had no right."

She laughs, and it is bitter. "Don't talk to me of rights. Una claimed you, and did you stop for a second to consider someone else knew a truth you didn't? You've grown arrogant, Alpha. You think you can't move this pack forward because they're too stubborn, but pup, you need to attend to the mote in your own eye."

"I didn't come for a lecture."

"You came for me to tell you what Una already did. Why take my word over hers?"

My back teeth clench so hard they ache. "You do not have the right to take my mate from me."

"You have no claim over something you so carelessly threw away."

"Put the bond back." I instill each word with alpha command.

"I don't know how."

My wolf howls, shaking the rafters, making himself known.

The crone narrows her eyes. "And even if I did, I wouldn't do it."

"Put it back!" I slam the table. The tea cups rattle, and a crack appears in the solid wood.

"I can't, but I'll make you an offer." Her lips curl. "I'll take the bond out of you, too."

My hand flies to my chest. It feels no different. There's no pulse, no burning fire like the mated males describe. There's—silence.

"I assure you, it's there." The crone calmly sips her tea. "You can't feel the blood coursing in your veins, either, but it's there all the same."

"No." The suggestion itself has my claws drawn.

"The bond can only bring you misery. Una doesn't want you now. And you won't force her."

Rage surges through me, and the crone is wrong. I *can* feel my blood—it's burning. "I am *not* my father."

"No, you're not. So since you don't want her, let her go. Let her be happy with someone else."

"Who?" It's a snarl.

She waves her hand. "Relax. I'm talking theoretically."

"You're playing Fate."

"And you don't, Alpha?"

We are silent a moment, glaring at each other as I force my wolf down, compel the rage to abate. The crone is a canny adversary. You don't go into the ring in a temper.

"There's no way to reverse what you have done?"

She crosses her legs and smooths her slacks. "I didn't say

that. I said I didn't know how."

"You have cost me my young, witch."

"You cost yourself. It's your head that's stuck up your ass." My wolf rumbles, and she hurries to add, "And we don't know that for sure. You could always, I don't know, woo her. The moon works in mysterious ways."

"Woo her?"

"You know. Dates. Flowers."

"That's human shit."

She shrugs. "They do it at Moon Lake."

I slowly exhale. "You have done me a grave disservice."

"Maybe," she says. "Or maybe I've done you a great favor. Go back to camp. Train your fighters. Let a female lure you to her bed. Nothing has to change."

It's the first lie she's told me.

I glance out the window at the packed car. "You're leaving?"

"I am."

"Stay gone."

"You're exiling me?" She arches an eyebrow.

"I'm advising you. You can come back when my mate's belly is round with my young."

She laughs and moves to clear the cups from the table. "You always were confident."

"I have always had cause to be."

The crone pauses and cranes her neck to search my eyes. It's the closest to a bent neck I'll ever get from her. "You really don't remember, do you?"

"Remember what?"

Her brow furrows. "I don't think I should tell you. I don't want to get in the way of the Fates."

I snort. "Crone, you're full of shit."

She shrugs. "It's hard to know what's helping and what's

meddling. There's no rule book."

I have no clue what she's talking about. There are rules. I made them. And folks don't need help or meddling. Nine times out of ten, they need a swift kick in the ass.

I don't think this conversation is going anywhere, though, and my wolf and I are agreed that we've been too long away from camp.

"Stay gone," I tell the crone's back as she turns on the faucet to rinse our dishes.

"I do what I want," she tosses over her shoulder.

I know when to tap out, so I toss my shorts on a bench, head out the door, and let my wolf take our skin.

I'm done with this vague, hippie shit. I am going to get my mate. My body warms. A faint, strange pulse tick tocks in my sternum.

My wolf raises his snout as we race back to camp, and I swear words ring in his howls.

Took you long enough.

I'm almost back to camp when another scent stops me in my tracks. It's rich. Delicious. I bound off through the underbrush, and it doesn't take long to discover the source.

Darragh Ryan is hauling a fresh kill on his shoulders. A buck. Eight points.

Before I shift, my wolf leaps up and snaps a chunk off the haunch. So fresh.

When I rise to two feet, I wipe blood from my mouth. "What are you doing down here?"

Darragh's twisting his neck to check out the damage. "Did you really have to? Couldn't wait for me to dress it for you?"

"You don't do it for me. You do it for Mari."

Mari's the mate he avoids claiming by living feral in the foothills. He says it's 'cause of the age difference—he wants her to have the chance to grow up before taking on his old ass—but it's something else. Don't know what, and since he keeps shit secure in our western territory, I don't care.

"She doing well?" Darragh schools his weathered face like he ain't transparent as hell.

"She is." I don't mention her squeal when she caught sight of my cock last night. That wouldn't go over too well. "What are you doing so close to camp?"

"Cutting through. I was following my nose. Took me out by the old dens."

"You smelled that buck all that way?" It's big, but it's not that big.

Darragh shakes his head, and his salt-and-pepper beard brushes his equally hairy chest. "Something else. Something unfamiliar."

My adrenaline kicks up. "Like what?"

"Dirt. Leaves. Pine needles. Not ours. From another territory. Baking soda."

"Like hunters covering their tracks?" It's rare, but occasionally humans are stupid enough to track an animal onto our territory.

"Yes, but I didn't scent human."

"Wolf?"

He shakes his head. "Once I got out there, all I smelled was this fella here." He resettles the buck's weight.

"Should I send a patrol out?"

Darragh snorts. "I don't know. You willing to waste good training time based on the overactive imagination of a wolf almost gone feral?"

"Hey, patrols are cardio."

"True enough." He sighs, his gaze turning toward the direction of the old dens. "I think it was a fluke—some strong scent carried on a strong wind. I tracked this big fella a few hours, covered a lot of ground, didn't scent anything out of place." Darragh pats the deer's haunch. "I'll bring this down later. Let Old Noreen know to expect it."

"I will." I clasp Darragh's hand and fake like I'm going in for another bite.

"Fuck off, man."

I chuckle. I made him flinch. I miss Darragh around camp. He taught me a lot of what I know. "You know we keep a seat open for you in the lodge."

"So you tell me." He jerks his chin and strides away, blazing his own trail through the thicket on a path toward the ridge. Anyone who saw him would mistake him for a member of the Last Pack. Long, snarled hair and beard, claws that never quite recede, ears that come to a point.

If he doesn't come out of the hills soon, he might not ever be able to. That's his choice, though. Every male is entitled to his own. I don't know how Mari handles her heat with him gone, but she does. It's a messed up situation, but they can do as they see fit—and if they don't want the rest of the pack to know, I'm not a gossip.

I shift back to wolf and lope back to camp. First, I swing by the lodge and tell Ivo to take a group up and comb the northeast quadrant, and then I head straight for Una's place.

Gael isn't where I left him. Jaime's there. He's wandered up on the ridge behind the cabin, squatting on a rock, playing on his phone. I leap and knock it from his hands while I shift back to my skin.

"Where's Una?"

Jaime scrambles to his feet. "Down there."

"No, she isn't." I smell Mari. Annie. Kennedy. That's it.

"I swear, Alpha. I've been here an hour. No one's left."

"Where's Gael?"

"Lochlan wanted him in the gym to spar with Finn. He

sent me to take his place."

What the fuck?

Jaime bends to get his phone, but before he can, I stomp it with my heel. It cracks. Doesn't make me feel better.

Where the hell's my mate? And what the fuck is Lochlan playing at?

I trip down the incline, cross the deck, and fling open the female's back door. There's a scream. I take a breath, slow my roll down the narrow hall. Una's not gonna like it if she comes home and her place reeks of female fear.

Mari and Annie are huddled on the couch, Kennedy standing in front of them in a defensive stance. They're all baring their necks.

"Where is she?"

"Don't tell him," Kennedy says at the exact same time the other two sob, "Chapel Bell."

I roar, the wolf coursing up my throat. I swallow him down. There will be time for rage. Later. After I have my mate in hand.

There's a footstep behind me. The females peek up. Jaime clears his throat.

His scent is in my female's space.

Oh, hell, no.

I barrel out the way I came in, seizing Jaime and hauling him out the back door, hoisting him into the sunflowers growing around the deck. There's a satisfying crunch.

Guess there's a little time for rage now.

What the fuck is Una doing in town? Who is she with?

When I get my female, I'm tying her to my bed.

No wooing.

I am alpha.

She is mine.

And all this bullshit is gonna stop here and now.

"Killian's not in camp." Kennedy rushes through the screen door, letting it slam.

Annie's having a panic attack on the sofa. She's wrung her skirt to the point it's wrinkled and damp with palm sweat. She's not going to be able to make the mushroom run. She was cool yesterday, but having Killian howling outside all night long jangled her nerves. And they're not steady on the best of days.

"Where is he?" I ease my backpack over my shoulders. I've carefully wrapped the jar of morels in a thick quilt.

"Old Noreen didn't know, and I didn't want to ask anybody else. I don't smell him anywhere, though." She squeezes Annie's shoulder.

"I—I'm s—so sorry." Annie's eyes are tormented. She hates herself like this, but once the poison gets in her head, you can't talk her out of it. Abertha's calming tea doesn't help. Even Kennedy's weed doesn't do much but blunt the worst of it.

"Nothing to be sorry about. We're a team, right?" I hold out my fist.

She wrinkles her forehead.

"You bump it with your fist. It's a human thing."

She's still hyperventilating, but she taps my knuckles.

"You gonna be okay?" I know she will be, but I worry. She's tough, but her brain kind of has a mind of its own.

"G-go g-get 'em." She manages a watery smile. That's my girl. A light breeze will knock her down emotionally, but she hauls herself back up every time.

"Are we clear?" I ask Kennedy, checking my phone. No new texts. About an hour ago, Shroomforager3000 said he was at the rest stop north of Chapel Bell.

"The males are all at the gym or the lodge. The patrols should be at the west and south perimeters. It's now or never."

"All right. I'll be quick. A half hour there, ten minutes or so to make the exchange, a half hour home. I'll be back way before dinner."

"We'll go down to the commons so if anyone's asking for you, we can say you're at the crone's." Kennedy peeks out the window.

"Has anyone ever asked for me?" I peer over her shoulder. The path is clear. I don't scent anyone.

"First time for everything." Kennedy holds up her palm, and I slap it.

"Keep an eye on Annie?" I ask her.

"You know I will." Kennedy lowers her voice. "If anything seems weird, bail. We can sell the mushrooms another time. They're dried. They're not going bad."

I lower my voice, too. "I'm a wolf. I'm not scared of a human man."

"Yeah, but that's not all that's out there." Kennedy and I exchange a look. We talk about this whenever she goes to her rented cabin to shift alone. There are still ferals outside our boundaries. Outcasts from the Last Pack. Humans who traffic in the fur trade. It's not like it used to be, but the dangers are still there.

But not at the farmer's market in Chapel Bell in broad daylight.

I give Kennedy the most reassuring smile I can muster, and she opens the door for me. After I hobble down the stairs, I force myself to walk at my usual pace. I look way too obvious when I hustle.

It's not far to the garage, and the path is empty. I don't run into anyone. It's a beautiful afternoon. The sun is bright but cool, and a steady, mild breeze flows down from the foothills.

Liam's not around when I reach the truck. He knows today is the run. I bet he's going after plausible deniability. He really likes the moonshine I bring him back from town, but he's not willing to take heat for us if he can avoid it.

I grab the keys from the corkboard in his office and go around back where the Ford is parked with the other junkers.

It takes a second to hoist myself into the cab. I don't bother adjusting the mirror. It doesn't swivel anymore.

Like I showed Annie, I really jam the clutch as I turn the key, and after a few wheezing false starts, the engine turns over. I give the dashboard a pat. She's a rust bucket, and she's temperamental, but she hasn't let me down yet.

I head for town by way of the north access road. The two miles or so on pack territory are bumpy, and I'm jumping out of my skin, imagining I hear engines coming up from behind. I have to go slow because the asphalt's busted with weeds growing in the cracks.

Road maintenance is not one of Killian Kelly's priorities. He's always fussing with energy efficient windows and solar panels, but there's a pothole that could eat a lawn mower in the middle of our only road, and it's been there forever.

Once I turn on to Rural Route 10, the ride is smooth. My hands are slick on the tacky steering wheel, and nerves riot in my belly, but I'm not as scared as the first few times I ventured into town. I'm not used to it by a long shot, but I can deal.

I am breaking pack law. Females are not allowed to leave the territory alone. That's carved in stone. I don't know what they'll do to me if they catch me. I've never known anyone but Mari, Kennedy, and I to go into town without a male.

A few of the younger males, including Fallon, got drunk at a human bar one time. One came home reeking of sex. Killian beat them all to a pulp in the middle of the commons, and the one who had sex with the human got busted down to maintenance crew. He's still not allowed to run with the pack at full moon. Fallon got off easy with an ass-kicking.

I'm smarter than them—I nearly scrub my skin off in the lake after I've been anywhere near a human—but I don't want a beating, especially not in front of the entire pack. Not again.

I'm sweating bullets. My knee shakes when I depress the clutch to shift.

But I want the money. More than I ever have before.

These past few days, I've been yanked this way and pulled that. My body does what it wants. My wolf. I want my life back. The one where I'm in charge.

I straighten my spine and turn on the radio. It only gets a few staticky stations, but I find one that plays Top 40, and I sing along. I love human music. More melody, less howling.

I'm in town before the commercial break.

Chapel Bell has three stop lights, six cross streets, and a

town square in the grassy expanse between northbound and southbound Main Street. That's where the farmer's market shares space with a weathered bandstand. There are also permanent shops on the street facing the park. An ice cream shop with a life-sized cow statue out front. A vintage jewelry store.

It's a nice town. Very peaceful. No sparring or wrestling.

I park and check my phone.

Here. At the honey table.

My belly swoops. This is it. This is going to be the biggest deal I've ever made. Who knows? Maybe the beginning of a mushroom empire. I force myself to steady my breathing.

I'm not new at this. I'm a business woman. I've got almost a thousand dollars in the trunk of an oak tree that says it.

And I am not thinking right now about what it says that my capital is stored in the hollow of a tree.

I've been selling for years. This is just another sale. Only a couple more zeroes on the price tag.

I make my way past the produce vendors and the other regulars. A few folks wave. I don't socialize, but I've been coming long enough that I'm recognized. The baseball card guy has his table laid out, and the cheese woman is here.

There's a man loitering by the honey table. I haven't seen him before. Shroomforager3000 said to look for a man with a beard, and this guy definitely has a beard. It's waxed and pointy like a goat's. His mustache swoops.

He's wearing a short-sleeve collared shirt under a brown velvety vest. He looks like a cross between a lumberjack and a yodeler.

He sees me, and his lips curl. I am a wolf, and his smile seems wolfish.

I don't like him.

I don't have to. I just have to sell him mushrooms.

He kind of canters over, hands in pockets.

"Una?"

I nod.

"I can't believe you got me all the way out here." He gestures around him. "I've never even heard of this town before."

I don't know what to say. Humans are into small talk between males and females, but I'm not used to it. It was different with the glassblower. He talked incessantly, and he didn't need you to reply.

I nod again and try to look friendly.

"Shy, eh?" He waggles his eyebrows. There's something wrong with them. They're tweezed. And arched to make him look perpetually surprised.

"I have the mushrooms."

He laughs. "Whoa, whoa. You say it like that, people are gonna think things."

I glance around. No one is close enough to hear us.

"Let's go over here. I can see what you got." He leads the way to a wrought iron bench at the edge of the lawn. I set my backpack down and carefully unfold the quilt.

Morels are ugly. They look like dried brains. Still, I hold the jar up proudly. They're all whole. No pieces.

For a second, ShroomForager3000's face lights up, but then his lips turn down, his thin, dark brows spearing together. "Oh, man. These aren't as big as they looked in the pics."

Yes, they are. These are the exact same mushrooms.

"Maybe it's seeing them in a jar." For the pictures, I laid them out on a table.

He shakes his head. "No, these are definitely, uh, you

know, on the small side." He scrubs his neck. "Man, this sucks. My guys, they're looking for a certain size you know? They want to stuff them with crab. Turkey mousse. That kind of thing."

"You can stuff these."

He sighs. "They're just not what I'm looking for, you know?"

My heart plummets. I want this money so bad I can taste it. I've been spending it in my head for months. Plenty of buyers are interested, but they want to pay online and have the product shipped, and whatever app you use, you need a checking account, and to open a checking account, you need identification. Shifter females don't have ID.

Kennedy and I have looked at it from every angle. We can't figure out a work-around. And this is the only guy who's been willing to drive down and pay cash.

I hug the jar to my chest.

ShroomForager3000 lays his hand on my shoulder. "But, hey. I mean, I drove all the way down here, right. I could take 'em off your hands. For maybe—" He licks his unnaturally red lips. "A hundred bucks?"

Oh.

He's playing me.

I tense.

He squeezes, like a massage. My wolf growls. His hand drops, and he looks at me, really looks, much closer than before.

"Holy shit. You're one of them, aren't you? A shifter. I wondered—since this town is kind of known for being close to a pack. Wow. You're a wolf, right?"

"Does that matter?"

His eyes flicker, and he licks his lips again. "Not at all. I vote pro wolf, all the way. You guys deserve citizenship. Most definitely."

I'm not up on the pro wolf stuff. That's more Moon Lake's bag. Still, I guess pro wolf is better than anti.

"You know, I have an idea. If you really need the money. I mean, I really can't do more than a hundred on the morels, but I did bring the whole three hundred."

He pauses, his gaze flickering around the market, like he's looking for something. My wolf's hackles are raised. She really doesn't like this guy. Neither do I.

"My van is just over there." He jerks his thumb to a white work van with rust along the bottom. "We could, uh, come to an arrangement, if you want the rest?"

"I'm not having sex with you for money." I hug my mushrooms tighter.

"No, no. You misunderstand." He lowers his voice and leans in. "Just pictures. A little video. You, uh, become the wolf. Shift back. Pose. I'll crop out your head. It'll take five minutes. Ten tops."

My stomach heaves, and a sour taste fills my mouth. "I'm not doing that. Give me the three hundred."

"Come on. It's just—"

My wolf growls, loud, a perfectly clear threat. He holds one hand up and digs the other into his pocket.

And then I catch a scent on the wind, and my heart leaps once, high in my throat, and then takes off in a gallop.

It's Killian.

He's close.

I scan the booths, and there he is, a blur rushing towards us, and I can't get a word out, I can't move an inch before he shoves me to the side and bowls into ShroomForager3000, sending him sailing into the air. My jar is knocked from my hands, and it falls to the sidewalk, shattering.

Killian's tan work boots land on the mushrooms, crushing them into pulp, as he bounds to loom over the human, fangs bared, claws unsheathed.

Screams pierce the air. There's the scent of piss. Shroom-Forager3000 scrambles backwards like a crab.

My mushrooms are brown goo. There are a handful intact, but they glitter with glass shards. Morels have so many ridges, even if I soak and rinse them, I can't be sure to get them clean. They are all ruined.

Three hundred dollars, down the drain.

No unlimited data. No mushroom farm. Nothing.

All that time, gathering and drying, scouring the online forums, wasted. Finding this creep. Listening to his creepy proposition. And I've got nothing.

My eyes prickle, hot with tears.

Killian looms over ShroomForager3000. "You dare touch what's mine?"

It's a roar. He's an enraged alpha. I should drop to my knees and simper, neck bared, but I don't. I don't care that my wolf is baring her neck and practically mewling. My hands curl into tight fists. He destroyed my mushrooms, and he doesn't even care.

ShroomForager3000 sputters. He can't manage a word.

"Stand," Killian commands. "Fight me."

ShroomForager3000 shakes his head hard, waxed beard swaying as a whole. "No way, dude. I didn't know the shrooms were yours, man. If I had known, I wouldn't have made an offer, hand to God." He raises his hand. "I don't want any trouble."

Killian just stands there, growling.

My wolf whimpers, and in the silence, it resonates in my own throat.

ShroomForager3000 glances at me.

"You don't look at her." Killian steps to the side to block me from view, puffing his chest, broadening his stance.

"Whatever you say, man. You're the guy with the fangs."

Killian looks at me. "You smell—afraid? But also like you're gonna puke? Why?"

I'm not telling him about the invitation to get in the shroom van. I loathe the dude, but I don't want him dead. So I don't say anything.

"Una?" Killian's voice is louder.

I stare at the brown fungi slush with the footprint.

Killian huffs in exasperation.

My nose is burning now. I'm gonna cry. In front of humans.

From the corner of my eye, I see the woman from the souvenir stand slowly approach, her hands raised, the bangles on her wrist clinking. "Hey, Una. What's going on over here?"

A siren wails in the distance. The humans have called their enforcers.

I'm not going to be able to come back. Everything I've worked for—everything—is busted and broken. A tear dribbles down my cheek.

"Are you safe, honey? You want to come over to my booth with me?" She offers her hand.

My heart cracks. A human can't help me.

I scrub my face with my sleeve and sniff back the tears. "I'm leaving. Don't worry. He won't hurt the human. It's against pack law."

And Killian *is* pack law. He decides, and it is so. I'm not his mate. I belong to him. Whatever he says.

My nails dig into the flesh of my palms.

It's not fair. None of this is. And I'm not standing here a moment longer with humans staring at me. *Pitying* me.

I turn my back, and I walk across the lawn toward the truck, back ramrod straight, leg dragging in the grass. Killian can do what he wants. I don't care. My wolf growls her accord.

And yet, every step I take, his scent dogs my heels. I want to scrub it out of my nose.

I reach for the door handle, and his hand is there, blocking me. He's crowding me, his chest pressed to my back, his breath on my neck.

"Keys," he says.

They're in my backpack. I don't want to hand them over. I want him to die and fall in a deep hole and go flying out the other side of the world. I want someone to ruin everything he worked for. I want him to have to ask permission and sneak around and hustle for every penny because he doesn't have a choice.

There's a zip and the backpack straps tug my shoulders. He helped himself. Of course he did.

"Come on." He grabs my elbow and pulls me around the hood of the truck. His grip has no give. I have no hope of pulling myself loose, so I hobble beside him and let him open the door and lift me into the passenger seat.

I'm frozen, not like ice, but like stone. Because if I ease my grip on myself, even the smallest bit, I'll burst into flames and burn him down. I'll go for his jugular—and I *know* I'm no match for him, and I'll end up humiliated again. Knocked down. Again.

He ruined everything. With one shove. That's all. He didn't even notice the crushed mushrooms. For years, I've been coming to the market. I learned bees. Jams. Herbs. I learned how to deal with humans, how to deal with the chemical reek of their plastic and Styrofoam and synthetic perfume.

The girls and I have a *brand*. Cottage Industry. That's what we've decided to call ourselves. Kennedy's designing us a logo.

We had a purpose and reason to get excited about the day. And Killian Kelly comes in like a wrecking ball and takes it all away without blinking, and there is nothing I can do about it.

I'm a hostage. He rules everyone and everything I love.

My fists are shaking. He circles the hood and hops in. Somehow, he gets the truck to start on the first try. He puts his arm behind me while he reverses, and it's all I can do not to rip it off and beat him with it.

What am I going to tell the girls?

No farmer's market means no money. No phones. No hotspots. No games for Kennedy and Fallon. No music and fancy shoes for Mari. Nothing to make life bearable. Nothing to look forward to.

I hate his guts.

He's glowering, all put out because I broke his rules. That's the worst thing that can happen to him. Somebody gets a little out of line. Maybe earns a little something for themselves that he didn't provide. He's such a big man, he has to keep everyone else small.

"You got something to say, say it." His jaw flexes. He doesn't even look at me.

I lift my chin and turn to stare out the window. The passing fields are blurry. My eyes are still wet. At least the tears aren't falling.

I make my eyes real wide and blink. He's not going to see me cry.

"You're in big trouble," he says. "You know that."

There is nothing he can do to me worse than losing the market. Also, fuck him.

He sighs, blowing out his cheeks. "What the hell were you doing? I could have killed that man."

I didn't barge into a situation I had no idea about and assault a human. That was him. I'm not taking the blame for his unhinged behavior. I was trying to sell some mushrooms. And I'm not sorry. I'm mad. Furious.

His huge hands tighten on the steering wheel. "You just gonna sit there and ignore me?"

Why shouldn't I? He's ignored me his whole life. And I'm grateful for it. He should go back to ignoring me. It's the best I can hope for in this shitty, backwards pack.

"You're acting like a child," he says.

And it erupts, bursts out of me so hot it scorches my throat. "*You* followed *me*. You *ruined* my mushrooms. You ruined *everything*. You're a—you're an *asshole*."

There's a beat of stunned silence.

And then he laughs. From his belly. Like I'm genuinely funny. If I had a knife, I'd plunge it into his throat and listen to him gurgle, and then I'd laugh, too. I'd laugh and laugh.

I clutch my arms to my chest, as if that'll hold my wolf in. She's snapping, lunging, bloodthirsty and wild. She's going to bite his face off.

When he's done laughing at me, he wipes his eyes and asks, "What mushrooms?"

My wolf surges at the same time I drop the reins. Our switches flip simultaneously, and we go off. She barrels through my skin, embodying me, and I welcome her, let her wiry strength join the fury seething in my veins. My spine snaps. My limbs realign. The sizzle of ozone fills the cab.

I can taste his face already.

Killian startles, eyes widening in alarm. "What the fuck? No. Shift back. We're in a fucking vehicle."

But I'm the wolf, and she doesn't recognize his authority.

We're tangled in the seatbelt, but that's not stopping her. She swipes at him, snapping her jaws, contorting her neck to sink her teeth into his thick thigh, ripping through denim so she can gnaw flesh from his bones. Make him sorry. Make him hurt.

What mushrooms? He's gonna learn.

"Holy crap, Una." He jerks the wheel, skidding onto the shoulder, and he unbuckles himself, trying to dodge my muzzle and my claws. I'm tearing up the upholstery. My good back leg nails the window and it cracks like a spiderweb.

"Stop. You're gonna hurt yourself." It's an alpha command. I fight harder, and I manage to rip his shirt, scrape his shoulder and draw blood.

It's sweet. It's what we want. We lunge again.

He throws open his door, and as fur sprouts on his exposed skin, he uses his claw to cut me free of the seatbelt, wrestling my writhing body out of the cab and then pitching me through the air. I land wonky, my bad back leg immediately giving out.

My wolf shrieks with pain.

His wolf howls.

Shit.

I crawl away, front legs dragging the back, as quick as I can, so when he bounds out of the truck, six hundred pounds of fur and fangs, he doesn't land on top of me.

I look over my shoulder, panting, to see how close he is. How angry.

I swear, his wolf smiles. He raises his snout and howls again at the clear blue sky. It's a warning. A promise. He's not holding back anymore.

I run.

We're in a fallow field, and I bolt as fast as I can on three legs, dragging the fourth. There's a windbreak in the distance, and I head there on instinct, even though it's not thick enough to lose him, and I'm small and lame and my human mind knows that if he wants to, he can catch me in one modest leap.

My wolf and I aren't scared. We're furious. We sprint, tongue out, and the sensation is still so new, and yet so natural, that it almost distracts us from our fury. The dirt is dry and clumpy beneath our paws, and the rich scent of life returning to the earth wafts from the ground.

There are squirrel tracks. A groundhog hole. Crows pecking in the distance. The pain in my bad leg fades as my limbs warm. The world is alive. It's bright and satisfying and soothes my bitter disappointment, tempers my rage.

There's a hawk circling high above, and a stream babbles ahead, the wet mossy slickness of it fizzing in my snout like soda pop bubbles.

We've been the wolf, but we've never run free before. And it's *amazing*.

It's so distracting, so wondrous, that at first, I don't realize Killian's wolf isn't chasing us. He's trotting a few feet behind, keeping an even distance. My wolf snarls at him over her shoulder on principle. He slows his pace so he's a foot further back.

This is what his wolf wanted last night, both of us in fur.

What is he going to do?

Whatever he wants. He's a giant.

Shit.

I pick up speed and duck into the windbreak, but of course, he has no trouble keeping up. The trees are spaced evenly, elderberry and dogwood, then arborvitae and oak.

My wolf isn't mad anymore. She doesn't really give a crap about mushrooms or the market, and now that Killian's wolf is trailing her heels, as she thinks is right, she's fine. She slows down and turns, letting out a series of sharp, bossy yips.

Killian's wolf skitters to a halt, standing still and tall, and then he lowers his head, baring his neck the slightest bit, a sly, unrepentant look in his bright golden eyes.

She better not fall for it. He's a jerk, and he does what he wants.

She pads forward and nips his exposed neck. He rumbles. She licks the fur where she pricked him with her delicate fangs. He nuzzles her, licking, nipping in return. She squirms, tongue lolling. She likes it. She wants more.

She fell for it.

His rumble picks up volume.

She whines and bats him with a paw. He rolls onto his back, cuffing her gently. She slides her flank against his exposed belly, an echo of his purr in her throat.

Oh, dear Fate. They're making out.

She's going to present. I can feel the urge rising. She doesn't care about anything except rubbing her scent on him. Everything is forgiven. Already forgotten. What does anything matter but that he's here, where he's supposed to be, and the sun is shining, and all is right with the world?

He prods us with his snout until we're on our belly, and he's above us.

Heat flares in our core.

He straddles us. My wolf arches her back and huddles her ribs to the ground. She pushes up on her good hind leg.

Oh, no. This isn't good. I grab for our skin, but she's inhabiting it totally.

Killian's wolf runs his snout down our spine, and then he noses our backside.

He's sniffing us.

I'm going to burst from embarrassment like a squashed tomato. Splat. Like the mushrooms. I am never telling anyone about this. Ever.

He nips our back haunch. She wriggles her hips. Her want floods my mind. It's joyful. Fated.

I tug as hard as I can, but she's on another plane. Blissed out and quivering with excitement. She gets real low, raising her hindquarters, whimpering. Killian's wolf purrs his approval, and she eats it up.

He covers us. Something hard brushes my good leg. I'm flailing, banging, screaming inside, and she's oblivious. She wants it so bad; she has for so long. He's hers, and she wants what belongs to her. It's only right.

There is hot breath on the crook of our neck. I whine.

Sharp teeth scrape our fur, and then they sink into our hide, piercing fur and flesh, deep, ripping muscle, clamping down and holding on. She howls. It hurts like hell, but we love it. We go limp. Pliant.

He slowly extricates his fangs, licking the wound gently and methodically with his raspy tongue, soothing the hurt.

I stretch my neck to test the tendon. It works. Everything is still attached. There's no pain.

Something thumps in my chest.

And then there's hot skin on my back.

"Shift, baby." Killian's human voice is gravel.

My wolf whines. He's above us, pushed up on his arms, shielding us.

"Come on, baby. Shift back." He infuses the words with alpha command. My wolf doesn't have a choice. Our body complies, breaks and remolds itself, and it aches, but not nearly as bad as my wolf's disappointment. She wails inside me.

Killian strokes my bare back. I'm lying on my naked

stomach. My neck throbs, and my muscles are limp. Wrung out. He's on top of me, braced on his forearms, nuzzling and lapping at the bite wound. He bit us. Claimed us.

No, he didn't. His wolf did.

I try to buck him off, but I have no strength. All I manage to do is press my bare ass closer to his groin. He groans.

"Baby, hold still."

And the haze from the shift clears some more. I register his weight, his hard cock pressing against my butt cheek. His thick thigh is nestled between my thighs. His knee is firm against my pussy. And I'm wet.

I don't want to be. I'm not my wolf. My brain's all muddled, but I'm pretty sure I still hate him. I want to toss him off, but I'm scared to move. His body is too entwined with mine, and the touch isn't bad. It's—interesting.

His licks slow and then stop. "You're not bleeding anymore. It's okay."

It's not okay. Nothing is.

His lips brush the wound. It's pulsing now. Hot. It makes me squirmy inside. Unmoored. The place where the bond was feels different. More raw. And prickly.

He continues down my shoulder blade, his lips brushing my skin, his nose skimming lightly down my spine. He's breathing me in.

A tangled web tightens in my belly like a cord was pulled.

I stay very still and screw my eyes shut.

I want this to be over.

And I don't want him to stop.

My wolf is demanding, prowling, angry now. *Mate.*

He ruined my business. He crushed my dreams. I have to hate him.

"You can relax," he says. "You're safe. I'm not angry. I'm not gonna hurt you."

I snort in the dirt.

He chuckles. "There's my grumpy mate."

Mate? Oh, fuck him.

"I'm not your mate."

"I talked to the crone. She says you are."

"I reject you."

He chuckles. "You can't reject me. My bite mark is on your neck."

Every word he speaks, his lips tease my skin. No one has ever lingered on my back like this. Shivers race down my spine, and my breasts are responding, growing heavy, aching where they're smooshed against the hard ground.

"Let me up."

"You presented." He brushes my hair to the side and kisses the back of my neck, right under my hairline. My knees clench, gripping his thigh tighter. I'm getting his leg wet with my slick.

"That was my wolf."

"The wolf and the man are one."

I draw my stiff arms closer to my sides, all my muscles clenching. Unease chases away the shivers. "Tell yourself whatever lies you want."

He pauses. Then he rests his nose in the crook of my neck, the opposite side of the bite. "You're scared."

I wasn't. But now I am. A little. I hate it. I don't want to be afraid of him.

He pushes up, and in one fluid motion, he sits on his butt, knees bent, a few feet from me.

It takes me a lot longer to get myself upright. I have to roll to my side, and it's awkward, and I can't stand that he's watching. I draw my legs to my chest, even though the bad one aches, and I wrap my arms around my calves.

He doesn't even bother to close his legs. His erection lays flush with his belly. It's purplish-red and thick and there's a drop of moisture on the tip. His balls hang so low they rest in the dirt. He stares at me, brow furrowed.

How can he just ignore—that?

"I'm not gonna hurt you," he says.

I lower my gaze to the ground between us, scattered with leaves and twigs.

"You don't believe me?"

I shake my head once.

"When have I ever hurt you?" There's a note of impatience in his voice.

"You trashed me in front of the whole pack. And then you had Tye throw me out." My voice wobbles, and I hate it. "Y-You stepped on my mushrooms. You ruined my deal."

"I—" I can hear his bafflement. "You're gonna need to explain that last one to me."

I clench my teeth.

"Una." It isn't a reprimand. It's—tentative. A hesitant prompting.

"Didn't you see them? You made me drop my morels, and then you crushed them, and you scared off my buyer, and you made a scene, so I'm never going to be able to go back to the farmer's market, and everything I've worked for is gone." I snap. "Like that."

When he speaks, his voice is very deliberately calm. "You were selling mushrooms?"

"Yes."

"Like *magic* mushrooms?"

"No. Morels. They're a delicacy."

"Have I had them before?"

How the hell would I know? My gaze flies to his face, and there's a softening at the corner of his lips. He's not being serious. He's not taking this seriously at all.

It feels like a slap. I stare at a fallen log over to his left. I smash my lips so they don't quiver.

"Come on, now, Una. Don't be like that. Look at me again." His voice is coaxing.

"Why did you have to come to town? You don't care what I do. How does selling some mushrooms hurt you or the pack? Why can't you just leave well enough alone."

"How long have you been doing this?"

I shrug. I'm busted. What does it hurt to tell him? "Almost ten years."

"You've been sneaking off pack territory for a *decade*?"

"I've been driving a truck five miles to a farmer's market to sell *honey* and *jam*." I snort. "I'm a criminal mastermind."

"You could have asked for an escort."

"You would have said no."

"You don't know that."

"Yes, I do. You don't get it." My gaze flies to his face, and I know there's hurt in my eyes, and I wish there wasn't. I wish I was unrepentant and bold and I didn't give a shit, but I can't help it. I care. More than I should. "You can live a few yards away and never really notice I exist, but you're the alpha. We all know you backwards and forwards. We have to for our *survival*. And no, you wouldn't have given me an escort to go to the farmer's market. You wouldn't have let a fighter miss training. Never."

"Yeah? You can read my mind?"

"Yeah. I can." I hike my chin.

"What am I thinking now?"

His cock bobs, the thick base swelling and flushing a

darker red. My cheeks flame. He chuckles. I want to bash him over the head with a log.

"I'm thinking that I have a mate," he says softly. "And she's cold and angry and sitting in the dirt. I'm thinking I'm an asshole."

I sniff the tears back. It is chilly in the shade. It hadn't really registered until now, but there are goosebumps on my arms.

"I'm thinking about how I'm gonna convince her to get back in the truck. And into my cabin. And my bed."

More blood rushes to my head, and now I'm dizzy. My wolf has gotten quiet, and her ears are perked straight up.

"I'm not getting into your bed. If you talked to the crone, you know she severed the bond."

"No, she didn't. Not all the way. I can feel it."

He can? His blue eyes hold mine, steady and cool. All the confidence he carries zips along a new thread between us. It's heady. Like a shot of whiskey. Is it real?

"Here," he says, laying his palm on a sculpted pec. A vein runs diagonally, past his pale brown nipple. It pulses with his heartbeat.

"What does it feel like?" I ask quietly. I can't remember anything but pain.

His lips turn down and a crease appears on the bridge of his nose. "Like I have another heart, and I didn't know I had it, and now I do."

"I don't feel anything."

He offers me a sad smile. "Yet."

"Ever."

"Come back to camp with me, Una."

"I hate you."

"I'll buy you more mushrooms."

Tears fill my eyes again, and he stiffens, his blue eyes

darkening. "I don't want your mushrooms. I want mine back."

He hisses, and then he hops to his feet, holding out a hand. "You don't have a choice."

I feel small and stupid, naked and huddled on the ground. There's dirt on my butt. I've ruined another outfit and pair of shoes. And it's all his fault.

"You can't stay here." He says it very reasonably. There's even a hint of compassion in his voice. I want to choke him to death with his patronizing bull crap.

"You're not my mate," I say. He can hear it as many times as I've had to. He winces, and my mean streak is happy.

He waits, though, patient, hand extended.

I roll to my hip, draw up my bad knee, push up on my good leg. I don't touch him. When I'm standing, I glare over his shoulder and wait.

"Have you always been this salty, shy girl?" His lips are turned up at the corners.

"You know everything. You tell me."

"I like a mouth on a female."

My belly fizzles. I clench my abs, and it doesn't help.

He draws in a deep breath, and his lips curve so high, he almost flashes his teeth. "You don't have to fight this. It'll be good."

I start back toward the truck, one arm wrapped around my breasts, the other covering my butt the best I can. "No, it won't."

He follows, and after a few steps, he takes the lead. He keeps his eyes straight ahead, and I don't have to worry so much about trying to cover myself.

"I don't see how you can say that," he says. "I've had no complaints."

"No complaints in Quarry Pack. Nut up or shut up." I throw his tired lines back at him.

He snorts. "You know, I say that, but the elders sure as shit don't think that rule applies to them."

He slows his pace a little so he doesn't get too far ahead. It's hard to navigate the furrows in human form. I keep tripping on dirt clods.

"Yeah, the rules are a sliding scale."

"What do you mean?" He sounds genuinely curious.

"High rank can do whatever they like. Low rank has to toe the line." The rules you can get away with openly breaking kind of reflects your rank, in a way.

"That's bullshit."

"Sure."

"It's not that way."

"Okay."

"Don't fuckin' do that." He's irritated. Good. So am I. I just twisted my ankle again, and we're getting close to the road. I don't want to be here, buck naked when someone I know from town could drive past.

"Do what?" I pick up my pace.

"'Okay' me."

"Yes, Alpha."

He's gotten far enough ahead that he waits for me to catch up. His arms are folded, and he's scowling.

I hold my head high as I pass him. I refuse to cover my butt. He's seen it before. And he can kiss it.

"The rules are the rules." He falls in beside me.

I don't bother arguing.

"For everyone."

We get to the truck, and he darts around me to open the passenger door. I ignore his hand and lift myself up to the seat.

He hops into the driver's seat, wincing as his bare ass hits the sunbaked vinyl seats. "You can't justify breaking the rules by saying everybody does it. That's weak."

I reach for the seatbelt, and then I remember it got sliced. The whole interior is wrecked. There are rips in the upholstery, my window is cracked, and the glove box is open and won't stay shut. I try a few times before I give up. Liam is gonna be pissed.

"Giving me the silent treatment now?" Killian jerks the truck into gear. It starts again on his first try. It's got to be luck.

"What did you want me to say, Alpha? You know everything."

He huffs, exasperated. I stare at the spiderweb crack on the window. My eyes blur. For a little while there, I forgot, but now it hits me again. It's all over. I'm not going to be able to casually go into town again. Not after Killian assaulted a human.

The girls and I have worked so hard. We built the bee hives. The herb garden. It took so long for the cuttings to sprout. We killed a lot before they took root. And then after we mastered growing them, there were the plagues: slugs, spider mites, whiteflies.

One step forward, two steps back. Another honey vendor showed up one day, and they had dandelion honey and sourwood honey and all different types, not just clover. Then another showed up. Then every farmer had honey, and our profits hit the crapper.

So we went back to the drawing board. Diversified. Mari learned to craft. Kennedy tried to make a still, but after two of them blew up, Abertha put the kibosh on that. Then I found the morels.

And now they're smeared on a sidewalk, my buyer is a

grade A creep and traumatized to boot, and Killian Kelly wants to lecture me like I'm a child.

I don't have any energy left to be angry.

Killian rolls down his window. He keeps glaring at me and glancing away. He's pissed, and it eats at me. You just can't totally ignore biology. An angry alpha is an overriding danger. But the whole suckiness of the day muffles the instinct enough that I don't feel compelled to show my neck and try to smooth things over.

He can stew. Dirty looks can't hurt me. Much. My belly does ache.

We're silent for a mile or two, and then he turns on the air conditioner to full blast. "It reeks in here," he mutters.

I sniff quietly. I don't smell anything besides old truck, which, granted, does stink. But it's not *that* bad.

He drums the steering wheel. His nails really are a mess. As if he bites them. He turns on the radio, flips through the stations without stopping, and then turns it back off.

Finally, he huffs, frustrated, "Can you stop? I'm getting pissed."

"Stop what?" And he's already pissed. So am I.

"You smell sad. It's stinking up the cab. And it's fucking with my wolf."

Un-freakin'-believable.

"Yes, Alpha." I close my eyes and picture the mushrooms smeared on the sidewalk. I picture the girls' faces when I tell them. I don't even try to fight the tears. I set them free to flow, but of course, now they won't.

He growls. "You're doing it on purpose."

My lips twitch, and I fight it with all my might. "Yes, Alpha."

I have to suck in my cheeks to keep from smirking.

"I should pull over and make you walk," he grumbles.

"Fine by me, Alpha."

"No male wants a female with a smart mouth."

"Don't want you either." I stare straight ahead. "And you said you liked a female with a mouth on her. Earlier."

He barks a laugh. "So I did." His smile is slow to fade. "So I did."

We fall quiet. He doesn't speak again until we turn off Rural Route 10 onto pack territory. "I like how you smell now. It's better."

He glances over at me and catches my gaze. "Better than better. Good."

Then, he schools his expression, and he doesn't say anything else until we pull up in front of his cabin.

"We're home," he says when the engine sputters to a stop. "Now do you walk in, or do I carry you?"

9

KILLIAN

S he chooses to walk. She won't let me help her up the stairs. I'm gonna have to get the maintenance crew out here to make a ramp.

She's been hopping up and down stairs this whole time. In the rain. In the dark. One wrong step, and she could fall and break her neck. Her wolf's not saving her. Not with how tortuously slow she shifts. It's like watching a baby chick fight its way out of an egg every time.

And there are stairs to every single cabin in camp. And the lodge. The commissary. Shit. Maintenance crew is gonna have to build a lot of ramps. How did so much escape me all this time?

Truth be told, I've got the sinking feeling that I've missed a hell of a lot. Like how our lone females have been running a side hustle in the human town for an entire *decade*. And it did not escape my notice which truck she was drivin'. It's the one I learned on. There's a trick to getting the engine to turn over the first time.

Liam and I have a date. I'm gonna hang his pelt from the flagpole in front of the lodge.

Later.

Right now, my mate is finally in my den. The rightness settles in my bones, and the bond pulses. It's growing stronger by the hour. It's more than a vague sensation now. It has a physicality, a location. The end anchored in my chest throbs with life, and then it dwindles into a cold nothing except for the slightest thread drifting toward her in the dark space between us.

I scrub my pecs. I'll fix this. My mate is here. That's all that matters.

She's almost across the threshold when she stops mid-step and sniffs. Her face screws up like she's sucking lemons.

"What?" I don't smell anything unusual.

"Nothing."

She's trying to cover her tits and her pussy again. She can hide those dark curls, but she's got too much up top. Her breasts spill from her arm, sweet and ripe. My cock swells to full length yet again. I try to keep my eyes above her neck. I don't need to antagonize her any more than I already do with my mere existence.

This is so fucked up. Every other member of this pack will bend over backwards to appease me. Everyone is always angling for an invite to my cabin. Making up excuses to drop by. And here's my mate. She won't even come past the welcome mat.

It's meant to scrub the dirt from your soles. It's gotta be rough on her bare feet.

And she's shivering. She's cold.

My wolf whacks me upside the head. Shit. I'm terrible at this mate shit. "You want clothes?"

She nods.

I stride to the back bedroom and find myself some track pants. I grab her a hoodie. I don't want her covered—my wolf in particular disapproves—but her unhappiness is sour, and it abrades my nerves.

I'm all jangly and uptight. I want to fight something. And I don't like her being out of my sight. I trot back to the big room. She's right where I left her, same prune-ish scowl.

I hand her the sweatshirt, and she practically dives into it. My wolf grumbles, but the tightness in my chest lightens a touch.

I like her in my clothes. It feels right. I don't like her body hidden from me, but her ass needs to be covered. Males come by all the time with one problem or another. They don't need to see her until she has my scent coming out of her pores. My seed inside her. Dripping from those dark curls between her legs.

My wolf surges, a giant wave that almost knocks me unsteady. He wants to mount her now, and he's losing patience. He was pissed as hell back in the windbreak when I forced him out of our skin. He was pushing too hard, though. Her wolf was down to fuck, but she was nowhere near ready.

Later. Soon enough.

I jerk back on the reins.

I can't handle her rough. She's—I don't know the word. Delicate doesn't seem right. But instinct tells me I gotta be gentle. Tread carefully. Unfortunately, that's not my forte. Nor my wolf's.

My hoodie comes to mid-thigh on her. Doesn't really hide many of the scars, and they're bad. There's a Frankenstein quality to them, as if the wounds were stitched in haste. Who tended to her? Couldn't have been the crone. The crone would've never abided such shoddy work.

Out of nowhere, Una makes a soft little harrumph, her

wolf adding a little growl. She gives me her back, shoulders up to her ears.

"What are you doing?" I ask.

"Thought you'd like the rear view. So you can take it all in."

She's shaking. Vibrating with anger and hurt. The thread may be slight, but the feelings stream into my chest, toxic and awful.

I didn't mean to upset her. Again. I suck at this. I tilt my face to the ceiling, cracking my neck. What do I do?

Usually, when a female drops by, she takes the lead, asks for a cup of sugar or suggests a game of cards or something. Or just gets on her knees.

I've got my mate in my den, and she's glaring at the front door, tense as hell, and her wolf's growling low, riling mine.

"Come on. Sit down." I back away, give her space. Gesture to the sofa. She finally turns back to face the room.

I take a seat. Put myself below her level. Try to calm her wolf. Let her take the dominant position for a while. Females love that feeling of power.

Una shakes her head. "No, thanks."

I almost say, "I don't bite." I swear, it's my wolf who stops me.

"We can talk," I say instead.

"I can't sit on that thing."

A bright red flush has crept up her neck and stained her cheeks. She re-braided her hair in the truck, but a strand's come loose, and she's winding it tight around her finger.

"Why not?" I try to smile. Let her know I mean no harm. I'm not really a smiler, though. She kind of grimaces in response. "Can't we have a conversation?"

Her blush darkens. "I can't. It stinks."

It's leather. It smells good. I draw in a deep breath. All I smell is her—her warm deliciousness and her tart displeasure. I almost like her scent better with an edge.

"Like what?" I ask.

Her gaze skitters wildly around the room. I hope she notices how big it is. I renovated it myself when I became alpha. Doubled the square feet. Added the loft. It's got Energy Star appliances.

"You gonna keep me in suspense, shy girl?"

She glares mutinously at the rug halfway between us. "Females."

"Nah." I give the cushion a good sniff. I mean, yes, I've gotten my knob polished plenty on this sofa, but I have the cabin cleaned on the regular. It's immaculate. "I don't smell it."

She closes her eyes. She's got her hands jammed in the hoodie pockets. "Haisley. Rowan." She scrunches her nose. "Maeve. Shalene. Finley. Siobhan. Tierney. Iona."

I, uh. Damn, she's accurate. "It wasn't, uh—" I don't know how to tell her that it was only oral. Does that even matter?

She grimaces. "Their smell is everywhere."

"It bothers you?" I kind of perk up. She minds. She cares.

She crosses her arms. "It's not my business. You can do what you want."

"Then sit down next to me."

She's shaking her head vehemently before I get the words all the way out. "I can't."

"You can't stand in the doorway forever."

She casts me a dark look. "Yeah. You're right. I'm going out on the porch. If I stay in here, I'm gonna throw up." And she turns on her heel and does just that.

She turns her back on her alpha. Me.

No one does that. *No one.* Even my father never walked

away from me. He was too good a fighter to make that kind of mistake. And here's Una, giving me her back at every opportunity.

My lip quirks up. She knows I won't hurt her. Maybe not consciously, but something inside her—maybe her wolf—recognizes that in our pack of two, she outranks the hell out of me.

If she ever realizes the power that gives her, I'm fucked. But I can't bring myself to mind.

My mate could stalk off up the hill to her place, make this a real fight, but she doesn't. She pokes around the front porch a little and then manages to lower herself to the top stair, stretching the hoodie over her knees as far as it'll go to cover herself. That's right. That body is only for me.

I'm gonna have to rethink the full moon runs. She can shift now, and I don't think my wolf will be able to handle her naked around the other males for the swim afterwards. I'd be cool. I don't have human hang ups. But my wolf, though. He definitely wouldn't be okay with it.

I watch Una from the front window while I make a few calls. A few packmates pass on the path. She ignores them. They eye her, curious, but not curious enough to talk to a low-ranking lone female. She looks like she's in time out on the alpha's porch.

Rowan and Tierney strut past, and they bend their heads close, whisper and laugh, and glance in her direction. She doesn't blink. Her back is straight, and her chin is up.

She's a tough female. It's a quiet strength. Not showy in the slightest. She's the kind of fighter that makes a killing on the circuit. Everyone bets against the standoffish, silent guy, and then he's always the one to come back with the KO in the fifth round.

Shy does not exclude fierce.

After I check in with our patrols—no news from the northeast quadrant—I call Ivo and tell him to post a male at the access road exit onto the highway. No one in or out. Then, I call Cheryl to get a crew over to do a deep clean. Replace the rugs and the sofa. I don't take females to my bed, but I figure a new mattress and linens won't hurt either.

Then, I check in with Tye. He's pissed that I disappeared. I'm supposed to be meeting with the lieutenants to finalize the plans for Cadoc Collins' training. The alpha of Moon Lake Pack is sending his heir to us for a few months to "hone his skills." It's gonna take almost the whole time to unteach him what he's already learned. Moon Lake pack fights like bitches.

It'll give me and Una a place to go, though, while Cheryl works her magic. I'll take her by her old cabin first to get something to cover her legs, and then we'll go to Tye's.

I want to throw her on my bed, and fuck the salty out of her, but I'm gonna have to be patient. She'll come to me in her own time.

Meanwhile, I satisfy myself by watching her out of the front window as she touches my bite mark with her fingertips.

WALKING TO TYE'S, it's like I'm driving straight down a goddamn rumble strip. My chest is numb from my wolf's constant growl. He doesn't like males anywhere near Una, and of course, like always, a half dozen folks crawl out of the woodwork as I pass through the commons. Everyone wants something.

I cut each one off before they have the chance to get started, but they all come too close. And apparently, too close is within five feet of Una. Then ten and then twenty. By the time we get to the path to her cabin, word has spread, and packmates are gathering in clusters, gossiping. But at least they're keeping their damn distance.

I've never felt this before. The growling rubs my nerves raw. My fangs have descended with no sign of retracting. Makes my mouth fill with spit. And then I get hungry.

Shit.

Does Una need to eat?

It's not dinner time yet, but she must've missed lunch with her little escapade into town.

She can miss a meal. It's not gonna kill her.

But now my wolf's grumbling about that, and truth be told, I'm uneasy about it, too.

Una needs to be fed. She's sturdy, but how long would that padding last in a survival situation? Not even a couple weeks.

I don't know why it's of essential importance to my wolf and I that Una be able to live through a hard winter right now, in this very moment, but it's at the top of my brain. She also needs to learn to fight. And how to shoot since fighting is probably hopeless with a wolf as small as hers. And a healer needs to see that leg. I can't believe that's as good as it can get.

Everything's fucking rearranging itself in the natural order—with Una crowding out every other concern—and it's disorienting as hell.

I think about the pack, twenty-four seven. The circuit. Which males need their asses kicked? Who's ready to move up? I think about threats and security and the goddamn utility bill way more than I want to, that's for sure.

And then there's pack politics. What's Moon Lake doing? How close to anarchy is the Last Pack today? When is

Lochlan Byrne gonna make his move? Would it make life simpler in the long run to kick the shit out of Eamon and those other old timers who are filling his head with dreams of a position he cannot possibly take? How wrong is it to give an elder a beatdown if it keeps the peace?

Except for in the gym, that's what goes through my head, an incessant whirl, mostly questions I can't answer and shit I don't know.

Not now. That's background noise. Una is the center.

Her wonky shuffle. Her swinging braid. Her downcast brown eyes.

She slows as she climbs the path to her cabin. Why did I never consider that I put the female with the bad leg halfway up the steepest hill in camp?

She won't accept help. I go to grab her elbow, but she tucks it to her side.

And how did I ever think she was plain? Her face is calm, like the surface of the quarry lake on a windless day, but it speaks volumes. And it's beautiful. Her lips have the sweetest divot at the top, her nose tilts just at the end, giving her a snooty air that's cute as hell. And she has honest eyes.

Everyone in the world wants something from me. Approval. Status. Protection.

And they're trying to hide shit, too. Failings. Weakness. Ambition.

Not Una Hayes. She would like me to fuck myself, and she makes no effort to conceal the fact. It'd be adorable if I knew without a doubt that this shit ends with us mated like Fate intended.

I need to put babies in that curved belly.

I need her to smile at me.

I need not to have fucked up the best thing that's ever happened in my life before it even happened.

I had accepted that I would always be alone. But acceptance is a stage of grief, isn't it? It's not joy. It's not *right*. A part of me knew this was out here, waiting. That's why I never got too close to another female.

Every moment with Una, my end of the bond thickens and surges. It was a shadow, a cloud floating across the sun, but now it's a living thing, strong, seeking.

How did I not recognize it?

Thankfully, my brain gives it a rest when we get to Una's place. As soon as she mounts the stairs, the door flies open, and Mari's curly mop boings out. Annie and Kennedy crowd behind her. Their eyes pop simultaneously when they catch sight of me.

"Oh, shit," Kennedy whispers. They shuffle backwards, necks bent. The stench of fear reaches me at the same time Una's back straightens.

"They had nothing to do with it," she says to me over her shoulder.

"Don't lie to me, mate." I walk her through the doorway, the others backing up, clustered tight together, guilt written all over their faces.

Do they think I'd hurt them? They're females. Everything I've ever done is to keep them safe.

But as soon as she crosses the threshold, Una scurries away, putting space between us. Every foot of distance raises my hackles higher, but I let her go to her friends. I want to grab her, yank her back to my side, but following my gut has not been standing me in good stead these days.

The females' arms reach for her and pull her close as they shuffle and fuss until they surround her. They're protecting her from me. They're terrified, especially Annie, but all of their wolves are close to the surface, rumbling a warning.

My wolf is smart enough not to take it as a challenge. He stays silent. The last thing I need is him ripping out a snarl that makes three lone females piss themselves in their own living room.

"W-what is he going to do?" Mari says under her breath to Una, those ridiculously big blue eyes trained on me. I get why Darragh thinks she's too young to mate properly. She looks like a living doll. It's kind of unsettling.

Una draws herself to full height and looks at me, raising her eyebrows. Now that's an unmistakable challenge.

What *am* I gonna do?

Females aren't allowed off the territory without an escort. If the Last Pack knew our unmated females roamed unprotected, they'd snatch them, and I can't say I'd blame them. If we can't keep our females safe, we don't deserve them.

But I'm not gonna shoot myself in the foot, either, and sentence Una and her girls to any kind of punishment.

I can't sweep it under the rug. I heard the police sirens back in Chapel Bell. Once the local officials grab their balls, they'll head out here for "a talk." It won't come to anything. It never does. The locals don't want the hassle of feds swooping in. But I won't be able to keep humans in our territory under wraps. The elders will be knocking on my door the second they catch wind of the aftershave and tobacco.

Luckily, Una saves me for the moment.

"He's not going to do anything." She hikes her chin and glares at me for a full three seconds before she slides her gaze to the side. My quiet lion.

"Not true. I'm gonna have a guard posted across the path from here, and if he doesn't scent three females at all times, I'm gonna move all of y'all into the basement of the lodge."

Mari's hand flies to her mouth, a sob escaping. Annie whimpers. Now I feel like an asshole. What's wrong with the lodge basement? It's finished. There's a pool table down there.

Una winds her arm around Mari's waist, tucking the younger female under her arm, shuffling her body to block Annie. "No, he's not."

"Yes, I am." I'm not gonna let them take risks with their lives 'cause they cry when they get busted.

"No. He's *not*." Una glares daggers at me, and it hits me— what used to happen in the lodge basement when my dad was alpha. Fuck. That's not what I meant. I would never—

"Shit, I won't put you down there. I, uh—" I scrub my neck, at a loss. I look to Una, and she's got her stance wide and shoulders squared like she'll fight me. "You're just grounded to the cabin."

"But we have to leave for work." Kennedy's face is turning purple, her fists balled. If she throws a punch, I'm screwed. She's ballsy for a female. There'd be no subduing her without a bruise or two, and Una would never forgive me.

But I can't backpedal anymore and keep any authority. "No, you don't. You stay here."

"For how long?" Kennedy asks.

"Until Una convinces me you all are never going to do something so stupid and reckless again."

Una's teeth grind. A cord in her neck strains, disappearing into the collar of the hoodie. She's got it zipped all the way up, and I can't see my bite, but I know it's there. My dick twitches, and at the same time, my brain refocuses.

Una.

Mate.

Unhappy.

Fuck.

"Or a week or so. Maybe a couple days. I don't know."

I glare at Una.

"Get dressed." My voice is sharper than I intended. Annie chokes off a yelp.

The females bend their heads together and murmur, more sound than words, before Una finally obeys and heads off down the hall. I force myself to stay in the front room, and after her scent clears a little and I can think, I start to notice shit.

There are obvious empty shelves on a console along the far wall, and a strangely placed candle, right in the middle of a dust-free rectangle. And there's a cord hanging out of a drawer. My guess is they've got themselves a widescreen TV, and at least one gaming console. Maybe a DVD player.

TV is allowed, but shifter ears are hyper-sensitive. We keep the media at the lodge, and most families don't have it in their homes.

The females have gotten away with a lot up here on the outskirts.

And none of them have been winning any fights. The money came from somewhere. Yeah. Dealing with humans. For ten damn years.

Holy fuck. My heart thuds with delayed panic.

Shifters are exotic; shifter females even more so. Shit happens. A North Border male was killed, his female taken and never recovered. A Moon Lake scavenger was lured off by a sweet-talking human, hooked on their drugs and turned out. When the pack finally found her, she was broken. Her wolf gone.

And those are the human dangers. Last Pack is always looking to poach females. They'll steal young, too, to lure away their dams. They don't care if the females aren't their mates, or if they're someone else's. They're animals.

It could have happened to our females. On my watch. Because of my lack of attention.

This is on me. I deserve the punishment.

Maybe that's how I present it to the elders. Ultimately, the females' transgressions are my responsibility, so I should bear the consequences. Lochlan's gang will get off big time, watching me take a beating in the commons, but it'd be a pleasure to go a round with each of them straight afterwards and whup their upstart asses. So they remember just who and what they're dealing with.

I guess the girls are getting accustomed to me in their space because slowly, their huddle disperses. Kennedy goes to lean in the kitchen doorway. Annie and Mari perch nervously on the edge of the sofa.

The cabin is nice. There are paintings on the wall. I don't recognize the artist, but the scenes are from Quarry Pack territory. The old dens. The river. The foothills. There are pretty curtains and embroidered pillows. It smells amazing —like Una's warmth is baked into the hardwood floors.

I lower myself into a recliner. It creaks, but it's comfortable. I resist popping the footrest. The way Kennedy's glaring at me, I'm pretty sure I've made myself at home in her chair.

In fact, all the females are giving me the stink eye.

"There something you want to say to me?"

Three sets of eyes go bigger and wider.

"Now's the time. Later might be too late." I go ahead and pull the lever on the footrest. Now I'm fully reclined. There's no way I can look less intimidating.

Mari draws in a deep breath. Her eyes are shining. If she cries, I'm waiting out on the porch.

"Don't hurt Una," she says.

"I-it w-wasn't h-her f-f-fault." Annie fights to get the words out. Her long face is a pasty green. "S-she did it for u-us."

"What do you mean?" I ask Kennedy. She's the least traumatized by my presence. She keeps her mouth shut, though, her expression mulish as hell.

It's little Mari who answers. "She did it so that we would have nice things. Something to look forward to, you know? And we helped. So if you punish her, you have to punish us."

A tear dribbles down her cheek. If Darragh Ryan knew I was here, making his mate cry, he'd kill me. Good thing he's still hiding from her up in the hills.

All three females look so defensive. So small and fierce and scared.

This isn't what I want.

My father was the one who wanted females to reek of fear. He got off on it. I never developed a taste for it. Smelled like defeat to me. Like a weak pack and weak males who confuse respect with mere compliance.

Submission—now, that's another thing. I wouldn't mind filling my nose with that. Later. When I have Una alone back in our den.

Now, though, I have to soothe these three before Una comes back and hates me even more for terrorizing her friends. And to be honest, their distress isn't sitting well with me or my wolf either.

"Was she the only one who left the territory?" I ask.

Not one of them will meet my eye. I sigh. They're not making this easy.

"What is it you need that the pack doesn't provide?"

Anyone can take what he needs from the commissary.

It's been that way since I took over. Cheryl might give you the stink eye and come bitch to me about it when folks get greedy, but there are no limits. No old carved up bench out back where females pay for extras with what's between their legs.

All three are blushing like a bushel of tomatoes, staring holes in the floor.

"Like, is it female shit you need or something?"

Mari squirms and looks at Kennedy. Kennedy's face is contorted in horror.

The air's so thick, it's getting hard to breathe, but I'm afraid if I stand, the stench will get worse. Fate, I hate the stench of fear. And what have I done to them to earn it?

I'm lounging here, very reasonable, feet in the air like an idiot. Never laid a hand on one of them. Or raised my voice. Much.

I shimmy down, make myself as low and small as I possibly can. "Come on. Help me understand. I'm not the enemy."

Kennedy huffs and stomps over to a closet, throwing open the door. Annie gasps and tucks herself behind Mari.

"See?" Kennedy cocks her hip, points a toe to the side, and glares mutinously. On the shelves behind her, there are a shit ton of cords, not a single one properly coiled. She huffs again, grabs a box, and turns to face me, glowering and unrepentant.

It's a PlayStation.

I try really fuckin' hard not to crack a smile. I also know that later, at the gym, I'm gonna absolutely lose my shit. My mate risked her life so she could buy her roommate video games.

But I'm not stupid. I keep my eye on the prize.

"Where's the TV?" I ask.

"In the kitchen cupboard." Kennedy tosses her head to get her shaggy bangs out of her eye.

"What games do you have?"

"*God of War. Uncharted 4. Cage Fight Takedown. Horizon Zero Dawn.*" She narrows her eyes. "Want me to keep going?"

"I'll get the TV. Let's play *Cage Fight Takedown.*" It was worth it to see how big their eyeballs popped.

I like being unpredictable. Once in a blue moon.

I hop up, find the TV stowed under a nice stash of girly liquor, and I carry it back to the living room. Mari jumps to move the candle back to a shelf that has the rest of the set. Kennedy rigs the machine up in no time, and we actually get to play for ten minutes or so before Una rejoins us.

Kennedy shows no mercy. She also calls me a "bitch-ass fuckboy" under her breath. I ask Mari to crack a window, and by the time Una joins us, the place smells like nothing but wholesome competition.

Una wanders into the room tentatively, keeping her distance. She took a shower, rinsed our scent off. My wolf growls. I don't like it either. She's folded my hoodie, and it's draped over her forearm.

I dig her outfit. A long corduroy skirt with buttons down the front that I can picture myself slipping one by one through the slits. Or popping all at once with a quick rip.

She's got a scoop neck white T-shirt on, and my bite mark is visible, red and jagged against her smooth skin. She fingers it self-consciously, tucking her chin, but it's too vivid to hide. It draws the eye.

I shift in the chair, hard again. The wolf is riding me. What am I doing? I need to take her home.

Hell, why bother? I could take her twenty feet down the hall and fuck her until she can't deny who she belongs to.

My wolf is all over that idea, but he doesn't know females in human form.

Neither do I, but I'm not stupid.

Una's wary, taking it all in. She sees the TV and the controller in Kennedy's hand. I can tell the second when she decides not to say one word about it.

She's got discretion. That's a good quality to have. Half of being alpha is dialing shit down when everyone around you is cranking it up.

When she can't avoid it any longer, Una crosses over to me and holds out my hoodie.

"Here." She sets it on the armrest when I don't reach for it immediately.

I stand. Her eyes drop to where my cock has popped my zipper. I can hear the glug as she swallows. The flesh under my bite hollows and smooths. I want to lick her. It's so natural, I have to consciously draw my tongue behind my teeth.

"Arms up," I tell her, stepping close.

She shivers, and her sweet scent thickens. She raises her arms begrudgingly. I slip my hoodie back over her shoulders, and I zip her up, but not all the way. I leave my bite mark showing.

"Your girls have been sticking up for you," I say quietly. The others are already making themselves busy elsewhere. I guess now that they know I mean their leader no harm, they've decided to give us a little privacy.

"I told you. It was all me. Don't listen to them. They had nothing to do with it."

"Do you play, too?" I hold up a controller.

She glares at me. "All of it was my idea."

"Now, that I believe."

"What are you going to do to us?" There's a tremor in her voice, and it's like nails on a chalkboard.

"You said it. I'm not going to do anything. And you're gonna convince me I don't have to 'cause you've all learned your lesson, and I don't need to ground your girls."

"How?" Her eyes narrow. What will they look like when she comes on my cock? I bet they'll blow wide open.

"You're gonna be a good mate," I say, guiding her toward the door. My phone buzzed several times already. It's Tye. I should've been at his place a half hour ago.

"I'm not your mate."

"You can make my lunch all the same." I don't wait for her to navigate the stairs. I gently lift her down, ignoring her prune face. She's gonna need to get used to it. Until I get those ramps built, I'm her elevator. "Wash my laundry," I go on. "Clean my cabin."

She's scowling. "That's what you think a mate is for?"

I stop her at the crest of the hill leading down to the commons, and I tug her close. She stumbles, but I've got her. I hold her flush so she can feel how hard I am for her. How my body knows her. Needs her.

For a moment, I let myself have what I crave. Her in my arms. Her chest rising and falling against mine. She shivers like a fawn, and she smells like heaven.

"No." I bend to whisper in her ear. "What I really want to do is take you back to my den and eat your pussy until you come, squeezing my head with those sweet thighs. And then I want to hear you wail my name while I tap that delicious, plump ass."

Yeah. Her eyes blow wide when she's astonished.

I keep going. "You're gonna come on my cock so hard, you're gonna forget everything but that you belong to me, and I was put on this earth to pleasure you and put pups in that little round belly." I rest my palm over her womb. "That's what I think a mate is for."

I bump noses with her and then I step back. "But I didn't figure you'd be down for that quite yet."

Her arousal teases my nose. It's faint, but it's there. I step back.

She tries to shove her hands in her pockets, but her skirt doesn't have any. She forgets the hoodie does and starts wiping her palms on the corduroy.

I know that was a lot. Frankly, I didn't know I had it in me. Usually, with females, I don't have to lay it out like that. They come on to me.

I'm willing to drop it—for now—but she exhales a long sigh, and her eyebrows gather, creasing her forehead.

"That's the whole thing, though. That's why I sell things at the market. I don't want to be just a female. Or a mate, or whatever." She says it slowly, as if she's working it out in her head as she speaks. "I want my *own* thing."

There are responses on the tip of my tongue. Of course she feels this way. She thought she was mateless. She had to make peace with her lot. She doesn't need mushrooms anymore. She's my mate.

Or I could remind her that mated females are happy. Satisfied. Complete. And she'll be happy, too, once she settles in. I believe that's true. I'm gonna work to make it so.

I know my pack thinks I'm a tyrant. When it comes to training for the circuit, I am. But I'm also a smart alpha. Coming up, I had the perfect example of what a 'dumb as shit' alpha does. I molded myself as alpha by thinking about what Declan Kelly would do or say, and then I did the opposite.

A smart alpha doesn't take something shared from the

heart and say, "You don't feel what you feel. You don't think what you think."

That's how you teach folks to lie to your face.

So I say, "Okay."

And I offer Una my hand as we walk down the hill.

Of course, she doesn't take it, but I grab hers. And she leaves it be all the way to Tye's cabin.

I will take my victories where I find them.

And it is shaping up to be a glorious day. The sun is shining, the birds are singing, and in their wisdom, Fate has given me a headstrong mate.

It's gonna be a sweet victory when I change her mind.

10

UNA

I don't understand Killian Kelly.

I thought I did, but now I don't know. We're heading back to the commons. Killian's slowed his pace to match mine, and he has a hold of my hand and won't let go.

Everyone is staring. Some folks are running to get other people so they can stare, too.

I guess I've never seen Killian Kelly hold a female's hand before. Not many males in our pack do. You're more likely to see a male striding somewhere oblivious to his mate hustling to keep up.

Holding hands is a human thing.

Killian's palm is rough. Calloused. It completely envelops mine.

When we pass the commissary, there's a rock in our path, and his foot darts out, kicking it aside before I have the chance to step over it.

He seems really worried about me falling over. I know I took a header at dinner the other night, but I was tripped.

My balance is great. It's my leg that gives out on me sometimes.

It just doesn't compute. Killian Kelly is hard. He starts training the males at six years old, and they do it seven days a week. The number of times the girls and I have been woken up in the middle of the night by the chanting of males sentenced to run the patrol routes because they didn't work hard enough or lost to an unworthy opponent—or, on one memorable occasion because a male farted in the weight room and no one would confess.

One, two, three, four. Crack a window or a door. Five, six, seven, eight. Take a dump then lift the weights.

I had it stuck in my head for weeks afterwards. Kennedy still hums it under her breath when she's painting.

And Killian's not only hard on the males. Pretty much every female under fifty has had a thing for him, and he doesn't care. He'll duck off into the woods with them if the mood strikes him, and if they get clingy or aggressive, he'll tell them to their face in front of everyone that he's not interested.

He makes zero effort. He just sits in his metal folding chair up on the dais, and the females go to him. He's an arrogant son of a bitch, right? Incapable of feeling like a normal person?

But he played video games with Kennedy. It was definitely his idea. The girls were terrified. And even though she doesn't show it, Kennedy freaks out about getting busted more than any of us. She has so much more to lose.

Right now, she's balanced on a knife edge. No one can know her wolf is male, but if she suppresses him, she'll go moon mad or worse. With no money, where will she go on a full moon? The foothills? She'll be easy prey to outcasts without a pack to protect her. She needs the rental we found. It's close enough to town that the ferals steer clear, and far enough from pack territory that no one will catch her scent on the wind.

Of course, with Kennedy, her fear smells like anger. That's, like, the first thing you learn about her. When I walked into our cabin, I had to breathe through my mouth. But then, after I showered and stole as much time as I could to collect myself, the stench was gone.

Kennedy and Killian were playing *Cage Fight Takedown*. I watched for a few seconds before I showed myself. Kennedy was sitting with one knee bent, her foot tucked under her butt like she does when she's comfortable. Killian was leaning forward, fingers jamming the buttons, teeth clenched, intent on taking her down. He reminded me of Fallon, cussing under his breath when he missed a shot.

Maybe Killian is being nice as a tactic, luring me into a false sense of security so I let him do what he wants.

Which is?

My belly clenches, and my cheeks heat.

He wants to have sex. Mate me. Knot me. Make me have his babies.

That's what all males want, right? Pups are a status guarantee. A male isn't likely to hold his rank forever if he can't prove his virility. There will be whispers. And then challenges.

Killian has never seemed the slightest bit concerned about his status, but folks change when they get older. And he did mention young. He stroked my belly.

I warm and tingle between my legs. I lengthen my stride, try to minimize the friction. It doesn't help much. This better be normal dumb hormones and not heat. No bond, no heat, right? I feel like that was part of the deal, but my memory of the blackberry patch is hazy.

Regardless, I'm not having babies with Killian Kelly. I'm not going to let him touch me.

That's exactly what I'm thinking when he lifts me up the steps to Tye's cabin—without asking permission—and hustles me through the door.

Oh.

No.

That is *foul*.

The instant the air inside hits me, I sink into his side. It's instinct. I try to breathe through my mouth, but it doesn't help. I claw at my collar, strain my neck, but it's no use. The smell is on my tongue, in my nose, my throat, my lungs. I retch.

"What is it, shy girl?" Killian curves his shoulder and leans down, blocking me from the males sprawled around the living room. His fingertips hover above my cheek, uncertain.

Tears stream down my face. "The air. It's too—*thick*. I'm gonna be sick."

I gulp down my spit, like that might get the nastiness out of my mouth, but all it does is roil my belly. This is awful. I press my nose into Killian's shirt. It helps, but not enough. I'd run, but my legs are noodles, and I'm dizzy as hell.

"What's the problem?" A gruff voice calls from across the room. It's Dermot.

My stomach lurches. I'm going to throw up right here. I can't even bolt for the bathroom. I'm stuck. "Can't you smell it?"

"What do you mean?" He sniffs, darting out his tongue to taste the air. He smooths my shoulders, rubs my upper back.

It's strange, him touching me like this in front of others, but I'm too nauseous to care. I plaster myself closer and screw my eyes shut, praying he does something, because I don't know what's happening to me, and I'm gonna hurl.

"Shit." There's panic in his voice. "Tell me what to do."

I can't. I can only shove my face into the seam where his bicep presses against his chest. He cradles me close. His wolf rumbles against my cheek.

A chair scrapes. Footsteps stomp across the room and a window is thrown open. Oh, thank Fate. A gust of blessed fresh air wafts in.

I blink and peek up. Dermot, the chief elder, is grinning at me as he drags a wooden dining room chair over to the window.

"Sit her there," he tells Killian. "It'll wear off."

"What is it?" Killian asks as he leads me to the seat. My knees wobble.

I sink down, breathing deeper as the clean breeze sweeps the nastiness away. I lean on the window sill, stretching my head as far out as I can get it, like a dog in a car window.

"Too many unmated males, too far along in her heat. Their scent's gonna make her sick." Dermot slaps Killian's back. "It'll get better the more heats she has, the more you fuck her, get your scent in her. The first heats are the worst. It comes and goes. Drags on." He smirks. "Enjoy it, my friend."

Killian frowns. He's still close, hovering. He touches my forehead like a dam checking her pup for fever.

"Open the other windows," he says.

Folks scurry to follow his orders.

Dermot doesn't know what he's talking about. I'm not in heat. I remember heat; it's seared into my muscle memory. It's unadulterated misery. Mind controlling. Madness making. This is not that. This is a queasy stomach.

Thankfully, my insides are settling now, and I'm starting to feel ridiculous. I shrink in the hoodie, tug the zipper up as high as it'll go. I'm not used to being the center of attention, and whenever I have been, it's not been a good scene.

Killian's hand wanders down and unzips the hoodie to my cleavage. He slides his finger up, lightly, very casually arranging the neckline so my neck shows. So everyone can see his bite.

He wants them to see.

I shiver to my toes. And I leave the zipper where he puts it.

Someone clears his throat.

Now that there's ventilation in the room, I recognize the individual scents—in addition to Dermot, there's Ivo, Tye, Eamon, Alfie, and Finn. They're pack. Their scents are as familiar as my own. They've never bothered me before, but now, and especially mixed together, they smell disgusting. Worse than a latrine. All kinds of wrong.

"I guess you have a mate after all." Dermot smirks from his perch on a stool at the breakfast bar. "Let me be the first to congratulate you."

There's a general choir of echoed congratulations. All for Killian.

The males studiously avoid looking my way. I swear that Finn Murphy actually scoots his chair further away from me.

"Why don't you, uh, put her out on the porch?" Alfie says. "Since it's bothering her in here."

Put me on the porch? Like a dog?

Dermot cackles. "He can't do that. You can tell you young pups aren't mated. You don't know shit."

Killian's wandering fingers are now fiddling with the tip

of my braid. "He's right. I can't let you out of my sight," he says low. "I'll have someone get you a glass of water."

Ugh. Gross. "No. Thank you. I can't drink here."

His eyebrows spear together.

"I don't want to put anything in my mouth here."

I brace for a smart remark—not one of my roommates would be able to resist, and they're females—but he places my braid just so over my shoulder, and strokes down its length one last time. "I won't be long."

I shrug. I kind of feel like his luggage at this point, and I'm getting exhausted. The shower wasn't enough time. I want to be in my own space. I need to clear the cobwebs from my head. They're getting thicker the longer we're together.

Killian joins the males, and their conversation resumes. I ignore it for a while, but eventually, as a steady breeze filters out the pheromones, my brain starts lazily paying attention.

They're arguing about Cadoc Collins, the Moon Lake heir. He's coming to train with Quarry Pack. That's not unusual. The high-ranking wolves from North Border and Salt Mountain also send their oldest to train with us. We're the best fighters. It's unquestioned.

With Moon Lake, though, things are always complicated. They're our closest pack in terms of physical distance, but the peace between us has always been tentative. They have ambitions for the five packs, and we have no interest in a united shifter nation where we're all under Madog Collins.

Life sucks now—it would be worse if we *had* to work in the human world and hand most of our profits over to whoever ranks higher. We live pretty basic here compared to the mansions at Moon Lake, but we provide for all. No one's scraping by for food because they rank low.

I'm bored, so I stare out the window and eavesdrop. It's basically come down to Ivo versus Eamon.

"All I'm saying, Alpha, is look down the road ten years. Cadoc Collins is our biggest threat. Would you hand a loaded gun to your enemy?" Eamon asks. Finn and Alfie murmur that no, they wouldn't. "We can show him the basics. Tell him he's a natural. He'll go home singing our praises."

"He'll go home and tell his father that Quarry Pack is weak. He's young, not stupid. If we hold back, best case scenario, he thinks we've lost our edge." Ivo stands and paces. Killian sits in an armchair across the room, facing me. He looks at his lieutenants when they speak, and then his gaze skips back to me.

Every time, I flush hot. Not heat hot, but—toasty.

"So what? Let them come at us, and we'll show them different," Finn says.

Ivo sighs, exasperated. "Because we're not going to be fighting Moon Lake in a gulch somewhere under the light of a full moon. They'll buy the properties surrounding our territory. Squeeze us out. Lure our females to their big ass fuckin' lakefront houses. Something like that."

Eamon waves a hand. "If our females can be lured, good riddance."

"We have so many, then, that we can spare them?" Ivo turns to Killian. "It's your call. We can argue for another hour, but it comes down to whether it's more dangerous long term to train our enemy so that he respects our strength or convince him we're chickenshit. You know where I stand."

"What's Cadoc Collins really gonna do if we teach him to fight?" Ivo adds. "He can't take us all."

"But he can teach his males. And I'm not convinced that

this doesn't end with claws and fangs in a gulch somewhere in the pale moonlight." Tye leans back in his seat. He's on Eamon's side. I didn't see that coming.

All the males grow quiet and look to Killian.

He's wearing his usual expression, lips a severe line, dusty blue eyes unreadable. He's very still. He's gazing in my direction, but I don't get the sense that he's looking *at* me. He's lost in his head.

I've never seen him like this. Killian Kelly makes snap decisions, curt and unapologetic. He doesn't tolerate argument. He certainly doesn't sit and patiently listen to them.

Finally, he lets out a long sigh, and says, "Mutual assured destruction."

Ivo instantly relaxes.

Eamon scowls. "What does that mean?"

"Didn't you pay attention in history class?" Killian raises an eyebrow.

Eamon sniffs. In his day, males only went to school until they could read and do long division. He never shuts up about the cost of gas to bus the pups to Moon Lake past elementary school. Says it's a waste.

"If Cadoc Collins goes back and trains all his packmates to fight like Quarry Pack—and that's a big if, he'd have to pry them out of their human office buildings first—the worst-case scenario is that he has a pack full of males with a deep respect for what we can do. And no incentive to test us."

Eamon Byrne shakes his head. "It's a mistake."

Killian levels his gaze at the male with the bushy gray muttonchops. Eamon's lips peel back from his yellowed teeth, and for a second, it seems like he might let his fangs drop. But then, he tosses a stooped shoulder and bends his neck.

"Besides, where's the fun in going easy on the pup?" Killian flashes a smile that barely shows his teeth. The other males relax. There are a couple chuckles. The tension dissipates, and the air thins.

My wolf shakes herself and plops down to lie on her side. I hadn't been aware, but she'd been on alert. She didn't like the vibe—males arguing, her mate the focus of the attention. She was ready to leap into the middle of something.

That would've been a debacle.

Not our mate, I tell her.

She yawns and rests her muzzle on her paws.

"All right." Tye claps. "Next order of business."

Oh. That's not it?

It is not.

It keeps going. There's a piece of gym equipment that needs to be replaced, but Alfie and Tye disagree on the vendor. There's an issue with the budget. Dermot and Ivo cover the coffee table in spreadsheets, and at one point, Ivo gets so pissed over an equation, he sprouts fur.

But it's mostly boring as hell.

I stare out the window for a while, but there's not much to see. Folks are getting ready for dinner. Old Noreen has put the roasts in the oven. The scent is winding up from the lodge. I lick my lips. I'm hungry.

A silence falls. I look up, and everyone's staring at me. Especially Killian. His eyes burn gold, and he's focused on my mouth. Without thinking, I gnaw my bottom lip nervously. His wolf growls. It rattles the windows in their frames.

As one, the males' heads drop. Then Killian clears his throat and asks Ivo to repeat himself.

I finger my phone. I tucked it into the hoodie pocket on my way out of my cabin. I have unread messages.

Dermot launches into a story about a time when Killian's father bought a cut of some kind of fight club up in North Border. It's supposed to back up his point about the spreadsheet, but it meanders. And meanders.

Has ShroomForager3000 trashed me on the locavore message board already? It's not like it matters. I don't know these people in real life. And the shroom business is dead in the water.

Did he tell everyone I'm a shifter? I guess people on the internet must love drama as much as a shifter pack because even on the Loca-voracious server, I've read posts putting people and restaurants on blast. Am I on blast?

Is he telling everyone that my boyfriend assaulted him, and I'm a sad, pathetic female shifter who isn't even allowed to sell the mushrooms she collected herself?

Aren't I a sad female shifter who isn't allowed to sell her own mushrooms?

Stuck in the naughty chair. Ignored. Because I'm a dependent, not a person. No value except my biology. I don't like thinking this way, but this chair is uncomfortable, and I'm hangry, and there's something weird going on in my body.

So I focus on being mad at Killian.

Yeah, my braid is fascinating now. Only a couple of days ago, I was buck naked in front of him, and he had his buddy put me out back with the trash.

But at least I had unsquashed product then.

Ugh. My own mind is a quagmire of squashed shrooms. I need a distraction.

I slip my phone out and tap in my code. I have a lot of missed calls. Annie and Kennedy and Mari. There's a text from Abertha about how she moved the dry cat food to the shed. There's nothing on the server from ShroomForager3000. I breathe a little easier and relax in my chair.

And then I notice that the room has grown silent again.

Everyone is gaping. What? Did I lick my lips again?

They're focused on my hands. Oh. Duh. Because of the phone. No phones for females.

Oops.

I guess shit is going to hit the fan now. I knew what I was doing. It's just my brain is so fuzzy. I didn't really *realize* what I was doing.

Eamon, Alfie, and Finn look indignant as hell. Almost horrified. Tye and Ivo have wiped their expressions clean. Killian's eyes are drilling into me.

"Females can't have phones," Eamon says, glaring at Killian expectantly.

I slide the phone back into my pocket. If they come for it, I'm going to let my wolf out. She's back up on her feet, not too keen on three males looking at us like that with our mate right there. She hasn't decided yet *who* she's pissed at —Killian or the others—but she's pissed.

She's content to wait a beat, though, and so am I. I honestly don't know what to say. Your sexist, backwards rules are bullshit? It's true, but I don't think the argument would go very far.

And it's not really my style to say that kind of thing out loud.

At least, it didn't used to be.

Killian rises slowly from his armchair. His face is inscrutable, mouth a slash, eyes narrowed so the blue is shadowed.

He stalks across the room to stand right in front of me. He gazes down.

He's going to demand I hand over my phone.

My fists ball in my pockets.

I'm going to have to give it to him, and it's going to feel awful. Worse than being beat in front of the whole pack. At least then I had a shot.

But he's strong. I'm not. I'm female. And he's the alpha. And this is his pack. His rules. I'm outnumbered. Outranked.

I lower my head.

He gently pushes my chin back up with his forefinger. His lips soften, curving at the corners.

"Guess females can have phones now," he says, never breaking eye contact with me.

My wolf yips.

Eamon, Alfie, and Finn erupt.

"Unheard of."

"Bad idea."

"What the fuck?"

Killian's smile widens, revealing wickedly sharp, extended canines. His tongue touches the tip of one as he pivots to stare at the males.

They shut their mouths.

And then he grabs my sleeve and gently, but insistently, draws the hand holding my phone out of my pocket. He wraps his fingers around the sparkly purple case. And then he waits.

He wants me to let him take it.

To trust him.

I don't.

He could take it and stomp it and say, "Hah, hah. Joking."

But he won't. My wolf and I both know that.

And that's not trust, but it's something. Enough so that I

loosen my grip.

Satisfaction flares in his eyes. They crinkle deeper at the corners. My heart skips.

He holds the screen up to me. "Type in your code."

I do. 5338. Bees backwards.

He taps away, and then he hands it back. "Now you've got my number."

I don't know what to say. I sneak a quick peek at my contact list. It's pretty short. He put himself in as "Killian."

Warmth spreads through my chest, a rush, like when you're in the bath and you turn the faucet all the way to hot when the water cools down too much. I feel seventeen. And silly. And flustered.

"The other elders will not tolerate this," Eamon says.

Dermot snorts. "Which elders? You know they all got phones, right? Cheryl. Nuala. Tippety tap. All night long. Sneakin' off to the kitchen. Air bombing each other." He shakes his head. "That horse has done left the building. We closed the barn door long after he left."

"It's called air dropping," Finn says.

Dermot waves him off. "It's called progress. You can't stop it." Dermot rests his folded hands on his round belly.

"Well, the mated males are going to have something to say about it," Eamon insists. He's not letting it go. Under the sideburns, his cheeks are red. His knee jiggles.

"Good thing I'm prepared for that." Killian smiles, and it sends a shiver down my back. It's a warning. Eamon is treading on dangerous ground. He bends his neck ever so slightly, but his disgruntled expression doesn't change.

My wolf snaps at him. The males startle. Eamon flashes his fangs and then snaps his lips closed, turning away. Then Dermot, Tye, and Ivo crack up.

"Better watch it, Eamon." Tye slaps him on the back.

"The alpha's female doesn't like you challenging her mate."

I watch Eamon fake a smile. This isn't a joke to him.

I remember the run-in on the path and goosebumps break out on my forearms. I hug myself and ignore the males as they go back to the spreadsheets. At one point, Ivo calls Killian over to the coffee table to show him something. At the same time, Tye bounces into the kitchen, asking if anyone else wants a beer. Alfie sidles up to Killian to peer at the papers.

I don't realize for a moment that Eamon and Finn used the general movement to wander over to me. They aren't close. I have no doubt that would grab Killian's attention. But they're near enough for me to overhear their conversation. I can't avoid it.

"It'll be a shame," Eamon says, turning his head left then right, loose-jowled.

"What will?" Finn asks like he's delivering a line. Badly.

"Females who don't know their place. They'll bring a strong male down, every time."

Finn sighs. "No one to blame but themselves."

"And when the dust settles, no one to call." Eamon skewers me with his cold, rheumy eyes.

"You don't need a phone when you're on your knees in a Last Pack den," Finn says, smirking.

Eamon smacks him upside the head and turns away as Tye comes back, announcing, "Beers!"

My blood runs cold.

Killian glances over, brows knit, but I'm sitting here alone. He frowns. He must not have noticed Eamon and Finn lingering nearby. He raises an eyebrow. I don't know what to do, so I lower my gaze. When Ivo nudges his arm, Killian turns back at the documents.

A steadying thrum comes through the thread between

us, though. Like a soothing scritch behind the ears. It's stronger now. No more avoiding the fact that Abertha was wrong. It wasn't forever. The bond is growing back, which is terrifying, but not the problem in front of me right now.

Should I tell Killian what Eamon and Finn said? I'm not scared of them. In a room with other packmates.

But Killian's not always there. He wasn't on the path that day. And he can't be everywhere at once. Right now, Kennedy, Mari, and Annie are alone at the cabin. And who's been tasked to watch the place? Lochlan? A B-roster male who wouldn't bat an eye if Lochlan told him to scram?

Right now, it's just words. Males who got taken down a peg, blowing off steam, asserting dominance so they aren't the lowest on the ladder.

If I told Killian, though, it'd become a challenge. He has too much pride for it not to be. Killian would win against either Eamon or Finn, of course, and I'd have an even bigger target on my back with the Byrnes and their backers.

And Killian is all about me today, but when was the last time he declared I wasn't his mate? Last night?

The reality is—when whatever weirdness is happening now is over—I'm going to have to live in this pack. Better keep my head down and my mouth shut. It's served me fairly well in life so far.

Killian flashes me another glance. The corners of his eyes are creased. I give him a smile. He looks even more worried.

"That's enough," he says, cutting off Ivo mid-sentence. "My mate needs to rest before dinner."

And at exactly that second, when everyone's staring, I spontaneously yawn.

The males laugh.

Eamon's laugh in particular is loud with a cutting edge.

11

UNA

The further we get from Tye's cabin, the more my tension eases. Killian lifts me down the stairs again, and then his hands don't leave my body. He guides me by my elbow. The small of my back. My hip.

I'm not used to someone so close to my back, so focused on me. I trip a half dozen times, way more than usual.

And despite the crisp evening air, the wool in my brain is thicker than ever. The sun has sunk below the foothills. It's almost dinner time, and I'm hungry, but as Killian and I walk side by side, I'm also drawn deeper, moment by moment, into a kind of tempting flow. I'm entranced.

I want to follow where Killian goes. Not for any reason, but because that's the direction of the current.

I grasp the place our bond used to be, and it's not empty anymore. The thread is a string now. The place where it roots into me tingles. Throbs.

Can it grow all the way back?

Abertha said the loss was permanent. No bond, no hope of children. Does she *know* for sure, though? She said she can't predict what might happen. That the Fates have a tendency of getting their way in the end.

And I'm definitely not myself.

I'm always thinking. Planning. What needs doing? How can I get or make a new beekeeping veil? Who can I trade for sticker paper for my Cricut? Where can I find that vintage game called *Street Fighter Alpha* that Fallon's been bugging me about?

But my brain's quiet now. I'm going along, and there's an ease to it. A pleasure and a peacefulness.

I walk beside Killian, his steps slow and measured so I don't fall behind, his fingers wrapped around my arm, right above the crook of my elbow. As if I might bolt. Or I'm being arrested.

But the touch is gentle. And I know—somehow—it's because if I trip, it's the best way to keep me upright without hurting me.

"I'm usually pretty coordinated, you know," I tell him as we pass B-roster's row of cabins.

"You can show me when we get back to our den." He smirks, teasing.

I roll my eyes. He tightens his grip on my arm. It's not a warning, and it doesn't hurt. It's just firmer. More secure.

My heart beats faster.

I'm not going to sleep with him.

Just because he let me keep my phone, and he's been decent for a few hours, doesn't change the fact that he's ruined my life. Or what happened the night I first went into heat.

You don't get to take back something like that because it turns out you were wrong.

And I'm not a moonstruck kid. Not having a happily ever after isn't going to break me. I already know that. I've gotten this far on my own, and it's not half bad. As a matter of fact, I'm free, and free is pretty damn awesome.

I've got myself well in hand by the time we get back to Killian's cabin. He lifts me up the stairs and throws open the front door like "ta da."

At the same time, I see the brand-new sofa and rug, the smell slaps me in the face.

I force down the barf, eyes bugging.

Killian's face falls. "What? It's all new shit."

"It smells like Cheryl now," I manage between shallow breaths.

Killian drives his fingers through his hair, ruffling chestnut brown tufts. I've never seen him tousled before. His gaze darts back and forth, as if he's looking for someone to bark an order at. There's no one here but us.

"Just let me go home," I say. Gently.

He heaves a sigh. "Stay here," he orders. Then he disappears into the house. There's a scraping sound. He emerges a few seconds later with a wooden rocking chair. It's beautiful, polished and smooth in the way only really antique furniture gets.

"Sit," he says.

I'm tired of sitting, but he looks at his wits' end, and I'm almost beyond exhausted now. I'm hungry. Fuzziness is descending on my mind like drifts of fluffy snow.

I hear Killian call someone on his phone, and then it's quiet for a while. I rock with my good leg and drift off. The sun sinks, and the foothills turn black against the pinkish orange horizon. Venus appears, super bright and all alone.

Thumps and thuds from the cabin wake me occasionally, but then I drift back off. Strange, almost waking dreams pass vaguely through my consciousness. A serious boy with

Killian's pale blue eyes, braiding my hair. Holding a cup of tea to my lips.

After what feels like a long time, but by the glow of the horizon, can only have been a half hour or so, the hum of a vacuum rouses me. I go peek inside.

Killian's cleaning. He has the new rug rolled up, and he's thrown all the windows open. Down the hallway, I can see the new sofa, armchair, and ottoman stacked by the back door. A mattress is leaning against them.

He has his shirt off. His chest, the slabs of his pecs, and the ridges of his abs are slick with sweat. The V that arrows down into his shorts. He moves so efficiently. So competently. He's not pissed. I wouldn't blame him if he was. I hate cleaning. But he's just—intent. And thorough.

Cheryl's scent has faded, replaced by lemon and pine.

And then a box truck comes down the path and pulls around to the back of the house.

When they cut the engine, Killian hollers, "Don't touch a damn thing. I'll get it."

I watch through the window as Killian hauls everything out, all by himself, and carries in a new leather sofa—black this time—and a new mattress covered in plastic.

At some point, whoever's making the delivery must step too close to the cabin because Killian's wolf snarls, and a male stammers, "Sorry, Alpha."

It's well past dinner time now. I'm starving, but I want sleep more than food. This day has been eternal. If he lets me, I'll pass out on the new sofa.

Killian disappears into the bedroom, and then, after what feels like forever, he comes out to the porch. I'm back in the rocking chair, dozing. He clears his throat, and I blink open my eyes.

He stands in the doorway, arms crossed. His chest is still

bare. It's perfect. Sculpted and strong. I want to lay my cheek against it and feel it rise and fall with his breath. The impulse yanks at something inside me. Synchronizes.

I smile drowsily. I don't have it in me to be prickly at the moment. It's too late, and I'm too damn tired.

"Beautiful mate," he says, gruff and grumbly.

"Not your mate," I murmur.

And there's a tug inside me. Small and sharp. Enough to send my eyes flying wide open. It wasn't my wolf. It came from outside of us. It came from *him*.

Killian grins. "Come on, mate. I've prepared your den for you. It should smell like nothing but Pine Sol and sweat."

He turns, expecting me to follow.

I rock the chair to the count of ten—because there isn't an almost nonexistent tether pulling me after him. I could walk away. There's no bond. Nothing that counts. I'm not gonna end up desperate and hurting again.

Once I've calmed the panic, I go to him. The walk home, all the way up the hill, is too far. And I kind of want to see the alpha's bedroom.

HE LEADS me down the short hall to the room at the end. It definitely belongs to Killian. There are no paintings on the wall. There's a utility bench and a rack of weights. A metal folding chair with a towel hung over the back. A plain chest of drawers, nothing on top. And a huge bed with a simple wrought iron frame.

The bed is made, covered in a thick Amish quilt. The room smells entirely of him. He didn't lie. His sweaty musk masks any other lingering scent.

I'm so sleepy, I let him guide me to sit at the foot of the

bed. He unzips the hoodie and slides it from my shoulders, his expression solemn.

Lazy swoops swirl in my belly, but I'm so tired. While he's tossing the sweatshirt in a hamper, I unlace my boots, kick them off, and crawl under the covers. The pillows are firm and cool. The sheets are soft.

It'll do.

I yawn so wide my jaw pops.

"I'm sorry," I mumble. "Just let me sleep a little. Then I'll go."

He growls low in reply. It's almost a purr. He flips off the lights, and a few moments later, he slips under the covers beside me. A faraway part of me wonders why I'm not freaking out. I don't want to sleep with him.

Right?

But he doesn't touch me. He lies on his back, an arm propped under his head, bicep bulging, staring at the ceiling. I can't make out his face in the dark. His body is alert, but relaxed. He's not getting ready to pounce on me or anything.

We lie side by side in silence for a while. Gradually, the tension seeps from my muscles. Looks like he's going to stay over there. I nestle my nose into the pillow. Yum. Toffee. The case smells like detergent, but it can't hide the delicious scent coming from the feathers.

Killian's voice, when he speaks, almost startles me. "I should make you eat."

"No, please. Eat tomorrow." My heavy eyelids sink closed. I don't know how late it is. It could be ten. Midnight. Later.

Time is inconsequential. I hover on the edge of sleep, but I can't let go quite yet. I don't want to lose this feeling.

The room is velvet black. It's quiet except for the occasional clatter of the fridge's ice maker in the kitchen. My body feels like it does after a long swim. *Good* tired. There's not a single worry skulking in the back of my mind.

And it doesn't make sense. My pack's alpha is lying in the bed beside me, and he expects things, and I think he might have taken his clothes off.

But I feel—safe. Completely safe.

For the first time in so many years.

This is what it felt like when I lived with my mother and father. I could sleep. The grown ups were on guard. I could let go and drift away. They'd never let any harm come to me.

I don't feel unsafe in my own bed at the lone females' cabin. I know the pack will protect me. But I don't sleep too deeply, either. A lot can happen while help is running to the rescue. I rub the scars on my thigh where the skin almost couldn't knit back together. Abertha did her very best, but the wounds were bad, and she told me infection set in right away.

A memory bubbles up in my consciousness, another bed with a soft quilt, a woman slumped and snoring by a fire, but the past is murky and far away, and maybe it's better to turn my face further into the pillow and close my eyes.

"Goodnight, Una. It's all right. Whatever you're worried about, you can worry about it tomorrow." Killian's voice rumbles in the dark.

And I do what he says. I let go.

I wake up hours later in the pitch black, panting. I know immediately where I am. Killian's bed. He's beside me. Closer. Awake.

I'm wet. Aching. My bra is twisted under my shirt, and my skirt's hiked, making an uncomfortable lump under my butt. The waistline digs into the flesh above my hip bones.

And I'm wearing my socks. I hate wearing socks to bed. My feet are hot. Everything's hot.

And there's something lodged in my chest. Between my breasts. It's not my heart, but it pulses. Slow. Steady. Insistent.

I push my palm against it as if that could stop it, but even with my brain cranking too slowly into gear, I *know*. It's the bond. It's all the way back.

No.

It can't be.

I sit straight up. I'm sweating, and I can't see a damn thing. I yank my collar away from my neck as if that'll help me catch my breath, but the problem isn't in my throat or lungs, it's in my head.

There's going to be terrible pain. I won't be able to handle it. I'll break.

Killian eases up to sit against the headboard. I sense the movement more than I see it.

"It's okay," he says.

"No, it's not."

"You're safe."

I laugh, and it has a hysterical edge.

"I'm not going to hurt you."

"Again?" I try to straighten my bra, but it's hopeless. The wire's twisted to hell.

"Yes. Never again."

"I hate you." It comes out a sob. Nothing's right. My skin is raw, and it's too stuffy in here.

He takes a second to reply. "Yeah. I guess you would."

"I don't want a mate."

"I do."

I— My brain kind of stutters. Males always complain about being tied down and leg-shackled and ball-and-chained. I can't count the number of times I've heard the older males wistfully expound on how Killian Kelly is the luckiest shifter alive—alpha, unmated, and drowning in eager pussy.

The only reason most males seem to want mates at all is to have pups and nail down their rank.

"You want young." I'm not disappointed. I have no expectation that Killian is different from any other male.

"That's part of it. I won't lie." He rolls to his side, folding a pillow and sticking it behind his head. "But I always wanted my female. The one who was mine, you know? Only mine."

He reaches out and flicks the tip of my braid. It's an unraveling, tangled mess. I don't know how the band is still there.

"Is that why you hook up with all the—everybody?" Not me, though. He never looked at me twice.

He shrugs. "They offer. I don't always turn it down. Didn't see the harm."

He's only being honest. I have no right to feel hurt. His love life or whatever you want to call it is not my concern.

I distract myself by smoothing my skirt. I liked the texture when I put it on. Corduroy is cozy. But now, the fabric is annoying. Too swishy when it rubs.

"The other females upset you," he says.

"It's not my business."

"It is. I'm your mate."

"Well, it's not like I can do anything about it."

"That's over now. You know that, right? You're it."

"I'm not asking you to, um, stop, uh—" I don't know why my face is on fire. He can't see me. And we're both adults. We have pasts. It's normal.

"You don't have to ask. I'm telling you. You don't have to

worry. Even if you never let me in, Una, I'm not gonna disrespect you. I'm in."

My mouth opens, but I forget what I was going to say.

He props his head on his hand. "You don't understand. I've waited, Una."

Bull crap. I've seen Haisley hanging on him, her hand shuttling back and forth under the water in the lake after a midnight run. And I've seen Rowan saunter out of the sauna, wiping her mouth, and Killian coming out a minute later, tugging up his shorts. He hasn't waited for anything.

"You don't believe me," he says.

"I don't understand what you mean. Waited for what?"

He exhales. "I don't know if it even makes a difference. I mean, I didn't touch a female for a long time. I figured my mate would come, right? After I put the pack to rights. So, I won some fights. Trained up Ivo and Tye so we've got enough money coming in to keep the kitchen stocked for the winter. And I figured now I'll get my mate."

He laughs, short and bitter. "Didn't happen. Then when I shut down that shit that went on in the lodge basement. And behind the commissary. I figured now it'll happen for me."

He looks over. It's dark, but I can make out his eyes. They gleam pale blue. "After a while, I figured I had no mate. The crone said 'your path follows a different way.' What the hell does that mean?"

I don't know. Abertha speaks in riddles. And when she's drunk, puns.

"I told myself if it's just a mouth or a hand, it doesn't count, you know? I'm not shutting the door. If my mate shows up from North Border or something, it'll all be good."

Is he saying he's never had sex? Like the penis in vagina kind? It's a good thing it's pitch black. My jaw just dropped.

This cabin smelled like a lot of fluids, but I guess that makes sense if he's been doing everything but. Messier out than in.

Holy crap. He's twenty-nine. I've had more sex than him. Two hundred percent more. The alpha is a virgin. Kind of.

My mind is boggled.

How does the whole pack not know?

But then again, Haisley and Rowan and Tierney and all of them get a nice bump in rank when everyone thinks they're banging the alpha. That's a lot of incentive to let folks think what they will. I guess none of the females are gonna lose status by admitting they only got to third base. If that's the blowjob base. I don't know that much about human sports.

Is it a big secret among them or do they all think the others are doing the deed, and they're the only one on "B-roster" so to speak?

This is wild. And also, how do I feel about it?

I don't know.

What I *do* feel—I probably shouldn't.

I'm a little, tiny bit, and very regretfully, pleased as punch. Or is it my wolf?

He waited for us. A little. He's never been inside another female. Well, another female's pussy. That shouldn't matter. I'm not more or less valuable since I've experimented. And if he thought I was, I'd drop him like a hot potato. That's bullshit.

But even that doesn't make sense. I can't drop him like a hot potato. He's not mine to drop.

But he's not any other female's, either.

There's a tingling in the bond. He reaches over and takes my braid, fisting it tightly but careful not to tug my scalp.

"I didn't ruin it, Una, did I? Did I break it before it started?" His voice roughens like tumbled rocks. It washes over me. "It was never what I wanted. It was never like this. Now."

My dumb heart melts into a gooey mess at the same time another part of me gets *hot*. Ragingly pissed. I jerk my braid out of his grasp, I don't even care that it stings.

His sexual history is not the thing that ruined this. And it's such a Quarry Pack male thing to think. *Must be my dick.*

He hurt me. He rejected me in front of everyone. He let everyone laugh at me when I was naked and bleeding. He didn't have my back when I needed someone more than I ever have in my adult life. And he thinks that him getting his knob slobbered on could hurt worse than that?

And the horrible, embarrassing, lowering fact is that I do hurt, and I hate it, and it makes me want to barf. I wish I could blame it on my wolf, but she's conked out and nowhere near this conversation.

And also, holy crap, Killian Kelly just admitted to me that he's a virgin.

Killian reaches out and grabs my braid again. Then he waits in silence. I guess I'm supposed to say something.

I don't know what to say; I'm so freaking hot. This quilt has too much stuffing. I kick my feet free. Then I wriggle higher—Killian has to adjust quickly to not pull my hair— and I try to adjust my clothes again, get comfortable, but I can't find the right position.

I need to say something. Killian is tensing, and I'm not such a jerk that I won't acknowledge he just opened up to me big time. It's surreal. It's the middle of the night, I'm alone with the alpha in his bed, and he's so close I can feel the heat radiating off his skin.

He's not barking orders for once. He's talking like a normal person. Telling me he's never gone all the way.

If this were a female confiding in me, I'd respond in

kind. Maybe I'd tell him about how—so deep down I'm not sure I've ever formed the words in my head before—I thought I didn't have a mate because Fate didn't want to curse a pup with a mother too weak to defend it.

How I don't want us to be ruined, either, even though we are.

How I needed him, and he let me down, so none of this can matter, and I hate that, and I wish I was like other females who can forgive and forget and be happy.

A wave of sadness, almost grief, rolls over me, but immediately, it's washed away by a wave of heat and the prickling of my skin. My thinking muddles. Narrows.

I don't have time for regrets. There's something I have to do.

My wolf is in total agreement. She's wide awake now and yipping.

I do a crunch and reach beneath me to rearrange the pillows. Everything is in the wrong place.

And my nerves are raw. Jangling. What am I doing lying here? I gotta get started. I'm going to be too late.

Killian sits up. "Una?"

He flicks on the bedside lamp. Three clicks.

The light drives a jolt of pain into my brain. I snap my teeth.

"Okay. No worries." He dials it down to the dimmest setting.

That's better. Now I can see to work. A flat sheet covers Killian's lap, and that's okay, too, for now. I press my fingers to his bare chest. It's firm. I squeeze his biceps. They're hard, too. Good. Very good.

I lick the smooth muscle. He lets out a throaty moan. He tastes perfect. He'll do.

Now for the nest. I kind of tumble out of bed, trailing

sheets, and I glare at it. It's all wrong. And he'll need to get up.

"Go stand there." I snap and point to the corner by the door. He can stand guard. That's where he belongs for now.

Killian frowns, and he doesn't go. Goodness gracious. It's not hard. "Go over there so I can fix the bed."

"It needs fixing?"

Obviously. I grunt. I don't have time for this, and frankly, the bed needs more than fixing. I'd burn it and start fresh if I could, but that would take too long.

"Are you okay, shy girl?" he asks cautiously.

I will be once the bed isn't all jacked up. I grab the fitted sheet and tug it free. Finally, he gets a clue and hops up, stalking over to hover by the hamper. *Not* where I told him to go. My wolf and I growl under our breath. At least he's out of the way.

I strip the sheets down to the mattress pad. It smells new. It can stay.

The position of the bed is okay. I push the frame a few feet either way to make sure, but it's fine. Unless it'd be better a little to the right. No. It's good. Centered.

Killian inches forward and moves the mattress in the direction I'm pushing. And now it's too far to the left.

What is he doing? I don't need help. This is my job. My wolf snaps her teeth at him. He raises his hands and backs away.

"All right. I'll stay over here."

He watches intently as I remake the bed, occasionally stroking his hard cock. That's okay. As long as he stays out from under foot. He'd only mess it up.

I get everything put together, but it's not right, so I take it apart again. At some point, Killian goes to his closet and comes back with a stack of blankets. Some are good, but some reek, and they have to go. I throw them out into the hallway, but even with the door shut, they bother me, so I take them out back and shove them into a metal trashcan.

Killian tails me, which is fine, because his scent masks the blanket stink. And the trashcan stink. And I don't like the smells coming from the nearby cabins, either. Too plastic, chemical, processed.

I need nose plugs like swimmers have on TV.

And food.

I'm ravenous.

I head back inside, stopping in the kitchen.

"I'm hungry."

"Okay." Killian already has the refrigerator door open. "What do you want?"

"Meat."

"I don't have any defrosted."

Frozen meat? That's wrong, too. I huff and head back to the bedroom. I'll finish my nest and then go hunting. There's just enough time if I hurry. The hour's growing late. But that doesn't make sense.

None of this does.

But that doesn't matter. The nest is the only important thing, and I'm almost done. I pile a down comforter in the middle and cover it with the best smelling sheets and the contents of the hamper. There's not much. A few pairs of jeans and T-shirts, but it'll have to do.

I stalk around the bed, examine what I've made from all angles.

"I need more." I catch Killian out of the corner of my eye. He's leaning against the wall, still watching. He's wearing drawstring pants now. When did he put them on?

"I need those." I snap and point.

"My pants?"

I snap again. He needs to listen.

"Una, I'm not sure you know what you're doing," he says in a very rational tone which makes me want to rip off his face.

I bare my teeth. Arrogant male. I know what I'm doing. And it's so damn *hot* in here. "Put them on the pile."

I let my wolf growl at him a few times so he knows we're serious while I throw open a window. The moon is full and high. I draw the night breeze deep into my lungs. It's cool and sweet.

My body is a live wire.

The ache in my bad leg is so faint it hardly registers. There are so many more things to feel.

Like my breasts. They're full and tender. And this bra has got to go. I peel off my top, fling it into a corner, and send my bra sailing after.

Out of nowhere, Killian plunges between me and the window, snatching the curtains closed.

"No." I slap his hand and go for the fabric.

"You're not giving a show to whoever walks past," he growls.

"I want to see the moon."

He's tense, and he grabs my wrists so I can't pull the curtains back open, but his voice is conciliatory when he says, "I know, shy girl. Next time, I'll take you out to the old dens, okay?"

Yes. That's where I'm supposed to be. Deep in the woods behind the old quarry. Surrounded by bark and brush and moss. Stone and soil. Running water and the hum of winged insects and croak of bullfrogs in the rushes.

That's the right place.

"Take me there now." I turn, and he's right there. So close. So sweet smelling. I brush my nose across his pecs, listening to his heart pound. Ka-thunk. I remember the sound, but it's fainter in my memory. He was smaller then.

"I can't," he says. "It's not safe without scouting first. I'd need other males to guard us."

"Okay. Go get males."

He chuckles, gently prying my fingers off of the curtain. "I wouldn't be able to tolerate other males around you like this."

"Like how?"

"You're in heat."

"No, I'm not. Heat hurts."

His eyes crinkle in sadness. "No, baby. It doesn't."

But I'm nodding. "Yes, it does. It's the most awful pain you'll ever feel." My eyes brim with tears.

I tug my hand from his and wander back to my nest. I don't want to think about it. The memory of the blackberry patch pierces the muzzy languor in my brain, and I don't want to go back to reality. I want this. Even if it's foolish. Even if I shouldn't.

I expect Killian to follow like he has been, but he stays at the window, although his eyes track me.

"I'm so fucking sorry," he says.

No. I don't want to go down that path. It's ugly, and I'll remember, and I'll hurt. That's not what I want. I unbutton my skirt, letting it drop to the floor, twisting my waist. That feels better.

I peel off my panties, too, and stretch my arms way over my head, arching my back. Now I can breathe.

Killian's wolf rumbles. I smile. I like him. He has never betrayed me.

The air in the room is thickening, and it's a heady scent, like incense. Toffee and sweets fresh from the oven. My tummy growls.

"I need to feed you," Killian murmurs, his gaze riveted on my body, raking down the slopes of my breasts, feasting on the slight swell of my belly, the curve of my hips. He scans my legs, and the scars are nothing to him—instantly dismissed—as his eyes travel past my knees all the way to my bare toes.

His cock is hard, and his wolf is loud in his chest.

He wants me. Which is right. As it should be.

I absently rub the throbbing behind my breastbone and climb into my nest, graceful for once because the stiffness in my leg is gone. My body is strong. The heat in my veins is powering me, charging me like streaks of purple lightning in an electrical storm. I'm a force. I can sway nature; I know it in my bones.

I kneel in my soft pile and smile at my mate. "Come on, now."

His eyes flash gold. He crosses the room in a blur, jerking to a halt inches from the foot of the bed. Why did he stop?

I pat the soft pillow next to me.

His shoulders bunch, and he grimaces as if he's straining against himself.

And then it's like someone flickers the lights on and off in rapid succession. He's standing; he's in mid-motion. His fangs glint; he's gritting his blunt white teeth. And there's a terrible sound—a garbled howl that rattles the dresser and the mirror on the wall.

I scramble to the headboard, huddle as small as I can, my power gone. Something's wrong.

He flip-shifts so quickly I can't track it. He becomes a blur. His naked body is a mirage.

And then it's over. He's standing as a man, panting, hands clenched. Trembling.

I wait a few seconds, but when he stays in human form, I slowly crawl to him. My wolf wants a closer sniff. She needs to know her mate is still in there.

He groans, balling his fists so tightly, all the veins in his arms pop. "You're gonna make me suffer, aren't you, shy girl?"

Yes, it's good that he's suffering, even though I can't recall exactly why. My heartbeat's calming down. The receding fear allows more feelings to flow through me—excitement, satisfaction, an exquisite anticipation.

I've never felt this amazing. Neither has my wolf. She's inhabiting me, melded in my muscle and blood, pure spirit. We're together in this. We need the same thing.

I lay back, propping myself up on a stack of pillows, and let my knees fall apart.

"Come on, then," I tell Killian.

"You want this?" His voice is gravelly, torn from his throat.

"Yes. Come now." I spread my pussy lips so he can see how wet I am for him. So he will come to me. I have no patience left.

He sucks down a ragged breath. "You're not yourself."

My wolf growls. My skin is flushing hotter than I can bear, and the pleasant pulsing in my pussy has crossed the line into an ache. He can make me feel better. Why is he just standing there at the end of the bed, staring?

The human can't be trusted. My wolf howls, calls to her mate.

"You don't really want this," Killian says.

I snarl. He won't come. My wolf knows. The human is not right. But I'm stronger than him. I hold more inside me —the moon, the night, the future. It doesn't matter if he's broken. I'm stronger than him.

I roll to all fours and crawl to him, kneeling at the very edge of the bed. Except for the rapid rise and fall of his chest, he's frozen. His jaw is a knife. I stretch my spine so I can reach it with my mouth, and I taste the harsh line, test the solidity of the bone with my teeth. He remains completely still, but his breath is ragged.

He should be still. I'm dangerous. He has wronged me, and I haven't decided yet whether he is forgivable or not.

I lick down his slightly salty neck, explore the knot of his Adam's apple, the ridge of his collar bone. His skin quivers under my tongue. An agonized rumble emanates from deep in his chest.

He suffers. I can taste it on the tip of my tongue.

He should suffer. He should cry alone with thorns stuck in his hide.

I press my heavy breasts to his chest so his hurt is closer to my heart. The grinding of his teeth is sweet in my ear.

I drag my sensitive nipples down his front, and it feels so good. Why do I want to torment him? He has what I want, and he needs to give it to me.

I need to take it.

I explore with my fingertips, my nails. The ridges of his abs. The valley below his hip bones. The hard, flat place above his cock bobbing in the air. Every muscle on his body is taut and straining.

"If I do this when you're—when you're not in your right mind, you'll hate me." He's panting.

"I already hate you." I don't remember why, but it's true, although less true than it was even minutes ago. Past wrongs don't matter. He's big and fierce. He can protect our young. And he can make me feel good, and that's what I need.

Everything else is inconsequential.

I wrap my fingers around his throbbing cock. He hisses,

abs clenching. I stroke down, let the velvet heat warm my palms. There's a drop of seed at the tip. I catch it with the fleshy base of my thumb, and then I lift it to my mouth and lick my hand clean.

Killian breaks, tossing me onto my nest, lunging after.

I laugh in victory.

My nest is soft and welcoming. I wiggle to get comfortable. My mate kneels between my legs, hovering over me, fangs extended. His eyes blaze blue and gold.

Is he going to bite me again? I touch the still tender marks on my neck and smile. I want that. He growls, and it doesn't stop, it rolls on and on like a distant engine, stoking the gentle spasms beginning in my core.

"Who do you belong to?" he snarls.

My lips curl higher. "My mate."

He grumbles, seizing my wrists and pinning them beside my head. My breasts graze his chest again, my nipples impossibly hard now and unbearably sensitive. Every glancing touch feeds a current surging to my aching pussy, priming it, readying it for his knot. I lift my torso, hunting more sensation, and he snaps, pressing me down to the mattress with his weight.

"Who do you belong to?" he says again, this time so close to my ear his incisor nicks my earlobe.

"My mate," I moan.

He pushes up on his arms, scowling. He doesn't like my answer.

"Who?" It has the resonance of an alpha command, but I can't tell him. His wolf has no name. And the question doesn't quite make sense. There's something we've forgotten.

He's not doing this right. I struggle under his weight, nipping at the flesh of his bicep and wriggling my hips until he lets me up. He sits back on his heels. Frustration pours from him.

He runs a hand through his hair. "What do I do to make this right?"

My cheeks are damp. It's not sweat. It's tears. I'm frustrated, too. I *need*, and he's supposed to *do*.

"Why do you ask me?" I sob. "I don't *know*."

It's too much. The air's too heavy. All the good feelings are twisting and turning and slipping away, and my head is full of wool.

I flop back and close my eyes. Why is this so hard? It always has been, from the second I knew he was mine, but I know deep down it's not supposed to be.

I plunge my fingers between my legs, finding my slick passage and the swollen nub that begs for attention. It's not what I want, but what else can I do? There's no relief from this male, only the stoking of a fire that somehow makes me hungrier, thirstier, and angry. So *angry*.

"Okay. Okay." Killian's talking to himself. I have no patience left for him.

And then his rough fingers slip through my folds, sending a shock of pristine pleasure through my belly. My channel squeezes on air. My clit throbs.

His hand covers mine, and for a while, he leaves it there, adding to the pressure as I touch myself the right way, stirring the breaking storm closer and closer, coiling it into a whirl of delicious shivers and cascades of molten delight.

Nothing has ever felt this good.

He gazes into my eyes, nervous and full of wonder, and the severe slash of his lips are curved because he sees that I need *him*—that I want *him*.

We breathe each other's air, eyes locked, together. *Finally.*

I'm almost there when his hand bats mine away. Now, he's the one teasing, circling, easing the terrible gnawing need inside me. His other hand cups my breast reverently, and he raises the nipple into his searing wet mouth.

"You can let go, baby. You can trust me."

And he suckles my tit at the same moment he slips a thick finger inside me, all the way to the knuckle. I groan, bucking, chasing the feeling. He slides in and out, testing speed and angle, and it's not quite right. There's something missing.

I growl and cant my hips, and then it's perfect, his finger crooked just enough to graze the sensitive patch in my channel wall that makes me bear down and tumble quicker and quicker toward ecstasy.

"Is that the spot, then?" he mumbles, smirking.

I spread my arms wide, hiking my knees so he can nestle his hips between them. I'm ready.

He pushes up on one arm to gaze down into my face, never stopping the rhythm that's turning my thighs to jelly.

He kisses my nose. I wrinkle it.

I want his cock. I want him to fill me up.

He brushes his lips across my cheek.

"You are so beautiful like this," he whispers in my ear.

I'm on the edge. I'm going to tip over any second. I can't take the circles anymore. I grab his tormenting hand and hold it in place while I grind my clit against the heel of his palm, taking what I need, what I can't wait for a moment longer.

He kisses the corner of my mouth.

"You'll forgive me for this, won't you?" He licks at my lips, and I welcome him, let him taste. Plunge. Own. "You'll forgive me everything, won't you?" he mumbles against my mouth.

And I combust—explode in a million directions—a starburst so intense it's not only happening in my body and my mind but in the air, the forest and the foothills, in the very fabric of the world.

I'm whole. And it is *wondrous*.

And then, like sand, the feeling slips away, almost imperceptibly at first, like the very beginning of a sunrise. As it fades, I grow aware of the thick cord in my chest. Strong. Whole. It begins in me, but it doesn't end there. It spirals outward like a fresh shoot toward the male sitting beside me, somber faced, forearms resting on his bent knees.

Cold seeps through my veins. Fear cascades inside me.

I just made a bad, bad bet.

I scramble for a sheet to cover myself. My eyes are bugging so wide, they water.

"What did we do?" I ask very quietly. It's not the question shrieking in my mind, but it's all I can manage to say.

"You're going into heat. We took the edge off."

"It's gone now, though. Right?" My brain is dull, but I'm thinking somewhat clearer. I need to get out of here.

But this is my nest.

So Killian needs to get out of here. How do I kick the alpha out of his own bedroom?

But we're so far past that, aren't we? He's not the alpha to me anymore. He's—more.

My head pounds.

"I don't think so. But, uh, I think it kind of comes in waves at first. Before the, uh, main show." He shrugs a shoulder. "I don't know. What do the other females say?"

I don't know, either. It hurt to listen to the mated females talk about something I believed I'd never have. I've always ducked out of those conversations when they get going. All I know is heat is intense and messy, it can come on out of nowhere, and you've got to make sure you prepare enough packed lunches for the pups ahead of time or your mother-in-law will give you crap.

I shiver. It's going to get worse than this, isn't it? I'm going to lose my mind entirely like I did in the blackberry patch. My stomach aches. I can't go through that again.

Killian shifts closer, so his leg rests against my thigh. He's facing the headboard, and I'm facing the foot. The blankets have piled into peaks around us.

His fangs have retracted. For some reason, he seems much younger like this. More his actual age, a guy in his late twenties.

"You hate me now," he says. It's not a question, but then again, it kind of is.

There's a shivery sensation creeping through the bond connecting us. A seeking. A hesitant presence. A soft knock on the door.

If I lied, he'd know. But I don't want to lie. I'm not spiteful. And I'm not a stone. But I am terrified and on the verge of panic.

"You hurt me," I say.

His face goes hard, and even though it doesn't betray him the slightest bit, I feel my words land like a blow.

He's used to taking hit after hit and showing no pain, but I have a keyhole now.

I grasp for the bond and follow it, feeling my way in the dark, navigating by an intuitive sense I didn't know I had. It's a path, but it's faint. Like trampled underbrush in the woods that has already sprung back straight.

The feelings are quiet, muted, but clear.

He hurts.

He regrets.

He's immersed in the kind of prideful fear that drives

males to posture and fight. And underneath it all, if I don't let the ugliness distract me, there's something else, glittering, strange and marvelous.

Gratitude.

In this moment, as the room turns gray with the first rays of a new day, I can feel what he feels, and he hurts, and he is grateful for it.

Because I'm here. With him.

I search his face, but there's no evidence of any of it there. Only in the whispering between us.

Does he know I can see into him?

What do I do with something so huge and impossible?

I fold myself tight, squeezing my knees to my chest.

He sighs, fishing a quilt from under a tangle of thin sheets and placing it carefully over my shoulders.

"You need to rest. It's okay. You're safe. I swear."

"I'm not tired," I say, and then I yawn. I release the bond, and as his being ebbs in my consciousness, a wave of exhaustion takes its place.

I guess it wouldn't hurt to nap a little. I'm too worn out to make any decisions. My wolf has already conked out. Now that I notice, she's been down for a while.

Killian's wolf growls softly, echoing the sentiment. *I'm here. No harm can come to you. Sleep, mate.*

So I do. I pull the quilt tight around me, and burrow into my nest. I'll figure everything out tomorrow when I'm stronger.

For now, I fall into a deep, peaceful sleep.

I'm not alone.

Killian keeps watch at my back.

And I am safe.

He's here.

And amidst all the wrong, that is perfectly, undeniably right.

WHEN I WAKE UP, I'm alone, and there's meat cooking. My stomach growls almost louder than my wolf ever has.

Killian's not here, but the bedroom door is wide open, and I can hear him in the kitchen. There's a thump, and he curses under his breath.

I'm buck naked, and I've kicked off the covers.

I should grab a sheet and cover myself. I should be embarrassed. Last night, I let Killian touch me. Oh sweet Fate, I ground myself against his palm until I came. My cheeks burn, but I also stretch, arching my back and reaching toward the headboard until I can touch the metal bars with the tip of my fingers.

My body feels *good*. And I don't feel like I did after the human or the male from North Border. I'm not in the wrong place. I don't need to scrub myself clean, hide the scent.

I'm good. This is *my* nest.

I sit up, cross legged, and adjust some of the blankets that have been shoved to the foot of the bed.

Even my leg feels fine.

Of course, last night was a bad idea, and it's going to smack me in the face as soon as I wake up fully, but in this moment, it's so peaceful in this room. The light streaming in the crack between the curtains illuminates the tiniest motes dancing in the air, and the wood floor and polished dresser shine. The stucco ceiling is crisp white, and the clattering of pans makes it not the least bit lonely. This is a good place.

I close my eyes and breathe deep. This is what it would be like if I had a mate.

I reach out with my mind and find the cord running through the sun beam, out the door, and down the hall. The farther I get, the more it tends to slip from my fingers, and I have to stop, fumble a bit and focus with all my might before I'm sure of it again.

It's like following a very old scent in the woods in spring. There's so much else clamoring for attention, and the trail is so faint, you have to lean on intuition and luck to take the next step and the one after.

I hit a point where all I can do is hold the bond. I can't follow any further. I'm lost somewhere in the hallway to the living room.

And then there's a sharp tug.

Killian.

And another. It's strong. Sure.

Meat.

Tug.

I grin. Breakfast is ready.

It's like playing telephone with tin cans and string. My empty stomach clenches, and I throw my legs over the side of the bed. I have no idea where my clothes are in the pile, so I snag a big T-shirt and pull it on. It comes down to my knees.

I wish I had panties, but from the smell of my nest, the pair from yesterday is ruined.

The back of my neck heats. I've never done the walk of shame in a male's house before.

Tug. This one is impatient. A little worried.

I run my fingers through my hair. I'd feel better with it braided, but I have no idea where my hair band went.

I make my way toward the kitchen, noticing all the things I didn't last night. Killian doesn't have anything hanging on his walls.

Correction. In the main room, the interior wall is nothing but mounted weapons. Bows. Spears. Swords. It's not decorative; it's utilitarian. There's also fishing rods, nets, and traps hanging from hooks screwed into the drywall.

There aren't pillows on the sofa or a coffee table. Several metal folding chairs are stacked in a corner. I guess for company?

Next to the sofa, where you'd expect there to be an end table with a lamp, there's a rack of weights, bigger than the one in his bedroom.

Overall, it doesn't really feel like a den. It feels like storage.

The kitchen is towards the back of the cabin. I vaguely remember standing there last night, wishing a meal would fix itself. I don't think I've ever been this hungry.

I still don't rush through the door.

Tug.

I let the bond go as I step through the door. Killian's muscular back is towards me. He's messing with something on the counter.

He's wearing gray sweatpants low on his hips, and there's a faint shadow where the waistline doesn't quite come up past the cleft of his ass. It's a nicely sculpted ass. I drop my gaze. He's barefoot. So am I.

My toes curl. I'm a mess of nerves, all the muzzy tranquility I felt in my nest gone. I'm in the alpha's kitchen, and last night, I let him touch my pussy. I *demanded* that he touch my pussy.

I sink into a seat at the table. Yeah, here's the embarrassment. It's not enough to mess with my appetite, but my face is on fire. I fuss with my hair so it covers my cheeks, and I examine the salt and pepper shakers with a great deal of interest.

"Here." A plate heaped with food slides under my nose, followed by a fork and knife. Scrambled eggs. Steak. Ham. He drops a second plate in front of his chair.

He stalks to the refrigerator and returns with a plastic carton of Greek yogurt.

"Shit." He goes to a drawer and comes back with a spoon, and then he glares at the spread. "Oh, yeah. Orange juice."

He grabs two cups and the OJ, and then he stands over the table, hands on hips. Is he going to watch me eat?

I'm starving. If he doesn't sit in a second, I'm going to dig in, and it's gonna be really, really weird.

But then he sighs and takes the seat across from me. He grabs a fork and starts shoveling eggs into his mouth.

I go for the steak. It's perfect. Almost mooing. No seasoning to get in the way of the flavor. My wolf is stoked. She gives a few appreciative yips.

Killian's stern lips lift for a brief second, and his fork pauses midair.

"There's more once you finish that," he says.

There are at least three eggs, twelve ounces of steak, and another eight of ham on this plate.

"This is good."

He makes a noncommittal grunt and goes back to conveyor-belting food into his mouth. His hair's stuck up in the front. I've seen it this way before. When he fights, he gets sweaty and disheveled. This messy is different, though. It makes me squirm. Makes my chest feel wide open.

It's just the two of us in this peaceful, sun-filled cabin.

I've never been alone with a male in his home. That's how things are arranged now, right? So that the lone females aren't ever alone with males. I'm either at my place with the girls, or up at Abertha's cottage, or we're at the lodge helping Old Noreen, or we're at the laundry with Cheryl and whichever protected females pulled the short straw that week.

In Killian's father's time, it was different. Lone females had to attach themselves to someone to get fed, a sympathetic mated pair or a male. Or males.

That would've been worse. But that doesn't make how things are now *good*.

There's a knock on the front door. I startle. Killian doesn't even turn his head.

"Ignore it," he says.

I sniff. It's hard to make out with all the food, but it smells like Tye.

Killian growls. His dusky blue eyes flash gold. He points his fork at me. "Don't do that."

"Do what?"

"Sniff."

I snort a laugh. "I can't not smell."

He glares. A tic in his temple flutters. "Try." And then he sighs. "It's Tye. He'll come back later. After you're fed."

I set my utensils down. I'm full anyway.

He glowers. "You're not done."

"I'm full." After a second, I tack on, "Thank you."

"You didn't have dinner yesterday."

I lift a shoulder. My nerves are too jumpy to get any more down, but I say, "You don't double up when you miss a meal."

"I do." He grins, pops a bite of steak in his mouth, and chews. I can't stop watching his jawbone work. It's cut so sharp, it's like watching a machine.

My stuffed belly clenches. Not with hunger.

Oh, crap. It's not heat again? So soon?

I flutter the collar of the T-shirt. I'm not particularly hot, but it can't hurt to get some air moving.

Killian's eyes track my movement. "You in need again?"

I gulp and choke on nothing. "No."

I push the plate away and cross my arms tight to my chest. And I stop looking at his jaw. And his throat bobbing as he swallows.

I should get up and start the dishes. That would give my hands something to do.

But my body is heavy. I don't want to move further away. I *can't*.

What's going on with me?

Panic flares, skittering inside me, and then there's a pulse through the bond, cool and calm.

My gaze flies to Killian's. He's watching me. And he seems confused, too. Perturbed.

He narrows his focus, and the pulse between us becomes a flow from him to me. The cool and the calm develops dimension, a smoothness, almost a scent. Toffee.

I press my palm to my chest. The sensation runs over the back of my hand, like a shaded stream in summer, a lazy current that soothes feverish skin.

I can't suppress a small smile. This is magic.

Killian feels it, too. I know he does. He's blown away, too, he's just playing it cool by focusing on his food.

Killian's lips curve the slightest bit, and he scoops up his last forkful of eggs. "After this, we'll shower and head to the gym."

We will? I thought I'd go home. Shower. Process.

"Can't leave 'em unsupervised for too long. They start brawling."

"Don't they go to the gym to train to fight?"

"Yeah, but if you don't watch them, they break shit."

"I can go back to my cabin."

He shakes his head before I finish the offer. "You know you can't, Una."

"Why not?"

"Heat," he says as if it's obvious.

Which it is.

I'm not even sure why I'm arguing. Yeah, I want to hide in my room, and tell Kennedy everything, and brush my teeth, and *think*. But the reality is that I can't even bring myself to walk across the room to the sink. I can't fathom being so far from him that I can't hear him breathe.

My wolf is pretty much rolling her eyes at me, but some weird biological event doesn't magically change everything. Yesterday, I had my own business. My own place. My own *life*.

So now, just like that, I'm tethered to Killian? Like the dog Eamon Byrne's mate keeps in their backyard so that when he sneaks out at night, she knows? I don't want to be Max.

If I'm going to try and figure this thing out with Killian, *I* want to decide—not my primal instinct.

Eventually, after the silence has stretched well past awkward, Killian sighs and lets his fork clatter to his plate. "We should get going." He reaches for my dishes and stacks them. Finally, I can stand, too. He clears the table, and I wander to the doorway.

The way out is right there. Less than fifteen feet away. Nothing but open space between me and the front door. I step toward it. The bond stretches. I take another. The bond is taut now, but it doesn't hurt.

"Una?"

I don't turn around. I don't choose this. Killian rejected me. I can't just say, "Oh, well. Everyone makes mistakes.

Now we're a couple." He controls everything in this pack, but not me.

I stagger forward on my good leg, dragging the bad. There's a sharp, shooting pain. I can bear it. As I cross the living room, it eases. See? I'm stronger than whatever this is between us.

I go on, and with every step, it gets better. I reach for the knob and throw the door open. It's past noon, and it's a glorious day. The sky is robin's egg blue, not a cloud in sight. The green leaves at the very tops of the tallest trees flutter in the breeze, but otherwise, it's perfectly quiet, fresh, and still.

I step out onto the porch.

Killian steps beside me.

I blink up.

He quirks the corner of his lip, ruefully.

"Were you following me the entire time?"

He nods, and then he exhales. "So I guess we're going where *you* want today then?"

He props his hands on his hips and surveys the cabins clustered further down the path, resplendent with his usual arrogance and command.

No one's out and about. At this hour, everyone's working. He's not standing like this to impress or intimidate. This is how he stands. The lord surveying his kingdom.

And he just followed at my heels while I tried to walk out on him.

"Maybe we could go back in first, though?" he says. "Get me a shirt. Get you some pants?"

He shifts to his heels and scratches his back as if we're ordinary folks, settling on our plans for the day. And oh, it's tempting. To let go. Let this new future carry me away. My wolf is already onboard.

But I'm stuck. And it's not only because of the hours in

the briar patch or Killian's rejection in front of the pack. Somehow—and I don't understand, but it's true anyway— the wound is a lot older than a few days. The hurt goes back to long ago before I can remember. And that doesn't make sense, but it's *real*.

I can admit it now. Every time he touched Haisley or one of the other females, I knew it wasn't my business, and it was wrong to feel, because I'm not a jealous person—I don't begrudge people happiness—but it *hurt*. In the back of my mind, I thought it was because I wanted what I'd never have, and I was ashamed to feel that way. But still. It *burned*.

It's too confusing. Too much.

"I don't want to be your mate," I say.

"You're stubborn as shit, aren't you?"

"Not usually."

"I am."

I bend my neck to squint up. Killian's still surveying his kingdom. He doesn't look down to meet my gaze.

"Pisses folks off, but comes in handy," he says.

An elder appears at the bottom of the path. I shuffle a step behind Killian. I don't have pants on, and I'm standing on the alpha's porch past lunch time with my hair a knotty mess. Maybe we should get dressed. Figure things out from there.

I can't solve anything here and now.

"I don't have any clothes."

"You do." He turns and gestures me back into the cabin. "I sent someone to get some of your things from Mari this morning while you were sleeping." He nods to a bag I hadn't noticed by a rocking chair.

I grab it and hold it to my chest. "Thank you."

He shrugs.

"And thanks again for breakfast."

"You don't have to thank me." His voice is gruff like I've insulted him.

"I guess we can go to the gym." We might as well. It's better than being alone together in this cabin with the nest nearby and the air growing thicker.

Fate, I wish Abertha was here. It's not like she'd definitely give me answers about what's happening—she's way too invested in her mysterious crone persona to give it to me straight, but she might. And I wouldn't feel so powerless. I'd have a friend who can kick ass.

That's the worst of this.

Everything I had control over is gone, and I can't even hide in plain sight, head down, like I've done my whole life. Killian's eyes are on me now. Always.

And I don't know what to do with that. It's like a killer lion is really infatuated with you—but not quite in a "wants to eat you" way.

Do you feel scared? Or excited?

"You can have the first shower," Killian says, interrupting my train of thought. "There are clean towels hanging up." He jerks his chin down the hall.

I nod and head toward the bathroom, expecting the bond to tighten again, but it doesn't. It's slack, almost imperceptible, even when I'm all the way across the cabin, ready to shut the door. I glance over my shoulder and check. Killian's still standing where I left him, his face is somber, deep in thought.

Even all by himself in the middle of the open floor, he dominates the space. He would look like a king anywhere. A light thrumming begins near the root of the bond, and I quickly turn my back. But not before I see the black band around his wrist.

It's my missing hair tie.

12

KILLIAN

Una's surfing the internet, and I'm having a meltdown.

All afternoon, every hour or so, a memory comes back, and I'm lost in my head, twitchy and sweating. She's scrolling like I'm not over here losing my mind.

I lean against the ropes and let Tye coach. I've got Finn and Conor in the ring. Tye's missed at least three fouls by Finn so far—in fairness, I caught 'em too late to call—but that's all right. Jimmy is watching, and he's up next. Finn's gonna go down the second after the buzzer.

It's better that I hang back. Between the flashbacks and Una curled in her chair in the corner, I have zero focus, and my wolf's—unsteady.

Una's ignoring everything, reading on her phone. That raised a few eyebrows, but I'm mostly working B-roster today, and none of them would say shit even if they had a mouth full. Fallon tried to check his voicemail messages, though, when he was waiting his turn on deck. Now he's gonna need a new phone. And he's gonna have to ice his tailbone where I kicked it, too. Rules have changed for females, not for training.

It's like I've lost control of my brain. My memories are all mixed up. There are flashes of last night. The taste of Una's cream on my fingers. The way she splayed her legs, urging me on. Demanding. I'm rock-hard in grey sweatpants, watching dudes spar. It's awkward.

There's no sign of bossy Una from last night now. She's back to reserved, tryin' to keep a low profile, but that's impossible because—besides the whole phone thing—she's the only female present, and when a male so much as glances in her direction, my wolf howls a warning. Not a growl. He's not being subtle. He shakes the rafters, and everyone's nerves are raw from it, including mine.

But it's good practice for the males. There's lots of howling on fight night.

I'd be cool if the memories were just from last night, but there are other ones, too. Faded. Old. Unfamiliar.

Una as a young girl, her body bloody and limp in the bright green grass. My wolf straddling her, snapping his teeth at my father as he commands, "Shift, boy. There's nothing you can do for her now."

Her slight weight in my arms as I lift her into a truck bed and then haul my broken body in after, terrified they'll peel off and leave me behind. It was the red Ford I learned on. The one with the trick engine that Una's been taking to town.

In my memory, when the truck finally comes to a stop, the crone lowers the tailgate, her crow's feet and silver hair exactly as they are now, tears filling her flinty eyes as she says, "Oh, Killian. Your mate. What have they done? I told them about Thomas Fane. I *warned* them."

In the present moment, my body primes to fight, but

there are no enemies. Only the familiar sights and sounds of the gym.

I reach out for the bond. It's there. My end is strong and sure, as much a part of me as any other organ.

And it always has been, hasn't it? It's not new. I know that now.

How did I not feel it?

What else is there that I can't see?

Una's too far away. I give the bond a tug, try to get her to come to me like she did at breakfast. She unburies her nose from her phone, blinking like an owl. I give another tug.

She frowns. Then she gives her own end of the bond a grumpy yank.

It's weak but unmistakable. It lightens my heart and calms my nerves.

I jog over to where she's sitting and squat so we're eye level. She draws herself up, flattening herself against the back of the chair.

I grin. She hikes her chin.

"Well?" I grab the sides of the chair so she's bracketed by my arms. My wolf and I both like her there. He simmers down, eases back. He's been riding me just below the skin. A little space is a relief.

"Well, what?"

"You called me. I came."

"I didn't, and you know it. I was telling you to knock it off."

I cock my head. "How was I supposed to know that? Felt like a 'come here' tug to me."

"It's never gonna be a 'come here' tug."

"Never's a long time."

She's scowling, and I'm growing lighter by the second.

Her warm, homey scent is in my nose, and I am where I'm supposed to be.

"You can go back over there." She waves at the ring.

I lower to my knees, sit on my heels. "I like it better here."

She glances over my shoulder. "Your males are staring. You better get up before they all challenge you. You're kneeling in front of a female."

"I am, aren't I?" I move my hands to rest them on her thighs. She glares, but she doesn't push me away. She clutches her phone tight against her belly.

"You're losing status as we speak," she says.

I shrug.

Her beautiful brown eyes darken. "It's a joke to you, isn't it?"

She's actually getting mad. I can feel it spark through the bond. Is she worried that there's a scenario where I'd actually lose alpha rank? That I wouldn't be able to protect her? That's never gonna happen.

"I'm not going to lose rank."

"That's right. *You* won't. You can do whatever you want, right?" Her jaw is so tight, her chin dimples. "But if he loses, maybe he has to sit with the maintenance crew." She points over my shoulder at either Fallon or Conor. "Maybe he and his mate have to move to a lowland cabin. One that floods. Maybe his mate gets stuck on laundry detail with me and the other lone females, and then no one brings their pups over to play with hers anymore."

Her anger grows hotter as she speaks. It's surging, insistent.

"I'm not busting a fighter down to the maintenance crew because he loses one sparring match."

"No, not one. But how many? Does *he* know?"

I don't know. This is not how I planned this conversation to go.

Shit. I didn't really plan this at all, did I?

"When we win, we eat. There has to be an incentive for hard work. Right?" That's obvious, isn't it?

"When we win," she says, drawing out each word. "We *eat*. That's not incentive enough?"

I huff a sigh. I want to tap the mat. She only sees things from her perspective. Sure, the reality of rank is harsh. But without discipline, without direction and motivation, you get Declan Kelly's pack—the strong feed, and the weak are food.

She should inherently understand this.

And I can hear myself explaining it, and pissing her off even more. That's not what I want.

I want my mate to respect me.

To stop fighting me, for fuck's sake.

I guess there's one way to make that happen. I can concede. My lips curl. Oh, yeah. I don't think my scrappy mate would know what to do with a win.

I flash her a wide smile, and then I do something I've never done before.

I bare my throat.

Behind me, the grunts and idle conversation stop.

"What are you doing?" Una hisses under her breath.

I don't answer. She knows.

"Get up." She squirms in her chair, her gaze darting over my shoulder. "They're staring."

I bend my neck a little further. I've only ever done this before in nightmares when I was a pup. Feels strange.

It's not humiliating, though. In fact, my cock is hard as hell.

"Una," I say gently. I can hear her heartbeat. It's tripping double time.

Her fingers reach out, tentative, trembling. She touches the place where my neck and shoulder meet, the place where—on her—my bite mark brands her smooth skin. My balls swell.

"You're moon mad," she whispers.

I twist to drop a kiss on the palm of the hand that touches me. "Want to go back to your nest?" I raise an eyebrow and wink.

She huffs and snatches her hand back to her lap. I laugh and hop to my feet. "That's a 'later'?"

"That's a 'no.'"

"Okay. Later." I wink again just so the pink on her cheeks blossoms bigger. My mate is so beautiful. So delicate, and so ornery.

I stride off to the ring, chuckling.

"Who's first?" I'm gonna drop every male in this gym to the mat in five seconds flat, settle their wolves, and then we can proceed with training.

It's a bit embarrassing that I'm gonna do it with a huge hard on, but at least it'll make it clear who's highest ranked in this pack.

It's the female stewing in the corner who can't help but watch as I dispatch five males, including my beta, in quick succession in tented frickin' pants.

She owns me, and that makes her the most powerful wolf in the five packs.

And I don't think she has a clue.

~

I DO CONVINCE Una to go back to our cabin before dinner, but she won't get in her nest. She insists on sitting on the sofa like a guest.

It's probably for the best. Her heat seems to have eased for the time being, and I need to feed her as much as possible before it comes on in full. It's true that I don't know much about a female's heat, but I do know some. Males brag about how much weight their females lose in three or four days. Sometimes as much as ten or fifteen pounds.

Una's healthy. She's got decent padding on her thighs and belly, but because of her leg, she doesn't have the best musculature. Muscle burns first, and I don't want her to lose more than necessary.

She'd rip my head off if she knew what I was thinking. She's real private. When she pisses, she turns on the sink so I can't hear.

She wasn't shy last night. She flung her arms wide and arched her back like pleasure was her due as a goddess on earth.

I can't wait to watch her come on my cock. Fill her up until my seed drips from her sweet pink pussy. Put my pups in her belly.

Rut is riding me, but I'm not so weak a male that I'm gonna give into it. It helped beating the shit out of B-roster. It's also good that Una isn't like Haisley or Rowan—she doesn't look for male attention. If she did, this pack would be in a heap of trouble.

Fate picked well for me.

She's got that leg, though, and that small ass wolf. It's not a problem. She's never gonna not have protection from this moment on. Still.

"Stand up."

She blinks at me.

"Put the book down and stand up." We've got some time before dinner. I want to see how bad the leg really is.

"Why?"

"I want to check out your leg."

She flushes and tucks the book to her chest. "No."

"Come on." I'm not the kind that's good at convincing people. I'm more of a doer. I cross the room and grab the book, setting it open and upside down on the end table so she doesn't lose her place. I don't know where she found it. I honestly didn't know I had any. I asked why she wasn't on her phone, and she said she doesn't have unlimited data.

Who doesn't have unlimited data? I've gotta put that on the list of shit to fix. I don't need to be up in the middle of the night worrying that lone females are gonna run out of minutes while they're off sneaking into town.

I draw Una to the center of the room and kneel, keeping a hold of her hands so she can't scurry away. She's got on a long flowy skirt like the crone wears and no shoes. Her top is loose around the neck so I can see my bite. When she blushes, it darkens. I like that.

"What are you doing?" Una bats at my hands as I raise her skirt.

"Hold these." I shove it into her arms and sit back on my heels. She's got her weight on the good leg, propping herself up on the ball of the other foot. The scars are awful. I skim my fingers over them as gently as I can. She sucks in a breath. "Do they hurt?"

"The scars? No."

"But the leg hurts." You can tell. If she's been standing or walking awhile, her face gets real serious and strained.

"Sometimes."

"Does it hurt now?"

"A little."

"Where?"

She huffs a small sigh. "My hip. My thigh. My knee. My calf. The joints are the worst, but sometimes, the bones ache."

"Why didn't it heal?"

"Abertha thinks because it was so bad, and it got infected right away, it just couldn't. Not all the way."

I want to kill Thomas Fane all over again.

Or I want to have been the one to kill him. Beat him to death with his own thigh bone.

Una half-steps backward, and I realize my wolf is growling. I cup her knee, stroke up, and try to give her a reassuring smile. "Don't mind him."

"It's hard not to."

"He's harmless."

She barks a laugh. "Now that's a lie."

I grin. It is.

"Okay, let's get started." I rest my hand on the outside of her knee. "Lift your leg to the side. I'm gonna apply pressure. Press against my hand as hard as you can."

"Why?"

"I wanna see what this leg can do. Then we'll see what we can do to make it stronger."

She's quiet for a second. I look up. There's pain in her eyes, and it's echoed in our bond. I scrub my chest. Shit. I thought since she's so active, she could take a little more.

I'm about to sit her back down when she says, "It's not going to get any better." She lifts her wobbling chin. "You just have to accept it."

I move my hand, testing the muscle. It's definitely underdeveloped, but it's not nothing. "I disagree. You've got a lot to work with here."

"I'm never going to win an alpha challenge, if that's what you're thinking. Even if my leg got better, my wolf's small."

I let my hands slide down the back of her calves and circle her delicate ankles. She's so damn lovely, still and somber, her brown hair in that neat braid.

"You don't need to win an alpha challenge. An alpha belongs to you." She gazes down at me with wide, disbelieving eyes, and I'd do anything—kill anything—for her to know I speak the truth. But I can't, so I change the subject. "I just want you to get a little faster is all. I can't walk as slow as you for the rest of my life. It's either you get faster, or we get you one of those human Segways."

"That's a really dickish thing to say." She doesn't smell like hurt anymore, though. She considers me a second, and then she grabs my hand, presses it against her knee, and steadies herself on my shoulder as she lifts her leg. "But I wouldn't turn down a Segway."

She smiles, and it's small and cranky, but it's the prettiest thing I've ever seen.

I work her out for another hour, testing her strength and range of motion and flexibility, and she lets me, and I'm grateful for it, but what I really want is another one of her tight, grumpy smiles.

An hour or so before dinner, Una excuses herself to the bathroom, and when she comes back, she grabs my hoodie from the hook by the door. She wore it to the gym earlier. I don't think it's registering with her that she's kind of claimed it, and I'm not bringing it up.

"Where are you going?" I shove the balance disc we'd been working with back in the corner.

"The lodge. It's time to help Noreen get dinner together."

"You don't do that anymore."

She rolls her eyes and puts her hand on the doorknob.

My wolf growls.

"Stop that," she snaps.

My wolf immediately offers a conciliatory whine. Sweet Fate. This is going to get out of hand.

I seize the bond, holding her in place while I stalk across the room. I crowd her, and she shrinks against the door. She smells like petulance and arousal, and I can tell her leg aches from the exercises. She didn't eat much when I fed her earlier. I bet she's hangry, too.

"Do you want a protein bar?"

She ignores the question, rubbing her temple like I'm not making sense, and then she asks, "What's your problem with me serving tables?"

"It's beneath you."

"But not beneath Mari? Or Annie? Or Kennedy?" She places her palms on my chest, and she shoves once, but when she can't budge me, she doesn't try again. Or move her hands. She absently kneads my T-shirt between her fingers. I don't think she's even aware of it. She's intent on her argument. "Is it beneath Noreen to cook?"

"Someone has to cook."

"But no one has to serve."

I arch an eyebrow.

She arches one back. "Ever heard of a buffet?"

I grin. "You think we should serve ourselves?"

"Why not?"

Excellent point. I drop to my knees.

"What are you doing?" she squeaks.

She knows. I can scent it when her pussy floods with cream. I hoist her up, bunching her skirt to her waist, settling her legs over my shoulders, massaging and stretching those aching muscles. We can kill two birds with one stone.

She wriggles, but with the door at her back and my head delving between her thighs, she's pinned.

She's not trying very hard to get loose. She's panting, her fingers plunging into my hair. I lower my fangs and rip the crotch of her panties. She moans, pushing her slick folds into my face. I have to quickly close my lips so I don't nick her with my teeth.

"We shouldn't be doing this," she murmurs as she tugs my hair. I lick her sweet, puffy seam, savoring the explosion of flavor on my tongue. Her thighs squeeze, compressing my ears to my head. I have to readjust so I can hold her open and keep her still. I need to hear her moans.

Before we leave this cabin, go around other males, she needs to know who she belongs to.

She's gonna say my name. She's gonna scream it, and I'm gonna walk into the lodge with her cream drying on my face.

"I'm mad at you," she gasps. "We're having an argument."

I spear her wet hole with my tongue, teasing her clit with the finger parting her folds. "That," she gasps. "There. Right there."

I go harder, flatten my tongue and lick in between flicks. She bucks as hard as she can, but she's stuck between the door and my mouth. I suck her clit while I grip her juicy ass, spreading those cheeks, opening everything to me.

Her hips rock harder. I'm straining my jeans, and I want more than anything to slide down my zipper and jam her onto my aching cock, spurt my seed into her until her belly bulges.

It's beyond desire. It's necessity. My eyes burn with the effort of holding back, denying myself the soft, sweet, slippery warmth I crave more than air or meat or a wild run under a full moon.

But I can't. I can't.

If I take her now, I'll lose her a minute later. My bond to her is steel. Hers is a tender shoot.

She has to come to me.

I know it in my bones.

So I devour her pussy like a starving man, explore every crease, every crevice. Her thighs quiver, and she pulls my hair as she rides my face.

"This doesn't solve anything," she moans.

Like hell. It fixes everything. I adjust my grip, seek out her puckered back hole with my middle finger. I've never tried this before. I move slow, giving her plenty of time to clench and shift away. She doesn't. She sucks in a breath, and I press against the tight ring. She squirms, mewling, panting.

I don't want to hurt her.

I swirl my tongue around her stiff nub, massaging her wet hole with my thumb, smearing her cream over her plump lips.

She's about to explode. Her abs are tight, and she's kicking my back with her heels like she's spurring me on.

I love her abandon.

She's not shy now. Not at all. She's wild for me. Only me. And her heat isn't riding her. This is all my doing, no assist from nature.

I press further into the tight muscle grasping my finger, try to be gentle and try not to come in my pants as I feel her inside, tight and hot and clenching. She shrieks, "Oh, oh, oh!"

And then she's jerking, spasming, and she hollers, "Killian!"

I spurt in my jeans, a massive gush, hot and sticky.

She blinks. Her eyes clear. And narrow.

Shit.

I sink immediately to my ass, wrap my arms around her and tuck her to my chest. Now is when she freaks out. Withdraws back behind that serious, reserved, humble expression that I realize more and more is a straight out lie.

Not now. I nibble my bite mark, and she shivers. "You belong to me, shy girl. You know that right?"

She tenses and struggles to put space between us. I'll let her. In a second. Once my wolf collects himself.

"I'm my own person," she mumbles into my T-shirt.

"I belong to you. Wolf and man." She's got to know, but it can't hurt to say out loud. Females need words. Even I know that.

"So you say now." She heaves at my pecs, and I let her get away. She lands on her butt, legs sprawled. "Maybe I don't want you."

I arch an eyebrow. Her thighs are chafed red from my five o'clock shadow. She huffs at me and tugs her skirt back down.

I don't let myself crack a smile. Instead, I give her a wink, hop to my feet, and go wash my hands in the kitchen.

I stalk the bond and listen as she scurries to the bathroom and then rummages around in the bedroom. She's probably looking for fresh panties. I ruined the pair she'd been wearing for good with my fangs, but she'd made a nice mess of them before we got to that part. They're lying in the foyer. I scoop them up before she comes back and gets all embarrassed. I like her better feisty than bashful.

Although making her blush does make me hard.

I head after her, stopping in the bathroom to clean up. Never came in my jeans before. Can't say I'm a fan. It's undignified as hell, and it makes the denim chafe.

I'm more than a little grateful that Una's too busy fussing at me to notice the scent of seed.

I grab fresh pants from the dryer, and then I go see what's keeping her. She's still in the bedroom. There's an odd sensation coming through the bond. A wistfulness. Longing. But not for me.

Her feelings for me are bold. This is a mild aching.

I pause at the door, careful to step heavy enough that she hears me coming. I don't know if she can track me through the bond like I can. Or if she bothers.

She's standing beside the unmade bed, fingering the Amish quilt. It's a knot pattern, soft and faded from washing. It was my grandmother's. My mother's mother. I've got no living kin on my father's side. Declan Kelly wandered into Quarry Pack territory one inauspicious day, killed the old alpha, and ruled with an iron fist until he keeled over with a chicken bone stuck in his throat, and not a soul moved to help him.

Not my mother. Not me.

Everything I've done since has been to ensure that history won't repeat itself. Every male in Quarry Pack can fight. And every outcast from the five packs knows better than to try to find their fortune here.

It's not been an easy path, but our females and pups are safe.

I lean against the doorframe. Una must know I'm here, but she doesn't turn her head. She's braided her hair again and changed into a flowing lavender dress. She's beautiful and calm, but her eyes are distant. Sad.

Are our females and pups happy?

I've never wondered before. I assumed. No one's getting beat. No one's hungry.

If they weren't content, would anyone tell me? Would anyone think I'd even care to know?

"What are you doing?" I ask Una because it's easier than following that train of thought.

"This is a lovely quilt."

"It was my grandmother's."

"She made it?"

"No. She wasn't the type to sew. She must have bought it."

"It's human-made?"

"Yeah."

"Your grandmother traded with humans?"

"She must have."

Una raises her eyes to me. Her usual defensiveness is gone. There's a vulnerability there now which scares me shitless. This female can be hurt. I can hurt her again. I can lose everything in this second, and I am not equal to the moment. At the end of the day, I'm nothing but a brawler. All fists and fangs.

None of those will do me any good here, with my mate considering her nest, her raw heart on her sleeve.

"Why can't we, then?" She adjusts the quilt so it covers the pillows she slept on last night.

My wolf's 'no' is loud enough it sounds in my throat. She startles, her fingers flying to her side. I stay still. Shove my hands in my pockets.

The picture of that smarmy human with the beard leering at her flashes in my brain. And her all alone, clutching that jar of mushrooms to her chest like it was treasure. It wouldn't take a rogue wolf to carry her off. Any idiot human could manage it if he promised her whatever it is she's looking for.

What is it that she wants?

"I'll pay for your phone. If you want to buy the others games or whatever, you can."

She straightens her spine. "I don't want your money."

"Then why do you want to sell shit to the humans?"

"I want *my* money."

"We're pack. There's no *mine*. No *yours*." Every pup understands this. Wolves aren't human. We rise and fall together.

She snorts. "That's bullshit and you know it."

"Everything I have is yours." It's the truest thing I know.

She takes a deep breath and tries again. "I don't want *your* stuff. I want *mine*."

"You're happy enough with *my* stuff in *your* nest." It feels like a solid point, and I know when it lands, that I shot myself in the foot.

Her eyes turn shiny, but she doesn't cry. She lifts her chin and steps away from the bed. "It's just biology. It doesn't mean anything."

"Una—"

"You don't understand, and you don't want to." She shrugs. "I guess it is what it is."

She sails past me, dragging her bad leg with the offended dignity of a queen. I'm an asshole, and I'm not really sure why.

"We can go to dinner now," she says over her shoulder. "I'll sit wherever you want. Alpha."

"Una." I follow her. "You're being bitchy."

"Sorry, Alpha."

I speed up to open the door for her. She shuffles past me,

chin high. I lift her by the waist and carry her down the stairs while she holds herself as rigid as a board.

"Damn it, Una. It's not safe for you alone in town. Let alone Mari and Annie. How many wins do you have between you?"

The answer is none. Females fight rarely, and then usually only those contending for alpha rank. Cheryl won her position more through lack of interest than prowess.

"We sell honey and herbs. It's not fight club. It's a farmer's market."

"You're not that naïve. You can't be."

She heads down the path toward the commons, and I shorten my stride to keep pace with her. She's hustling a little more than usual, but the speed is still painfully slow. At least by the time we get to the lodge, dinner will be served, and our original point of disagreement will be moot.

I'm grouchy, starving, and even though I know she's trying to pick up the pace, we're basically taking one step at a time like a bride toward the altar.

And I wouldn't want to be anywhere else in the world. My heart soars, and Una looks over at me. Her brow wrinkles. She felt that through the bond.

I offer her a wry grin.

"What are you so happy about?" she grumbles.

"Smells like venison tonight." The rich, gamey scent is in the air.

We both know I'm lying, and she grunts, but she lets it be. We're approaching the lodge now. There's more than the usual number of males hanging around on the front porch. We're a good half hour late. Everyone should be digging in right about now.

It's not until I escort Una through the front doors that I realize I've thrown a wrench in the works. Cheryl's standing by the dais, arms folded, glaring down her nose. No one's been served.

Annie, Mari, and Kennedy are standing at the kitchen door, laden trays propped on their hips, looking tired and pissed. There's a general grumbling and more than the usual number of squalling babies.

"What the hell's going on?"

Una looks at me like I'm an idiot. "Cheryl doesn't let us serve until you're here."

"No?" I hadn't noticed. Of course, I'm rarely late for a meal.

And then inspiration strikes. Didn't my mate say something about a buffet? Instead of heading for the dais, I make my way toward the kitchen.

The table furthest back is a bunch of pre-shift males. I moved them back here the first day I became alpha. They eat like animals.

"Clear off." I snap and point to another far corner. They scramble, leaving a half dozen gum wrappers and a weird puddle. I grab the slowest one by the back of his shirt. "Go get a bucket. Wipe down this table. You have sixty seconds."

I let my wolf growl his displeasure. The pup gets it done in forty-five.

Then I take the tray from Mari. "Come on." I nod for Annie and Kennedy to follow.

I unload the plates on the table, buffet-style, grabbing the best-looking cuts of meat on my way back up front.

"Help yourselves." I gesture to the overflowing table. "Elders first. Then pups and females. Males last. Like you're getting on a life raft."

The grumbling gets louder, some growls thrown in. My wolf alerts, his fur prickling up my spine. He's not mad. He's ready for a challenge that he can actually win. He's on a solid losing streak with Una Hayes.

I soothe him with the promise of venison and our mate. She's still standing in the entrance, baffled and blushing as she worries the tip of her braid.

The elders are lining up with their plates, perfectly content with the new set up.

I grin at my mate, and I restrain myself from asking if she's happy now. Instead, I gesture her toward my accustomed place in front of the fireplace.

Her gaze darts to the back of the room, but her roommates have disappeared into the kitchen. I duck aside for a second and tell Tye to keep an eye on the back exit. Make sure none of our lone females use their new free time to run off and do shit that gives me ulcers.

Una makes her way to the dais. She's self-conscious. Her leg's dragging pretty badly at this point.

At the dais, I lift her. There's only one folding chair. Cheryl's off overseeing the new buffet, and everyone else is either bitching or staring at us like we're the floor show.

I guide Una to sit. She does, all stiff and twitchy. I snap at the B-roster table, and they all surge to their feet. Gael's the fastest, even though he's with A-roster. He turns, snatches Finn's chair from under his ass, and hands it to Jimmy to bring over.

I knew I liked that kid.

I sink down, smirking, and tear a hunk of meat off a backstrap filet. It's good. Smoky.

I rip off another bite and hold it up to Una's mouth. She makes me wait a few seconds before she goes for it with her fingers. I snatch it back.

"Open up."

"You're not feeding me."

I give the dish in my lap a meaningful look. "Yes, I am."

"You're not putting it in my mouth."

I don't smirk, but my dick rises hard and sudden. I have to steady the plate.

"You wanted a buffet. You got a buffet." I wave at the anarchy below us.

A-roster has cut the line. A scuffle has broken out between two pups. Cheryl's given up. She's commandeered a table and filled it with a few purloined plates. Her usual court is gathered around, whispering to each other, glowering with well-fed disapproval at the general disorder.

"It's not a buffet."

I raise an eyebrow. "Oh? Then what is it?"

"You said it yourself. A sinking ship."

I bark a laugh. She scowls. I finish the filet and lick my fingers. She can't tear her eyes away. Her throat swells gently as she swallows.

A whiff of her arousal teases my senses.

I'm suddenly twice as hungry as I was before I ate.

A few male heads turn from their food, noses twitching. Oh, hell, no. Not for them.

My wolf lunges. Somehow, Una manages to grab the plate of venison as he leaps through the air, snarling and snapping, landing hard enough to rattle the empty chairs. He bares his fangs, pacing the open floor, forcing the males back to their tables further away and scoot their chairs.

He's like a rabid sentry, patrolling a line, getting up in the faces of random males whose necks aren't bent quite far enough for his satisfaction. I should rein him in. This is our pack. They are no threat to me. And we're wolves. There's no such thing as a private scent.

And I am inordinately proud of the proof of Una's impending heat. It marks her as mine.

And it's not like Una's trying to lure a male. Or any would have a chance of getting within twenty feet of her. My wolf has made damn sure of that.

I need to put him back on the chain. I'm stressing the pack, upending the natural order, and that way inevitably leads to a challenge.

I want one. I want an enemy I can slay. The wolf and I both. But it would cause havoc when I need shit calm to focus on Una.

And my pack is showing their necks as they go about chowing down. I'm out of control, and they're unsurprised. Mildly put out by the inconvenience but unfazed. Am I so unreasonable that this is par for the course?

I release one last howl for good measure and pad back to my mate. She's feeding herself. She's almost cleaned the plate. She grins at me. There's a smudge of grease at the very corner of her mouth. I shift and as I go to sit, I grip her neck and lick her clean. Then I plop my bare ass on the cold metal and hold out my hand. Gael tosses me a pair of shorts from halfway across the room. Dude has excellent aim, too.

Thank Fate he's wearing boxers.

"You full?" I ask.

Una lifts a delicate shoulder, and her neckline falls so my bite peeks out. A growl vibrates in my chest. It isn't hunger. Not the kind that can be satisfied here.

I don't know how much longer I can hold out. My cock aches, my balls throb, and there's a constant urge inside me —drag her closer, bite her again so everyone sees, take her back to her nest.

Is this rut? I thought I was immune. I've never had a problem resisting temptation before. I'm a flip-shifter. I have full control over my physical body. I operate on a higher level. The good of the pack. The safety of our future.

Oh, I am a prideful fool.

My palms are damp, my face is flushed, and I'm hanging on by a thread.

If it comes down to it, I will beg this female. I will give her anything she wants. I am weak for her, and I don't give a damn.

I will go fetch her another plate of venison.

"Want more?" My voice is husky. There's a lot of the wolf in it.

She clenches her thighs, her dress clinging to her lush curves. She shakes her head no. "I'm good."

Her eyes are downcast. The sweet, warm smell of her grows stronger. Intoxicating. She flutters the neckline of her dress, cooling her flushed chest, drawing my eye to the pattern of my fangs in her rosy flesh. Is her heat back?

I don't think so. She's perspiring, but her eyes are clear. She's watching the pack. She seems nervous. Jumpy.

Makes me jumpy.

And then—so gradually that it takes a few seconds to register—a hush falls. Lochlan has pushed his chair back, and he's standing at the B-roster table, chest puffed. Finn and Eamon are standing at his back, in formation.

My wolf growls low in anticipation. A challenge. My fangs descend. I lick the tip of an incisor. My wolf basks in the collective gulp of our packmates.

I will very much enjoy finishing off Lochlan Byrne.

But it's not Lochlan who speaks. He glowers while Eamon strides forward to the middle of the open floor.

"Alpha," he calls. "A word."

My mouth waters.

Eamon's hair might be gray, and his hands, especially, are mottled with age spots, but he hasn't begun the rapid decline that marks the end of a shifter's life. He still has bulk, and his stoop doesn't slow his gait.

He hunts more than fights these days, but he still puts in hours at the gym, usually late at night with Lochlan and his crew. Telling them stories about the good old days when he was beta to my father and folks knew their place.

I have his number. He can't win against me in a fight, so his challenge has to be more insidious. I know he's been poisoning the well, gathering the disaffected. It'll get him nowhere. All the males in this pack banded together can't beat me.

But it will be sweet to remind them.

I wave my hand at him to speak.

The elders perk up and hush each other. He is the greatest of their generation. They put up with Dermot as a mouthpiece, but Dermot's loyalties are with me at the end of the day, not them. Eamon is their champion. The last vestige of their waning strength. My father's male.

He clears his throat. "You've taken a mate."

Una tenses. I nod. "You know this."

"You have our congratulations. I am sure I speak for the pack when I wish you many, healthy sons."

Una's teeth squeak when they grind. I incline my head, acknowledging his words. And I note what he does not say. He did not wish Una well, nor bend his neck to her in deference.

That was a mistake.

And this farce of congratulation is not why Eamon has stepped forward.

"Speak your piece," I tell him. Generally, my lieutenants will corner me in private to bitch so as not to risk rank. I like this new direct approach. I can shut down whatever nonsense this is in public. Once and done.

"We had visitors this afternoon. Human enforcers. From the town."

My gaze flies to Tye. His expression is contained, but his temple tics. He didn't know either. I shift forward in my chair. Well, this is some bullshit. Since when does my pack keep secrets from me?

Una shifts in her chair. Well, I guess some have all along.

"And?" I keep my gaze on Eamon, but I clock Lochlan in my periphery. He's the fool with ambitions. The mutt who chases the car and wouldn't know what to do if he caught it.

"They came to offer a friendly warning. Apparently, you assaulted a human at their market?" There are gasps.

Eamon can hardly mask how much he's getting off on calling out the alpha.

I shrug. My wolf pushes forward. He wants out. He knows he can make quick work of this half-assed challenge. An image flashes in my brain, three mangled, bloody bodies piled in front of Una. A tribute.

She wouldn't like it.

Her wolf would, but she wouldn't.

I sigh. "And?" I prompt Eamon when he doesn't go on.

"Your mate left pack territory without protection." Murmurs erupt around the room. Nuala shakes her white head. Yeah, I don't like it either.

"We were told she has been doing this for some time. And on occasion, the other lone females have, as well."

The murmuring increases in volume. Gazes fly to the erstwhile buffet table where Mari and Annie had been clearing dishes. Now they're huddled together, frozen. Scared.

Unacceptable.

I clear my throat, drawing attention back to me. "What's your point?"

"And your mate is permitted a phone."

I wouldn't use the word "permitted," but yeah, I suppose so. I nod.

All the females burst into stage whispers. Eamon has to raise his hand for silence.

"And we're to take it that *any* female may do likewise? Gallivant around the human town, bury her nose in a phone, ignore her young, get seduced away from her mate and her duties to the pack by the cesspool of the human *internet*?" His voice gathers volume until it booms on the last word.

The females collectively lean forward with bated breath.

Una has become very still beside me. She is waiting for me to disappoint her. The bitterness taints our bond.

I lean forward and steeple my fingers. It would be so much easier to beat some ass. I still might.

The end goal is so clear. Protect the females and young. But the way there is so damn muddy.

I'm not stupid. I know that just because you forbid a thing does not mean it is not done. It means it's done in secret. I've been content to tell myself the lone females only indulged in a little wine, a little smoke. The young only sneak off to the border of our territory to steal a bone and win a dare. Elders only cuff females and young every once in a while, and not too hard. Not like they used to.

Nothing's perfect. But it's better. I've made it so.

And then, as they have been all day, a memory flashes to the forefront of my mind. The bed of a truck, metal slick with blood. Una, slight and pale as death, her brown hair soaked a rust red. My mother and the crone at the tailgate.

"Let us have her now." The crone beckons with her hand.

I bare my fangs and crouch lower.

My mother leans as close as she can, laying a slender hand on my massive paw. "You can't protect her like this. You need to trust us. We know what to do."

I remember now. It's the hardest thing I've ever done. Letting the females take my mate away.

And how I knew then what I needed to do. How I could make sure no one ever hurt her again.

I had to change *everything*.

They took her, and I collapsed, and there are no other memories until I woke up weeks later. My father told me I'd caught a terrible fever after shifting younger than any male in recorded history, and I'd beat it because I was the strongest of my generation, destined for greatness.

And I figured then it was good I was the strongest because it was gonna take some big balls and righteous ass-kicking to fix this backwards pack.

I never questioned why I needed to do it. It seemed obvious. The pack was fucked up.

This is fucked up.

Why am I overthinking? This is a challenge. I know what to do with them.

I stand. Eamon shuffles almost imperceptibly back on his heels. I grin.

And then I look down at my mate. Her eyes are eating up her face, her wolf close to the surface, ready to follow me into battle. My wolf grumbles. He's insulted that she thinks he needs help.

I don't mind. She's not gonna lift a finger, but the way she's subtly measuring the distance between her and Eamon makes me hard. And weirdly warm in my chest.

I need to teach her to fight. Her wolf's obviously the sort that's gonna keep getting her in trouble.

"What do you say, mate?" I ask her. "Can any female go gallivanting around town?"

Her eyes spark. She draws herself up. "Yes. If they want to."

I expect a few shouts and a lot of pearl clutching, but it's so quiet, you could hear a pin drop.

"But what about outcast wolves? Humans with bad intentions?"

She shifts a little in her seat, but she doesn't lower her head an inch. "We can go in partners. Or with a male if he's free. But we shouldn't have to ask permission."

"Seems fair."

"It *is* fair."

"And any female can have a phone?"

"Yes," she says firmly. And then she casts Eamon a black look. "And mothers are not going to neglect their young, and I think that's pretty rich coming from a male when everyone knows the fathers in this pack don't lift a finger to help until their sons are old enough to go into the ring." She folds her arms.

At the elder tables, wizened faces turn bright red.

Eamon coughs. "All due respect, but Una Hayes ain't my alpha," he says.

I crack my neck. This is not going to be my proudest moment—handing an old wolf his ass in front of the whole pack—but I'm going to enjoy it all the same.

I crack my neck again, twisting to the other side.

And then, a murmuring from the A-roster table erupts and a chair screeches across the linoleum. There is a collective gasp. I fully expect to see Alfie or maybe that lost pup Fallon throwing his lot in with the opposition, but it's a female. Haisley.

I haven't spoken to her—or thought about her—since

my wolf dumped her from our lap when he leapt to attack Gael. She's not looking at me. She's got Una in her sights.

My wolf snarls, and it's all I can do to keep him down, but this needs to play out.

I search for Cheryl, and she's hanging back by the elder table, nose in the air. So Haisley has the alpha female's blessing for whatever's about to go down. Noted.

Beside me, Una stiffens. I ball my fist so I don't reach for her, but I focus on the bond, send her every reassurance I can. She is the strongest wolf here. I've got her back. No matter what.

She waits while Haisley struts forward to stand in the middle of the open floor. Haisley's dressed for her moment, high-heeled black boots, tight red top, and tighter jeans. She comes to a halt, smiles, and sucks her front teeth like she's checking for lipstick.

There's simmering rage coming through the bond. The wolf is loud in the mix.

Tell her to sit her ass down, I send through the link, but I don't think it works that way. It's not like text messaging.

Una ignores me, tracking Haisley's every move. The flip of her poofy blonde hair. The hip cock. The room is silent except for the occasional cough.

Finally, Haisley speaks. "I have a question, Alpha." She's looking at Una though, a smirk playing on her red stained lips.

"Go."

"I was attacked—unprovoked and unchallenged—by Una Hayes."

She pauses. I don't know for what. We all saw it. I grunt to move shit along.

"I won. By our laws, I rank. And I demand to be heard."

Everybody's fucking listening. I gesture for her to cut to the chase.

"I say females must not be allowed to risk our males' lives for foolish escapades off territory. Last Pack will stop at nothing to restore their numbers. They don't care if a female is mated. They just want bodies. Mark my words, they will attack, the human authorities will come down on us, and there will be war among the packs. And for what? What is so hard about the lot of a lone female with no pups to tend and everything provided for them?"

That's an interesting complaint from a mated female with no pups and everything provided for her.

There is some rumbling from the younger females at the tables toward the back.

"Una Hayes—who has *never* won a challenge—wants to destroy our traditions and put our males in danger—put our very territory in danger—and for what? Her fucking *hobby*?"

This sounds nothing like Haisley. I've never heard anything from her mouth but purring and flattery. These are Eamon's words.

I glance down and over. Una's maintaining eye contact with Haisley, and her stance is solid. She's clearly pissed, but she's also uncertain. I can feel it all—including her wolf's instinctive fear of an adversary who bested her. It pains me, and riles the hell out of my wolf, but I hold course.

Folks don't fully understand this quite yet—Una doesn't either—but my mate is the most powerful wolf here now. She can make her own calls.

And then Haisley adds, as if it's an afterthought and not an obvious incitement, "Maybe the lone females need to spend a night back in the basement so they can remember to be thankful for what this pack allows them."

The room was quiet, but now it's absolutely silent. Not even the creak of a bench. You can hear the lights hum.

Una's eyes seem wider until I realize the brown has changed. It's a mellow cognac now, shining and alive. It's her wolf.

She steps forward. "You shut your mouth."

Haisley draws herself up and smirks. "Or what?" Now that sounds like her.

"I'll shut it for you."

The entire pack looks at me. They know. Even Cheryl's starting to look green around the gills.

Haisley doesn't give an inch. Whoever's put her up to this has done a thorough job of messing with her head. Her instincts should be screaming, but instead, she laughs. "Don't you remember my fangs in your neck, bitch? That's what's wrong with you and all your misfit friends up in the reject cabin. You think 'cause Alpha pities you that you're safe? Strength rules in Quarry Pack, and everyone knows your wolf is a sad, scrawny loser."

There's the sound of a hundred simultaneous drawn in breaths.

Haisley glances over to her brother, proud and high on her own audacity. There's a shine in her eyes. I wouldn't doubt but that she's high on something else, too. I catch Cheryl's attention and nod for her to come get her girl.

"He's gonna breed you and leave you, and then you're gonna be back on the bottom with *Toddlers and Tiaras*, weepy Annie, and the freak who doesn't even know if she's a boy or a girl." Haisley jerks her thumb over her shoulder toward the kitchen door where Mari, Annie, and Kennedy are gathered.

Una snarls from the back of her throat, a clear warning,

and I'm just about to step in when everything happens at once.

Una tugs the bond so hard I can feel it in my breastbone. *Come on.*

"I told you to shut your mouth. Now you're gonna lose your teeth." The words are garbled by Una's lengthening fangs, but we can all make them out. The pack edges backwards, riveted. Dams hiss at pups to back up.

There's another yank at the bond like I got a goddamn leash attached to my solar plexus. *Come, mate. We attack.*

I can't stop the stupid grin. Good thing Una's focused one hundred percent on Haisley. "Alpha doesn't pity me. Alpha *belongs* to me."

Hell, yeah, I do.

As Una's body breaks, I become the wolf, and howl the truth to the rafters. Finally, the insolence in Haisley's eyes dims, and her gaze darts around the room. Cheryl's waving wildly, but Eamon and Lochlan are still standing, unbowed, so she hesitates.

Big mistake.

I bolt for Haisley. Females scream. Haisley abandons her skin to her wolf who promptly panics as she registers the enraged alpha leaping for her.

Haisley should thank freakin' Fate that Una shifts slow as molasses, and I beat her wolf across the floor. If Haisley raised a paw to her, I'd rip her head from her spine.

As it is, all I have to do is snap my teeth, and Haisley's wolf skitters backwards and crawls under a table, mewling for her mother. Cheryl has backed off to huddle beside her mate in human form. No help coming from those quarters.

Dermot's looking uneasy, but he's not gonna make a move. Not for a "strictly for heat" mate. Not against certain death.

It takes a second for Una's wolf to catch up to me, and she nips my haunch as she passes, howling and growling and letting the whole damn lodge know that no one touches her girls, and Haisley better come out and fight us.

Haisley cowers closer to the floor, neck bent at a right angle. Eamon and Lochlan exchange glances, but they don't move to help her. She's a female. In their eyes, she doesn't rank. Not enough to risk skin or fur. They want to live to plot another day.

Una's wolf yaps louder, unsatisfied with Haisley's submission. She wants a pound of flesh.

Drag her out so I can kill her.

I love how her wolf doesn't hesitate to boss my ass around. She knows how it is. But you can't always get what you want, especially when you're in charge. The sooner Una and her bloodthirsty wolf learn that the better.

I bite the scruff of Una's neck and draw her back to the dais. She growls in the back of her throat and stays stiff as she lets me pull her away. It's freakin' adorable.

I shift back to human first. Gael's right there with another pair of shorts. This pair rides up my ass. I don't look around. I don't want to know what scrawny whelp he got 'em off of.

Una's wolf rumbles a little longer to make sure her point is taken, and then she plops on her rump and gazes up at me expectantly. I squat, my back to the room, so that no one will see my beautiful mate in her bare human skin.

I know we're shifters, and it's normal and everything, but if shit's changing, maybe we all need to get more modest. Fit in better with the humans or whatever. I'll figure out a justification. No one sees Una's tits but me.

Finally, Una takes back her skin, and she's flushed and breathless. Magnificent. Gael lays a sundress on my shoulder and scurries away. That one is smart. The fabric smells like an unmated, protected female. Not ideal but acceptable.

I help Una tug it over her head. Her braid's undone, and her eyes are still flashing with temper.

"No one touches my girls," she says.

I turn to direct my response to the pack. "No one touches the lone females."

"Or threatens them."

I nod in agreement.

She lowers her voice, and her brow furrows, like she's working something out. "She wouldn't fight me."

"Nope."

"Because your wolf would kill her."

"Yeah. Without hesitation."

I can see the wheels turning.

"No one in this pack will challenge me now, will they?"

I shake my head. "Nope. They know I'd rend them limb from limb."

"So I'm the de facto alpha female?"

"You're the alpha female."

Through the bond, I sense the confusion and awe as she comes to understand. I lead her back to her chair. Cheryl rushes over to coax Haisley out from under the table.

A few low conversations start, but mostly, there is uneasiness in the hall. Eamon and his contingent have taken their seats. No one seems certain of what comes next.

Truth be told, neither am I.

Una absently rebraids her hair, frowning. I don't like it. Maybe some more meat would perk her up. I snap and point, and Gael brings over a platter. Una ignores it.

After a long time, she finally speaks. "It *is* dangerous to go into town."

"Alone, yes." There's no way around it. Last Pack and human traffickers are a real threat.

"I was putting the girls in danger."

I don't answer. I can't soften the truth. I feel her guilt, and I wish I could soothe her, but living with your own shitty decisions comes with being alpha.

"But it isn't fair to keep us locked up and beholden, either. It isn't *right*."

I grunt. Sometimes the choice isn't between right and wrong. It's between the bad and the less bad. She knows this. She's been leading her own little pack for almost as long as I have.

She thinks for a time. Folks relax and get up for a second helping. Mari and Annie come around with tea and coffee. Voices rise.

"A pack's strength is in numbers," she finally says. "We'll just have to go to town in a big group."

She's so serious, I fight my smile. It is the logical conclusion, and there's gonna be no shortage of unmated males who'd like to take a morning off training to escort a bunch of females to market. I'm gonna have to come up with a rotation. Maybe an incentive system. Now my wheels are turning.

There's still an unsettledness in the air. Maybe there's no time like the present to show the folks that change can be good—and impress upon them all one last time that the highest-ranking wolf in any pack is that one who rules the alpha.

"If we were to go to town now, mate, what could we do there?"

"Now?"

"Yes."

"You want to go to town now?"

I nod.

She searches my eyes, and I feel her nosing around the bond, trying to ferret out my intentions. "I don't think much is open this late except maybe the bars?

"We're not going to a bar. What else is there?"

She thinks. "Well, we could get ice cream."

"Yeah?" Wolves aren't that big on dairy.

"Mari and Annie love it."

"It's from cows right?" If it comes from a cow, it could be good.

"Yeah."

"All right. Let's go for ice cream in a big, safe group." I help her to her feet and address the lodge. "Who else is coming to town for ice cream?"

The place erupts. Pups start begging. Half of the elders shake their heads, aghast, while the other half help each other up and grab their shawls and hats.

"Bring your girls," I tell Una. I'm not leaving them alone with a frustrated Eamon and company. Lochlan's sulking at the B-roster table, about to blow. He's got a 'roided up look about him.

Una smiles and waves her girls over. My wolf begins to relax. The pack is acting like itself again, each member worried about himself. Challenge averted. For now.

I have no doubt that this shit will come to a head soon, but not tonight. I wave Ivo over and tell him to tap Gael and a few other trusted wolves to stay back and keep an eye on Eamon's faction. Then, I escort my mate toward the door. Her roommates trot along behind us, and as we go, the sound of scraping chairs and arguments rise behind us.

Tradition versus change.

The same-old, same-old versus ice cream.

Not for the first time, I marvel that such major shit

hinges on such small things.

I park in the lot by the commissary, and it's a short walk. I send Fallon for my keys. The packmates choosing adventure follow as we make our way slowly down the path toward the commons. The sun is setting, and the foothills are a solid black outline blending into the deep purple of the evening sky. It's a beautiful night.

My tension isn't set aside; it's gone. My enemies' machinations have no consequence when Una leaves her hand in mine after I grab it to help her navigate a root in the path.

Behind us, there are whispers tinged with excitement. I hear Conor and Jimmy. Dierdre and Liam. Nuala. Dermot. Old Noreen. Ashlynn. Tye, oddly enough. And behind them there's a parade of other mated pairs with their young. The longer we walk, the freer their laughter, the louder their voices.

"What's ice cream?" a small voice asks at the top of his lungs.

"Like thick milk," an elder female replies.

"That's gross."

"Yes, but I'm not missing this for nothin'."

Una hides a smile. Our bond pulses. "You're really taking us for ice cream," she says.

"Yup."

"Eamon's crew is just going to get angrier."

"Don't care. There's a new order. They'll fall in line or leave."

She sighs, and worry threads through our connection. "You know I can't win against any of them in a challenge."

"No, I don't know that."

She huffs. "You won't always be there."

"Yes, I will."

She rolls her eyes. She doubts me, but time will tell.

"Your little wolf might not be able to take all comers—yet—but you rule me. So, you rule the pack. Get used to it. It's a pain in the ass."

"I rule you?" She scoffs, but she also adds the slightest sassy sway to her walk. Even in the dark, I don't miss it.

"You lead me on a leash." I slap that swaying ass. Can't resist.

She yips, and she gives a good, salty yank on the bond. Much stronger than she has before.

The early rising stars have never been more beautiful, nor has the susurration of the night critters in the woods. Her lightness makes me drunk.

Yeah, I don't want to fight. I don't want to be in charge. I want to feed my mate thick milk and then race her home through the fields, stopping by the old dens for her to ride my hard, aching cock.

Yeah. That's the best damn plan I've ever had.

We reach my Jeep and Fallon's waiting, leaning against the door, keys dangling. He grins. "There's not enough room, Alpha. Can I get the keys to the Mustang and take the others?"

The others? I finally notice Annie, Mari, and Kennedy close behind us. Tye, too, his eyes flashing silver.

"I don't think so, pup." Tye puffs his chest.

Fallon's wolf yips. Not big enough to growl, not smart enough to keep his muzzle shut. Tye's wolf responds with a snarl.

These assholes are not ruining my night. I don't know what's going on, or what kind of mismatched pissing contest this is, but I do know we own vans.

"All of y'all go together. You can go in the Windstar, or you can take the Astro." I gesture at our two fine, working tributes to the 90s. Liam is a truly talented mechanic.

I don't waste time listening to them groan. I open the Jeep's passenger door and lift Una in. Her smell is sharper than it was in the lodge. It's a stimulant. I drag it in with the night air, and my muscles tingle.

We're riding with the top down, or I'm not gonna make it all the way to Chapel Bell.

The moon is waning, and it hangs above the tree line like a giant glowing hook, set off by the last golden orange streaks of sunset.

Una lifts her face to the night sky. Her braid hangs down her back, thick and inviting. I grab it. She doesn't startle. She glances over at me, lips curving, and then she closes her eyes again, letting the cool wind bathe her face.

There's a fire raging inside me, a longing that crackles like embers.

She is the one. Fate saved her for me. To be mine alone. The reward for all the sacrifice, all the cracking of thick skulls and sleepless nights worrying over shit that seemed impossible to change.

Tonight, I get to know what it feels like to sink deep into my mate and seed her belly so she belongs to me like I already belong to her.

I don't want fucking ice cream.

I want to pull over onto the shoulder. I want her to flee again, and this time, I won't stalk her. I'll catch her. Take her. And she'll cry my name. Her wolf will howl it to the skies.

I adjust my cock before it punches through my zipper, grateful for the dark and Una's distraction.

I might have never mounted a female before, but I'm no pup. My body is a finely-tuned instrument, and I can read a partner in the ring. Una won't be dissatisfied.

These aren't nerves. It's anticipation.

13

KILLIAN

Our caravan pulls into Chapel Bell as the clock tolls eight. There aren't many humans around, but the lights blaze at the stand in the square with the cow statue in front. It's a prime specimen. Nice haunches. Really gets your mouth watering, and then you see the menu, and it's instant disappointment.

We park our makeshift caravan, and I help Una out of the Jeep. Maybe I linger. The nip of her waist and swell of her hips are sweet as hell. Made for my grip. Her hands flutter to my chest. The lamplight shines in her eyes. I can't tell if her pupils are blown wide like before when the heat overtook her.

"Everyone's staring," she whispers.

"Let them."

She ducks her head, unconsciously flashing my bite. The sight makes me even harder. When I spill inside her tonight, I'm going to mark her again. Deeper. And then I'm going to mount her again and again until she marks me back.

I lick my lips.

"Ice cream," she murmurs, voice rough.

"Ice cream." I force myself to step back. Grab her hand. Lead her after Nuala and her sugar-happy grandson.

We're the last to order. I get chocolate. Una gets vanilla.

It's disgusting. The pups like it, but pups will put anything in their mouths. I see many males surreptitiously tossing theirs in the garbage while their females bravely force down what their males have provided for them. There's an analogy there. I'm not so dense that I don't see it.

Maybe we're overdue for a change. I might have accidentally started things moving with this impromptu jaunt to town. A lot of females joined us, as well as all of B-roster. Not so many elders. Even excluding those I left back on purpose, A-roster is underrepresented.

I reach behind the bench and offer my cone to Nuala's grandson as he tears past, and I smile. I won't mind a good fight. In a few days. Once Una's heat is over, and she's sated.

She's actually enjoying her ice cream. She savors it, swirling her tongue around the base and then mouthing the cream into peaks.

The back of my neck sweats. We're sitting together on a wrought-iron bench, and I swear, I'm heating the metal. She has a dollop of melted white on her bottom lip. She darts her pink tongue out and dabs it clean.

I'm done.

I stand, throwing her over my shoulder.

She yelps, and her ice cream plops into the grass. She whacks my back.

"Hey!"

"You've had enough."

"I wasn't even to the cone!"

I smack her ass, and it jiggles so sweet. I'm not making it

back to camp. It's gonna be close getting to the boundary of Quarry Pack territory.

I want her first time to be in her nest, but it's so damn far away. The dens are closer. The dens are *right*.

"See you in a few days, Alpha," Tye calls, chuckling. He's sitting between a scowling Kennedy and a blushing Annie, crowding them into the corners, his legs sprawled wide, arms resting along the back of the bench. "I'll see the girls home."

Kennedy's wolf grumbles.

I grunt my thanks and place Una into the Jeep, careful of her leg.

"Did I hurt you? Carrying you that way?" I grab her chin and search her face for traces of pain. I tried to keep her leg free and not jostle it too much, but I'm a rough guy. I don't always know my strength.

Her eyelashes flutter against her pink cheeks. "I'm okay."

"You'd tell me if you weren't?" It's an order, not a question. I know she wouldn't, and her leg's a pretty constant bother, the ache is always there in the bond, so I don't know if it's worse or not.

She ignores me, straightening her skirt and buckling up. "Why are you in such a hurry to leave?"

I'm already in the driver's seat, turning the key in the ignition.

"You know."

I expect more protests, but she grows quiet. I make it out of town in record time. Our connection is alive, coursing with energy. It's undeniable. Is that why she's speechless?

Because she knows she can't deny it anymore?

I don't want her to surrender.

It would relieve, but it wouldn't satisfy. What do I want?

I guess what should have been. I want to go back to the

moment she claimed me in the lodge, and I want to accept her then. What would it have cost me to hear her out? Take her aside and talk?

My soul would have recognized her. With the way I feel now, there's no way it wouldn't have.

But that's rewriting history.

Maybe the way this is unfolding is what Fate intended. Me pulling my head out of my ass. Her giving me a chance. What if screwing up was necessary so that I could truly recognize the grace I've been given?

We've waited for each other our whole lives. And despite my epic fuck up, we're still here together now.

I'll be gentle. I'll make it good for her.

My cock strains, the urge to chase rising, even in this human contraption.

I force the rut down, call on my wolf to restrain the lust in my blood. My mate will want her nest, not the dens. I can hold out a little longer, take her to the cabin, not some cave in the woods.

I obey the speed limit. I won't jostle her leg more than I have to in my haste. I won't hurt her ever again.

I park right in front of my cabin, and I scoop her from her seat. She's hot to the touch, eyelids at half -mast. She wasn't feeling the heat back in town, but she is now. Her eyes are hazy, and she's fiddling with the buttons on her top before I get her to the front door.

Her need beckons to me.

"I can't stop," I tell her.

"I don't want you to," she says, breathless.

I carry her across the threshold like a human bride, and she wriggles in my arms, trying to get closer, to press her swollen breasts to my chest. I kick open the bedroom door and place her reverently in her nest. Her hands fumble at her waistband, and she shimmies her skirt down. I rip off my own clothes, feasting my eyes on the skin she reveals, inch by inch, the curves and swells, every perfect line of her.

Her fingers are already stuffed between her legs, her eyes screwed shut. There's a sheen of sweat on her chest and forehead.

My heart thuds. There's no more dance. No courtship. This is happening now. I wipe my palms on my thighs. I can do this. You put part A in slot B. Simple.

She glances up at me through hazy brown eyes and moans low in the back of her throat. It's a command.

She climbs to all fours, sticking a pillow haphazardly under her bad knee. Her braid dangles over her shoulder, sweeping the mattress as she stretches her neck and arches her back. Then she folds, resting her forehead on her arms, and she lifts her hips, angling her pussy so it's open to me, pink and slick and plump with her arousal.

I kneel behind her. It's a simple matter of easing my cock inside. If she whimpers or stiffens or anything, I'll stop. Play with her clit 'til she's ready for more. It's not a race.

She growls and shuffles her knees further apart.

I trace the bumps of her spine, smooth my hands over her round hips and hold her tight in place. I can't bear the thought of hurting her, but her body seems to know what it wants. There's no fear in the bond, no tension in her muscles. She's presenting like Fate intended. She wants this as badly as I do. As if that's possible.

I just need to go slow. It's her first time, and I want her to remember only pleasure. I don't see a barrier in the shadow between her folds. I've heard females lose it riding bikes. That's good. I don't want her to feel any pain at my hands. Never.

I draw in a deep breath, steeling myself. And then I ease

my hard and aching cock into her slippery entrance. She gives for me perfectly, accepting me, groaning her delight. I sink to the hilt in one, smooth thrust, and her channel grips me tight. Before I can breathe again, tamp down my animal urges so I can stroke into her sweet heat like a male in control of himself, she bucks.

I shatter.

She rocks into me, and I slam to meet her hips, going deep, so deep, and she screams and clutches the sheets, bucking faster, harder. She's not shy. Not scared.

She wants it all.

I grab her braid, twist it around my fist, make her lift her head, exposing the elegant line of her neck.

My beautiful, greedy mate. She works my cock, seeking her pleasure, using me, pushing back and up, widening her knees and angling her pussy so every thrust hits a place that makes her contract and squirt cream.

She's wild. Demanding. Like she knows exactly what she wants from me.

I curve an arm around her waist, sit back on my heels, and lift her so I can drive into her from below. She tilts her head back and rests it on my shoulder. Her needy whimpers tickle my ears.

She's perfect. She matches every thrust, takes everything I give her. I don't have to hold back. She's not delicate or breakable. She's voracious.

My balls contract, and there's no stopping it. I can only go harder. She screams, and her core clamps on my cock, milking my seed, her whole body trembling, spasming. Then she goes limp. My knot swells, notching behind her pubic bone, binding her to me.

My heart explodes in pure joy, and then I panic.

She's not moving. Her eyes are closed.

I slap her cheek gently, and then with a sharp tap. Oh, Fate. I broke her. What do I do?

I tap harder, and she jerks her head to the side and grumbles drunkenly, "What're you doin'? Knock it off."

My heart starts beating again.

Her eyes are open now. Her pupils are still the size of dimes, but her muscles aren't lax anymore.

We're naked, slick and sticky. Despite the thickness of my knot, which swells the plane above her pussy, cum leaks, trickling down her thighs.

"Are you okay?" she asks and reaches up to wind an arm around my neck.

"Are you? Is this comfortable?" I stroke her stretched belly.

"Yeah." She offers me a small, shy smile. "I'm good."

"Are you hurt?"

She shakes her head, still smiling. "No. Why would I be?"

"Because it was your first time." I'm oddly nervous. It was good. She said so herself. But still.

I glance down where my cock splits her wide, and I don't see any blood, but we're still stuck together. After my knot shrinks, I'll get a warm washcloth. Clean her up and check to make sure she's okay.

"I wanted to be gentle." But I wasn't. My shoulders bunch. I was an animal.

She lazily strokes my jaw with her fingertips. I'm clenching my teeth pretty hard. I try to relax. I don't want to freak her out.

"I wanted to respect the fact that it was your first time, too." I know it's not good enough, but I need her to know.

"It wasn't my first time. It's all good." Her lips curve higher. "Great, actually."

What?

It wasn't—what?

I bend my neck. I can't get enough distance to meet her eye. We're locked together. "What do you mean?"

She giggles. "Okay. It was really great."

"No. You said it wasn't your first time."

Her smile immediately drops. A crease appears between her eyebrows.

My gut sours. Acid scores my throat. There's a scramble in my brain as the words translate and my wolf comes to understand what our mate has said.

He loses it. He snarls. His fangs flash. Una startles. She lunges forward, ripping herself off my knot with a scream. Sharp pain shoots through the bond. She scrambles up the bed, turning to cower at the headboard, gaze darting wildly around the room, knees clamped tight and drawn to her chest.

My wolf fights for our skin. He needs to attack. Protect what's ours.

She's ours. There's a threat. He can't see where it's coming from, and I can't explain, so he snarls louder, rattling the window panes.

"Who?" The word comes out a jagged growl. My mouth is full of fangs.

"I—It's n—not your business." Her fear blooms, overpowering the scent of our mixed juices, driving my wolf and I crazier. "I—I d—don't ask you about Haisley. Or the o—others."

Our mate is scared, and that's not right.

But is she ours?

She's fucked other males. They need to die.

"How many?"

Her nostrils flare. "N-not your b-*business*."

"Were you willing?"

"*Yes*," she sobs.

My wolf goes nuts. He howls. The walls shake. She scrambles for the edge of the bed. Our vision flashes red.

She's trying to leave us.

My wolf lunges for her neck. He needs to sink his fangs into his mark, bite down until he hits bone. Until she submits. I struggle to hold him back, and he tears at me, raging. She screams, burrowing into her nest, her cries muffled by the pillows.

Oh, Fate, this is wrong. She's so scared. I fight for control, and it slips from my grasp. The wolf drags her back to the center of the bed. He wants to mount her. *Needs* to. Other males have touched her. Tasted her. They'll take what's ours.

We'll die without her.

She doesn't belong to us. She's given herself away.

My wolf lifts his muzzle and bays his misery, straddling her so she can't run to another male.

She whimpers and rolls to her side, tucking her knees to her belly.

She can't leave. She's ours. She wears our bite. How could she have allowed another male to touch her?

The wolf glares down at her, confused, heartbroken, and she trembles, curled like a shrimp.

This is wrong.

This is not how mates are supposed to work.

I know I have to take back our skin before the wolf hurts her, but the loss is so strong. So all-consuming. I grapple for the bond, and it ends in nothing. Empty space.

A heavy sadness falls on us both, dampening my wolf's temper, giving me the space to haul him in, take back our skin.

Una is terrified. Her scent agitates us both, exacerbating

the wrongness in the air. I reassume human form, and now my wolf is happy to fade back. He has lost, he has failed, and he doesn't know how to fix what's broken.

He can't. There's nothing either of us can do about the past.

I back away from the disheveled nest and our sobbing mate. Una struggles to sit upright, back and shoulders curved, huddling as small as she can. The tears pooled in her eyes reflect the moonlight.

I pace the room. Slam the wall. Dent the drywall.

I'm gonna puke.

All these years, when I have been waiting, even without hope, my mate has let herself be mounted by other males. And it's nothing to her. She can say, as if it's inconsequential, "It wasn't my first time."

I have no right to be angry, and the fury eats at my soul.

I didn't recognize her as my mate. I rejected her. I cannot blame her for what she's done in the past.

But I do.

I'm a hypocrite and an asshole and what can I do?

"Don't you have anything to say?" I spit the words. It's not what I mean, and not the tone I ever want to use with her, but I am powerless in this moment, and I can't see my way forward.

I have to fight. It's the only thing I know.

"F-*fuck* you." Una buries her face in her knees.

I plunge my fingers into my hair, turn my back to her and her nest. I can't be in the room anymore. I'll make it even worse.

I snatch my jeans from the floor, tug them on, and walk out. Her wolf yips once as I go through the door.

It's as clear a 'yeah, fuck you' as I've ever heard.

I deserve it.

I am to blame. I know nothing else—but I am confident of that. It is my fault, and I have no idea how to fix it.

I DON'T GO FAR past the porch. I can't. And I wouldn't, even if I could.

I just need to calm down.

My heart's pounding, fur is prickling my back, itching like hell, and I've got too many teeth in my mouth. I pace up and down the path. I need a run. I need a fight.

And then I scent a male on the wind. Close. A little more than a yard away.

Yes. He's dead.

My claws snick through my fingertips, and I relish the pain. It clears the garbage from my mind, the sourness in my gut. It mutes the pain flowing through the bond.

"Come out and fight," I roar at the shadows.

"Can't. Hands are full." Darragh Ryan steps out of the tree line with an armload of venison steaks wrapped in butcher paper.

Fuck.

My adrenaline crashes, and I'm left drained. What have I done?

My shoulders slump. I force down a deep breath. A few of my brain cells start firing again, and I pull myself together.

"Now? This late?" Darragh shows up at strange times, but this is odd even for him.

"I get done when I get done."

"Kitchen's closed." Old Noreen's definitely passed out.

"That's why I'm here."

I grunt, scratch my ribs, and trudge out back for my

wheelbarrow. There's too much meat for my freezer. I'll have to haul it down to the lodge myself. Which means bringing Una. If she'll come with me. I doubt she will. She hates me. I can't blame her. My wolf was out of line.

I was out of line.

We both know it.

And I'm sorry.

And not sorry.

Fate, it's hard being even this far from her. What do I do if she says she wants to leave?

Of course she's going to want to leave. She didn't want to be here in the first place.

Is she hurt? She ripped herself off the knot. I didn't see a tear or smell blood, but what if the damage is internal? I seek out the bond, feel for pain, but it's all a kind of —shrieking.

I have never fucked up anything this badly before.

I roll the wheelbarrow to Darragh—who's wisely staying just outside my property line—and he dumps his contribution with a loud thud. Then he carefully places a thick, double-wrapped package on top. It's labeled "Mari" in thick black grease pencil.

"You'll make sure she gets it?" he asks.

His white T-shirt is covered in blood. He peels it off and drops it in the path. His sweatpants follow. He's become so uncivilized, I'm surprised he can still write.

"You know she throws it in with the rest," I tell him with maybe more sympathy than I have in the past. It's not the first time I've told him Mari wants nothing to do with his gifts.

Darragh and I go back a long way; I'm real with him. He backed me during my alpha challenges, and more importantly, he didn't step up to challenge me himself. I would've won, but it would've been close.

"That's her prerogative." He sighs, scrubbing his furry chest. Dude spends so much time as a wolf, a lot of hair stays when he shifts.

"That doesn't piss you off?"

"She's well-fed. That's all I care about."

"You don't care what she's doing when you're not around?"

A glowing bronze ring appears around his pupils. "You tryin' to tell me something?"

"No, man, no." This is my own shit. I don't need to fuck with his head.

"Does she need anything?" he asks.

"No. She's got everything she could want." I snort, remembering the stash of contraband at the lone females' cabin. "She's got herself a cell phone and a video game system."

"Who?" The syllable is a deadly promise, and I recognize the tone.

"Not what you're thinking. Seems Mari and her roommates have been running an underground honey and mushroom ring. Una's the ringleader."

"What the hell?" He's not as amused as I am. I've had time to get over the initial freak out. "They've been selling shit? Where?"

"Chapel Bell."

Darragh groans and rubs his gut. I've become familiar with the gesture. Let the acid indigestion begin.

"And you're letting them?" he asks.

"We're working it out."

He raises a thick eyebrow.

"You want to take away Mari's spending money?" I ask

him. "Confiscate her phone?"

"Hell, no."

"We're working it out," I say again. "They'll be protected." The statement's more hopeful than true, but I've calmed now. I'm not in the fever of a looming rut. It's ebbed for the moment, leaving me room to think. To feel.

I threatened her. Dominated her. Scared her.

I acted like my father. The shame is bitter in my mouth.

"So who's 'we?'" he asks.

"The ringleader and I." I cast a glance at the cabin. Her scent is subtle but obvious. I attend to the bond. Sadness. Fury. It makes my skin burn. Still no pain, though. Because this wasn't her first time.

"And you're hanging out here while your mate's inside because—" Darragh's really enjoying kicking me when I'm obviously down. Dick.

"It's a nice night." The clouds have thickened, hiding the moon. It's humid, and the mosquitos are out. "I'm getting some air."

"You want some advice?"

I lift a shoulder. Not sure what the pack's mountain man can tell me about females, but clearly I don't know what I'm doing.

"Oil the meat, not the pan. And you want to use a low, wet heat." Darragh nods sagely as he smirks through his salt-and-pepper beard. Then he winks. "Did you think I was gonna tell you what to do with your female?"

I chuckle. "Maybe."

"I know shit-all about females." Darragh jerks his chin toward the porch, asking permission. I nod. We walk over, lower ourselves to the steps. Wish we had cigars. I've got some in the cabin, but I haven't got the courage to go back in yet.

I lean back, resting my elbows on the rough porch boards. "What would you do if Mari, uh, took up with some other male?"

His chest rumbles, and his nails lengthen into claws. "Give me a name."

"I don't mean *Mari*. She's got no interest in—in that sort of thing. I'm asking, like, *for example*."

"You tell me if some asshole starts sniffing around her. Kill him first. Then let me know." He's not joking. I understand completely. I nod, and we're silent together for a while.

Somewhere, there are males who know what my mate's pussy feels like. They've seen her—felt her—come. And what was I doing?

Training. Fighting. Busting skulls so half-feral males would fall in line? Doing the bills?

She could've been hurt. She could have been stolen.

But she wasn't.

Haisley, Rowan, a whole bunch of other females are willing to do whatever with a high-ranking male. I don't disallow it. It's better that the females choose. Better than how it used to be when males took.

Una chose. I hadn't claimed her. I have no right to feel this way. I don't change what I believe day-to-day to justify whatever I want to do in the moment. That was my father's way.

If I was okay with females spreading their legs last week, I can't have a problem with it today. That's logic.

I don't actually believe a word of it.

"There's no rule that females have to save themselves for their mates," I say out loud, test if it has the ring of truth. "This isn't the old world."

Darragh grunts. It's an acknowledgement of fact, but not an endorsement of the idea.

"Males mount whoever's willing before they mate." That's a fact.

"Some keep going afterwards," Darragh points out. He speaks the truth.

I've had plenty of opportunities to get my dick wet over the years. I always told myself I didn't because it'd mess with rank in the pack. The natural order of things. And that's true, as far as it goes. But I also didn't want anyone who wasn't mine.

I was waiting. And I knew I'd wait forever, and some nights were long, and I'd wonder why I was making such a big deal out of something every animal does when the mood strikes him. But I never changed my mind.

I never wanted anyone until Una Hayes, and it came on so gradually. She slipped into my hands, and I am so very painfully aware that she can slip right out again. Maybe she already has.

I'm an idiot, but I feel what I feel.

Why couldn't she have waited?

I sigh. "I want to kill someone, and I don't ever want to know who he is."

"Did she want it?" Darragh asks carefully.

"Yeah. That's what she says. She says it's not my business."

"You're her mate."

"I am." Everything about her is my business.

"Heard you rejected her in front of the whole pack. Had Tye throw her out back by the trash."

My chest aches. None of this has been auspicious. None of it has been right.

"Yeah. I made a mistake."

"And now you're losing your shit because—I don't mean to presume, but—she, uh, has seen a little bit of the world?"

I don't think I'd put it that way, but I grunt. I don't want to be talking about this, but at least with Darragh, he'll take it to the grave.

"Alpha, I don't know another way to put this, so I'm just gonna say it—she's, what, twenty-eight years old?"

"Twenty-seven."

I wait for his point.

He coughs. "Twenty-seven," he says again. "In the old world, she'd be a couple years away from being a grandma."

"This isn't the old world."

"No. It's not. It's your pack." He pauses a second and then he plunges ahead. "I don't know. I don't keep up with the comings and goings so much down here. You keep the lone females in the lodge basement for the males' entertainment like your father did?"

"Fuck you." My fists ball, fur sprouting up my spine. Those are wrongs I have long put to rights, and everyone knows not to speak of it.

"Why change things?" he pushes.

"You have to ask?"

"It's a—what do you call it—like Socrates did? To get at the truth. Just answer the question."

"You're fuckin' Socrates?"

"Not lately. We're on a pause." He smirks again. Asshole. "Just answer the question—why did you change the way things were done in this pack?"

"It was wrong."

"Why?"

"She wasn't safe." And then the memory sails into clear view like a galleon, canvas billowing, churned up whole from the black storm of the past. The memory that had been there all along, waiting, biding its time.

In the bed at the crone's cottage. Bundles of lavender and Queen Anne's Lace hanging from the wooden rafters to dry. Una huddles into my side. The moon shines through the thick glass pane. My mother is asleep in a rocking chair, head tilted at an awkward angle, snoring.

My body is raw, my muscles torn and weak. All I have the strength to do is lie on my back and stroke Una's soft shoulder with my fingertips. She shakes with fever. She's swaddled in blood-soaked bandages. I'm feeble, painfully aware that in this state, I can't protect her or myself. My brain is churning. I need a human gun.

I killed the male who attacked her, but there are others, always waiting in the wings for an opening, and I'm paralyzed. Thomas Fane has friends, males who covet my father's rank, and who won't hesitate to take out his son to deal him a blow. I don't trust rat-faced Eamon Byrne. Who will protect Una if I'm gone?

Panic gives me energy, but not the strength to move my shredded limbs. I try anyway, but I jostle Una, and she whimpers in pain, so I stop.

My brave mate. She's so small. And fierce. Perfect.

The crone rises from her stool by the fire. She quietly shuffles over, a chipped china teacup in her weathered hand. She sits on the edge of the bed and smooths my hair from my forehead. I jerk my head away. I'm not a pup. Not anymore.

"You did well, boy," she said. "You protected your mate."

"Will she live?"

"I think so."

"How long will I be like this?"

The crone shrugs. "I've never seen a male shift so young. Maybe a week, a month, a year. Only the Fates can say."

"I need a gun."

She arches an eyebrow. "What does a shifter need with a gun?"

"I have to protect her. I can't fight. Not like this." I try to lift an arm, but I can hardly raise it an inch.

"You can't shoot them all, Killian Kelly. You'll have to beat them, one by one."

"Like this?"

She smiles, the crinkles in the corners of her eyes deepening. "You'll need a little more bulk, I think. Especially to best Eamon Byrne."

"I don't want to be alpha." I want to spar with Tye and hunt for Una. Make her strong. Maybe teach her to fight so my heart never again stops in my chest like it did on the commons when I heard her scream. I knew in that moment she was mine. And I've never known such fear.

"That's why you'll make a good one," the crone says.

"No." What do I want with a bunch of ass kissers and two-faced males lying in wait to take me down?

"Oh, Killian." She shakes her head, not unkindly. "You don't have a choice. Do you want to protect your mate?"

"I will. No one touches her. Ever again."

"How can you say that? In this pack?" And then she looks at my mother.

My father's mate. The bruise on her cheek has faded yellow, but there's no doubt in my mind, she has fresh ones somewhere else, somewhere she can cover with her long skirts and sleeves.

"I'll never hurt Una. I'll never let anyone hurt her."

"You couldn't stop it today." Her voice is gentle, and her words cut to the bone.

I push Una's hair out of her face. It's sticking to her clammy cheeks. "What do I do?"

"You put things right."

"How?"

"*Everything has happened out of order. We need to pause time. Give you space to do what needs to be done.*"

She's speaking mystic nonsense now. I need to know who to kill, and in what order.

She presses the cooling tea into my free hand. "*You can't protect her like this. You need to grow into your strength. You'll need all your focus to root out the evil in this pack.*"

"*Tell me what to do.*" *I'm so tired. So terrified. My wolf prowls inside me on shaking limbs. He's weak, too.*

"*Drink,*" *she says, glancing down at the dark brew in the cup. I sniff. It has no smell.*

My grip is unsteady. The liquid sloshes over the rim. "*What is it?*"

"*A choice.*" *She covers my hand with hers.* "*Let her go—for now. Let her be happy while you grow strong so you can make her safe.*"

"*Or?*"

"*Be selfish. See your mate as a possession, not a gift. You won't be alone. You'll be in good company in this pack.*"

"*And if I drink this, she'll be safe?*"

The crone's gray eyes grow moist. There's a deep sadness in them, a hopelessness that riles my wolf. He doesn't surrender, and the sight pisses him off.

"*Yes,*" *she says.* "*That's what I'm betting.*"

"*But are you sure?*"

"*No. I can't see the future. But I'm depending on you. And so is she.*" *She nods at Una.*

My mate is so pale, she's almost gray. I can't sense her wolf at all.

"*She didn't shift.*"

"*She couldn't. She's not like you.*"

"*Where's her wolf now?*"

The crone's lips wobble before she forces a smile. "*Hiding for now. She'll be back in time. Usually, the wolf is braver than the girl, but in this case, the girl has the heart of a lion."*

It's true, but the crone's words provoke my temper. "She doesn't need the heart of a lion. I'll protect her."

"I know you will." The crone gently guides the cup to my lips. "Drink."

I don't. I am not one to do what I'm told. Instead, I watch my mate.

She squirms, restless, fighting the sheet. Her hair is tangled from her head turning back and forth. She's feverish.

I rest my free hand lightly on the spot above her belly button, the only part of her that Thomas Fane's claws missed. This must be where she tucked the baby.

A fierceness surges through my veins. Pride. A gratitude so powerful it's a hallelujah.

"Will it hurt her if I drink?"

"Some might say so. I wouldn't."

"Why not?"

"She'll be free. She won't be waiting. She'll find her own way."

I comb my fingers through her hair, gently loosening the tangles. Some strands are stiff with dried blood. "She's mine. She should be with me."

I expect the crone to argue, but instead, she gives me a sad smile, pats my shoulder, and takes the cup and sets it on the bedside table. Then, she shuffles off to stoke the fire.

What do I do?

The path forward is so unclear. There are so many enemies. So many dangers. The only certain thing is that Una belongs to me.

And I would do anything to keep her safe.

Last winter, when I was on a run with my father, we came across an old wolf up in the hills, a male gone feral in his youth.

He'd triggered a landslide somehow, and he was at the bottom of a ravine, dragging himself along with his front paws, trailing blood in the dirt.

He must've been trapped by a falling rock. He'd gnawed off his own hind leg to free himself.

My father put him down. Ripped his throat out as the old wolf bared it in deference. My father had called it a mercy. There is no place in our pack for a defective wolf.

I think of that old grizzled male as I finish with Una's hair, braiding it as best I can so she doesn't work it into knots again. I don't have anything to tie the end, so I lay it carefully on her chest. She has pretty hair. Brown like a chestnut.

Her wounds are deep. Despite the crone's best efforts, there is no way they won't leave marks. The pack will see her as defective.

But she is perfect.

There is only one choice.

I can't change what happened, so I have to change what will.

I take the cup and drink deep. It's bitter, and it burns my throat. And then I hook my elbow behind Una's neck, prop her up, kiss her clammy forehead, and coax her to open her lips. I pour the rest down her throat.

She grumbles and bats at me with a small hand.

As blackness rushes toward me, roaring, I pray that when I find her again, I will have made the right decisions.

That I won't have done this for nothing.

"Where'd you go? You all right, Alpha?" Darragh claps me on the thigh.

I blink, shaking away the cobwebs. "Yeah."

I leap to my feet. My heart pounds. I remember. My arms feel empty, like I realized too late I let everything slip away.

Where's Una? How could I have left her alone, even for a minute?

14

UNA

I pick myself up.

It's easier this time because if there's pain, I can't feel it. All my wolf and I know is rage.

That asshole.

That hypocritical, backwards *bully*.

Why did I expect any different? I've known Killian Kelly my entire life, and what exactly in his illustrious past convinced me that he'd be any better than this?

The lifetime spent beating the shit out of other shifters?

The throne on the dais where he lounges while females throw themselves at him and he barks orders at us lesser folk?

I'm a fool.

I *knew* what he was, and here I am with his jizz still dripping down my leg.

I grab a blanket from the nest and scrub, but now his scent is *in* my skin. It's everywhere. The nest. The air.

What if he knocked me up? What have I done?

I can't blame heat. It's there, in the background, receded now, crowded out by fury and hurt. But even in the moment,

I wasn't lost to it. It hasn't come on in its fullness yet, thank Fate.

Can I stop it?

I have to. I have to go see Abertha, but she's gone on walkabout or a spirit quest or a spa retreat or whatever.

I pace the room. I have to do something. I can't stay here and wait to lose my mind like in the blackberry patch. What would he do if I begged him now? Call me a slut?

That's what he thinks, isn't it? That I'm damaged goods? My jacked-up leg he can overlook, but my missing hymen's the end of the damn world?

Well, screw him and his double standards. I'm not standing here and waiting for him to come back. I head for the door, bound and determined, but when I pass the bed, my steps slow.

No, this is wrong.

I can't leave my nest.

Not here, in Killian's house.

He doesn't deserve my nest.

Asshole.

The rage crashes through me again, and I grab a sheet and start stripping the bed. I fill my arms, over and over, shoving as many blankets and quilts as I can into the hamper until it's overflowing. I lay a comforter on the floor and pile pillows and clothes and towels into it. Then I tie the ends and drag it down the hall toward the kitchen.

Killian has his own washer and dryer in a mud room at the back of the house. I've got at least ten loads here, but I can get it started before I blow this pop stand.

I cram sheets into the washer, fill it up well past where I should. I hope it gets off-balanced. I hope I burn it out.

My nose itches. I swipe at my face with a fitted sheet, and it comes away damp. I'm crying.

I don't want to be.

Killian Kelly isn't worth it.

And you know what?

Screw doing his laundry. I'm gonna throw it all in the garbage.

I limp back to the bedroom. My bad leg is stiff, and I'm cold. I'm only wearing the gray T-shirt I pulled on after Killian ran like a scared pup. After I take what's left of my nest out to the trash cans, I'm going home.

Killian probably won't even care now that he's filled me with his baby batter. He's been outside all this time, talking to some male like nothing's wrong. Oh, Fate. Was Haisley right?

It makes no sense, but that makes me madder than the rest of it.

I shove the linens down into his trash can as hard as I can. I don't want to make too many trips.

That's what I'm doing when I scent Killian in the doorway.

I turn, chin high, ready to tell him to go fuck himself again.

He takes a step forward. He looks at the bare mattress. He looks at me. He glances behind me, down the hall, toward the kitchen. The washing machine is filling up.

Something happens to his face.

It hardens at the same time pain floods his blue eyes.

I've seen this expression before. In videos of fights. When he takes a blow that would lay a lesser shifter out, but he keeps his feet.

His nostrils flare. He balls his fists.

I don't move.

He comes for me.

My wolf yelps and ducks. I don't move. I let all my hate

and hurt and pain and disappointment stream through the bond. He might not care, but he's gonna *know* what he's done.

He puts his hands on my shoulders. I brace myself. Then he gently moves me to the side.

He bends over, fishes a fitted sheet out of the hamper, and sighs. Then he goes to the bed, corner to corner, slipping the elastic on, lifting the mattress to tuck the sides tight.

He comes back to the hamper and grabs a sheet. He squints at it, considers the bed, and then he balls it up and puts it on the right side near the headboard.

It belongs a little further down.

Then he comes for a wool blanket. He folds it and puts it in the middle where I had it.

He goes back to the hamper, over and over, and despite myself, my anger flows out through the bond like sand through an hourglass, and eventually, I run out.

I can't help but watch. He leaves for a minute and comes back with the bundle that didn't fit in the washing machine. He doesn't speak. He doesn't even look at me while he remakes my nest.

Everything is more or less in the correct general area, but it's also all wrong. Like a painting by Picasso.

When he finally finishes, he sits on the edge, forearms braced on his thighs, and bows his head.

"I was wrong," he says.

I wait for the next part.

Down the hall, the washing machine's agitator begins swishing. I squeeze my crossed arms tighter to my chest. I can feel the bond now. There's hurt and pain and frustration and fear. None of it mine.

"You had no right acting like that."

"I know." He meets my eyes.

He knows I can feel what he feels.

His grasp of the bond is so much stronger than mine, and it's unfair. All of this is unfair. I want my anger back. I want him to be the bad guy who fucked up beyond redemption.

'Cause then I don't have to forgive him.

And I'll never get my heart ripped out again.

"I'm not a thing. I'm not ruined 'cause I've been used." My voice wobbles.

"I know that." The bond flares, ugly and jagged. I hope he gets mad. I want him to stand and flex. Spout off like I've seen him do with his males a hundred times. I want his wolf to snarl.

But he just sits there in my shabbily repaired nest, gazing steadily up at me, and I realize something so big, my arms fall to my sides, and I blink in wonder.

To him, I am perfect. The most important thing in the world.

I do have his heart in my hands.

We're both not safe.

Or only as safe as the other will keep us.

Killian frowns, sitting taller, scanning the room. "Why are you scared?"

I could lie.

I could refuse to answer.

I could turn my back on this thing between us.

But although I've been weak before, I've never been a coward.

"You could hurt me again."

He rises to his feet, and I can see him searching for words. I can *feel* it, along with the pain and the hope and the guilt and the soaring, swooping, bright thing I can't name.

And then there's a boom, and a scream echoes from the hill.

KILLIAN BOLTS FROM THE ROOM, making a beeline for the front. His phone is at his ear. He's barking orders as he throws open the door, and above us, just below the ridge, a huge fire lights up the night. It's my cabin.

My girls.

I run, but Killian's got me around the waist, hauling me toward him. I fight. The phone falls and cracks. He drags me back into the house.

"Let me go."

"Stop." He pins me to the wall, grabs my chin. Over his shoulder, I see flames lick into the black sky. There are shouts. More screams. Mari.

"We have to go."

"Listen." His voice is so deep with alpha command, it rumbles. "You have to stay here."

"No."

"Listen!" He tightens his grip. "If you go, I'll be worried about keeping you safe. I won't be able to do what I have to do. Protect the pack. You have to stay here. Please, Una." He kisses my forehead, over and over. "Please."

An alarm sounds from the commons. Declan Kelly's voice rings out from the grave. *Emergency. All females and pups report to the lodge. All males to stations.*

"Una, please." Killian's eyes are wild. There's a pop, then a bang, and then the roof crashes down in flames.

"Go!"

He shifts as he sprints, bounding down the steps and up the path, disappearing in the dark and the smoke. There are shouts and howls, but no more screams. I pace the porch, straining to see more. Ivo and Gael rush past with bunker gear. I force myself not to call out and delay them.

Mari, Annie, and Kennedy are fine. They have to be. Their wolves are strong and quick.

I squeeze the railing, my claws splintering the wood.

Killian will do whatever needs to be done.

I expect comfort, and fear slaps me in the face. I can't stay here, no matter what I promised. I can't let him go.

I make for the steps, but as I do, a familiar husky voice calls from behind the cabin. "Una! Come here."

"Fallon." I rush toward him. "Are you hurt?"

"Come quick."

He sounds like there's something very wrong. I round the back, and out of the smoke, three ATVs roar up. Fallon. Alfie. And Lochlan Byrne.

15

UNA

My body hits the rock wall at force. Mari screams. Annie clutches Kennedy's black coat, using her whole weight to hold the wolf back. There are too many—he can't take them all. I stagger back to my feet, limp forward until I'm back in front of my girls.

My heart thuds, panic momentarily deafening me. I can't show fear.

I'm surrounded by wolves and males. The males are ours. The wolves aren't. They're huge and shaggy and yellow-eyed. There's only one of their kind in human form. He looks like a castaway. His long hair is matted, and there are claws jutting from his mud-encrusted hands and feet. I can't make out his features behind his tangled brown beard, but I can see his fangs.

I've never seen one, but I have no doubt they're Last Pack. On our land.

Terror skitters up my spine, but I stay stock still. If I show fear, they'll attack. The air is thick with aggression.

Eamon sneers down at me. "Tell the freak of nature to shift back, *Alpha*." The word drips with scorn.

Kennedy's wolf is not going to listen to me. He's a beast, and he'd never leave us undefended.

"Do it, or we kill it." He snaps, and six Last Pack wolves stalk forward, so close that their musky filth burns my nose. Kennedy's wolf bares his teeth, and he doesn't give an inch, but he knows he's outnumbered.

"Now, or I put it down." Eamon's cold, rheumy eyes bore into mine. He's not bluffing.

Anger and fear make my voice tremble. "Shift back."

By some miracle, she does. Kennedy pops straight to her feet, fists balled, guarding us with her body as if she were still in her fur. She is a fierce wolf.

Eamon laughs and calls over to the castaway. "Justus, you sure you don't want the broken one, too? She can control the others for you."

Justus spits and then scratches his hairy chest. "No. We trade for unmated females. She stinks like alpha." Justus shuffles closer and sniffs the air. "And you promised us three. There are only two."

"You can fuck the freak in her human skin just fine."

"Not talking about the blessed one. Talking about the blonde." He points at Mari.

Mari's not mated.

I glance at her. Her eyes are downcast. Her cheeks are pink.

Mari's mated?

No way. I'd know.

"Take her anyway," Eamon says, sneering. "She might not bear y'all pups, but that means you'll get more use out of her, right?"

Mari sobs. I stiffen my spine, praying she sees and follows suit. Already, there are a dozen yellow-eyed wolves tracking her, salivating. Her fear even tickles my nose.

Get mad, girls. Get mad, I think at them as hard as I can. I wish I was magical like Abertha.

I need magic to get out of this shit.

They're going to ambush Killian, and of course, he'll kill them all, but what will happen to my girls while he does?

"You got so many you can use them thus?" Justus spits in the dirt and stalks back to his wolves, grumbling.

Eamon shrugs at Lochlan, and they wander off to sit on a log beside a cold fire pit, knives in their hands. Last Pack and a half dozen males, including Finn and Alfie, lounge around the clearing. In the woods beyond, I scent more Last Pack and a handful of other A-roster males and elders. And Fallon.

That traitorous rat.

That *idiot*.

What did they promise him? A shortcut to A-roster? He'd fall for it. He's always wanted more, faster, easier.

After he helped Lochlan dump me at Eamon's feet, he scurried off to hide. After this, I'm going to bring him back to life to beat him to death with my shoe.

The girls were already here when I arrived. They're bruised and shaken and scared out of their wits, but there's no sign they were in the fire. It must have been a distraction.

This was clearly an elaborate plot, and it's going to fail so quickly, if I blink, I'll miss it—if I don't get killed in the chaos when Killian attacks.

The males in the woods are trying to hide their scents with pine needles and acorns, but Killian won't be fooled. He won't come in his human skin, and his wolf isn't going to fall for hunter tricks. He *is* the predator. This is going to be a bloodbath.

Have they not been watching Killian all these years? It

doesn't matter if they outnumber him twenty to one. He's a monster, and he is relentless.

And he saved himself for me. Kind of. And he apologized to me sincerely. And he remade my nest.

And he's a backwards Neanderthal who loses his marbles when he finds out a grown ass woman had a lover or two.

Did he think I was home crocheting all this time?

I mean, I was. A lot. My escapades were few and far between. I wasn't sneaking off into the bushes after every moonlight swim like his cousin Ashlynn does. No judgement, not from me, but damn, Killian is as big a hypocrite as any male in this pack.

Of course, he is. He's the alpha. And I got caught up in his scent and his muscles and his growly "mine" bullshit that I forgot that I *know* who I'm dealing with.

Killian Kelly has always been a caveman, and if I had any pride, I would sit back and watch the Quarry Pack's version of the Roman Senate try to "et tu, Brute" his ass.

Except accidents happen. Fate is capricious. What if he gets hurt?

I need him.

And—maybe something else.

He did ruin a magical moment back at his cabin. *Again.*

In the nest, I'd been perfectly content for the first time since I was a very little girl. I was where I belonged. Knotted and held by my mate who belongs to me. My leg hardly ached at all. I'd been lost in a hazy daydream.

I had a family. A place. A person. I had actually been eyeing Killian's throat. I was going to bite him. I would have if he hadn't thrown a temper tantrum because we're not living in the nineteenth century anymore.

But he did.

And then he came back.

And he tried to make amends.

Because despite what he's about to do to these males, he isn't a monster.

He's mine.

And he knows exactly where I am.

Our bond is hella strong now. I can't shut it off. It's like a troglodyte newsfeed. *Find. Kill. Destroy.*

He's getting closer every second.

I called him when Fallon threw me onto the ATV. I did it without hesitation. Killian will come for me, and he'll prevail.

He'll know he's walking into a trap. This isn't high quality plotting the Byrnes are doing. It's about what you'd expect from males who get their heads knocked around for a living.

At first, in the panic of the moment, I worried the bond wouldn't work, but it's not delicate anymore. It's as sturdy as a sweet potato vine. Tender and new, yes, but when I reach out, Killian's there. All of him. Like I'm a glass bottom boat in his brain.

I don't think he's entirely aware. If he was, he'd hide some stuff.

I can see *everything*. I'm trying hard not to, but it's just there. And the Byrnes are sitting quietly, picking at their claws, and the other males are squatting, scratching their balls. The silence is jangling my nerves.

I try to stay mad. If I stop for a second, I'm scared. My wolf is not big or strong. She's no match for any of the males here. Killian is fast, but he's not supersonic.

I think Fallon would help me if it came down to it, but I can't believe he got pulled into this nonsense in the first place. He clung to me so much when I lived with the Campbells because he's the fourth of five kids, and he was pretty much neglected. I bet Eamon and Lochlan paid him lots of attention. Fed him a bunch of garbage. And they're going to get him killed.

My anger surges, and my wolf grumbles. I swallow the sound. I have to keep cool. Soon enough, everything's going to go down, and I need to be clear-headed. I need a distraction.

The bond is right there.

Wide open.

I shouldn't.

But I want to.

I find the cord and follow it, wading through the blare of Killian's current panic. When I'm all the way in, I peek around, peering into his dark, cobwebby corners. It's not pretty.

I thought there'd be more backwards thinking, but it's almost all worry. Like ninety-nine percent premium, high-octane, all-consuming preoccupation.

Is Gael's left hook weaker than his right? Why is Tye distracted and pissy for no reason? Nuala's bloodwork came back not looking so great. The heating bill is going up and new windows are expensive, but if he doesn't lay the money out now, will they only get more expensive? Was the smaller purse last month at Salt Mountain a sign of things to come or just Salt Mountain being cheap?

It goes on and on like a library with endless shelves of unsolvable problems and things he can't control.

His panic and rage in this moment scream like a fire alarm, but underneath, the vibe is not much better. How does he function this way?

I go searching, poking around for something that'll

temper this new understanding. I don't want to feel bad for Killian Kelly. He's a dick. And his wolf's a dick, too, he's just a little smoother about it. Making me think he was chill. He's the one who really lost it back there, going for my neck with his fangs.

Over on the logs, the Byrnes are muttering to each other. The scent of fear is beginning to mingle with the reek of aggression. It makes my nerves jumpier. Scared, panicking animals are more dangerous than aggressive ones.

I calm myself by rooting around in Killian's psyche, looking for something that isn't anxiety, but when I find the good stuff, I don't feel any better.

It's a new memory. The images set my skin on fire. I'm grateful Lochlan and Eamon have their backs to me.

I can see earlier from Killian's point of view—my boobs bouncing, my belly jiggling, my fingers furiously rubbing my clit. I look—wanton. Unlike myself. As if I don't have a care in the world. Like I'm *enjoying* myself.

And I know what he felt when he sank inside me. The overwhelming awe.

He felt at peace. All the noise faded, and there was nothing but my breath, my soft cries. His soaring heart.

I am his reward.

And in a burst, I know why he's done all the things he's ever done. Every win in the ring. Every beatdown outside of it. Every hour of training in the brutal heat or cold. Every time he roused the males from their beds for a midnight run through the mud and rain and snow. Every rule. Every piece of justice dispensed with his fist or claw.

It was for me. To make me safe.

I see the echo of a memory—a faint glimmer that ignites an answering memory buried deep inside me.

Killian and I are children, huddled together in a bed,

bandaged, dried blood still caked in our nail beds and hair. Abertha and Killian whisper, but I can't follow the gist. I'm in too much pain. I have to trust him. When he raises a cup to my lips, I have to believe he is doing the right thing. And I do. Because he is my mate. I trust him in my bones.

And then I understand it all.

I sway. Kennedy steps forward to brace me up.

Killian did it all for me.

He changed this pack and everyone in it through the sheer force of his will, for me. Because of the kind of world he wanted for me to live in. Not our young—*me*.

In his imperfect, clumsy, hypocritical way, he made a pack where I could build beehives alone without worrying about a male coming by and taking advantage. And Old Noreen is in charge of the kitchen instead of begging for leftovers outside of the lodge. Where Dierdre can go on runs with Liam, and Conor and Jimmy can live together, and no one would consider driving them out of camp because we don't do that kind of shit anymore.

And Killian didn't even mean to change everything. It's just when you start insisting that folks behave decently to each other—I guess it kind of snowballs.

I'm not sure how to feel now.

When we were children, he gave me up. We could have fought together, side-by-side, but he took the choice away from me.

But we were so young. Too young to make those kinds of decisions.

It all clicks into place.

I need him.

I need to go away with him, be alone, piece this together. Remember everything.

But we're in the middle of a coup, and Killian is going to

blaze in any second, rip the heads off half our fighting males, and roll them at my feet.

I know this because the image is flashing through the bond now. He's close, approaching from the north, upwind, and he's scouting the situation through my eyes.

I try to let him know the positions of the other males, but I'm not sure if I succeed. I don't know how to work this connection between us, especially since he's sending me a flood of desperate reassurances tinged with bloodthirsty rage. It's hard to get anything through that mess.

I signal I'm okay. To be calm. Smart. I have no idea if it gets through.

My shoulder aches from where I hit the rock wall, my leg throbs from rough handling, and my heart lifts in happiness. Here comes my mate. He's racing to me, and he's going to do what he's always done—protect me. Rescue my girls. Make the pack safe.

And he's going to decimate our numbers. None of these males are leaving these woods. There's no doubt in my mind.

My wolf's hackles raise. She senses her mate closing in, and she's eager to watch him bleed out her enemies. I want that, too. They put their hands on me. They terrorized my girls. Destroyed our cabin.

Worse, this whole plot is about taking us back to a time where the males are the only ones with a say, and there's no need to work anything out with a female because might makes right. They look around at happy females, and think: *There's something wrong with this picture.*

It's a little ironic that my mate is about to shut down their little insurrection with the might of his fists. Or claws. Probably both. But I have no pity for Eamon or Lochlan.

They're trash. The Last Pack males are enemies, pure and simple.

But for the other Quarry males—especially Fallon—it doesn't have to be this way. They must have been convinced somewhere along the line that females with phones and ice cream dates are a hell of a lot more dangerous and offensive than they are, and that points to them being stupid, not necessarily evil.

They're going to die in these woods, too, though.

A lot of females will lose mates. Ma Campbell—who took me in when she already had five of her own— will lose her son.

And in the chaos, what happens to my girls? The one called Justus is still laser focused on Annie and Kennedy.

I can't let this happen to my pack. For good or ill, this is my family. We rise and fall together, and that's a lot harder, and a lot messier, than it sounds.

I have to stop my mate from slaughtering a dozen misguided males who don't want my friends and I to have phones. Because they're going to change. We're going to make them. We're not leaving them behind. Like I'll never leave my girls.

But Killian is flying in with claws unsheathed. He won't hesitate. There's only one thing that'll make him pause.

I *really* don't want to do this. And I am going to regret it so hard for the split second it'll take for the Byrnes to kill me if this goes south.

I can't think of another plan, and time is running out.

Fuck it. I'm reckless in a tight corner. That's my origin story.

I step forward, heading for the firepit. Lochlan and Eamon look up.

"Una," Mari hisses. "What are you doing?"

"Bitch, sit your ass back down." Eamon points his knife.

I keep coming, sucking down a deep breath. My bad knee hurts like hell, but I make my way toward the pair of them. They're still sitting like they haven't got a care in the world. The Last Pack wolves are sniffing the breeze, growling low in their throats.

Killian's almost here.

I don't want to do this. My leg drags more than usual, but I put one foot in front of another.

I round the log the instant Killian's wolf breaks into the clearing. Lochlan seizes me at the same moment. There's a prick at my neck. His arm crushes my chest, and his knife presses against my carotid.

This is the worst idea I've ever had.

Killian's wolf rears back, lifts his muzzle, and goes insane, howling at the sky, lunging and snapping his fangs. He doesn't come any closer, though.

The other males creep out of hiding, careful not to get too close to his beast, surrounding him in a loose semi-circle. Last Pack backs up to form a cordon around the perimeter. Our males are all in human form, and they carry weapons. A tire iron. Knives. They reek of fear.

Adrenaline gallops through my veins. I'm betting on Killian, but what if he's already been pushed too far?

I have to trust him.

How do I do that?

I shout down the bond with all my might—*simmer down. Think. Don't kill everyone.* It's like hollering into a paper towel tube, muffled and garbled. There's too much static from his panic and rage.

So I try something else.

"Shift." I make my voice sound as much like his as I can. "Shift *now*."

With a righteous howl that sends birds as far as the foothills into the sky, Killian shifts back to a man. His shoulders heave, and he curls his lips back to show his fangs. He is every inch the fighter who's never lost a bout.

"Let her go." There is all the force of an alpha command is in his voice, and Lochlan's hold loosens for a split second.

"We will," Eamon says. "Once you're dead." He slaps a wrench against his palm.

Killian eyes it and snorts. "You weak males need weapons to defeat me? Aren't twelve of you and the trash you brought in from Last Pack enough?"

He hasn't spared the others a glance, but he knows their number. I have no doubt he's decided the order he's going to kill them.

Finn and Alfie's eyes are eager, but some of the others flick uneasy glances at each other. This must be getting real for them. There's a whine coming from the back of Fallon's throat that he can't quite stifle. He's trying to catch my eye, like I can get him out of this mess. I'm gonna try, but if he gets a beatdown before it's over, I'm not crying over it. All those video games we've hooked him up with, and he chose these idiots over us.

I bet reality is a lot different than sitting in a basement, blowing off steam about how bitches rule everything these days, and someone should do something about it.

"None of you have the balls to challenge me one-on-one?" Killian sneers.

"You're the one who changed the rules." Some of the others lower their gazes, but Eamon has no shame. "So have we. It's never been a fair fight with you—wolf versus flip-shifter. And now we all see the consequences of letting an aberration lead the pack. Anarchy."

Is he calling females with phones "anarchy?" But it's fine to invite Last Pack onto *our* territory? To barter with them for *our* females?

"Shut up," Killian snarls. "I'll kill you in a minute."

He focuses on me, and I can feel how hard it is for him to hold himself back. I don't even need to grapple for the bond. It's just there, as if it always has been, and it's blasting at me. He's pissed, and he's terrified to his marrow.

Killian's eyes are a searing blue, ringed with gold. There is raw pain there.

"Why did you do this, Una?" His face is drawn, tormented. "Is it because of what I said back at the cabin? If you don't—If you want to get away from me, I'll let you go. You don't have to do this."

He paces, but away from the Byrnes. As he moves, the other males shuffle backward. I don't think they're even aware they're doing it. Most are still trying to look fierce, but the longer the minute stretches, reality seems to sink further in. More faces blanch. Gazes dart around the clearing, searching for a way out.

They must have made Killian small in their minds while they groused in their basements, but he's larger, faster, and stronger than all of them—than any shifter before. They'd need a hundred more males to have a hope of taking him down.

This will be a bloodbath if I don't figure out what to say. Last Pack is eyeing the woods. I bet everything they're out of here as soon as the fur flies.

If I don't stop this, no one else will. And it's a real bitch that I'm the one who has to save their sorry, backwards asses.

While I'm stuck on words, Killian goes on. "I'm sorry. I said it before, but I—I need you to know, I mean it."

"Weak," Eamon spits.

Behind me, Lochlan tenses, readying for an attack.

Killian totally ignores him.

"But please don't ever put yourself in danger, Una. I can't bear it." He pounds his bare chest with his fist, pacing still. "You can feel it, Una. I know you can. Don't do this to me ever again, shy girl. I can't handle it."

He's so worked up that fur sprouts along his happy trail. Crap. I need him to stop and think.

"I had to do something. You were going to kill everyone."

"I still am." A whiff of terror rises from the males behind him.

"I don't think you should."

Lochlan readjusts his grip on his knife. I freeze, willing Killian not to attack. I send every calming thought I have down the bond. He roars, but he stays where he is.

"You're done, Killian," Lochlan says. Under the braggadocio, there's a tremor running down his arms. And his weak leg. He's been favoring the right one since Killian kicked his ass. It's the kind of thing a female like me notices. "Bare your neck, and we might exile you."

It's an obvious lie. He wants to humiliate his alpha before he kills him.

Killian doesn't pay him any mind. "They took you," he says to me.

"Because the Byrnes poisoned their minds."

He sneers at the young males surrounding him. They've edged way back at this point. Last Pack is clustering around the one called Justus. "If these shits were worth a damn, they wouldn't be so weak-minded that a bitter old fuck and a

B-roster wannabe could convince them that females are the reason they can't win a fight."

Killian spares a glance over his shoulder at the gathered males. "And don't think it's escaped my attention that all of you have been losing your bouts. Ever bother to think that it's because instead of hustling, you spend all your time bitchin' about how messed up things are nowadays?"

He snorts in derision. "You want me to spare these pieces of shit?"

I can't nod with the knife to my throat. "Yes." I send my answer through the bond, too, so he knows it's not because I'm afraid.

"Why?"

It's so hard to say. The idea is new in my head. I struggle for a moment to find the words. "Because you're the alpha. And I'm your mate. This is my pack. They're my pack. Even the dumbasses. Not the Byrnes though. Fuck them."

Lochlan begins to speak, and Killian roars him down. Leaves high in the tree tops flutter.

"You're my mate?" His temple twitches, and he finally stops in his tracks. There's a surge of pure, sparkling energy through the bond.

"You know I am."

"You forgive me?"

"If you're sorry, yes."

"I said I was."

"Because I have a knife at my throat."

"You're not nearly worried enough for a female in your position." Killian is smirking now. Finn and Alfie exchange nervous glances.

"It's because I know something Lochlan here doesn't."

"Yeah?" Killian's smiling so wide, his eyes crinkle. His

muscles are ready. We're in tune now. The bond is flowing both ways. He knows my mind, and I know his.

Lochlan clears his throat, but I say my line before he can ruin it. "I know exactly how little pressure it takes to buckle a fucked-up knee."

I slam my heel into his calf at the same time I shift, using the energy flowing through the bond to do it quicker than I have yet. Lochlan jabs with the knife, but my wolf is small. She's not there anymore. She's wriggling loose, tearing at him with her small but sharp fangs.

There's a bone sticking out from Lochlan's leg. I don't know where I found the strength to land a blow that sharp. It must've come from the bond. Lochlan barely balances upright on the other one, and his gaze darts around the clearing in pure panic.

The instant Killian knew I was safe, he went on a rampage. He leapt—his body rippling as it became his wolf. He tore out Eamon's throat in one bite, and he kept the bloody meat in his mouth as he dashed from male to male, ripping with claws in a frenetic blur, until each one lies groaning in the dirt, hands pressed to gaping flesh and gushing wounds.

The Last Pack wolves flee. Justus throws a Quarry male into Killian's mouth so he has time to shift and bolt.

When it's over, the dirt is red with blood, and the screams still ring in the foothills. Only Fallon is spared with nothing but a claw mark across his hairless cheek. He's still plopped on his ass and crying.

Lochlan raises his knife. I sink my teeth into his good leg and shake. The knife thuds to the ground. Killian's wolf lands on his chest and snaps his jaws around Lochlan's head, crushing his skull with a horrible crunch. Things squirt.

The wolf grins at me. Blood and brain matter drip from his fangs as he wags his tail.

I sink to my butt. My wolf hangs her tongue out as far as it'll go. She'd spit if she could. She doesn't like the taste of viscera.

Killian's wolf pads closer.

My wolf ducks her head. She hasn't forgiven him for trying to dominate us in our nest. She's pleased that he smote our enemies and spared Fallon and the lower ranking males. She's protective of the pack in a way I'm not. The males' lives are precious to her, even if she thinks they could use a little more roughing up to put them firmly back in their place.

Based on the amount of blood and moaning, they're good.

Killian's wolf noses mine. She nips at him. He lies down on his belly. Even like that, he's three times our height. She's not appeased.

My wolf lets out a long series of snarls, yips, and growls.

He bares his neck.

She growls more emphatically. I think she means something like "you'd like that, wouldn't you."

I test her, see if she's ready to give up our skin. I have the urge to be in human form again.

She gives me an equivalent of the "wait a minute" finger, and then she launches into a fierce diatribe that makes Killian's wolf slink backward and lower his muzzle. He looks like a very sorry killer wolf.

And then she gives a sniff, and she lets me take over again. Now I'm sitting in the dirt, naked, covered in blood. None of it is my own.

Killian immediately shifts to male form.

"Shirt," he barks at the field of moaning males. Some

have managed to get themselves upright. Not a single one has dared try to leave.

The nearest male peels off a blood-stained polo shirt and holds it out.

Killian and I both stare at it in disgust.

"I won't wear it," I say at the same time Killian throws it back at the male.

He leaps to his feet and stands in front of me, shielding me from view.

He coughs. Every pair of eyes are glued on him. A fog of dread hangs in the air. They know the moment of judgement is here.

"All of you. Go back to camp. And *decide*. If you stay here, you're Z-roster. You're trash crew. You're the asshole I call when we gotta drain the sewage tank. Got that?"

He waits for every male to grunt assent before he continues.

"You aren't allowed within fifty feet of any female. I don't give a shit if you're mated. You lost the privilege. Or get the fuck out. Maybe Last Pack will take you. If I find you in our hills, though, I'll kill you."

He glances back at me. "Okay by you?"

I'm caught by surprise, so I nod.

"We clear, Z-roster?"

There's a general muttering. The males who've made it to their feet help the others.

And that's when Tye, Ivo, and Gael—magnificent in their wolf forms—race into the clearing. Tye goes straight to Kennedy. His wolf is at her eye level. His wolf blinks at her. She glares back. He nudges her shoulder with his snout. Kennedy's wolf growls. Tye ducks his head, ever so slightly.

And then Annie and Mari are running to me, and I'm hugging them, and Kennedy is joining us, and there's a great hullabaloo. Mari and Annie cry. I wipe their cheeks, but all I do is mix dirt in with the tears.

"W-we th-thought we were gonna be traded to Last Pack," Annie says.

"I thought you were gonna die." Mari clings to my neck.

"They blew up all our stuff," Kennedy says. Mari and Annie crowd close to her, covering her nakedness as best they can. Kennedy puts up a good front, but she's not comfortable around other packmates in her bare human skin.

"W-where are we going to live?" Annie breaks down in fresh sobs.

"Whichever of those asshole's cabins that you want. How about Alfie's? His is catty-corner from mine and Una's." The girls fall silent and look up at Killian.

He attempts a smile.

Annie sniffles.

"Is that okay?" he asks.

One by one, the girls nod.

"Can Ivo and Tye take you back? Help you get it set up?" Killian is trying to speak gently, and it makes my insides warm.

"Ivo, yes. Tye, no," Mari answers.

Killian raises an eyebrow, but Mari doesn't elaborate. Kennedy stares at the ground. Mari is an excellent friend.

"Okay, then. I'll bring Una over later. All right?"

They look to me. So does Killian.

I could say no, I want to go with them now. He'd listen. He'd walk us back to camp. He'd let me go with them to a new cabin, and he'd sit on the porch, but he wouldn't say another word. I know this in my heart. It streams through our bond. I outrank him. I am his alpha.

This must be what it feels like to fly a fighter jet. Or a space shuttle. The pure power.

Killian opens his hand and holds it out. "Come with me?" he asks.

I don't know where he wants to go, but yes.

I'll go with him.

I take his hand.

He leads me away, and I follow.

16

UNA

Killian takes me further up the hill, past the other dens, to the very last one to be occupied. When I was a little girl and my parents were alive, my mother would bring food up to the elders who lived here. I was fascinated by them. They split their time almost evenly between fur and skin. They hunted their own food, and bedded down with the rest of the pack in piles. I always got the sense when I talked to one, I talked to all of them.

We don't live like this anymore. We have our own cabins, keep to our own little groups. There's a thread that still runs through us all, though. No matter how we change. We're swept along by time together. We share a past and a future.

Killian has carried it all on his shoulders for a long time now. When we first moved out of the dens, we split. Under his father, we divided into winners and losers, the strong and the weak. Rank ruled. Killian figured out a way for our males to fight for us, not amongst each other. He couldn't change rank, so he slowly made the strong the protectors and the weak, the protected.

Imperfect. Infuriating. Downright maddening.

But he kept us together. And what he did, he did alone.

I squeeze the calloused hand still holding mine. He glances down, surprised.

I offer him a small smile.

His grin splits his face.

I scent Gael and Tye on the wind, hanging back, but following. Guarding us. And for some reason, I catch a whiff of Kennedy, too.

I don't have the chance to puzzle that out before Killian pulls me through the entrance to the cave we call "the over-look." It opens facing the old quarry. There's a view of the emerald green rainwater collected at the bottom, and in the distance, the wooded hills that lead to the border of our territory to the south. It seems high above the world, and when there is a moon illusion, it feels like you can reach up and touch it.

The ceiling is low, but Killian can still stand without stooping. The caverns go back a long way, but you can't tell from the first room. It's like any other cave with a narrow split in the rocks at the back.

I haven't been inside in years. There aren't cozy nests on frames strung with ropes or fires with kettles hanging above on tripods anymore. The space has been swept clean. There are waterproof plastic tubs along the walls. I guess that's where the bedding is stored for females who do their heat up here. It's supposed to be auspicious to conceive young in the dens.

Is that what Killian is thinking? The excitement earlier —and the scent of other males—tamped down my heat, but it's returning now, stronger than before. I can't see how it can ebb again. I think when it comes this time, it's going to carry me away until it ends.

My belly is unsettled. Last time with Killian was good—

until it was awful. And Killian and I haven't really worked things out between us. Have we?

I fuss in my head while he guides me through the back caverns. The floor slopes downward, and the ceiling rises higher. Now there are stalactites dripping down, slick and pearlescent. There's a pitter patter ahead, like raindrops.

It's the pool. The elders used to take us young down here while our parents chatted around the fire. It's bigger than a bathtub. Almost the size of a small swimming pool. The water is perfectly clear.

The elders explained how the rainwater is cleaned as it sinks through the bedrock and how it collects and never evaporates because there's no sunlight down here, only the bare lightbulbs rigged up on a string along the walls. They're not quite fairy lights, but they cast a warm glow around the cavern.

Killian leads me to the edge of the pool. It's chilly this far down, but my skin is hot. Inside, I'm a furnace. My heat is coming on hard.

"Wait," he says. He jogs back the way we came, and for a few minutes, I'm alone, deep underground. It's a surreal place, magical and shadowy and silent.

This whole day has been strange. I should be reeling, but I'm not. I feel steadier than I ever have before. I made a choice. I claimed my place in this pack. With Killian.

I'm not living one foot in, one foot out anymore. This is my life. For good or ill. And it doesn't feel like giving up or making do or accepting that which cannot be changed. It feels like fate. A fate that isn't a trap but a path.

I run my fingers along the smooth, cool walls. We came from here, and we keep coming back. Not because we can't get away, but because there's power in where you come from. What made you.

Fate made me Killian Kelly's mate. That doesn't mean what I thought it did. I'm not his to do with as he pleases. He is mine.

I think these big thoughts while my body goes haywire waiting for my mate to return. My nipples peak, aching. My skin shivers and there's a bubbling in my belly.

I want my mate.

"Hurry," I send through the bond.

"Yes," he answers me instantly.

When Killian returns, his loud steps give me plenty of warning. He brings a pile of clean blankets, towels, and washrags.

"I thought we should get the blood off before we take a dip," he says, arranging the linens in a pile. It's all wrong. I'll fix it once I'm clean.

Killian stalks over to the pool, oddly bashful. He tests the temperature and scrubs his own hands. He's not meeting my eyes.

Then he dips a cloth in the pool, wrings it out, and comes to me. I stand very still, flushing hot, breathing quicker and quicker.

He wipes my neck first, lingering over his bite mark.

"You almost killed me back there," he says, his voice low and smoldering.

He traces the pink scars of his claiming bite. They look like the wounds on my legs, but they don't hurt at all.

"Don't ever put yourself in danger like that again, Una. Promise me."

"I knew you'd get Lochlan before he had a chance to hurt me."

"I didn't though. You took him down." He smiles as he smooths the cloth down my shoulder and arm.

"Yeah. I don't know why he used a knife. If he'd used his claws, it would've been a lot closer."

Killian tenses, but his strokes remain calm and even.

"It's a tactic. In case of invasion, wolves expect to fight wolves. If you outnumber the attacking force, armed males have the advantage."

"You taught them that, didn't you?"

He huffs a sigh. "I taught them everything they know."

"Who taught you?"

He moves to my other side. His touch becomes brisker and more efficient. I've got goosebumps up and down my arms, and they seem to bother him. He uses his other hand to rub my clean skin, as if to warm me, but I'm burning up. My skin is prickling from anticipation, not the chill.

"Everyone."

"How so?" He lowers himself to his knees to wipe my legs.

"Dermot. Eamon. Quill. My father. Moon Lake. North Border. Salt Mountain."

"Not Last Pack?"

"They don't know shit but how to sniff ass."

My lips curve. Poor Last Pack. Always lowest rung on the shifter ladder. And yet here we are. In our bare skin, in a den. No different than them.

"If you listen, and you watch, you pick stuff up." Killian places my hands on his shoulders, and then he lifts my bad leg to wipe off my foot. I wiggle my toes. He grabs them and squeezes. "Behave."

"It tickles."

"I'm quick."

"And bossy."

He arches an eyebrow. He looks so damn pleased with himself.

"You're not the boss of me. Just so you know." I put more of my weight on his shoulders as he lifts my good leg.

"I know."

"I'm not going to stop selling mushrooms."

"You've got more?"

"I'm going to grow more."

"Okay." He places my foot carefully back on the smooth rock floor, and he sits back on his heels, gazing up at me. He's smiling, amused, and his cock is hard.

"And any female who wants to sell things at the market, can."

"Agree."

"And we need a rotation for laundry and kitchen duty. One that's fair."

He nods.

"And if a female wants to fight, she can."

"Who wants to fight?"

Kennedy, for one, but I'd never betray her confidence. "It's a hypothetical."

"If I let females fight, the males are gonna band together and come after me again."

"Are you worried?"

Now he grins wide enough to show his sharp incisors. "Not at all."

"And females can drive if they want to."

"Seems they already do." Killian gazes up at me, and even in the dim light, his eyes twinkle. "Are those all your demands, Alpha?"

My stomach flips. Oh, I like him on his knees in front of me, calling me that, looking at me like that. It's heady.

"I want land near the commons. For gardens and a new greenhouse."

His smile already tells me yes.

"I might not want to go all the way to Abertha's cottage when I have a pup."

His eyes turn molten and lower to my bare belly. My heat surges.

"A pup?"

I shift. "Well, yeah. I guess. Yes? That's what mates do, right? Have pups?"

"Not always."

"But most of the time."

He nods. His face is serious now. "If you don't want it yet, I can pull out."

My hand flies to my face. This is so weird. We've known each other all our lives, we're connected by a bond as real as muscle and bone, and in some ways, I'm still the nerd at the front of the bus, and he's the cool kid in the very back seat.

And he just said "pull out."

He reaches out and cups my calves, stroking with his thumbs. "I want you to carry my pups, Una. I want that more than anything. You know that, right?"

I lift a shoulder.

"But if you want more time, you have it. If you need me to prove myself, I will."

His intention flows into my chest, powerful and true. He's waited for me almost his whole life. Maybe his mind forgot, but his heart never did.

Now I understand that mine didn't either. Not really. But I didn't have a choice, so I made my own way. Like he did. And we found each other again. Neither of us innocent anymore, but maybe better off for it.

"Are you still mad that I didn't wait for you to have sex?" For the first time in the cave, I feel naked.

"Not mad."

"Disappointed?" I cross my arms.

"Jealous."

"We weren't together. We didn't know we were mates. Neither of us."

"I know." He rises to his knees and gently takes my hands, pulling them away from my chest. "I feel what I feel. But it's not on you. And I don't want you to regret anything. I wanted everything in your life to be good and perfect."

The memory floats up between us. The crone's bed, her soft quilt, the horrible pain, and the cool tea.

"It wasn't. But it wasn't bad, either. It's the path I had to take to get here."

"To me," he says.

"To you," I agree. "Do you remember? Abertha's cottage? After the attack?"

"I do." He tucks a flyaway behind my ear. "You were so brave."

"You were so strong." And in my memory, I see how very young he was, too.

He brushes a kiss across my lips and lowers himself back to his knees, drawing me down to wrap my legs around his waist. He's hard against my belly, but this isn't about that. He squeezes my hands, and through the bond, I feel his nervousness and hope.

He bares his neck and casts his gaze down. For me.

His vein throbs.

I have a choice, but it feels like I made it a long time ago. When—I'm not quite sure. But it's natural for my fangs to lengthen. My wolf yips and bounds. She's all on board.

I open my mouth and test his skin with the tips of my fangs. He shudders in my arms. His longing teases my nostrils.

He wants this so bad. Worse than I have ever wanted anything.

It's knowing that—the truth of it pulsing through our bond—that lets me let it all go—the fight with Haisley. The night in the blackberry patch. The dumb rules and frustrations and bull crap that I blamed him for over the years.

It was all his fault, but it's not the whole of it.

I remember curling beside him in bed. I remember him reverently braiding my hair. We've been without each other too damn long. And I want him back.

I sink my teeth into his neck, and his groan of pure pleasure echoes off the ceiling. He tastes like a copper penny. His blood sizzles on my tongue, and then it lights my every nerve on fire, and I'm burning now, hotter and brighter than ever before.

"Mate," I moan.

He blinks at me with bleary, blissed-out eyes. He holds me tight, and I lap at my bite, healing the wounds as I admire them. They're not as big as mine, but they're perfect all the same.

I wriggle in his arms. Why are we kneeling here?

"What's wrong?" he murmurs. "What do you need?"

"You *know*. I'm hot." My skin is on fire, and my insides are cramping, spasming on air.

"Do you want the pool?" He stands, lifting me, and strides over to the pool to lower me in. The water is cold, and I sink down until it licks my chin, but it's not enough.

He steps in after me, and I turn, climb him, gnaw at the beautiful mark I've made. He rinses my hair with palms full of cool water.

"*Killian*." I rise up, try to sink down on his hard cock, but he twists to the side.

"You need to build your nest. And you'll need food and water. I have to go back up and get some. It'll only be a minute. Okay?"

He's frowning, and he's talking nonsense. Except the nest. Yes. We do need that.

I push out of his arms. He lets me go, but he follows close behind. We're dripping on the rock, and I slip, but his hands are already on my waist, steadying me. The pile of blankets is not very big.

"Don't move. I'll be quick." He's at the crack leading out of the cavern. My wolf snaps at him to stay.

"But you'll need food."

My wolf growls. I swear it sounds like she says if he leaves, she'll chew his leg off.

Killian stays. I fix the nest. Thick wool blankets on the bottom, fluffy comforters on top. They smell like detergent and lavender sachets, which isn't perfect, but it's acceptable for now, especially with the scent of the cave in my nose. It's dark and private and full of the essence of wolves from ages and ages ago. It's pack.

I fluff a pillow and ease myself down. The heat is a beat in my chest, a cresting, crashing wave.

This is right. Everything is aligned. The moon is rising. My wolf can sense it.

I move onto my knees and arch my back, opening my chest, welcoming the bond. I close my eyes.

Killian comes to me. His steps fall heavy on the stone. My mate is strong and tall. He's vicious, and wise, and he belongs to me.

I bend deeper, showing him that I'm ready. Inside, I blush, but I'm not only Una. I am Una and her wolf. We are shameless and demanding.

We've waited for this moment for a very long time.

Killian covers me. His cock prods my slick opening. I moan.

He whispers in my ear, "Everything I've ever done, I've done for you, Una Hayes."

And he sinks inside me, plunges deep, and my pussy is already fluttering, urging him on, to seed us with our pups and to make him ours again.

EPILOGUE

UNA

Change is hard.

That's why there is a leather sofa half in and half out of our front door and a very pissed off Killian pacing in the kitchen, trying not to lose his shit.

He's going to lose it.

We've been together for eighteen months, and relationships are hard. Especially with males who have always gotten their way and previously only used one way to settle an argument.

Tye is supposed to be helping me get rid of the sofa, but Killian gave an alpha command to "stop," so now Tye's standing at the top of the ramp Killian built to replace our front steps, blocking me from shoving the foul thing the rest of the way out of our cabin.

Of course, if I try to do it myself, Killian will restrain me. Very gently, but effectively. He'd never hurt me, but I haven't been able to convince him that manhandling me is harmful. If he doesn't like the look of something, he hauls me up like a sack of potatoes.

He doesn't like the looks of most stairs, hills, freshly mopped floors, or trails with too many roots showing.

And he's definitely not cool with his almost-ready-to-pop pregnant mate moving furniture. He's caught me doing it a lot these past few weeks. It's a sign the pup is coming soon if the aching hips, the ginormous belly, and the permanent indigestion weren't enough advance notice.

I'm past ready. My ankles are swollen, my boobs are leaky, and I'm horny and mad at the same time—all the time. I'm not in the mood to suffer fools, and that's what Killian is if he thinks I'm going to tolerate this repulsive thing in my space for another day.

"What's wrong with the sofa again?" Killian's using that "reasonable" tone of voice that I want to smack out of him.

"It *stinks*."

"You never had a problem with it before."

"It didn't stink before."

Tye bends over and takes a whiff. He shrugs at Killian like I'm nuts.

"It's dead cow carcass treated with smashed brains, urine, and chemicals. I'm not nuts." I hike my chin. My mate moves so the breakfast bar is between us.

"Where am I gonna sit, Una?"

"Sit on this." I flip him the middle finger. I've picked up the habit from the males at the gym. When we were first mated, Killian liked me to hang out with him a lot—and I wanted to be around him all the time, too. I picked up tons of useful, new cuss words, and I was starting to learn how to fight when Killian caught a whiff of me one day, declared me preggo, and forbade me from doing anything more dangerous than weeding.

He'd probably be pissed if he knew the girls and I have dedicated the locked backroom of the old greenhouse to growing mandrake, hemlock, and henbane. The more I learned about Killian's defensive efforts—the patrols, the contingency plans, the bunker under the commissary—the more I realized the threat from Last Pack and Moon Lake isn't as far-fetched as I thought. If they are ever dumb enough to come for us, we'll have more than fangs and claws to greet them.

Banning me from the gym was our first major fight, though. It ended with Killian buying me a Subaru and building me a raised garden in our backyard. I don't remember exactly how it unfolded. I was shifting to my wolf a lot, and we were not using our words.

On the porch, Tye sighs, sinks to the sofa, and takes out his phone. "We've got a reconciliation match in a half hour," he calls over his shoulder.

Those were my idea. You can't leave ten males in the proverbial doghouse forever. You need to provide a path back to the pack's good graces, or they stop bathing, spend too much time as wolves, and terrorize the chickens.

Hence—reconciliation matches. If a wannabe insurgent can beat an A-roster male—or go five rounds without getting knocked out—he can start eating meals in the lodge again.

Fallon was first to come back. It was a good day. I cried, but I waited until I was alone to do it. The pack is always looking at me now, but in a different way than before. I don't want to call it awe, but it's close. It's how you look at a snake handler or a lion tamer, I guess. Like they're insane, but also kind of magic.

Handling Killian Kelly isn't magic. It's all tenacity, an ability to ignore nonsense, and the willingness to tell him no a few times a day for his own good.

It turns out I'm pretty good at all of those things.

"Tye, put the sofa back." Killian adds a growl to the order. Tye looks up.

"No." I put my hands on my hips. Tye drops his gaze back to his phone.

"There's not enough furniture in this camp to make you happy, female."

"That's a gross over-exaggeration, and you know it. This is the only thing I want out of the house. The rest I just moved around."

"I have no idea where my good hand grip is."

"What's a hand grip?"

"Exactly!" Killian slaps the counter.

I'm screwing with him. I know what a hand grip strengthener is. It's in the junk drawer behind him. I put it there after I almost knocked it into the toilet. He had been keeping it on the tank. And he thinks I put things in weird places.

This has gone on long enough. My feet hurt, and Killian does need to be at the gym. This match is important to Garrett and his family. His mother has been torn up since the failed coup. She started dropping by Abertha's garden to plead his case, and now she comes over to help with my backyard garden every day.

She has a wicked green thumb. She said she never knew it before. She'd always been stuck in the kitchen. I'm not sure what exactly stuck her there, but she's unstuck herself now.

A lot of females are branching out. Rowan convinced Ivo to teach her how to fight. Old Noreen is learning French cooking from Julia Child videos on the internet. Annie showed her YouTube, and it's a good thing we all have unlimited data now.

Killian emerges from the kitchen. He knows by my tone

that we're done messing around. He's wary. His hands are on his hips, too.

I narrow my eyes. "It's either me or the sofa."

"I pick you."

My insides melt. It's the baby. But also because I know it's a hundred percent true. Killian is not an easy male to live with, but loving him comes as natural as breathing.

We're fated mates, but that's mere biology. It's not respect. Care. Loyalty.

We have that. And maybe we've never said it, but it's there, growing stronger every day as we navigate this strange connection that both of us now protect with our lives.

I didn't know what I was doing when I let Abertha sever the bond. It wakes me up in a cold sweat sometimes, the thought of what I almost lost forever.

This blunt, bull-headed, arrogant male who would move mountains for me.

Who already has.

I rub my big belly, and worry furrows Killian's brow.

"Braxton-Hicks? Do you need to sit?" He casts a pained look at the sofa stuck in the door.

"I'm fine. Baby's bopping around. Everything's okay."

His panic recedes, and the bond fades to its usual reassuring presence. "I'd feel better if you sat. Your ankles are fat."

"Screw you."

"Hey, don't threaten me with a good time." He grins as he pulls two dining room chairs into the living room.

I sit. My dogs are barking. My wolf has been very quiet since the baby started moving. It's like she's afraid to bother him. Sometimes, though, like now, she rumbles in my chest, a soothing purr that calms the baby and his tiny, flickering wolf.

Killian sits beside me and rests his hand on the top of my mound. His wolf starts rumbling, too. It vibrates his fingers.

The baby kicks in delight, gets me hard in the ribs. I wince.

Killian's wolf growls once, not scary, just bossy, and the baby goes back to squirming lazily.

"It'll take a day or two to get a new sofa," Killian says. "I'll have to send someone to town."

"I'll pay for it."

He rolls his eyes. All the females who want one have an online bank account now. Mine is growing at a greater rate than my belly. We can sell online now, too, and I was right—wolf branded goods are hot.

Killian doesn't argue. He also won't give me the chance to pay for it. That's going to be a huge argument a few years down the road when the girls and I are making more money with farm-to-table stuff than his males earn at the fights. I can't wait.

"Hey. I want to pick the fabric." I wish I could give it a sniff, too, but neither my wolf nor Killian's—nor Killian himself—will let me leave pack territory this close to giving birth.

"I'll have whoever gets it text you pictures and you can pick. That work?"

It does. I lean my head on Killian's upper arm. He drops a kiss on the top of my head and grabs the bottom of my braid.

"I liked that sofa," he sighs.

I kiss the bulging muscle under my cheek. "I'll make it up to you later."

Abertha says sex is really great at this stage of pregnancy

for moving things along. Also, I'm completely, utterly addicted to my mate.

Killian's wolf purrs like a pleased pussy cat. The dirty voyeur.

"Una, I'd get rid of every stick of furniture in this place if it made you happy."

I giggle. "I know."

He nuzzles my hair. "I'd do anything for you. You're the reason, Una."

"For what?" I know, but I want to hear him say it.

"Everything. I love you, shy girl."

"I love you, too, mate."

Our hands find each other as we sit side-by-side, our wolves quiet and content, everything the way it ought to be —because we made it so.

THE FIVE PACKS saga continues in *The Heir Apparent's Rejected Mate*. Want more Cate C. Wells? Check out *Charge*, the first book in her motorcycle club series, or *Hitting the Wall*, a small-town, secret baby romance.

WANT A BONUS EPILOGUE?

Sign up for the Cate C. Wells newsletter for a bonus epilogue and meet Killian and Una's pup.

You'll also get free novellas, updates, bonus content, and special offers!

ABOUT THE AUTHOR

Cate C. Wells writes everything from motorcycle club to small town to mafia to paranormal romance. Whatever the subgenre, readers can expect character-driven stories that are raw, real, and emotionally satisfying. She's into messy love, flaws, long roads to redemption, grace, and happily ever after, in books and in life.

Along with stories, she's collected a husband and children along the way. She lives in Baltimore when she's not exploring the world with the family.

She loves to chat with readers! Check out the The Cate C. Wells Reader Group on Facebook.

Facebook: @catecwells
Twitter: @CateCWells1
Bookbub: @catecwells
Instagram: @authorcatecwells

Printed in Great Britain
by Amazon

55759849R00212